I0634868

SUCH A GOOD MAN

ALSO BY KATE FLORA

SUCH A GOOD MAN

A JOE BURGESS MYSTERY
BOOK 8

KATE FLORA

ePublishingWorks!
love what you read.

Without limiting the rights under copyright(s) reserved below, no part of this publication may be reproduced, stored in, or introduced into a retrieval system or transmitted in any form or by any means (electronic, mechanical, photocopying, recording, or otherwise) without the prior permission of the publisher and the copyright owner.

This is a work of fiction. Names, characters, places, and incidents either are the product of the author's imagination or are used fictitiously, and any resemblance to actual persons, living or dead, business establishments, events, or locales is entirely coincidental.

The scanning, uploading, and distributing of this book via the internet or any other means without the permission of the publisher and copyright owner is illegal and punishable by law. Please purchase only authorized copies, and do not participate in or encourage piracy of copyrighted materials. Your support of the author's rights is appreciated.

Copyright © 2023 by Kate Flora. All rights reserved.

ACKNOWLEDGMENTS

A million thanks to the beta readers who took the time to read the manuscript and help me make this a better book. A writer always reaches a point where she cannot see her errors or where she knows her characters so well she forgets to fully disclose them to her readers. You help me fix these issues, catch my typos, correct my character screw-ups, and fix my timeline. I couldn't do this without you. Thank you John Clark, Nancy McJennett, Marian Stanley, Kait Carson, Dorothy MacKeen, Diane Englund, and Alice Dashiell.

To Hugh Holton, Carl Johnson, Joe Loughlin, Brian Cummings, and Bruce Coffin, the police officers who have been my advisors and inspiration along the way.

ONE

For once, the call hadn't come in the middle of the night or in foul weather. It had come in on a sunny, end of September morning at a civilized hour when Burgess had already had his coffee. A homicide detective learned to be grateful for small things.

As he stepped through the door into the neat and airy condo, he had something else to be grateful for: the place didn't reek of decomp, and the air wasn't buzzing with flies. The sun's reflections off the busy ocean waves danced on the high ceiling. Tall, open windows allowed in fresh sea air, which mingled with the faint smell of cleaning products. Unsurprising, since the body had been found by the housekeeper when she went upstairs to clean the second floor.

The woman, who had called the police and immediately left the premises, was now sitting outside on a bench weeping while his teammate, Terry Kyle, tried to get her story. Before Burgess left the conversation, he'd gotten basic information on the victim. A doctor at the local hospital. Single. Lived alone. She'd been cleaning for him for about eight months.

As Burgess rose to head inside, the weeping woman gasped, "But he was such a good man. How could anyone do that to him?"

Soon, Burgess knew he would understand what "that" was. Her reaction suggested something shocking and horrible. According to the cleaner, a small, sturdy, middle-aged woman named Lena Nowak, the front door had been locked when she arrived, and the windows were open. She reported that open windows were unusual. The owner was scrupulous about keeping things locked. Living in the city had made him paranoid about being robbed. Since she was a regular visitor to the condo, she had her own key.

Burgess thought it was crazy to buy a place right on the ocean in Portland, Maine, and not open windows to let the sea air in. But if he knew anything at all, it was that people often made strange choices or choices he would never make. He wouldn't have to worry about this one—he'd never be able to afford a place on the water on a cop's salary.

The third member of their team, Stan Perry, was back at 109, as they called Portland's police headquarters, researching their victim's background. The medical examiner, Dr. Lee, was on his way. Burgess was about to climb the wide, blond wood stairs to the second floor and meet the victim, Dr. Eliot Spence.

As he pulled on gloves and shoe covers and started up the immaculate stairs, Burgess was grateful for the absence of frightened animals, feces, bags of trash, and other clutter and for air that was breathable. The information that a cleaner had been through the downstairs before discovering the body and calling 911 was troubling, though. It might mean a nicer situation for cops to work in, but any evidence of the killer, if, in fact, this *was* a homicide, had probably been dusted and vacuumed away. He might hope that she was a careless cleaner, but the pristine rooms suggested she was not.

At least the upstairs, where the body was, hadn't been touched, except by Lena Nowak's footsteps as she approached to change the bed. Her vacuum and bucket of cleaning products and rags still sat just beyond the top of the stairs where she'd left them.

There's always a moment at or en route to a crime scene, before seeing the body, when a detective catches his breath in anticipation. A moment when the imagination, running on the meager facts supplied by dispatch—in this case, a name, address, and the fact of a body—begins to throw up possibilities about what is waiting. The deceased person was a doctor. Did that mean a possible overdose? A suicide resulting from guilt over a medical failure? A homicide perpetrated by an aggrieved patient or the patient's family? A death related to the victim's secret life? Even a natural death incomprehensible because of his age? The doctor was only in his forties. But that last wouldn't explain the housekeeper's, "How could anyone do that to him?"

Over three decades, Burgess had seen plenty, but every case was new. Assuming he'd seen it all or that there were no surprises was dangerous. It could make an investigator careless when those first neutral impressions mattered most. Now, he moved slowly, taking in his surroundings as he climbed the stairs, focusing on what they might tell him. It was a two-story condo on the waterfront. Huge windows, especially on the second floor, with sliders to a balcony. The furnishings were modern, and the art was large and dramatic. The décor was expensive and carefully chosen either by the occupant or a decorator. Burgess would bet on a decorator, but what did he know? Until his life had been invaded—and improved—by the presence of Chris and a family, his own style of decorating had been merely functional.

There was a sparseness to the place, only the essentials of furniture, rugs, art, and lighting. No books, throws, or decorative objects on the surfaces. Burgess thought there was also darkness. Maybe it was just the contrast between the brightness outside and the dark colors inside. Given Maine's long winters, plus the shoulder seasons when the trees stayed depressingly bare, all that onyx and gray and dark plum would have been too depressing for him despite the lightness of the wood.

The staircase was lined with large black-and-white photos of glamorous women. All taken from the rear with the women looking back over their shoulders. Seductive. Smiling. In a few, looking nervous. All the women had long hair—mostly dark, some with highlights, sometimes wavy, sometimes straight. All appeared to be undressed. At least, no clothes were shown, but that might just be the way the women had been dressed and the photos cropped.

Spence's work or someone else's? According to the cleaner, Dr. Spence wasn't married. Burgess wondered how a woman ascending the staircase might feel. Would she compare herself? Feel inadequate? Would she wonder whether a man who chose to decorate like this viewed women as objects, or would she see it as a challenge?

At the top of the stairs, he paused and sniffed the air. Along with the distinctive, stomach-turning smell of decomp, fresh death also had a scent. More subtle but often present. He didn't smell that here. What he did smell was the scents from the cleaner's work downstairs. A pleasantly sweet something she'd probably used on the hardwood floors and the scent, familiar from his own home, of lemon furniture polish. There was also the slightly astringent scent of glass cleaner. No air freshener. No diffused scents from the oils that were so common these days. And no grooming products. Was there something else? He couldn't tell.

That done, he stepped into the room.

The upstairs was one large open room. A sitting area, black leather furniture on a tufted black and white rug facing a gray marble fireplace with a large flat-screen TV mounted on the wall above it. A pair of tall, ornate screens made of carved dark wood separated the seating area from the sleeping area.

He stepped carefully around the screens over a pile of bedding probably dropped by the cleaner, and there was Dr. Spence. He was sprawled face down on a fluffy white duvet, his face buried in the fabric, his glossy dark curls set off by the pristine white. His clean, pale feet were bare and hung off the side of the bed. He wore a white tee shirt and black jeans. The jeans had been pulled down below his hips, and he had been sodomized with a bottle.

There was no blood. No sign of a struggle. Nothing in the immaculate room was out of place. Except that he'd been violated with that bottle, the doctor might simply have thrown himself down on the bed and gone to sleep.

Close to six feet tall, Burgess figured, and fit. Maybe a hundred seventy-five pounds?

Burgess studied the carpet for footprints. The thick, coarse pile, rough underfoot and not as pleasant and yielding as he would have expected, didn't show any. Although the housekeeper had probably done it before she called them, he checked for signs of life. The body was cool. There was no pulse. Here, as downstairs, the windows were open, letting the fresh morning breeze, the sounds of moving water, and the crying of gulls into the silent room.

No blood. No visible bruises. No signs of violence to the body. No signs of a struggle. Quite a contrast to other crime scenes. This one gave Burgess little information. He'd have to wait for the medical examiner to tell him what he was seeing.

Burgess wondered if Dr. Spence had enjoyed the good life when he had it. The décor told him that the doctor had been precise with discriminating taste, had an eye for detail, and that no expense had been spared to make the place luxurious and very personally his.

The black leather headboard matched the furniture in the seating area. The bedside tables were shiny, dark wood. A small number of books, fiction and nonfiction, were neatly stacked on one of the bedside tables. A black cell phone rested on a black charger.

On the other bedside table, there were tissues in a shiny black box. There were no visible fingerprints on all those shiny surfaces. Unreal.

Even with a frequent and diligent cleaner, it didn't seem possible that Dr. Spence could have lived in this place and left no traces of himself anywhere. The cleaner had told them she hadn't gotten to the upstairs yet.

Burgess wondered if the killer—assuming there *was* a killer—had cleaned up before departing. If there might be cleaning rags or crumpled paper towels in Dr. Spence's trash? He made a mental note to be sure the techs collected it. Or in a trashcan on the street? Maybe a killer had carried it away.

He reminded himself that he didn't yet know if there was a killer or whether the violation of the body had simply been opportunistic after Spence was already dead.

He'd seen a variety of crime scenes over his three decades, yet this one stood out. It was too pristine. Too clean. Too uninformative. Of course, for a seasoned investigator, all of that was information.

Straightening from the body, he surveyed the rest of the bedroom.

Black bedside lamps were mounted on the wall. The platform bed frame sat on a rug that matched the one by the fireplace. Near the body, a pair of black slip-on shoes were tucked halfway under the bed. Once the techs had taken their photos, he'd check the size.

He stepped past the bed and opened the door that led into the bathroom. It was bright and modern. An open rainfall shower with pebbled walls and floor. Those pebbles looked really cool, but he cringed at the thought of standing on them. That, plus the uncomfortable rug, suggested someone who elevated style over comfort.

The black granite surrounding the sink had raw edges, and matching granite had been used on the floor. One wall was entirely mirrored. The wallpaper was a bold black-and-white geometric design. The sconces were deco.

Like the bedroom, the bathroom was unnaturally neat. Nothing on the sink except a black toothbrush holder with brushes, a black soap dish with a cake of black soap, toothpaste, and a black drinking cup. He wondered if the toothpaste was black, too. The fluffy white towels were dry, except for a damp one in the hamper. The toothbrush and soap were dry, and the soap dish was clean and dry. The shiny black wastebasket was empty. The air was neutral, not scented with deodorant, shampoo, soap, or aftershave. Nothing was out of place except one of the medicine cabinet doors, which was partially open.

When he carefully finished opening it with a gloved finger, he found everything neatly aligned except a single bottle of prescription medicine for erectile dysfunction. He photographed its placement and the label.

Depending on what the ME learned about the cause of Dr. Spence's death, he might need to speak with the prescribing physician. In a man this young, ED drugs were often used to enhance sexual performance rather than for any medical need.

Before he left the room, he paused and studied it again. It was now ten in the morning. A Friday in September. Dr. Spence had either gotten up this morning, gotten dressed, and then somehow died, or he'd died some-time last night or early this morning. His clothes—jeans and a tee shirt—were casual. Not something he'd be wearing to work. But Burgess realized he didn't know that. Spence might well have spent his day in scrubs, and the jeans and tee were what he wore to the hospital. He needed to know a lot more about the doctor's schedule and whether he'd been expected at work today.

Another question for Burgess's growing checklist.

Leaving the bathroom, he opened a second door. It led to a large walk-in closet tricked out with racks and shelves and a blond wood bench where someone could sit to put on shoes. Everything was neat and orderly. A single pair of new-looking athletic shoes were aligned under the bench. A bright blue shirt, a white tee shirt, and pale blue cotton boxers were in the hamper. Nothing appeared disturbed except a rack of ties where one seemed to be missing, and others were slightly crumpled as though they'd been hastily shoved aside. Clinging to one of the ties was a long blonde hair.

It was all a little too much like walking into a store display before opening time.

Nothing else to learn here. He'd need to learn about Dr. Spence from his colleagues and friends, as well as from the distraught woman down-stairs. Perhaps from his neighbors.

Burgess returned to the bedroom and checked the drawers in the tables beside the bed. On the side where the phone rested, he found an interesting collection of lubricants, a variety of condoms, and several different dildos. There was a lower drawer, but it was locked and would have to wait.

He checked the drawer on the other side. The top drawer was empty except for a sleek, zippered black leather pouch—Coach brand—that held a few tampons and some pads. The lower one, as on the other side, was locked. There were no other signs of a woman in the apartment—no clothing or toiletries—but evidently, the doctor enjoyed an active sex life with a partner. Or multiple partners. Nothing except that long blonde hair, those feminine products, and the photos on the stairs to suggest the sex of the partners. Even that was far from conclusive.

He went back down the stairs to wait for the medical examiner, going slowly as he took a second look at the row of ladies. *No*, he thought, *if he were a woman, he would not enjoy walking past them.*

As he reached the bottom of the stairs, there was a commotion of voices and the sound of a blow against flesh. A woman who had shoved her way past the officer guarding the door ran into the room. She was tall and slender. Brunette. Beautiful. Moving fast, despite the four-inch stilettos, what Dani Letorneau, their lab tech, called FMPs, or fuck me pumps, and a tight white pencil skirt.

She stopped when she saw Burgess.

"Who are you?" she demanded. "And what are you doing in Eliot's house?"

Right on her heels was the medical examiner.

TWO

The officer who'd followed the woman and the medical examiner in shook his head at Burgess. "I tried to stop her, sir. She wouldn't listen."

Burgess nodded. If he was interpreting what he was seeing—and had heard—correctly, the woman had not simply pushed past the officer's attempts to stop him; she'd hit him. With her hand? Her handbag? A cell phone? Definitely with something. There was an ugly bruise already blooming on the officer's face.

"Hold on a second, Remy, okay?" Burgess said. He'd worked with Remy Aucoin many times since the officer was a rookie. While he admired Aucoin's forbearance here, as the woman was clearly distraught, no one got away with striking one of his officers. The situation had to be dealt with. First, though, he needed to send the ME upstairs.

"Your client is upstairs in the bedroom, Dr. Lee," he said. "Curious to hear your reactions. I'll be along in a minute."

The ME, a Harvard-educated pathologist who was brilliant at seeing what others often missed, nodded. "You rarely let me down, Joe," he said and started for the stairs.

The woman had been waiting for her chance. Now, she flashed past Burgess and tried to elbow Dr. Lee out of the way.

Big mistake. People didn't elbow Dr. Lee. Nor did people mess with Burgess's crime scenes if he could help it.

"Remy, help me," he said and dove for her. Together, he and Aucoin pulled the woman back down the stairs and led her into the living room. "Your cuffs, Remy?"

The officer handed over the cuffs, and Burgess cuffed the woman. He hated to do it. If this woman had been involved with their victim, as appeared to be the case, she could be a valuable source of information, a source who might not be nearly so cooperative after this. But it was clear she wasn't going to comply with any commands Burgess might give. She needed to be restrained, or who knew what havoc she'd wreak upstairs?

Burgess studied the woman, who was glaring at him as though looks could kill. "Sit down," he said.

"I will not sit down. I need to go upstairs. I need to know what's happened with Eliot."

"Detective Sergeant Joe Burgess, ma'am," he said. "You can't go upstairs. This place is a crime scene. You need to sit down and settle down so we can have a civilized conversation. Otherwise, I'll send you down to the station, and we can talk when I'm finished here."

She glared at him again, a look he thought often got the woman her way. She said, "Down to the station? You have got to be kidding."

It was interesting how much less beautiful even the loveliest of women looked when they were glaring or sulking or just generally acting entitled. She'd obviously chosen to skip wheedling or a charm offensive. Not that that would have worked, either. It had all gotten old long ago. So long Burgess had started referring to himself as a dinosaur.

"I don't have much of a reputation for kidding, ma'am." He got out his notebook. "What's your name?"

"None of your business."

"Everything about this place, and Eliot Spence, has become my business."

He didn't have time for this, for a stupid ping-pong match of words with an entitled woman evidently way too used to getting her way.

Burgess turned to the officer who'd tried to stop the woman's advance. "Remy, did this woman strike you because you were trying to prevent her from entering the premises after you instructed her she could not?"

Aucoin looked at the floor. What cop wants to admit he let a woman hit him?

Burgess nodded. "It's okay, Remy. Happens to all of us, but..." He switched his gaze from the officer to the woman. "But that doesn't make it okay. Call for someone to replace you, please, then take this woman to 109.

And get that mark on your face photographed first thing, okay? We'll need the photos for evidence."

"Photos? Evidence? You have got to be kidding," the woman said again. "Do you know who I am?"

"Can't know, can I, because you refuse to tell me. Don't care because justice isn't about how important people are or who they know."

He reached for the woman's purse, ignoring her squawk of protest, and opened it, looking for some ID. Found her license and wrote her name and address in his notebook.

Aucoin, his back to them, was on the phone. He closed it, turned, and told Burgess a replacement was on the way.

"Thanks, Remy. Put her in your car. She can wait there. I need to get upstairs and see what the ME has to tell me."

Aucoin nodded. "On it, sir." He stood before the woman. Picked up her purse and tucked it under his arm. "You need to come with me now," he said.

"Her name is Deidre. Deidre Lovejoy," Burgess said.

"Right," Aucoin said. "Ms. Lovejoy?"

With a flounce, Deidre Lovejoy rose from the couch. Good core strength, and strong thighs, Burgess noted. She didn't need to use her hands. "You haven't heard the last of this," she told Burgess.

"We've only just begun," he agreed, thinking it sounded like a sappy song. He followed them outside in case Aucoin needed assistance getting her into the car.

When the cruiser door was shut on her, Aucoin outside leaning against the car, Burgess crossed to where Kyle and the housekeeper were sitting on a bench. Indicating the woman they'd just arrested, he said, "Ms. Nowak, do you know that woman?"

"Oh, yes." The housekeeper frowned. "Miss Lovejoy. Miss Deidre 'Don't ever call me Dee Dee' Lovejoy. She is thinking she is Dr. Eliot's fiancée and that they will be married, but she is dreaming. There is only one woman in Dr. Eliot's life, and that woman is his wife."

"He has a wife and a girlfriend?" Burgess asked.

The housekeeper shook her head, then looked down at the work-worn hands knotted in her lap. "I am sorry. I am confusing you. He used to have a wife. Lenore. Mrs. Eliot. She died two years ago. Those are her pictures that are on the stairs. Dr. Eliot took them. All of them. And this woman… Deidre Lovejoy? She has been after him all the time to take them down because they make her uncomfortable. He only laughs at her."

She looked down at her hands and corrected herself. "Laughed, I mean. She even tried to get me to take them down while he was away at some conference for doctors. Of course, I would not."

Burgess nodded, annoyed with himself for not seeing that those pictures on the stairs were all the same woman.

As if she understood his confusion, the housekeeper said, "They were taken over the twelve years that they were married. That's why they look so different. I never knew her. She was gone before he moved here. Before I started working for him. But when he spoke of her, it was always clear that he adored her."

The housekeeper nodded toward the cruiser. "That woman there? He did not adore her. But he is...he was a man...and like many, enjoyed having a beautiful woman that other men envied." She shook her head. "But they would fight—"

She broke off, perhaps remembering that people weren't supposed to speak ill of the dead.

In Burgess's business, people who spoke ill of the dead could be very useful. For now, he would leave it to Kyle to follow up on what she'd said. He had to get inside and learn what Dr. Lee was seeing. He'd already missed those initial moments, moments when Dr. Lee often had valuable observations to share.

Burgess thanked her. He was about to head back inside, but Aucoin was still standing there, so Burgess motioned him away from the car.

"Something you wanted to tell me, Remy?"

Aucoin jerked his chin toward the car. "You know who that is?" he asked.

Since Aucoin knew him well enough to understand a person's status didn't matter when Burgess was conducting an investigation, Burgess asked the obvious question. "No. I don't. Is she someone I...or we...need to worry about?"

Aucoin shrugged. "Might be. She's the chief's niece. His sister's daughter. In case that matters."

Burgess sighed. Not the first time that he'd tangled with someone who had VIP connections to the chief. The last time, it had been a spoiled, entitled brat whose father was a senator's brother. The brat had been driving while eating a bowl of cereal, run up on the sidewalk, and nearly killed a mother walking with her baby. Under pressure, Burgess had backed off, or at least told his nemesis, Captain Cote, that *he* could decide how to handle the situation. Instead of pulling her license, Cote had let the brat off the hook. The brat had later run her car into a tree and nearly killed herself.

Burgess looked at the woman in Aucoin's cruiser, who was glaring at him through the window. He weighed the pain in the ass sending her to 109 would be against the value of her information. She was evidently in some kind of relationship with the deceased, an intimate one, even if her version of it and the deceased's had differed. She could be a valuable source of intel about many aspects of Dr. Spence's life.

As he debated, he watched a pair of gulls drifting over the water, riding air currents. They seemed to be enjoying this beautiful day. As they rose and fell, he considered which might get him better results—sending the sulking woman to the station or bringing her back inside and asking his questions now. He figured if he sent her to 109, the chief might hear about it and release her before he got a chance to question her. At least, here, he had a chance. But first, he needed some time with Dr. Lee.

Sighing, he said, "Thanks for the heads up, Remy. Let's let her cool her heels a bit…twenty minutes at least, while I consult with the ME…then you can bring her back inside. But only on the first floor, okay? She may not go upstairs."

Beyond Aucoin's cruiser, he saw the crime scene van arrive and park.

Aucoin nodded. "Got it," he said. "Okay, if I wait out here? That perfume she's wearing is strong enough to choke a horse."

Or a cop stuck in his car on a warm day. Burgess nodded. "Fine with me. Probably not fine with her. Oh, and you can take the cuffs off. Just don't let her bolt, okay? Not…" He looked in at the woman's massive purse, sitting on the front passenger seat. "Not that she's likely to go anywhere without that. She could probably go camping for a week with whatever she's got in there."

If people went camping with bulging wallets and overstuffed makeup bags and spare glasses, a scarf, an iPad, a pair of fold-up flats, and whatever else she was carrying.

He added, "When your replacement comes…you can let him babysit her. I still want you to get that bruise photographed."

Aucoin started to protest.

"Do it for me, Remy, okay? Because when the chief, or Captain Cote acting for the chief, calls me on the carpet, and he probably will call me on the carpet for this, I want to be able to show him those photos. They might take a bit of wind out of his sails. Hard for him to condone someone attacking an officer, even if that someone is a relative."

Aucoin nodded reluctantly, and Burgess went back inside.

This time, when he climbed the stairs, he studied the photographs more carefully. Assuming they were in an order—he thought youngest to oldest—Spence's wife had aged beautifully. If it could be said that she'd aged at all. He wondered what the story was. Who she'd been and how she'd died. He wondered whether Spence was only attracted to beautiful women. Whether Spence had led Deidre Lovejoy to believe there was more to the relationship than he intended because he liked the company of a beautiful woman.

So much to learn about their victim.

He found the ME bent over the man on the bed.

"About the best I can tell at this point, Joe, is that your victim is dead. Not that you needed me to tell you that. The how will have to wait for autopsy unless we turn him and find something definitive then." Lee turned and looked at Burgess. "Your team here? Because the sooner they get their photos, the sooner we can turn him and the sooner we can send the body to Augusta."

The ME smiled. "Looks like you might have a real mystery on your hands."

As though many of their cases weren't real mysteries. It was just that, usually, the mysteries were not about the victim's cause of death.

"Not that I don't enjoy a good mystery from time to time," Lee added. "What do you know about the man?"

"We're just getting started. His name is Eliot Spence," Burgess said. "Surgeon over at the hospital. Lives alone. We're told his wife died two years ago. There's a girlfriend. Deidre Lovejoy. No sign that she lives here or even keeps any of her things here. The housekeeper found him when she came to clean. For now, that's about it."

"It's too clean. Too neat. No struggle. The bedclothes unwrinkled. The sodomizing was postmortem. But the rest of it? The arrangement of the body? It's..." Lee considered. "It's odd." He added what Burgess had been thinking, though the two of them weren't always on the same page. "It's a message of some kind. Was it meant to degrade your victim or shock whoever found him?"

A question it would be Burgess's job to answer. "Any thoughts on how long he's been dead?" he asked.

"Rigor is setting in." Lee raised the tee shirt to reveal the torso. "And lividity. It's a cool day, and with the windows open, it would have been cooler in the early morning hours. I'd say seven or eight hours. But that's a guesstimate, Joe. A lot of things can affect the onset of rigor and lividity."

As Burgess well knew.

Again, Lee articulated what Burgess had been thinking. "Up early and already dressed or never went to bed?"

"Like you said, it's a mystery."

As the sounds of the crime scene team were heard on the stairs, Dr. Lee had one more thing to add. "Part of your mystery will be that bottle," he said. "It's not a common brand. Or at least it looks vintage. I wonder if that's part of the message?" He paused, then asked, "Do you think this killer...assuming you have a killer and not simply someone who took advantage of a postmortem opportunity...wants to be caught?"

Burgess had no idea.

He stepped back as Wink Devlin and Dani Letorneau entered with their gear.

THREE

"Wish you could arrange to have all our crime scenes look like this, Joe," Dani said as she turned slowly, admiring the space. "Wish I could live in a place like this. Or even one half this nice."

Wink, ignoring her, set down his gear and got out some gloves. Wink Devlin, their senior crime scene tech, was a quiet workhorse. Perpetually grouchy, always overworked, and beset at home by a wife who wanted him to retire and travel, he was always happy to be called out, day or night. He particularly liked being called out on weekends when he would otherwise be swept into Devlin family events. Wink's description of escaping the task of decorating a onesie just in time had been hilarious.

After a moment, he grudgingly said, "Guess we can't complain about the working conditions, can we?"

"Place is too clean," Burgess said. "Too neat. Too void of fingerprints. It's as though no one lived here. Or the perp was meticulous."

"Or your vic has the world's best cleaner," Dani offered. "I could also use a little of that at my place."

"Couldn't we all," Dr. Lee chimed in. "Somehow, despite my wife's best efforts, three little Lees can make an awful lot of mess."

Burgess had often heard the Lee children referred to as the "three little Lees," which sounded to him like a children's book. He realized he had never heard them referred to by name, nor did he know their sex or their ages. Now curious, he asked, "How old are your children? And what are their names?"

Lee shrugged, like it was a struggle to remember, then said, "Samuel is ten, Jennie is eight, and Michael is six. My wife wanted a fourth for a while, but she's found that three is more than enough. Especially when my schedule can be so uncertain."

"If you can get your photos and measurements," Burgess told Wink, gesturing toward the waiting Dr. Spence, "then we can turn him."

He and Lee stepped aside so Wink and Dani could work.

After what seemed like too short a time, Wink said, "He's ready for you."

Wink Devlin, catching his surprise, only said, "Annie Liebowitz of crime scenes, Joe. You know that."

It was easier, Burgess thought, when they didn't have to step around clutter. When the only sign of violence was a discreet bottle, and they weren't photographing the floor and the walls and all the stuff on the floor. When they didn't have to collect a lot of random items before they even got to the victim, and when there was no need to create a path through the clutter that everyone had to use. Still, he wondered if the unfriendly carpet might give them something—a hair or fiber or something dropped that had lodged in its thick pile.

Ever hopeful, wasn't he?

"Ready when you are," Dr. Lee said, stepping toward the bed.

They carefully turned the body so they could examine the front. It offered no further clues or discoveries, beyond the information that there was no blood, and it appeared that Dr. Eliot Spence hadn't been shot or stabbed. There was an odd bruise on the chest that brought a murmur from Lee about needing to examine it further. Under the body, there were a few long blonde hairs like the one Burgess had seen in the dressing room. He gestured for Dani to collect them.

"There's this," Dr. Lee said, pointing to the man's wrists. "Looks like he might have been tied up. With something soft, though, not a rope. I'll check for fibers when we get him back to Augusta. Sexually, maybe. The bruises would be more defined, or deeper, if he'd been struggling."

Burgess thought about the space on the tie rack, where a tie seemed to be missing. Had their killer—he corrected himself, their potential killer—taken the tie as a trophy? These early hours were always so filled with speculation. He also thought about the sex toys in the bedside tables. And what might be in those locked drawers.

He preferred doing this with Kyle or Perry, the other detectives on his team, because having observed the same situation, they could act as sounding boards for each other. One might spot what another might miss, and the search went faster. But it made sense for Stan Perry to be back at 109, getting a warrant to search the condo, Spence's office at the hospital, and his vehicle. Then, doing research on their victim. If time allowed, heading over to the hospital to speak with Spence's colleagues. Just like it was practical for Kyle to be sitting down with the cleaner now while she was available and finding the body was fresh in her mind. Valuable to talk with her now when observations might pour out rather than giving her time to censor what she should and shouldn't reveal about a customer. A sensible allocation of resources that left him alone with his speculations.

"What's the matter, Burgess?" the ME said. "Scene not bloody enough for you?"

"Maybe it's not bloody enough for you," Burgess suggested, deflecting the question. He hadn't yet decided why the scene troubled him so much. He ought to be grateful for these working conditions. Indeed, he was. It was also concerning because it was so pristine. What kind of a killer took the time to leave everything so neat? Who was comfortable enough around a dead body that they could take the time to wipe surfaces and possibly remove evidence? In a busy area like the one around these waterfront condos, could it have been done unseen?

Also, in his on-again, off-again relationship with the ME, he wasn't sure what the needling meant. Was Dr. Lee expecting him to see something he was missing? Reading something in him that Burgess didn't know was there? Was he giving off some insecure vibe? Decades on the job and an experienced and competent reader of crime scenes, Burgess was rarely insecure.

Sending the ball back into Lee's court, he said, "Although I expect the mystery of it intrigues you."

They had stepped away so Wink and Dani could take their photos. Once the location and condition of the body had been recorded, Dr. Eliot Spence could be sent off to the ME's office, and they could process the rest of the scene.

"I admit I am intrigued," Lee said. "The whole place is intriguing. There's a darkness to it, don't you think? Darkness and something cold."

Burgess did think. It was the first thing that had struck him on entering the condo. The place felt dark and cold, even with the open windows admitting sunlight and fresh ocean breezes. Reflections off the bouncing sea danced across the dark furnishings like they were trying to cheer the place up. It felt to Burgess like the place stubbornly resisted that cheer. The housekeeper had expressed surprise at finding the windows open. That wasn't usual. Dr. Spence had been very security conscious.

Though it probably didn't need saying, he turned back to Wink. "Be sure you fingerprint the windows and windowsills. The housekeeper says he never opened them."

Wink, concentrating on a photograph, waved an assent.

As Burgess stood at the top of the stairs, looking around at the somber space, something else struck him. At a recent crime scene, his sense that the interior of a storage shed didn't match the exterior dimensions had led him to a secret room and an awful discovery. Now, he realized that while the downstairs of the condo extended a full room's width beyond the stairway, an area that held the kitchen and dining area he'd not yet explored, up here, there was a wall about eight feet to his right, beyond a built-in desk with an office chair.

There was a large hanging on that wall, an elaborate quilt in the same dark colors as the rest of the place. Lots of shades of black and gray and plum with bits of cream, quilted with silver stitching. An abstract of mesmerizing dark swirls, continuing the dark theme of the rest of the condo.

It could be that the wall demarked the end of the condo on this floor. Or, the developers had given more space on this floor to another tenant. But he wasn't going to take that on faith. He stepped over to the quilt and carefully lifted it up from the bottom. Behind it, there was a door. Not a properly framed door like the woodwork in the rest of the place, but a flimsy wooden pocket door with a cheap recessed handle.

He looked back at Dr. Lee. "And here we have ourselves another mystery."

Lee nodded. "And you will have the happy task of uncovering why Dr. Spence had a secret room."

Burgess thought very few of his tasks could be described as happy, but he nodded. "We sure wouldn't want anything that came easily, would we?"

The discovery ramped up his need for that search warrant. Nothing plain sight about this door. He pulled out his phone and called Stan Perry to check on the status of the warrant.

FOUR

He got a brisk, "Perry. Investigations," from which he assumed that Stan hadn't checked the number before answering.

"Burgess," he said. "Also investigations. Checking on the status of the warrant."

"On its way, Boss," Perry said. "Soon as it gets here, I'll send it over to you. How are things on your end? From what I'm learning, seems like Dr. Spence was pretty much a closed book. People don't seem to have much to say about him."

"Maybe they'll be more forthcoming in person. You should head over to the hospital and talk to some folks. Before you do, though, we've been told that Spence lost his wife about two years ago. Her name was Lenore Spence. They didn't live here then. See what you can find out about her, including how and when she died."

"On it," Perry said. Then, "What's your scene like over there? Should I be feeling left out?"

Stan Perry was the youngest member of Burgess's team. Until recently, when his girlfriend Lily got pregnant, and he found himself married and with a baby, Perry had been kind of a wild man, his dating habits sometimes leading him into trouble. He'd also been kind of wild and insubordinate on investigations, frustrating Burgess until he was ready to kick the kid to the curb, only to have Perry turn up, like a retriever, with a critical piece of information. Marriage and his new daughter, Autumn, seemed to have settled him. Burgess hoped so, for all their sakes.

"Lovely condo. Pristine scene. Almost disturbingly so. We'll have to rely on Dr. Lee for the cause of death. The guy looks like he just fell asleep. Except for being sodomized with a bottle."

"Interesting," Perry said. "Can't wait to see the pictures." He changed the subject. "So, to clarify. You want me to look into Lenore Spence's death before I head over to the hospital?"

"I do."

"On it," Perry said again.

Burgess had another thought. "And look into Deidre Lovejoy, too. She's our victim's current girlfriend."

"And the chief's niece," Perry said.

Burgess wondered how come everyone knew that but him. He wasn't usually so far out of the loop. He wasn't political, but no one could be a cop in Portland without knowing something about the players.

Before he could ask, Perry explained, "Had a run-in with her once. Careless driving. I got the 'Do you know who I am?' question. I learned who she was."

"You give her a ticket?"

"You bet I did. One of my policies. If they pull the 'I'm someone important' card, I always give them a ticket."

Burgess had the same policy. Let the people upstairs who got paid the big bucks do the fixing. "Gotta go," he said. "Soon as we get that warrant, I'm going to investigate Dr. Spence's secret room."

"Don't," Perry said. Because the last time, what they'd found had traumatized all of them.

Sometimes, it seemed like getting traumatized was just part of the job. Other times, they could go months without anything so horrific. The roller coaster of homicide work. Or personal crimes. People didn't have to be killed for what the cops uncovered to be horrible. Burgess, Kyle, and Perry were all recovering from a terrible case in the summer. He shouldn't be joking about a secret room. Not now. But joking was how they kept it light.

"Have to," Burgess said. "But maybe I'll spend some time with Ms. Lovejoy first. She promises to be a charmer to interview. When he wouldn't let her into the condo, she slammed Remy Aucoin with a purse the size of a baby hippo. Left a nasty bruise. I'm sending him back to get it photographed."

Even as he said it, he realized that he had Wink and Dani right here, and they could take the pictures.

"Better you than me," Perry said. "I haven't slept in a month, and it tends to make me short-tempered. Not that Autumn isn't a darling baby. She's just nocturnal. Lily is a wreck, and she's supposed to go back to work next week."

"We could all move to a country where they respect parenthood and childrearing."

"Too late for that. We'll all just have to muddle along."

Burgess left him to his muddling, disconnected, and went outside to fetch Ms. Lovejoy for her interview.

First, he took a moment with Remy Aucoin and told him he didn't have to leave the scene and that Dani could take the photographs they needed. Aucoin was pleased. He was an ambitious lad who hoped to follow in Burgess's footsteps and become a detective one day. He'd make a good one, so long as he was diligent in learning to be careful. Plenty of times, Burgess had worked with ambitious young officers who were too eager and skipped necessary steps like learning to take things slowly and be observant.

He sent Aucoin inside to get his picture taken, then opened the rear door and invited Deidre Lovejoy out of the car. She wasn't out two seconds before she opened her mouth to complain about her treatment. She got as far as "Took you long enough—" before Burgess cut her off.

"Don't!" he said.

She rocked back on her flimsy heels and glared at him.

"We're going to go back inside. We're going to sit down, and we're going to have a conversation in which I ask you questions about Eliot Spence, and you answer them. You are not going to complain. You are not going to threaten. You are not going to interrupt to ask your own questions or make demands. When I am done with my questions, you may ask yours, and if I can answer them without jeopardizing the investigation, I will. Understood?"

"I am not—"

"What did I just say?"

She tossed her hair and looked away, possibly assessing her chances of escape. They were nil. She was surrounded by cops, and even if there was some slight avenue of escape, she was wearing shoes and a skirt that made it impossible for her to run. "You have no right to keep me here."

"Maybe not keep you here," he said. "But you assaulted one of my officers. I have every right to arrest you and send you to headquarters for booking. I'd rather not do that if it can be avoided. The best way to avoid it is to cooperate." He gave it a beat, then added, "Besides, if you genuinely were in a relationship with Dr. Spence, and someone has killed him, I would think you'd want to help the police catch the person who did it. Why wouldn't you?"

Burgess put genuine curiosity into the question. Because he was curious. He was often curious about why people who should want a crime solved chose not to cooperate with the police. It was what his late mother would have called "wrongheaded."

In a book called *Homicide* by the author David Simon, about police investigations in Baltimore, he'd read a truth that all cops understood: everybody lies. Some people lie because they have something to hide, either connected to a case or in their own lives. Some people lie simply because they don't want to help the police. His mother was right. It was definitely wrongheaded. He often wondered how those people who lied just to screw around with the police or to make some anti-police point would feel if the crime was committed against them or someone they cared about.

She hovered there, back to him, balanced on one precarious heel, as she considered her response.

Fine with him. It was pleasant out here in the sun, with a cooling breeze off the water. The summer had been too hot. Miserably hot. Normally, he felt a bit sad at the approach of fall, but this year he was grateful.

After she'd hesitated long enough for his patience to run out, he said, "I'm not getting any younger, and the day isn't getting any longer, and I have a lot to do. So, inside and cooperate or an arrest and back to 109?"

"You are a very unpleasant man," she said.

Lady, he thought, *you ain't seen nothing yet.*

"I'll need my purse. I have some calls to make. There are people who—"

"You can make your calls when we're finished, but I'll have to ask you not to speak about what's happened here nor to share what we discuss."

"There's this thing called freedom of speech," she said.

Burgess wanted to shake her, an impulse he'd learned to squelch. "Inside or back to 109?" he repeated.

"Oh. All right. I suppose the sooner I speak to you, the sooner I can leave, right?"

He didn't answer. Instead, he opened the cruiser and got out her purse, which he tucked under his arm.

She tried to grab it, and he gave her a look. The patented Burgess glare, his team called it. She dropped her hands.

"After you," he said.

She swiveled on her heel, and with a twist of her hips, finished turning her back on him and stalked toward the condo door.

FIVE

When she was settled on the couch, Burgess across from her, her purse on a table beside him, she said, "I'm thirsty. It was hot in the car. Hot and smelly and awful. People shouldn't be subject to—"

Ignoring her request, Burgess smiled. "I'm afraid police cars aren't designed for comfort. So…" He checked his notebook and read her name and address back to her. "Is this information correct?"

She nodded.

"And your phone number?"

She told him, adding, "That's my cell. I have a landline. And an office number." She gave those, as well. And waited.

"Are you employed, Ms. Lovejoy?"

"I have a consulting business. Media relations. Lovejoy Associates."

"Do you have an office address?"

"I work from home. From my condo. I've turned part of it into an office. I thought you wanted to talk about Eliot."

"We'll get there. Background is important. How long have you known Dr. Spence?"

She considered. "It's what? September? We met at a party last Christmas. At my mother's house. She knew Eliot's boss, uh, department chair? Whatever they call them in medicine. From some charity things she does, and she asked him to bring Eliot along. She thought the two of us might hit it off. Which—" She smiled. "We definitely did."

"A dating relationship?"

She nodded.

"Exclusive?"

"Absolutely."

"For how long?"

"Almost immediately. We just knew, I guess, the way people do some-times. It got pretty serious very quickly, despite his hesitation about getting involved again." She paused. "You see, Eliot is...uh, was, still recovering from the loss of his wife. Lenore. Those are his photographs of her on the stairs." A grimace. "I've been trying to get him to take them down. I find them..."

She considered, and Burgess leaned forward a little, curious about what she'd say.

She looked down at her feet in those awfully impractical shoes. Uncrossed and recrossed her ankles. "I don't know whether to say insulting or intimidating. Lenore was beautiful, and I can't help feeling, when I pass them, that I don't quite measure up somehow."

This time, the pause was while she waited for him to reassure her. He didn't pick up his cue. Burgess thought she measured up just fine. It wasn't her looks that were the problem.

"A feeling you got on your own or something you sensed from Dr. Spence?"

She shrugged. Definitely not going there.

"Tell me about Dr. Spence. What was he like?"

An open-ended question. How she answered would tell him about her as well as about Spence.

"He was handsome, of course. And fit. Very fit. He was meticulous about his person, his home, and his possessions. You've probably already realized that. Meticulous, not fussy. He just had a very strong sense of how he wanted his home, well, his life, actually, to be, and was comfortable being assertive about it. He was a work-hard, play-hard person. It was important to him to be successful at whatever he put his hand to. He was—"

Another hesitation. Something important she wasn't at ease saying. "He was a bit controlling. He liked to have his way, and he wasn't always nice about it. I mean, he was fine with me. With friends. Peers. He could be abrupt with what I might call the smaller people. People he worked with who weren't doctors. People like store clerks and waiters. I guess pretty much anyone he considered beneath him."

A lot like her. Burgess wondered if she was aware of that.

She knotted her hands together. "Look, I love…loved Eliot. I expected that, eventually, we would be married. Of course, he was reluctant to commit again, having lost Lenore. But I can be very patient. Talking about him, telling a stranger about him, it's difficult. I'm afraid I won't paint a fair picture of him. That if I tell you about his controlling nature. Or about how obsessed he was with making this place perfect. Or about his occasional irrational…in my opinion…flares of temper, you won't see the Eliot that I know."

She gazed toward the window. "It's strange to see the windows open like this. He never liked to have the windows open. He was very strict about it. I told him it was silly. That he lived right here on the waterfront and should let that lovely fresh air in. But he…" She considered. "It sounds odd to say this, but it was almost as though he was afraid someone would get in if he left them open."

"He was afraid of someone or something?" Burgess asked.

That stopped her for a moment. She considered, then said slowly, "I don't know. Really. I don't know whether he was a little paranoid or whether he was genuinely concerned. He wasn't the type of person to be fearful. He was very much an in-charge type of man. And yet, there was something."

Burgess waited for her to describe that something.

After another moment, she said, "There must have been something. He was scrupulous, you might even say over-scrupulous, about checking locks. He always looked in the backseat and under the car before he would get in and drive. And he…well, he did that thing I've read that cops do, where in a restaurant, he would always sit so that he could watch the door. That kind of thing. It was surprising, given what a masculine guy he was."

"Did you ever ask him about it? Ask whether there was someone who was, or had been, threatening him?"

She nodded. "I did because it was otherwise so unlike him. I mean, he was the kind of man who loved extreme skiing and sailing on a day when the wind was high. He loved the thrill of coming close to danger. Anyway, I asked, and he pretended he didn't know what I was talking about. But it was definitely a thing with him."

"Did he ever talk about anyone who was threatening? Anyone whose behavior he was concerned about?"

She shook her head.

"What about threatening phone calls or messages?"

"Nothing that I ever saw. But he was pretty private about his messages; he always stepped away to take phone calls. I figured that was because they involved patient care."

"Private or secretive?"

"What's the difference?"

She knew the difference.

"What about enemies? People he'd had run-ins with or disputes? Did you ever witness any angry confrontations?"

"I don't know of any." She looked away as she said it, telling Burgess there had been something.

"Anyone who seemed to be watching him? Did he ever seem concerned about being followed?"

"Not that I noticed. I mean beyond that careful checking. He checked the rearview mirror a lot when he was driving. But people do that, don't they?"

"He was a doctor. What about angry patients or patients' families? Was there any trouble you knew about on that front?"

She shrugged. "He never mentioned anything. But Eliot didn't talk much about his work. He said he liked to leave that at the hospital. He liked our time together to be just that—together time. He didn't like it to be interrupted by his work. Or anything else."

"What about colleagues? Anyone at the hospital he didn't get along with?"

"As I said, he didn't like to discuss his work. Or his workplace."

"Any disputes with neighbors?"

"No."

"What about his family? What can you tell me about them?"

"Disputes with his family?"

"Sorry. That was a poor transition," Burgess said. "What can you tell me about Dr. Spence's family?"

She considered. "He wasn't close to them. I know that. He was the oldest of three. He has a younger brother, Billy, and a sister, Kara. They live in the DC area. That's where he grew up. In Maryland. His parents are both still alive. Jack, short for Jackson, and Carole Spence. I have their address somewhere. I can find it for you."

"I'd appreciate that. Got their phone number? The parents?"

She shook her head.

"Brother or sister?"

Another shake of the head.

"You met any of his family?"

A simple, unembellished "No."

"So, not close to his family. Who was he close to?"

"Me."

"Besides you. Who were his close friends?"

She named two doctors at the hospital. A Gordon Webster and Adam Schenk.

"Outside of work?"

The ankles uncrossed and crossed again, those sharp heels scything through the air. He was glad he was five feet away.

"I don't see why any of this matters. Why are you wasting time with all these questions when you should be out looking for his killer?"

"Because killings are often personal, and knowing about the victim becomes essential to locating someone who believed they had a reason to kill. Because somewhere in Dr. Spence's life, there is a person who wanted him dead. We need your help, help from the people who knew him well, to locate that person."

Burgess didn't add that the violation of Dr. Spence's body made it highly likely the killing was personal. Very personal. That was not something they would be sharing. He waited for an answer to his question. Realized without another nudge, he'd probably be waiting all day.

He nudged. "Who were Dr. Spence's friends outside of the hospital? Friends from high school? College? Med school? Friends he did sports with, that kind of thing."

After a bit of hair tossing, and when she'd inspected her fingernails and found them satisfactory, she said, "Jeff Gilbert is his financial guy. They play golf together. And he and Coleman Travis sometimes run together. Maybe grab a beer. Coleman runs a restaurant in South Portland. I wouldn't say either man was that close to Eliot. See, men don't have friends like women do. I expect you know that. Beyond that? Sorry. I really don't know."

Burgess nodded. "What about people you socialized with?"

"Look, you're wasting your time, Detective. There's not anyone who knew him better than I did who could help you with questions like this. I mean, why would he confide in someone he played golf or went skiing with? He just wasn't that sort of person. He wasn't a confider. He kept things to himself."

"Do you know where he lived before moving to Portland?"

"In the Boston area. Weston, I believe."

"Do you know of any friends from Weston we should speak with to get a sense of his life before he moved here?"

She shrugged. "He rarely mentioned it. Or anyone from there. As I told you, he was trying to leave that life behind. Trying to move away from his sorrow over Lenore's death. Staying in touch with friends from there would have made that harder."

"If you know, how did Lenore Spence die?"

She held out one foot and studied her shoe, as though somehow that would help her shape an answer. After twisting her ankle right and left a few times, she said, "It was a freak accident, really. Eliot said it should have been him. That he was always the one who got up in the night to answer the phone. They...uh...he said that because he was interrupted so often, they had a pact that they wouldn't keep their phones in the bedroom. Their phones—the landline and their cell phones—were on a small table near the top of the stairs. Anyway, this particular night. I guess it was very late—like one or two in the morning—the phone rang, and he was sleeping so soundly he didn't hear it."

Another glance at her feet. "He said that he was exhausted that night from a particularly long and grueling surgery. He just didn't hear it. He repeated that so many times, always in a kind of disbelief, that he didn't hear the phone. He said that it kept ringing, and eventually, Lenore got up to answer it. He said their housekeeper must have used some wrong kind of polish near the top of the stairs. Maybe the furniture polish on the floor by mistake? The floor was very slippery that night, which it never was. Anyway, Lenore was half asleep, going to answer the phone, and she tripped over the dangling ties on her robe, and the floor was slippery, and she couldn't stay on her feet, and she fell down the stairs."

She looked at Burgess. "He's never gotten over it. The guilt. He slept right through the phone call and her fall and didn't know what had happened until the next morning when another phone call woke him. He saw that Lenore wasn't in the bed, and when he got to the phone, he looked down the stairs, and there she was, crumpled at the bottom. A total tragedy because if he'd heard the fall or woken sooner, she might have been saved. That is why, if you really must know, he kept to himself. He was a total bundle of guilt over what had happened. He never could forgive himself. It was the reason—"

She broke off, staring at the open window as she shaped her words. "The reason he was so solitary. Sometimes, so cold and distant. Because he was carrying that memory and that guilt. So, of course, he was reluctant to

37

form a new relationship with me, even though he wanted to, and we were close. And why he threw himself into his work, doing as much for his patients as he could. He was trying to save as many lives as possible to make up for the one he'd lost."

Very interesting insight, Burgess thought. He wondered if it was true. Or how much of it was true. And about a man who'd share that with his girl-friend. How he'd go about doing that. It did suggest a relationship more intimate or close, perhaps, than he'd gotten an impression of from the cleaner. At the same time, he wondered about a man who'd share some-thing that intimate but didn't share details about friends, family, and his former life. He also wondered whether Lenore Spence might have had a family member or friend who held grudges. Someone who blamed her husband for her death?

He switched to a different set of questions.

"What can you tell me about his routine? About his schedule? Was it regular? Were his hours predictable, or did they depend on his patients and the hospital's needs?" The information would help them know whether someone might have stalked Dr. Spence, looking for an opportunity to attack. He'd be asking these same questions of his housekeeper if she knew, and his colleagues, as well as friends they could locate.

He made a mental note to be in touch with the Weston police depart-ment to learn the details of Lenore Spence's death.

She shrugged. "He worked a lot. I don't know whether it was required or by choice. Sometimes, we'd have something scheduled, and he'd have to cancel. I wasn't very happy about it, and I let him know. He said there was nothing he could do about it."

"Did he have regular arrangements with friends for activities outside the hospital?"

When she didn't answer, he added, "If you know."

"I don't know. That is, I sometimes knew when he was going to play golf, or in the winter, when he'd be going skiing. I don't ski, so he made those trips without me." A pause. "He went to the gym, of course. And tried to get in a three- to five-mile run three times a week."

"Running partner or solo?"

"Mostly solo. Sometimes with Travis. He wanted me to start running so we could do it together. I guess he and Lenore used to run together. It wasn't something I was interested in. I have my yoga and Pilates, and that's enough for me. I don't like—" She broke off, glared at Burgess, and decided not to answer.

Burgess figured he'd exhausted her utility, at least for now. There were so many other things calling for his time. He had one last question. "Except when he's skiing or at work, do the two of you typically spend your weekends together?"

She nodded.

"But not last night?"

"He said there was someone he had to see. Some business thing that came up suddenly. We were supposed to try out a new restaurant. I'd made reservations, which, by the way, were very hard to get. I was dressed and ready for him to pick me up, and then he called, said this thing had come up, and totally blew me off without any further explanation. I suggested that he take care of business, and we get together later, but he never called, and when I called him, he didn't answer."

"What time did you call him?"

"I called at nine. He picked up that time but said he was busy and couldn't talk. Then I called at ten, and eleven, and twelve. He didn't answer, so I gave up and went to bed."

She held up both feet and studied her shoes. "I'd gotten these shoes specially, because he likes me to wear stilettos. Not picking up? That wasn't like him. He always takes my calls. Well. Almost always. Not at the hospital, of course. Or when he's running. Or—"

Another pause as she realized that there were a lot of times when he didn't pick up. She glared at Burgess like that was his fault.

"What made you decide to come to his place today?"

"It's obvious, isn't it?" she said. "He never answered any of my calls, and then he stood me up again for brunch. I mean, he offers brunch since we couldn't have dinner last night, and then I'm there waiting for him for more than an hour, and he never shows up. Never answers his phone. That wasn't like him. I knew something had to be wrong."

"You have no idea who he was meeting last night?"

She sighed. "I already said that, didn't I?"

"But whoever it was, canceling your date was unusual?"

She nodded.

He had one more question, or questions, that she wasn't going to like. "Those photographs on the stairs. Of Lenore Spence. Dr. Spence took them?"

She nodded, not looking at him but staring toward the window.

"Did he take photographs of you?"

Her gaze shifted back to him, her face angry. "Yes, he did. A lot of photographs of me. At first, I found it flattering, but gradually, I grew to dislike it. The pressure. The way he was always arranging me. It couldn't just be a spontaneous picture. It had to be…I had to be…perfect. I told him he had to stop it. It was making me too uncomfortable."

"And did he stop?"

"Not entirely. No. But it did get better."

Burgess wondered where those photographs were and what other photos they'd find.

"Are we done?"

They were done. He'd seen enough of the twisting foot, and the way twisting her foot made her mid-calf skirt hike up to above her knees. He didn't think it was deliberate, but he wasn't sure. What he was sure of was that she knew a lot more than she was sharing, and he wondered why she was holding things back. Partly to protect herself, her privacy, her memories of Spence and their relationship? People did that. But there was more, he was sure. Maybe he'd learn the next time they spoke. She probably thought done meant done, but he knew it often took multiple interviews with a subject to get all the information they knew.

"Thank you for your time, and I'm so sorry for your loss," he said. "You're free to go."

She rose, tugged down the skirt until it was wrinkle-free, and gave him one last glare for the road. "I was always free to go." She stalked away, leaving him annoyed with her attitude and impressed by her ability to walk in that outfit.

He followed her out. He had some questions for the housekeeper and hoped she was still out there talking with Kyle.

SIX

Just in time. Kyle and the housekeeper were both on their feet. She had her bag on her shoulder, and he was bent down, evidently thanking her for her time.

"Excuse me," he said as he approached. "Got one more minute for a question?"

"Whatever I can do to help you with this awful thing," the woman said.

Kyle stepped back to let Burgess take the lead. "Actually, a couple of questions," Burgess said. "Would you like to sit?"

She shook her head. "I am already late for my next job. They will understand when I explain the circumstances, but I must be going soon."

"I understand. My first question, if you know, is whether Dr. Spence had many visitors to the condo?"

She shook her head. "Once in a while, I can see that someone else has been here. Extra glasses or dishes or bottles or takeout containers in the trash, things like that. He doesn't have guests to stay over because there is only the one bedroom. Except for the women, of course."

Burgess exchanged a look with Kyle as he asked, "Dr. Spence entertained women other than Ms. Lovejoy?"

The housekeeper shrugged. "She doesn't know, I think, but yes. Sometimes. Sometimes, there would be signs that a woman had spent the night. Or been there in the evening. Extra towels used, and...well, the sheets or hair on the pillow. Or things in the trash or makeup on the sink." She grinned, a sly, insider's grin. "Housekeepers know, you know. We see things even when our customers think they've cleaned up."

"Did you ever see any of the women?"

She shook her head. "My time to clean is at nine-thirty on a weekday. He is gone by then. His guests as well."

Burgess was getting the feeling that he wouldn't have liked Dr. Spence very much. In truth, except for his favorite ER doc, he didn't like doctors very much. Not that it made any difference. Like or dislike the victim, his job was to solve their murders. Sometimes, he thought he worked harder on the victims he didn't like just because he didn't like them. As though he had to prove something to them.

He nudged himself back into questioning mode. This woman needed to leave, and he was letting his thoughts wander. "What about his schedule? Was Dr. Spence very regular about his schedule?"

"I wouldn't really know, Detective. Only that, from what I saw, he was very precise. Very much on time, and he expected me to be as well." She hesitated, as though she wasn't sure she should share, then gave a nod—to herself, Burgess thought—and added, "Even when he wasn't here, it was as though he knew whether I was."

Cameras, Burgess wondered? In the rooms they hadn't searched yet? In the room or whatever it was that lay behind the hidden door?

"We understand he didn't like to have the windows open?"

A vigorous nod. "I couldn't understand it…why he wouldn't want fresh air…but he was very specific. I was never to open the windows." Another small grin. "Of course, on one beautiful day, I opened them to air the place out, but I was very careful about closing and locking them before I left." She hesitated, then added, "And he specifically reminded me about not opening them after that day."

One question inevitably became several.

"When you arrived today to clean, were there any signs that Dr. Spence had had company last night?"

She nodded.

"What were they?"

"Very small things," she said. "Two glasses were out of place. They'd been washed but were put away in the wrong place."

"Anything else?"

"Just that. As I say, small things. But Dr. Spence was very particular."

Two glasses suggested two people. But they'd been washed, so they wouldn't be much use unless they had the fingerprints of whoever had put them away. If that person hadn't worn gloves or been Dr. Spence. Since she didn't want to go back inside, he asked her to describe where to find the two errant glasses.

"Do you collect the trash when you clean?"

She got slightly indignant. "Of course."

"What do you do with it when you're finished?"

"There is a garage beyond the kitchen. I leave it in the can there."

"Today, when you were interrupted by finding Dr. Spence's body, did you still take out the trash?"

She hesitated, suggesting she must have left the trash she'd collected somewhere that had deviated from Dr. Spence's very particular rules. For a moment, he thought she was going to bolt away from them and dash inside. Then she sighed and shrugged. "It is still in the kitchen because I never finished."

"Do you know anything about the door upstairs behind that tapestry?"

She shook her head but looked away. A tell. She might not know what was behind that door, but she'd peeked behind the wall hanging.

Those small grins, admissions of breaking her employer's rules, and the way she'd looked away—suggested this woman might know more than she was sharing. They might have more questions for her, as well. But for now, Burgess thought they were done. He looked at Kyle. "You have any more questions?"

Kyle shook his head, giving Burgess a look that said he, too, expected they'd be questioning the woman again. "She can go." Burgess knew Kyle wanted to get inside. To see what Burgess had seen. Get a sense of the place, as Burgess had. No one objected to sitting outside on such a lovely day, interviewing a witness, but as Burgess had once put it, he and Kyle were like pieces of blotting paper. They walked through scenes, absorbing what they passed. Kyle needed to be able to get inside and absorb.

Thinking about the vacuum and bucket at the top of the stairs, Burgess asked her, "Do you need anything from inside?"

She shook her head. "Those things I left at the top of the stairs are his. Dr. Spence's. And anyway, I do not want to be in there anymore. Not after—" She shook her head again, more vigorously. "No. I am done here. But do you think..." She hesitated, as if it was an improper question under the circumstances, then decided to ask it anyway and said, in a rush, "...will I get paid for today?"

Burgess didn't know, so he told her that. She shrugged and hurried away. The shrug was an eloquent version of "Why should I be surprised? People always take advantage of the help."

"Interesting woman," Kyle said. "At first, I thought she didn't know anything. She had that air of 'Don't ask me, I'm just the cleaner,' but as we talked, there were hints. Well. You know. You saw. She kept tabs on Dr. Spence. I think she actually enjoyed knowing that Deidre Lovejoy thought she was a serious girlfriend while Spence was entertaining other women. I'm guessing Lovejoy wasn't exactly kind to the help?"

Burgess nodded. "And she described Spence as not being very kind to what she termed 'the little people.' Kind of unselfaware in that department."

He led the way inside. At the bottom of the stairs, he hesitated. "Looks like maybe we've got ourselves another secret room."

Kyle took a step back. He shook his head. Took another step. "No way, Joe. Just no way."

"It won't be anything like last time, Terry."

"Sure. You say that now, but you have no idea, do you?"

Terry Kyle was lean, a little over six feet tall, and whippet-thin. He had fierce blue eyes and a shock of unruly black hair. When he was upset, he trembled like a whippet, and he was trembling now. A visible vibration that, combined with those eyes, could be seriously intimidating.

Burgess put a hand on his shoulder. "Easy, Ter. Easy. We won't know what's there until we open the door. Stan's coming down with a warrant. But it won't be like last time. Just look at this place. What's on the other side of that door may be weird. Or creepy. Or criminal. But in this neighborhood, and with a girlfriend and other women coming and going? It's not going to be like that."

"That" was a horrific case of trafficking young girls for sex. Burgess believed, based on his cop's gut, not that it was always right, that what had gotten Dr. Spence killed was something far different. Something very personal.

Kyle settled and followed Burgess up the stairs.

Wink and Dani were still recording the scene. Dr. Lee was waiting impatiently, shifting from foot to foot, waiting for Wink's nod to tell him that they were ready for the body to be removed. Lee could have gone already. He'd done what he'd come for. Burgess wondered what he was waiting for.

He let Kyle go first. Kyle hadn't had a chance to observe the body yet, and he wanted Kyle's unfiltered first impressions.

Kyle stopped about eight feet from the bed and studied Dr. Spence. The immaculate covers, now slightly disarranged when they'd turned the body. The bottle. The trim figure and slightly overlong dark curls. His gaze then shifted to take in the room. After a long moment, he stepped back.

"Nobody lives like this," he said. "Place is like a high-end decorator's showroom." Then, "Someone was making a very personal statement here with that bottle. But whether it was to us—a challenge in the form of 'See if you can figure out what this means' or a final 'Fuck you' to the victim?" He shook his head. "I guess that's our mystery to solve."

He stepped back away from the bed and around the edge of one of the screens. "This whole damned place is a statement about something. It's so damned curated. I know. We know that people use decorators, and those decorators often have a unified vision for a place. But there is such a darkness to it, especially for a waterfront condo. If I lived here, I'd be too depressed to get out of bed in the morning."

He gave his wolfish grin. "And right now, I am happy to get out of bed in the morning, even if I am scared to death about getting married again." The grin widened. "And very happy to get into bed at night."

Kyle had married young and quickly had two girls who were the light of his life. His ex-wife, on the other hand, had been a manipulative harridan, known to Burgess and his team as the PMS queen. Or the bitch from hell. When they'd separated, the ex had made plans to take the girls to Texas. Kyle had had to fight bitterly to get custody of his girls.

"So where's this secret door?" he said, looking around.

Before Burgess could show him, Dr. Lee joined them. "Well, Gentlemen, I am off. You can send Dr. Spence when you're ready. I'll see you tomorrow for the autopsy. I'm thinking bright and early, like eight? I do enjoy starting my day with a good mystery, and Dr. Spence presents one. I'll call and let you know."

He sketched a wave and headed down the stairs.

"He's in a good mood," Kyle said. "Must not have been on the golf course when the call came in."

"I think it's the puzzle," Burgess said. "As he said, he does enjoy a puzzle, and the cause of death appears to be one. No wounds from gunshots or stabbing. No signs of strangulation. The only sign of violence is that bottle."

"Oh boy. Captain Cote is going to be disappointed. He's probably back there right now, salivating over the expected gory details."

Burgess rolled his eyes. Captain Cote, his boss's boss up the food chain, was the bane of their existence. A man who'd worked all the jobs under him but never seemed to have learned anything about how to do them. Either that or he'd forgotten. He was famous for ferreting out the details detectives wanted to keep hidden from the public—details only a killer would know—and then blurting them out at press conferences. Burgess and his team had learned to hide them within the most boring documents. Or not write them down anywhere that Cote had access to. It didn't always work, but they tried.

Cote also had a beyond infuriating habit of barging into crime scenes and tromping around like the proverbial bull in the china shop. Only in his case, it was the bull in the blood spatter or whatever else there was at a scene for him to mess with.

Once again, Burgess found himself needing to drag his wayward thoughts back to the business at hand. Lately, he'd begun to refer to himself as a dinosaur, slowed down by age and weariness. His favorite ER doc had prescribed some thyroid pills, which were supposed to give him more energy. Between the pills and an actual vacation, he should be raring to go these days. Things were better, but he still felt like an engine that needed a tune-up. Possibly because that vacation had come with as much drama as any of his days here in the city.

"Where's this secret door?" Kyle asked again.

Burgess pointed toward the wall hanging. "Behind that."

"Let's see—"

However, the inspection of the mysterious door was delayed by the arrival of the removal team, and once the body had been removed, they inspected the bedcovers where the body had been. A few more of those long blonde hairs and little else.

"But who knows what we'll find back in the lab," Wink Devlin said.

"Yeah. Like the killer's name written in invisible ink?" Kyle suggested. "Or maybe a confession hidden among the bedclothes?"

"Oh, ye of little faith," Devlin said. "Stan Perry isn't the only one who can pull rabbits out of hats. If our victim was entertaining a lady or gentleman friend before his demise, we might well get DNA from the sheets."

Which they all knew was true.

"We will leave you to it," Burgess said. "Find us rabbits. Please."

Another interruption, as the third member of their team, Stan Perry, arrived with the search warrant. Burgess and Kyle went downstairs to meet him.

"I could have sent it over with patrol," he said, "but I wanted to see things for myself. Got appointments over at the hospital, but you know how accommodating they are. It'll be a few hours before anyone deigns to receive me."

Burgess quirked an eyebrow at Stan's use of the word "deigns."

It was going to be one of those cases, they all knew, where they would have to press those who knew Dr. Spence to make themselves available. Doctors were always overworked and often had staff who protected them from the annoying intrusions of the constabulary. He didn't expect the denizens of these pricey condos would be much more forthcoming. It wasn't an absolute ratio, but there was definitely a negative correlation between wealth and privilege and the level of cooperation the police got.

Maybe that was unfair. These days, cooperation often seemed to have flown the coop everywhere.

"You just missed one doctor," Kyle said. "He had to go up to Augusta."

"Yeah. I saw someone getting into a black car. Looked kinda like a hearse."

Perry looked around and echoed what they had thought. "Gad. If I lived here, I'd be chronically depressed. Where's all the blue and cream upholstery and the fabric with seaside motifs? The paintings of beach grass or lobster boats or little pine-dotted islands?"

Funny how they were all on the same page about that. Burgess thought the word for the dark décor was funereal. It had definitely proved so for Dr. Spence.

Time to move along. Now that they had the warrant, they could legally explore things like Dr. Spence's locked drawers and what was behind that hidden door. All they needed were the man's keys.

"We need keys," he said. "Terry and Stan, you two look downstairs. I'll look up here."

He'd already done a quick scan of the place. Now, he regretted not asking Dr. Lee to check the victim's pockets. They could get a locksmith in, but it would be an unnecessary complication for exploring locked spaces if they'd just sent the keys off to Augusta.

Plenty of places to still check here. The dressing room. The desk. Burgess recalled that there had been a black lacquer box on a small table in the entry. The kind of place a meticulous and habitual person who disliked clutter might leave their keys. As he headed for the desk, he leaned over the partition and called down, "Check that black box by the entry."

Black box. The term made him pause. Sometimes, cases needed to be given names, and often, surprisingly, those names presented themselves before the cops even had time to think. Given the preponderance of black in this place, and the mystery Dr. Spence's death presented, black box seemed appropriate.

He'd start with the desk. A pristine eight-foot expanse of blond wood with a high-tech black desk lamp and nothing else on the desktop. Nothing obvious in the drawers. He figured a man who had a secret room—or at least a secret door that might only lead to a closet—might have secrets in his desk as well. Never mind how inconvenient it would be to have to delve into a secret compartment every time he wanted to drive his car. Burgess pulled out the center drawer, wrestling it free from its rails, and checked behind it and under it. Experience had taught him to check the bottoms of drawers. Sometimes, they yielded very interesting finds. Here? Nothing.

He moved on to the top drawer on the right. And yes. The drawer had a false back. Anyone pulling it out or feeling around would think they'd come to the back of the drawer, but when he wrestled this drawer off its rails, there was a four-inch space behind the false back. No keys were in there, but a stack of letters held together with a thick rubber band was.

He left the letters sitting on the desktop and moved to the bottom drawer. It was full of files. He felt the back. No secret compartment. And the files could wait.

On to the other side. No secret compartment in the top drawer. Or in the middle drawer. The bottom drawer held a stack of the kind of instructions and information that came with appliances and electronics. A big stack that probably matched a lot of things in the kitchen, a space he hadn't checked yet. Behind this drawer, there was another secret compartment. Still no keys, but there were a bunch of legal papers. Those might prove fruitful. For now, they, too, could wait. He put them on the desktop with the stack of letters.

He stood up, flexing his bad knee a few times as he apologized to it for holding it in that bent position for so long. Then, he looked around. Dressing room? Or was there something else here that he was missing?

He decided two secret compartments were probably the lot and headed for the dressing room.

SEVEN

Burgess paused in the doorway, thinking he shouldn't search here until Wink and Dani had had a chance to process it. Those bruises on Spence's wrists and the possibility of a missing necktie, along with that long blonde hair, suggested someone besides Spence had been in here. Someone who might have been more careless about fingerprints away from the bedroom. He was saved from making a decision by Stan Perry's voice from downstairs.

"I've got 'em," he called.

Burgess went to the top of the stairs and leaned down. "Let's take a look at that mysterious door, then."

Stan Perry climbed the stairs, the keys dangling from his hand. Kyle was right behind him. While they might normally be handling separate tasks, the mystery behind that locked door was something they were all too curious about.

After Dani had photographed the wall hanging in its place, Kyle and Perry reached up and carefully lifted the dowel that held the hanging in place down from its hooks and draped it over the desk chair. The door that was exposed was in stark contrast to the rest of the condo. Instead of impeccably finished woodwork, this was a slab of thin, unpainted plywood with a cheap inset brass handle. A pocket door. Instead of a regular lock, there was a bracket held shut by a padlock.

Perry handed Burgess the keys. A rather large bunch that didn't include a car key.

"You find a car key as well?" Burgess asked.

"I did. Left it there for later."

Burgess nodded and examined the key ring. Ten keys. He chose a smallish one that looked like a padlock key and tried the lock. The lock clicked. He opened the padlock. For a moment, the three of them hesitated, reluctant to take the next step, their curiosity about what lay behind the door warring with their experience of what might be. Then Burgess slid the door open, exposing the space that lay beyond it.

The room was approximately eight feet from the door to the wall, and, to their right, it widened and became almost the length of the condo's second floor. Two doors at the long end suggested closets or possibly another bathroom. Immediately to the right, there was an armchair, a side table, and a floor lamp. The floor was carpeted in a thick beige Berber. The chair, table, and lamp were the only furniture in the room. The wall directly ahead, the wall the chair faced, was covered in photographs. All the same woman—the woman on the stairs. The woman Burgess had been told was Lenore Spence.

They were looking at a shrine.

"I don't get it," Stan Perry said. "Why all the secrecy? Why a cheap door when the rest of this place is so nicely finished?" He turned to Burgess. "Do you know who this is?"

"Dr. Spence's late wife, Lenore. She died in a fall two years ago. Those are his photographs of her on the stairs."

"Wow," Perry said. "She was so beautiful. But this? And those photos? Must have made it hard to bring any other woman home."

"He had a girlfriend," Burgess told him. "Deidre Lovejoy."

"The chief's niece?" Perry said.

It was Kyle who answered. "The very same. Joe has discovered that she's quite the feisty one. Even slammed Remy Aucoin in the face with a purse the size of a baby hippo when he wouldn't let her through the door."

"Bet Joe didn't like that much," Perry said.

"Remy didn't, either," Burgess said. "I had Dani take some photos. Remy wasn't happy about that."

He stepped farther into the room, studying the wall and then the large empty space where a bed would have been if this had been a second bedroom. Then he tried the two doors at the end of the room. One was a small second bathroom. The other was a closet. Part of the closet, where a rod for clothes had been removed, was stuffed with boxes. The other half was a surveillance setup with cameras to watch the street outside and all the rooms in the condo.

"Aha!" said Kyle from behind him. "Surveillance equipment. This is a job for Super Rocky."

Ricky Jordan was their computer expert, a man who got excited about internet searches the way Burgess and his team got excited about leads toward catching a killer. Rocky would love to get his hands on a setup like this.

Kyle already had his phone out. "I'll see if he can come over now. Wouldn't it be great if Dr. Spence recorded his own demise?"

"Demise?" Perry said. "Aren't we getting fancy?"

"Oh, I am fancy," Kyle said. "Surprised you've never noticed." He looked at Burgess. "Doesn't look like you need me here. You want me to search downstairs?"

Burgess nodded.

Kyle returned to his phone, held a brief conversation, and said, "Rocky's coming over."

Burgess said, "Good."

Perry checked his watch. "And I am due at the hospital, where I expect I will be met with open arms and an outpouring of helpful information about the character and habits of the late Dr. Eliot Spence."

Were they cynics or just realists?

"We meeting later?" Perry asked.

He nodded. "We are. What's good? Can we do eight?"

Since Kyle was trying to show his fiancé Michelle that he could be a good dad to his girls and not leave their care to her, and Stan Perry was a brand-new dad, their meetings now had to be scheduled around family responsibilities like dinner whenever possible. Despite a career spent pushing his way through investigations, often without food or sleep, Burgess was learning to build in breaks. He had a family at home now, too. Still a surprise. A few years ago, he'd been a monkish bachelor. Now, he had two teenagers and a ten-year-old. A fiancée who refused to marry him. Balancing work and family did not come easily. He still sometimes felt dazed by the change.

"I can," Kyle said.

Perry only shrugged. "Depends on Autumn," he said. He didn't mean September. He meant his newborn daughter.

Before they left, Kyle and Perry both paused to study Dr. Spence's memorial wall. It appeared to be arranged in chronological order, from early photos of a young Spence and his lovely girlfriend through a bunch of wedding photos and then years of vacations and domestic scenes. They made a very handsome couple.

"Is it strange that they never had any kids?" Kyle wondered.

"Lotta people don't have kids these days," Perry said. "Way the world's going to hell, who can blame them?"

"We've got kids."

Which made their lives better. And harder. And put pressure on them to maintain a decent world for their kids to inherit.

They went back to studying the wall. Plenty of pictures of Spence and his wife together that others must have taken, as well as all the obsessive photos of her. Burgess thought "obsessive" because there were so many and because they were all too perfect. Maybe Spence had thrown out any that weren't perfect. Had Lenore Spence shared her husband's obsession with her beauty? Had she posed for him? Been constantly aware of being watched and photographed and been willing to adjust her clothing, hair, and makeup accordingly? Or, like Deidre Lovejoy, had she found Spence's focus on her looks annoying and resented the pressure?

As though echoing his thoughts, Kyle said, "I wonder how she felt about being constantly photographed? Whether she liked it or resented it? Whether he was pushy about it, or it was just a thing between them?"

"We have much to learn about Dr. Spence," Burgess agreed. "The condo says controlling and of a dark turn of mind, I think. And his obsession with keeping the windows and doors locked, plus the surveillance system, suggests he was concerned about his safety. I wonder why?"

"Or concerned about his possessions," Kyle said.

"Haven't seen much of value here," Burgess said. "Of the kind of value that would merit this level of caution. I'm told he was also cautious in public. When entering his car."

"Nothing much of value unless there's another secret room?" Kyle suggested.

"I'm off," Perry said. "You can fill me in later if you find another secret room." He left them to their musings and went to keep his appointment at the hospital.

Burgess and Kyle continued to study the wall.

"He had a steady girlfriend," Burgess said. "She thought they were on track to get married."

"And, if the housekeeper's information is correct, he also had a series of random women he spent the night with."

"So, grieving widower. Serious boyfriend. Guy who played around," Burgess said. "So, how does all that fit together? Do you suppose he photographed the casual women as well?"

Kyle's grin was more wolf than humor. "I expect we'll find out when we get to those boxes." He headed for the stairs.

EIGHT

Wink was working on the bathroom while Dani did the dressing room. Burgess reminded her about the tie rack and the long blonde hair and got a nod. Dani was Wink's protégé, and he was training her in his own mode. That meant when she was working, her focus was entirely on the job. That nod was all he got when he mentioned the tie rack.

Nothing more for him to do up here. He might as well go downstairs and join Kyle in searching there. First up, he figured, was the trash. He might not like being the trashman, but a person's trash could often be very revealing. Besides, he figured that the trash from a place where the owner was as meticulous as Dr. Spence wouldn't be a sordid nightmare. He'd put in his time sifting through sordid nightmares. Could give an entire speech on the worst things he'd found in people's trash.

That was for another day.

He headed downstairs and went right out the door, treating himself to a few moments in the sun before diving into a search. The sun was warm, but there was that faint undertone of cool that arrived shortly after Labor Day. It was a portent of colder days to come. He wasn't ready. He wanted another month of summer. July had been savaged by a terrible case that had made any kind of pleasure impossible. Even his vacation had been interrupted by crime. When he wasn't labeling himself a dinosaur because he was so slow and lumbering, he applied another label to himself: trouble magnet. Maybe all cops were trouble magnets. It just came with the territory.

Warmed and with no excuse for lingering, he reentered Dr. Spence's dark cave, pulled on gloves, and began to explore the trash. It wasn't hard to find. The housekeeper had left the bag in the middle of the kitchen floor.

To get out of Kyle's way, he took it into the dining area, spread out rows of overlapping paper towels, and began to remove items from the bag. Nothing too exciting. Some takeout containers, meticulously washed. An empty wine bottle, also washed. A few used paper napkins, two of which had lipstick on them—lipstick of two different shades, one pink and demure, the other bold and red. Did that mean two different women? He thought back to Deidre Lovejoy. She'd been wearing bold and red.

He dove in again. A few pieces of junk mail. Some pink message slips that might yield something since Spence had taken the trouble to bring them home. He set them aside and went on.

There had been almost nothing in the trash upstairs, suggesting either that Dr. Spence never blew his nose, used a Q-Tip, or discarded an empty container, or that he emptied his own trash between visits from the house-keeper. An empty toothpaste box and a few tissues suggested the latter. He debated with himself about the tissues and decided to collect them. At the bottom was one of those brownish-orange pill bottles. Empty. The label said that it had once held Ambien, and it had been prescribed for Dr. Spence. He hadn't seen Ambien in his quick check of the medicine cabinet, but he might have missed it. Or it might be in one of those locked drawers.

Despite the colorful array of condoms in the bedside tables, those blonde hairs, and the housekeeper's information about female visitors, there were no condom wrappers in the trash. At the bottom, among a pile of discarded junk mail where he almost missed it, was a postcard.

The picture was of a fierce-looking Celtic woman in ancient dress, holding a sword and shield. The legend told him he was looking at Boudicca, an ancient English queen who led her people against the Romans. The address was printed and pasted on the card, and the message, created from cutout letters, was a single word: **Unforgotten.**

This was definitely something. Was this part of a series of threats and a reason for Spence's concern about security?

He put the card, the messages, and the napkins and used tissues aside for Wink and Dani to collect and returned the rest of the trash to the bag.

Kyle was systematically working his way through the living room, so

Burgess decided to search the kitchen. He found the two misplaced glasses the housekeeper had described and took them to the table. Then he began to search.

Kitchens generally didn't yield much, but they could never be discounted. People hid a lot of interesting things in the flour and the sugar. Useful phone numbers and addresses were often stuffed into junk drawers, and drugs and ammunition were often found in the freezer. He didn't expect that Dr. Spence even had a junk drawer, never mind drugs or ammunition, but people often defied his expectations. Today was no exception.

Dr. Spence did have a handful of joints in his freezer. He also had a plastic container labeled Soup, which contained a tight roll of fabric wrapped around several thousand dollars. There was also a medium-sized plastic tub, unlabeled, which held some very expensive-looking jewelry. Perhaps it had belonged to his late wife. But why hide it in the freezer? Was he afraid one of his lady friends might take it, which made Burgess wonder what kind of women Spence was bringing home. Was he afraid of having this or other things stolen, and that was the reason for his security system, or was it something else?

When people were unlikely victims, it could be a challenge to figure out why they were killed. There were cases where the attacks were stranger on a stranger, but they didn't usually leave a message like the one the sodomizing of the victim's body did here. Nor did they take place in pristine settings, where everything was left undisturbed. There was usually violence and little effort made to hide evidence of the crime.

Burgess liked a good puzzle now and then. He enjoyed the challenge. Or he had before he got so lumbering and tired. Still, Dr. Cohen over at the ER said he would feel better, though it would be gradual, and he trusted her.

"Hey, Joe…" Kyle, from the doorway. "You finding anything?"

"A lot, actually. A possibly threatening postcard. Drugs. Money. Jewelry. And some stuff we'll need to look at later. You?"

"Squat. Nada. Zilch. Nothing under the sofa cushions. Nothing interesting in the drawers. The books on the shelf are just books. No notes, secret messages, hollow books with secrets tucked inside. Mind if I go out to the garage and look at his car?"

"You finished with the living room?"

Kyle shrugged. "Looks like it. Unless there are some secret compartments I haven't found yet."

"You may. This guy was weird. There were secret compartments upstairs in the desk. I'll be curious about what young Stanley learns at the hospital. And we need to talk to his friends and neighbors. See if any of them have a read on him."

Burgess considered. The downstairs was the one large room Kyle had searched, plus the dining room and kitchen. He could finish those.

"If you want the car and the garage, go for it. We still have to do the upstairs. Finish the desk, see what files we might need, and do the bedroom and the dressing room. There are locked drawers in the two nightstands. Who knows what might be hidden in there? I hope the keys are on that key ring, so we don't have to look for more keys." He shrugged. Keys could be anywhere, given Dr. Spence's penchant for secrets. "Somewhere in this place, there's a camera. Or cameras. And I would bet a lot more photographs. I think that memorial wall is just the tip of the iceberg."

He tried to recall whether there had been anywhere else in the shrine room where photographs might be stored—or hidden. Remembered there was still that stack of boxes in the closet with the surveillance equipment. It was pleasant to be doing their searches in a clean and decent place but unpleasant to have to assume anything they wanted or needed to see was going to be hidden or difficult to find.

The universe gives with one hand and takes away with the other. Burgess sighed.

"What?" Kyle said.

"All those boxes upstairs in the closet."

"Oh. Right. We could get Sage over here and have him go through them. He loves it when we call on him."

Sage Prentiss was the newest detective in personal crimes and was eager to prove he was up to the task. He was also up to his ears in other cases that needed his attention, especially when they were tied up here. But this was a homicide, and a doctor, which would grab press attention and make the taxpayers nervous. Burgess was surprised the press hadn't arrived yet. They tried to keep things low-key and off the channels that the press monitored, but there were always blabbermouths in the department.

"Good idea. Call him," Burgess said.

Kyle got out his phone as Dani called from upstairs, "Bedroom and dressing room are all yours, Joe. Wink's just finishing the bathroom. Not a lot here. The place is as sterile as an operating room. Whoever wiped it down was very thorough." Knowing that was not what he wanted to hear, she added, "I did get a good print off that tie rack. And, strangely, some off the wood at the edge of the bed, like someone braced a hand there."

She grinned down at him. "No matter how careful they think they are, people generally slip up somewhere."

"Thanks, Dani. Let's hope."

"Hope is what we live for, right? Hope and results."

"I live for results."

"And heaven help anyone who gets in your way."

That made Burgess smile. "I'm not that bad, Dani, am I?"

She laughed but didn't reply. Burgess went back to his search of the kitchen. The freezer had surprised him. The rest of the kitchen didn't.

He moved on to the dining room. Here, instead of carpeting, there was dark hardwood flooring with an elaborately patterned rug in colors that matched the black, purple, and white theme. This was leavened here with a bit of teal. The table was rectangular, with six chairs upholstered in teal. There was a purple runner down the center of the table and a large ceramic bowl in the center. The bowl was empty. Burgess figured it was always empty, and there had never been a time when six people had sat at this table for a meal.

He could be wrong. The kitchen had contained state-of-the-art appliances, large and small, and high-end equipment. For all he knew, Dr. Spence had been a gourmet cook. He'd have to ask.

He made a note in his notebook. Notebooks were essential in cases like this. Actually, in all cases. Sometimes these days, he made notes on his phone, but he tried to record those notes later in his notebook. Phones kept changing and weren't always that user-friendly, while a notebook was forever.

Apologizing to his knee and wishing he'd worn his knee brace, he got down and peered at the underside of the table. It wouldn't be the first time he'd found something under a table. Drugs, knives, guns, papers. People liked to tape things under their furniture. Not this time.

He turned his attention to the sideboard. Dark wood to match the table. The drawers revealed a lot of silver. A service for twelve. Table linens. China for twelve. Lots of glasses. And no secret compartments or unexpected objects.

The dining room was done. He was heading upstairs when Rocky Jordan arrived. Rocky was carrying what looked like a small suitcase and wearing a pleased smile. "Dr. Rocky on the case, Joe. Where is my patient?"

Burgess was glad someone was in a good mood. He'd begun in a good mood, but between Deidre Lovejoy's attitude and a house full of secrets, it had eroded.

"Follow me," he said and started up the stairs.

"Nice place," Jordan said.

Burgess stopped before the door to the shrine room. "We found this room hidden behind a wall hanging, the door padlocked shut. Think it's a shrine to our victim's deceased wife." He pointed toward the end of the room, where the large closet full of equipment waited. "He had an elaborate surveillance system in that closet. We're hoping maybe the murder was recorded. Also curious about what his equipment was recording in general. He seems to have been extremely concerned about security, always checking the windows and doors, things like that. So far, we have no idea what he was nervous about."

"I'll see what I can find." Jordan stepped into the room, pausing to study the wall of photographs. "This the deceased wife?"

Burgess nodded.

"Beautiful, wasn't she?"

Surveillance equipment held more allure for him than a beautiful woman, though, and he hurried toward the closet.

Turning the other way, Burgess pulled Dr. Spence's key ring from his pocket and went to inspect those two locked drawers.

NINE

Burgess tried the drawer on the side closest to the bathroom first. It seemed logical that was the side a single man would sleep on. It was also the side where the drawer of condoms and sex toys was. The key slid in smoothly, turned easily, and Burgess opened the drawer. Like the items he'd found in the freezer, what he found in the drawer surprised him. A handgun and ammunition.

His first reaction was: why would someone keep a gun in a locked drawer beside their bed but leave the key downstairs? Particularly a man who seemed extremely concerned about security?

He shot Perry a quick text, asking where the keys had been found. Made a note in his notebook.

Maybe there was another key, hidden, according to the "hide in plain sight" theory, among the flotsam of sex apparatus in the top drawer.

There was nothing else in the locked drawer besides the gun. He didn't touch it; only called for Dani to come and take photographs. When she was done and had collected the gun, she remarked that guns and sex toys didn't seem like an appealing mix. He closed that drawer and opened the top drawer again.

His theory was right. Nearly lost among the various colored and ribbed condoms was a small black velvet pouch. Inside the pouch, another key to that drawer.

Still damned hard to find in an emergency. Or in the dark.

He made a note, then moved to the other side of the bed and found the key that unlocked that drawer. He hesitated a moment before opening it, wondering what surprises awaited him there. Nothing so concerning as a handgun.

This drawer was a jumble of luxury items—cufflinks, watches, expensive men's wallets and belts, even a gold neck chain still in the box. The helter-skelter jumble, compared to the obsessive neatness of the rest of Dr. Spence's things, looked like someone had robbed a high-end men's store and stashed their ill-gotten gains in the drawer.

Presents from Deidre Lovejoy, Burgess wondered? It definitely looked like gifts rather than something Dr. Spence purchased for himself. Gifts that hadn't been appreciated.

He closed and relocked the drawer and checked to see if a second key for this drawer was stored in the drawer above. It wasn't. No need to reach for a gold chain in an emergency. Nor a fancy leather belt.

Time to move on to the dressing room.

As he had before, he stood in the doorway, surveying the room. Partly, it was just to take it in—the obsessive order and what it said about the man. Partly, he was looking for anomalies, for places where another secret hiding place might be found. Probably, he was too sensitized to secret hiding places these days, and it was just a dressing room. His partner, Chris, would have swooned over a room like this. She was orderly. The place they shared was always as neat and tidy as a home with three kids could be. But she had a fondness for shoes, and Dr. Spence's shoe racks were elegant.

He kicked shoe racks and family matters out of his head and started examining the room. He'd gotten as far as checking inside each of those fancy shoes when his phone rang. Chris. Had thinking of her summoned her call? Not that he believed in summoning calls or anything like that. He was a rational man. Except cops believed in all sorts of unexplained things. Like Divine Intervention. They definitely believed in evil. And probably the spirits of the dead. He knew few cops who weren't haunted by a death scene, or a victim, or a case that couldn't be solved.

But Chris wasn't dead, and she didn't often call him while they were both at work. He felt a spike of anxiety as he answered. Had something happened to one of the kids?

"Hey," he said. "To what do I owe the pleasure?"

"Hey, right back. And sadly, not pleasure."

"What's up?"

"You aren't going to believe this, Joe."

He read the anxiety in her voice.

"Wait," she said. "Is this an okay time to talk?"

"In the middle of a homicide," he said. "Homicide investigation," he corrected. Though it was true that his temper and the ugly things they saw had occasionally made him want to commit, not investigate. That was what self-control was for.

She swore, which she never did. "Dammit! I'm tied up here for at least another hour, and I was hoping you could—" She sighed. "Wishing and hoping, right?"

"What's happened, Chris? Is it one of the kids?" He didn't have time to chat, though he knew she liked to take some time working her way to what she wanted to say.

"Nina got into a fight at school. She's in the office, and they need one of her parents there."

"Nina?" That *was* a surprise. Dylan, he might have expected. His son had a penchant for getting into trouble because he couldn't help stepping in to protect those weaker than himself. Since Dylan was Burgess's son and Burgess's size, about six foot two and burly, almost everyone was weaker. Burgess was proud that his son had inherited his protective instincts but still working on helping Dylan use his judgment about when and how to intervene.

He might even have expected a call about Neddy. Now, at age ten, asking them to call him the more formal Ned. Ned was impish and impulsive. But Nina?

"Nina?" he repeated. "Fighting?"

Nina, the foster daughter they were in the process of adopting, was petite, a good student, and generally of a quiet disposition, though firm in her views. Like her brother, if someone was being picked on or a situation was unfair, she wouldn't hesitate to speak up. But fighting didn't sound like her. He wondered what the school considered fighting.

"That's what they said when they called. They wouldn't tell me anything else. They were being real pricks about it." There was a tremble in her voice. Chris was a nurse, and she was practical and matter-of-fact, but being a parent was new to both of them. "Joe. I need you to handle this. You know how she's been with me lately. I know it's a normal mother-and-daughter thing, but...but I don't want to be sitting there crying in front of school officials, losing my cool, and unable to stand up for her if that's what's called for. And I'm afraid I will."

She hesitated, then rushed on. "I know you're tied up. But could you… it shouldn't take long. And I—"

He could. An hour ago, while the ME was there and Wink and Dani still recording the death scene? No. But right now, he could.

The dressing room could wait. So could talking to the neighbors and everything else that needed to be done sooner rather than later. No sense in vowing that family came first and then blowing them off when work called. Not when things had been rocky between him and Chris, and were getting better now.

"I'll deal with it," he said. "Who am I supposed to see?"

She gave him a name he recognized as the assistant principal in charge of discipline, Dr. Alyce Jorgensen. A woman he'd tangled with before. Maybe that's why she'd call Chris? Well, too bad. Burgess expected good behavior from his kids, but if the system was being unfair, he absolutely had their backs. The last time he and Jorgensen had tangled, she was definitely being unfair.

Actually, when Dylan had tangled with the administration, they hadn't called him or Chris. They'd called the department, which had failed to share his cell phone number or give it to the school. Of course, the school had it; they'd just gone with the first number in their files. At least this time they'd made an effort. Unless Nina had given them Chris's number. She was a very organized kid.

He tried to push the memories of that last meeting away so that he could approach this one with an open mind.

They wouldn't be pushed away. He could be rational and objective when it came to his work, striving not to let his assumptions get ahead of the facts. But Nina? Nina wasn't combative.

He reminded himself again: wait for the facts. What he'd tell a junior detective. Don't let your suppositions get ahead of the facts. And getting the facts would have to wait until he got to the school. His two older ones were in Catholic school because it was where he had gone. It was still a good school, with high academic standards and a culture that frowned upon violence. He hated to think that Nina had seriously broken the rules.

He also knew that even if he and the administration weren't on the same page, they were on similar pages: the pages open to maintaining power and control.

He went to tell Kyle that he had to leave for a while.

He found Kyle in the garage, the lights on, down on his knees, feeling underneath the front seat of Dr. Spence's car.

"Hey," he said, and Kyle's head popped up.

"Finding anything?"

"Not even dust. This guy was scary, Joe. No one lives such a sanitized life."

"We've found stuff. And we'll find more. Guy had a gun in the drawer beside his bed."

"Well, that is interesting. I wonder if it's registered. Where he got it. All the fun things a firearm can tell us."

"I gave it to Wink and Dani. So perhaps, soon, we'll know. Look, I hate to do this, but I've got to leave for a while."

"Leave?" Kyle stood up, his expression somewhere between curious and concerned, said without speaking, *You never leave in the middle of an investigation.* What he did say was, "What's up?"

"Chris called. School says Nina's gotten into a fight. She's in the office, and they need a parent."

"Which would be you because you can scare the pants off 'em while Chris would be polite?"

"Something like that."

"Well, go and do what you've got to do. We'll be at this for a while. A little time away won't hurt." Kyle gave his wolf's grin. "Long as no one sees you bringing them in, you might bring back some of Melina's sandwiches. I know one hungry detective who would very much appreciate it."

Detectives being seen eating at a crime scene was a huge no-no. Never mind how many hours it could take. The operative word was "seen." "I can guess who."

"And cookies."

"And cookies."

Burgess told Wink and Dani he had to leave for a bit. At least they didn't ask for sandwiches. But Kyle ran at very high revs, and if he wasn't fed frequently, Burgess worried that he'd break down. Or consider taking that transfer to an easier position that his fiancée, Michele, was always nagging him to take.

On his way, he called the school, reached Dr. Jorgensen, and told her he was coming from a homicide and was about twenty minutes out. He was more like ten minutes out but wanted to stop by Melina's sandwich place and put in an order. She made the best sandwiches, particularly her meat-loaf one, and often ran out because they were popular.

She picked her head up from sandwich-making when he came through the door and smiled. "Detective Joe. How good to see you! How was your vacation? You look like you got some rest."

"It was good. Thank you. The kids had a ball."

"And Mrs. Joe? Did she enjoy herself?"

She'd assumed, as people did, that he and Chris were married. He hadn't bothered to correct her. One of these days, or one of these years, he would make Chris Mrs. Joe. Right now, she'd taken to referring to herself as Almost Mrs. Burgess, which she thought was hilarious and he disliked.

"She had a grand time, Melina." He knotted his fingers together in a prayerful gesture and said, "Any chance you still have meatloaf?"

"Oh, yes. Because I save it for my favorite customers. I am making it for you and Terry and Stan, yes? And you will want cookies?"

She looked at the clock. "Can you give me a little time? I am working on a big order here."

"Is an hour good?"

She nodded. "An hour is very good. I see you then."

She returned to her work, and Burgess headed for the school. Bad guys he could handle. He'd rather have a root canal than tangle with Dr. Jorgensen again.

TEN

Nina was sitting in a stiff leather chair outside the office door. When she saw him, she jumped up, ran to him, and threw her arms around him. "Thank goodness you're here, Dad. They won't listen to a word I say."

He gave a nod toward the office. "Give it to me short and quick, okay?"

In a shaky voice, she said, "There's this boy. His name is Dexter. He's a real creep. Always grabbing at girls, and the teachers won't do anything about it. They say that we need to be understanding because he has issues with impulse control."

She shook her head vehemently. "Like that is supposed to be our problem?"

He put a calming hand on her shoulder. "Go on."

"He sits behind me in History, and he's always muttering these foul things under his breath. Foul, as in sexual, Dad. Foul, as in what he'd like to do to me. I've told the teacher, Mr. Harrison, about it and asked to have my seat moved, and Mr. Harrison won't do it. He says he thinks I can handle it."

His daughter shrugged, anger replacing the tremble in her voice. "Why should I have to handle it? That's my question. Anyway, today it was uglier than usual, and I was feeling kind of fragile, you know, and after a while, I couldn't take it anymore, and I got up and grabbed my history book and slammed him over the head with it. And Mr. Harrison sent me to the office for fighting. Which is so unfair."

"Okay. I think you should come in with me."

"Dr. Jorgensen said I should wait out here."

He said, "Well, your dad thinks this is very much your business, and you need to be in the conversation."

He and Nina headed into the office.

The last time he'd seen Dr. Jorgensen, she'd looked too young for her job. The couple of years since had aged her. Now, she looked worn out and unhappy. *Not a good frame of mind*, he thought, *for whatever was coming*.

He gestured for Nina to sit, then, still standing, extended his hand to Jorgensen. She took it with a reluctance that told him she remembered the last time he'd been in her office.

"I would prefer to have this conversation between the two of us, Mr..... uh.... officer...uh Detective Sergeant Burgess."

He nodded. "I understand. But from what Nina's told me, the facts, *her* facts, are important for an understanding of what happened. Her facts and the fact that she's attempted to deal with the situation in a more appropriate manner and been unsuccessful. Now," he sat in the chair beside Nina. "Tell me what the school's version of the event is."

Little frown lines between the woman's eyes told him she didn't like his use of "the school's version" at all. Naturally, she wanted to control the message. The last time they'd met, she'd concluded by saying, "Detective Sergeant. I sincerely hope we do not meet again." And now, they were meeting.

"Your daughter Nina attacked a fellow student. She struck him in the head with a book. She knows the penalty for hitting another student is a suspension." She looked at Burgess, as though expecting him to understand, as she added, "The boy has some mental health issues."

Beside him, Nina shifted, getting ready to defend herself.

Burgess put his hand on Nina's arm. "Patience, Nina. You'll have a chance to speak," he said. To Dr. Jorgensen, he said, "Have you been told the context of the incident?"

She didn't reply. Probably rerunning their last encounter and hoping it didn't go the same way. But all she said was, "It doesn't matter."

"Context always matters."

He shifted in his chair, a sudden shift toward Nina, knowing that the suddenness, and his size, would make Dr. Jorgensen uneasy.

He'd meant to give Dr. Jorgensen time to explain the school's position, but her rigid, rule-bound statement, "It doesn't matter," told him that would be a waste of time. And time wasn't something he had a lot of right now. "Nina, can you explain the circumstances that led up to your actions today, please?"

Did his daughter already have a cop's face? She didn't look at him, crack a smile, or show any emotion as she launched into a more detailed version of what she'd told him out in the hall.

"Dr. Jorgensen. Dexter Wiggins sits behind me in history class. Nearly every day, he spends the class muttering ugly things under his breath." Nina paused. Took a breath. Her face might be unemotional, but the shake was back in her voice. This was hard for her. "Ugly and vulgar things…sexual things…that he would like to do to me. It's…honestly, it's terrifying. This week, he's been talking about how when he's done doing those things to me, he's going to kill me, and then he tells me how he's going to do it."

Nina stopped again and looked at Burgess. "Dad, this is awfully hard to talk about. To repeat the things he's been saying, I mean."

"I know, Nina. But sometimes, in order to make people understand what I was referring to as 'the context,' it's necessary to step out of our comfort zone, however hard that is."

His daughter nodded and got out her phone.

"We don't allow the use of phones during school hours," Dr. Jorgensen began.

"I know that," Nina said. "But because Mr. Harrison won't listen and won't help me, I've been recording Dexter for a while."

She looked at Burgess for his approval. He nodded. "That was very smart, Nina."

Dr. Jorgenson looked like she'd just tried to swallow a slimy frog, and it had gotten stuck in her throat. But how could she complain about a young female student who was being sexually harassed taking reasonable steps to protect herself?

"Go ahead and play those recordings," he said. "We're listening."

Nina found the first recording and played it for them. By the time it was done, Burgess was as angry as he could ever remember being and very grateful that Dexter Wiggins wasn't with them in the office. And this recording was just one of six. Six that were recorded out of who knew how many days of poor Nina having to listen to that boy's foul utterances despite having taken responsible steps to protect herself?

Why hadn't she told him or told Chris so they could have acted sooner? Had she believed she deserved this? Or that it was her job to be able to handle it? After all the violence she'd been through, it was an outrage that she should have been subjected to this.

He forced himself to stay silent as Nina played another, then said, "And this is where he talks about killing me."

Partway through the first of those, he lost it. "You can stop now," he said. He glared at Dr. Jorgensen. "Apparently, neither you nor Mr. Harrison have even the slightest understanding of sexual harassment and its impact on victims, or something would have been done about this boy long before now."

She opened her mouth to speak, but he cut her off. "When we came in here today, you implied that this boy, this monster, should be entitled to understanding because he has mental health issues. Were you saying that my daughter Nina, or any girl, should be required to put up with this behavior because of that? That he gets a pass on threats of sexual and physical violence, a pass on making death threats because he has issues?"

Burgess hadn't noticed that he'd left his chair nor that he was bent over the desk as he spoke. Not until Nina put a hand on his arm and said, in a small voice, "Dad. Dad. Sit down. Please. You're scaring Dr. Jorgensen."

Burgess stepped back, took Nina's phone, and sent copies of the recordings to himself. No way did he want them inadvertently lost.

He was trying not to be a bully. He forced himself back into his chair, returned Nina's phone, and waited for Dr. Jorgensen to respond. Those recordings had to have influenced how she would handle this.

But she didn't say anything. He said, "This isn't simply a case of needing to be understanding of the boy's mental challenges, whatever they are. It's clear you have a serious problem here. If the boy is doing this to Nina, he's probably doing it to other girls as well. In my experience, boys who talk like this, who fantasize about violent rape and torture and killing, often escalate to the real thing. May already have escalated."

He forced himself to stay calm, to keep his voice low and unthreatening. "Have there been other complaints about him?"

He had his notebook out and his pen ready. Yes, this was still about Nina and making sure she was safe and not wrongfully penalized for protecting herself. But based on what he'd heard, it was also about protecting other girls, in school and outside of school. He needed a lot more details because whatever happened with Dr. Jorgensen, public safety concerns about Dexter Wiggins didn't end at the schoolhouse door.

When she finally broke her silence, instead of addressing what ought to be a mutual concern, Dr. Jorgensen said, "The matter of other complaints is not at issue here." Her face was neutral, but her voice was almost as shaky as Nina's.

He couldn't fucking believe it. His temper was like a kite in a high wind, threatening to blow out of his control.

"The last time you tried unfairly penalizing one of my kids while planning to let far worse actors off the hook, we were able to reach a reasonable accommodation once the situation was viewed in its entirety. I'm hoping we can do that again."

He gave it a beat, watching her closely, waiting for a sign that they could move to less tense ground and reach that accommodation. Again, she had no response. There was something going on here besides what Nina had shared. Maybe Wiggins's parents were connected, putting pressure on Dr. Jorgensen? But that shouldn't affect the result here.

He didn't have time for this, time to parse the politics of this situation. He needed to set things right for Nina and get back to work. He said, "Do you mean that despite what you've heard in that boy's own words, how persistent the threats have been, and despite Nina's attempts to handle the situation by asking to have her seat changed only to have that very reasonable request denied, you still think this meeting is about Nina smacking him with a book? Seriously? It has gone way beyond that."

Jorgensen danced a few papers around on her desk without looking at him.

Nina *was* looking at him, her no longer opaque cop's face asking what was going on. Asking him to help her. Her lips were trembling, and there were tears in her eyes, though he wasn't sure whether they were frustration, rage, or emotional overload. It had been extremely hard for her to share those recordings, however brilliant it had been to make them. It would have been hard for a seasoned adult to hear them once, never mind having them on repeat day after day. Did the woman before him, charged with the task of dealing with adolescents, not get that?

Maybe she was paralyzed and didn't know what to do. Or could it be that the school, in some misguided PC way, was bending over backward to accommodate this boy, Dexter Wiggins, no matter how much harm he caused?

He said, "Imagine if this happened to you when you were sixteen."

No response. She turned to the shelf behind her, got out the student handbook, and started thumbing through it. By now, she should know it by heart.

Maybe it really was that she didn't know what to do. Maybe strict adherence to a narrow parsing of the rules was her solution when she was overwhelmed. That wasn't going to work well here.

He waited, feeling the minutes tick by, minutes he couldn't spare.

Enough with the dancing papers and the obfuscation. If Jorgensen wouldn't take charge, he would.

"I'm sorry," he said, "but a man has been murdered, and I have a crime scene waiting. So, here's how this is going to go. You will revoke Nina's suspension. You will make sure that starting tomorrow, she is not seated anywhere near Dexter Wiggins. I will send our juvenile officer, Andrea Dwyer, to meet with you to explore the matter of Wiggins's behavior further. If you stonewall her, as you've tried to stonewall me, I will refer the matter to the county attorney. If Nina is threatened in any way by that boy after today, we will obtain a restraining order preventing him from coming anywhere near her. I guarantee that after hearing those recordings, any judge will grant that order. And believe me, trying to manage that will be a bigger pain for you and your staff than having to deal with me."

He took a breath. Checked that Nina was still okay. She looked like she was barely holding on. "Are we clear?"

Jorgensen said, "You don't get to—"

He cut her off. "Maybe you've not been informed about his behavior before now. Or maybe you've been willfully ignorant. Maybe, in some la-la bureaucratic universe, you even think you have been dealing with him. You haven't. You're on notice about his behavior now. You know what he says he will do. If anything happens to any of the girls in this school..." He raised his voice. "...any of the girls in this school, and you haven't taken steps to prevent him from acting. If you haven't cooperated with the police department in ascertaining whether he is a genuine threat, then you are complicit in whatever happens. Complicit. You understand that, don't you? You can't just put your head in the sand and pretend it's okay because you're accommodating his mental health issues or because his mommy and daddy have leaned on you. You can't accommodate harassment, death threats, sexual assault, or homicide. Are. We. Clear?"

She continued to flip through the book, not meeting his eye.

He raised his voice even louder and repeated, "Are we clear?"

"You are such a bully," she said. "I pity the people who have to work with you."

"I could flip that and say I pity the students who have to rely on your protection. On you doing your job responsibly. I know you have a hard job, and I know situations like this are particularly challenging. I know that you feel you have to balance the rights and interests of a student with mental health challenges against the rights and interests of your other students. But you can't come down on the side of condoning his behavior. If he can't... or won't...control it, he can't be a part of your general student population. It's that simple."

"Oh, Detective Sergeant Burgess, it's not simple at all. We have rules—"

She looked ten years older than when he'd come into the room. Was that, perhaps, his superpower? Forcing people to age before his eyes? What was he supposed to do about that? Never call anyone on anything?

He sighed.

She sighed. She closed the student handbook, looking defeated, and said, "You win."

He hadn't come here to win, only to protect his daughter if that needed doing. He said it aloud. "I didn't come here to win, Dr. Jorgensen, only to ensure that Nina got a fair hearing."

She wouldn't look at him. "Nina's suspension is revoked. I will make sure that she is moved to a different seat in history class. Are we done?"

They were so far from being done. But he wanted to consult with Andrea Dwyer, affectionately known as their "kiddie cop" and the department's attorney, for starters, before he took this any further. Maybe someone in the DA's office. He also wanted to check the department's records and see if Dexter Wiggins was already on their radar. Kids like him often were. Sometimes from quite an early age.

She didn't need to hear all that. He'd already told her about Dwyer and reminded her of her duty to her students. Now, he had a homicide scene to get back to.

He turned to Nina. "You okay to finish the day here, or do you want to come home?"

She sat up very straight. "Thanks, Dad. I appreciate your standing up for me. I'll stay."

His lovely little Nina, so young and so brave, and lately, becoming such a beauty. He could understand a boy having a crush. He'd seen it enough that it didn't surprise him, but he'd never understand a twisted creature like Dexter Wiggins, nor why people accommodated monsters like him instead of insisting they get help.

He added to his follow-up list to check out who Dexter Wiggins's parents were.

He stood. "Got to get back. First twenty-four hours and all that."

Trying to soften things, he added, "I'm sorry if you think I've trespassed on your patch, Dr. Jorgensen, but I have a lot more experience with young men like Wiggins than you do. Plus, I'm as bad as any father when it comes to threats against my daughter."

Jorgensen was unmoved. She didn't come from behind her desk to see them out. Didn't offer her hand. Never said a word, comforting or otherwise, to Nina. He could talk to Nina about that later. He motioned for her to leave before him and walked out of the office.

ELEVEN

Out in the corridor, he paused. He was feeling the weight of time passing but needed to know that his daughter was all right. "Seriously, Nina, if you want to go home, give yourself some time to process this, it's more than okay."

She managed a feeble smile. "I'm okay, Dad. Really. Shaky, but okay. I just hope that she…" A nod toward the office. "…isn't going to hold this against me. I didn't think I had any choice. I couldn't stand it another day, and I knew asking him to stop would only feed into whatever sick fantasies he has going. I was just…you know…feeling so helpless when Mr. Harrison wouldn't help me."

Another smile, slightly stronger this time. "I suppose I could have sicced my brother on him. Dylan would have straightened him out. Dexter, I mean, not Mr. Harrison." She ducked her head, then gave him another smile. "But I didn't want to get Dylan in trouble, either. He's kind of had enough of that, here and at home."

"We would have helped you."

"I know that. I was…you know…trying to handle it myself. Guess I didn't do a very good job, huh?"

"You did fine. Making those recordings was brilliant. Going forward, though, you need to talk to us. Especially if there are any further issues with Dexter Wiggins. Understood? You don't suck it up. You don't take any crap from him. If he even approaches you, you tell us. Okay?"

Now, the smile was genuine.

Then she said something that surprised him. "The thing is, I don't want to go through my life being the poor, damaged girl who always needs protecting. I want to learn to protect myself."

"Well. This is a good start. So long as you don't get in the habit of whacking people."

"Okay. Thanks, Dad." She made a shooing motion with her hands. "Now go back and fight crime."

He went back to fight crime, stopping en route to pick up Melina's great sandwiches. They were in an anonymous brown shopping bag that could have been anything. This way, he could carry them inside without the press snapping a photo of a detective bringing an easily identified picnic to a crime scene.

As he drove, he called Andrea Dwyer, their "kiddie cop," and relayed his experience in Dr. Jorgensen's office. "I told her that you'd be coming by to get more information about Dexter Wiggins. Do a deeper dive into the situation at the school. Whether Wiggins has been in trouble before, etc. I want him on our radar if he isn't already there." He hesitated. "That's something you should check on. Whether there are reports about him. A kid like that, acting like that, and the things he's saying. It's very concerning."

He pulled over and shoved the truck into park. "Wait. Nina was smart enough to record some of the things Wiggins was saying, both the threats of sexual assault and death threats. They're pretty ugly. I'm going to send them to you so you know what we're dealing with here."

"Always such a pleasure to do business with you, Detective Sergeant," she said.

"And with you, Andrea. Once you listen to them, you'll see why I'm concerned."

"Besides the fact that Nina is your daughter?"

"Yes. And because other people have daughters in that school...and out of school...around this boy and my trouble radar is going off big time."

"I'm on it, Joe. I'll let you know if we have anything on him. Of course. See if there's any gossip on the street. And give the school the heads up if that's the case." Silence. Then, "You think they're trying to sweep this under the rug because he's got mental health issues?"

"I do. And I get the impression that his parents are somehow involved. Maybe connected in some way that puts pressure on the school?"

"Dammit. I get so tired of that. Who your family is doesn't excuse people who commit bad acts."

"Let me know what you learn. And thanks."

"Anything for you, Joe," she said. And she meant it. He and Dwyer had great respect for each other.

As he passed the news trucks and the crowd that had gathered at the crime scene, he was feeling uneasy. Hours had passed, and he hadn't had a call from his nemesis, Paul Cote. Cote always wanted the details long before Burgess's team had had time to finish a scene and had an infuriating habit of sharing those details with the press. Burgess and his team had developed strategies for hiding important details, but sometimes, Cote managed to get them anyway. Not so long ago, Burgess and Kyle had rescued Cote from the brink of death. Doing their duty, as they were trained that all victims mattered. The rest of the department never let them forget the mistake they'd made.

Maybe Cote had called Kyle, though that seemed unlikely. Kyle was no more chatty or forthcoming than Burgess. Lately, Cote's focus had been on their third team member, Stan Perry. Perry might be impulsive sometimes, causing consternation and headaches, but Burgess was confident that he wouldn't share any more details than the rest of them. Still, he was perfectly happy to have Perry the focus of Cote's probing. It kept the man off their backs. For now.

Once Cote knew that the victim was a doctor—meaning, in his mind, an important citizen of their fair city—he might even show up at the condo and start mucking around. Mucking was the operative word. Whatever knowledge he'd once had of crime scene protocols had long since left his brain.

Burgess was also uneasy because the confrontation with Dr. Jorgensen had left him feeling torn. Torn and distracted from his investigation when he needed all his focus to be here. He had been a bully to the school administrator, and he was sorry. But the alternative would have been to abandon his daughter to their arbitrary decision-making. He was also sorry because this had definitely been causing Nina distress for some time, yet she hadn't come to him or to Chris for help. Had they done something to discourage her from doing that, or was it simply, as she'd said, that she was trying to learn to navigate high school life on her own, trying to resist being labeled as the poor little damaged girl? They needed to talk about that. He supposed he should trust her parting revelation: that she wanted to learn to stand up for herself instead of being a victim.

He parked, but before he went inside, he gave Chris a quick call and an even quicker summary.

"The poor kid," Chris said. "I wish she didn't feel she needs to be so brave."

"Maybe it's empowering," Burgess said, using a word he disliked but seemed to fit the moment. "We can talk tonight. I have to get back to work."

Back to work. Such a banal term for searching a homicide victim's home. But it truly was his work.

"I don't know if I'll be home for dinner."

"I've heard that before," she said, but there was no edge in her voice. "See you when we see you."

He grabbed the sack of sandwiches and headed inside.

He found Kyle and Perry in the dining room waiting for him, a pile of napkins on the table, and gave Perry a curious look.

"Aren't you supposed to be interviewing docs?"

Perry grinned and ducked his head. "The first two had very little to say beyond what a wonderful guy Dr. Spence was. A very good surgeon and well-respected by his colleagues. Loved by his patients. Neither man could imagine why anyone would want to harm him. If what they say is true, our victim was practically a candidate for sainthood. My third interview gave me the impression that she wasn't a member of the Spence fan club but weaseled away with a 'Sorry. Too busy now,' before I could probe. There's also an assistant who worked for him, but she's playing hard to get. My well-honed cop's gut told me if I came here, I would find Melina's sandwiches."

"That's some cop's gut."

Perry patted his lean stomach. "Ain't it, though."

Burgess handed out the sandwiches.

Kyle sighed and smiled. "Melina is an angel. A food angel."

"So Spence was a saint, huh? Think that might be why the third person blew you off? She didn't subscribe to the general sainthood theory?" Burgess said.

"Maybe there's something in that," Perry said. "I rescheduled for around four, and this time, I am not taking 'too busy' for an answer." He balled up his sandwich wrapping and reached for a cookie. "I wonder if she'll try to blow me off again?"

Despite how delicious the sandwiches were, they ate like cops who'd learned they could be interrupted at any moment. The sandwiches were gone in a flash, and soon after, the cookies were just a small pile of crumbs. Good thing, too. As Kyle was disappearing the remains of their meal into the plain brown bag, and Perry had gathered the napkins and swept crumbs off the table, there was a commotion at the door, and Paul Cote's voice could be heard arguing with the cop who was maintaining the crime scene log.

No matter how many crime scenes he visited nor how often he was reminded of protocol, Captain Cote needed to assert his importance by arguing that his status exempted him from the formalities.

Kyle and the evidence decamped for the kitchen while Stan Perry followed him to exit through the garage. Burgess got to be the unlucky winner in the "Who will handle Cote this time?" contest.

He usually was.

He met his boss at the door, using his size to prevent an impetuous spill into the rest of the condo. They'd finished their search down here. Just the dressing room, the desk, and the memorial shrine room upstairs to go. But Cote didn't know that.

He arrived as Cote pushed past the protesting officer at the door and nearly ran right into Burgess.

"Crime scene, Paul," Burgess reminded him. "Gloves. Booties. And don't touch anything."

Cote, who had an aversion to protective gear, took a step back and glared. "Update me, Burgess," he said.

"Not much to tell at this point. Dr. Spence's body's gone up to Augusta. The ME says we'll have to wait for an autopsy to determine the cause of death. No immediate suspects. We're hoping interviews will lead to someone. Kyle and I are finishing up the search here. Perry is over at the hospital interviewing Spence's colleagues. We'll be talking to the neighbors soon."

He shrugged and decided to give Cote something to gnaw on, something that might be a useful distraction. "Spence had a girlfriend." He corrected himself. "Woman friend. Deidre Lovejoy."

He gave it a beat, then added, though he assumed Cote would have recognized the name. "Chief's sister's daughter? So we'll want to keep this low-key, of course."

"She's a suspect?" Cote's tone implied this was impossible.

"For now, everyone's a suspect," Burgess reminded him. "We haven't got much to go on here."

"Well...keep it tight, okay?"

Like Burgess had ever done anything else?

Cote stood on tiptoe to peer over Burgess's shoulder. Nothing to see except the dark, immaculate living room.

"No cause of death?" Cote sounded disappointed. He preferred the gory crime scene, the details he could smack his lips over in private, then blurt them out to the press. Nothing to see here. Nothing to blurt except the one detail Burgess had shared, and that was one he wouldn't blurt.

Burgess took a mean bit of satisfaction about that.

"Body's gone?" Cote said.

Burgess nodded.

Cote studied him, maybe trying to decide if it was worth pushing past and examining things for himself. He peered at the dark room beyond. Immaculate and undisturbed. Swung his gaze to the dining room. Nothing to see except a few out-of-place chairs. From here, if there were crumbs, they weren't visible. "I'll want your reports as soon as possible," he said.

Predictable. He'd prefer that cops be at 109, police headquarters, writing reports than be out gathering information that might help solve a case.

Burgess ignored the comment and waited. After another scan of the room that garnered him nothing, Cote sighed. "Autopsy scheduled?"

"Dr. Lee is going to call to confirm. Likely eight tomorrow morning."

"I'll want a full report as soon as you get back."

Of course. Unless something came up. Whenever possible, Burgess arranged it so something *did* come up, if it didn't happen in the normal course of things. "We may have to wait for toxicology for the answers," he said.

Disappointed, Cote turned and walked out. When he was gone, the air felt lighter.

From the kitchen, Kyle said, "Wow. How did you do that? He never walks away when he can mess up a crime scene."

Shrugging, Burgess said, "The place was disappointingly clean and empty. Plus, I played the Deidre Lovejoy card."

"Whatever works. What's left? We done here?"

"Almost. Dressing room. Spence's desk and the shrine room."

"I'll take the shrine, then," Kyle said. "And check with Rocky, see how he's doing with the surveillance system."

"Deal."

They trudged up the stairs. These days, Burgess felt like he was trudging far too much. He wanted things to happen faster. He'd been born impatient.

Upstairs, he decided to do the dressing room last and headed for the desk while Kyle stepped past him into the shrine room. He heard Kyle ask Rocky Jordan how it was going. Thought he heard a noncommittal murmur from Jordan.

Then, Kyle's voice. "Nothing from last night?"

And Jordan's deep, "Still working on it, Terry."

He focused on the desk. What he wanted to check first was what had been stored in those secret compartments, the materials he'd left on the desktop. Next was information about Spence's phone records, which could give them additional contacts who might have information about Dr. Spence. Then, his financial records, since a person's finances were often a window into their lives and sometimes a window into why someone might have wanted them dead. Wealth, debt, and spending could be all clues. He'd also be looking for anything that might help them confirm what Deidre Lovejoy had told them about Spence's next of kin. And their phone numbers.

He gathered bank statements and investment statements. Added phone bills to the pile. Remembered that Spence's phone was still on the charger next to the bed. Something else they needed to collect.

Before he moved on, he checked the files for insurance policies. Spence might have them through work and a work office, which might yield further information. But Spence had been meticulous, so if he had policies, Burgess expected to find something here. Without checking the contents, he added a file labeled "Insurance" to the growing pile of papers, along with one labeled "Condo mortgage." Plenty of material for them to work with.

Curiosity, though, pulled him back to the legal papers he'd taken from the secret compartment. He scanned them quickly. On top was a lawsuit against Spence filed by Belinda Carlisle, his late wife Lenore Spence's sister. The substance seemed to be that she was suing Spence, claiming he wasn't entitled to inherit his late wife, Lenore's, estate. A similar suit had been filed by Mark Carlisle, Lenore Spence's brother.

The siblings of his dead wife suing him to obtain her estate? That, he figured, would go straight to the top when he began working his way through the papers.

He made a note, then added the items he'd identified to the list that would go with the search warrant as a record of what they were taking. Then, he headed for the dressing room.

TWELVE

As Burgess stood in the doorway, he composed a message to the late Dr. Spence. "Dear Dr. Spence. Please stop with all these secret compartments and rooms and all the weird stuff you like to hide around your condo. We are just poor small city cops with too much work to do already. Got it?"

A useless message, of course, since whatever Spence had done was already done, and anyway, cops didn't get to dictate the terms of their jobs at crime scenes. They just got to suck it up and get to work.

He sucked it up and started on the room. Dr. Eliot Spence had more clothes in this room than Burgess had owned in his entire life. Nice expensive clothes, too. Cashmere. Linen. Fine cotton. Expensive shoes. He'd checked the shoes already. Now, he worked his way through the pockets of suits and sports jackets and beneath stacks of sweaters and shirts still folded from the laundry. And between the boxer shorts and among the socks.

Nothing. Nada. Zilch.

He was grateful.

It was in the middle of a stack of neatly folded gym clothes that he found the only thing there was to be found, but it was kind of a big deal. Between the tenth and eleventh tee shirts, between pale blue and medium blue, as they were arranged by color, there were more postcards like the one he'd found downstairs in the trash. All the same. All with the same message: **Unforgotten.**

Why keep these and discard the one he'd found in the trash unless Spence hadn't been the one who'd discarded it? Was whatever the sender indicated was unforgotten a clue to why Spence had been killed? Was the threat implied in those messages the reason Spence had been so paranoid about safety?

Burgess wondered if Deidre Lovejoy knew about the postcards? If anyone else did? He wondered who had been Dr. Spence's confidant, if anyone, or if the doctor had kept his secrets to himself. Everything about this place suggested Dr. Eliot Spence hadn't been a happy man or one who lived an easy life. It was all darkness and secrets.

Finished with the dressing room, he went to see if Kyle was done with the shrine and how Rocky Jordan was doing.

Kyle was on his knees beside one of the boxes that had been stored in the closet. It looked like it was an entire box of photographs. He looked up when Burgess approached.

"Well, you said there had to be more photographs than the ones on the wall, and boy were you right. This is the third box I've gone through. Hard to believe any man would ever say this, but I am awfully sick of photos of beautiful women. It's like eating too much chocolate. After a while, the pleasure is gone."

"The wife or many different women?"

"Many of the wife and many of other women. Many other women. He definitely favored brunettes, but there are blondes and redheads as well. No Asians or persons of color, if that means anything."

"Any kind of order to it? Dates? Places? Anything to help identify the women?"

Kyle shook his head. "Not really. That is, the first box is all the wife. The second and third boxes are more mixed. Some outdoors. Some in bed. But not naked pictures, just suggestive ones." He waved a hand toward the closet. "And I've only started. Help yourself to a box. You'll see what I mean."

Burgess stared at the neatly stacked boxes. Four stacks of banker's boxes, eight boxes to a stack. He hoped they weren't looking at thirty-two boxes of photographs. "You think they're all photos?"

Kyle shook his head. "Dunno. I just started at the top and been working my way down. You might start at the other end. Maybe you'll get financial documents or the pages of his novel. Lurid love letters or his diaries or his old books from medical school." He paused. Said, "Did you notice there aren't any books in the place except for that row in the living room, and they look like something the decorator picked, not something anyone has read?"

Burgess eyed the stack of boxes gloomily. He was already tired of this place. Not that protocol cared. It cared that searches were done in a careful and systematic way. Careful and systematic enough to find postcards hidden in a stack of tee shirts. He hefted a box from the fourth row and set it on the floor. Left it there while he went to check in with Rocky.

"Getting anything?" he asked.

"Working my way through yesterday. Slowly. One thing I can tell you… despite having a lot of cameras in the place, the one area where there isn't surveillance is the bedroom."

Which made some sense if the guy was a player. Probably figured there was enough surveillance to keep him safe before someone got there. Only was there some way he could monitor the cameras without going through the hidden door, into the secret room, and into the closet?

"Could Dr. Spence have surveillance data sent to his phone?" he asked. "Something that would alert him if someone approached or entered the condo?"

"Sure."

Burgess had more questions, but they could wait. He had many boxes waiting for him. Annoying. What he wanted to do was get out on the street and start interviewing neighbors. Review those papers about lawsuits and call the police down in Massachusetts to learn more about Lenore Spence's death.

He went back to his box, raising the lid and finding not photos but lots of old file folders, each carefully labeled, looking like they'd been lifted from a filing drawer like the ones in Spence's desk, put into the box, and never touched again. Most of the categories were the same. Home repairs. Insurance. Financial statements. Bank statements. Bills. Taxes. A few, though, caught his eye. Funeral expenses. Condolence notes. Lenore's life insurance. Medical bills, misc. And a very strange one that wasn't labeled. For someone as anal as Spence seemed to be, that one stood out.

Burgess opened it. A stack of handwritten correspondence. Written in several different hands. After reading one or two, he decided it could have been labeled Hate Mail. There were definitely some people out there who had very harsh opinions of Dr. Eliot Spence.

He slid the file toward Kyle. "Take a look at these."

Kyle skimmed a few and nodded. "Such a good man. A medical angel. Couldn't be a nicer fellow. Seems not everyone's on the same page. These definitely deserve attention." He stared unhappily at the stack of boxes. "And there are still twenty-eight boxes to go. Could be nothing or could take hours. I think we'd better get young Stanley back to help."

He got his phone out. "Wonder if that third doctor blew him off again?"

Stan answered on the first ring, a crisp, "Perry. Investigations."

"You almost done over there? Because we need you here," Kyle said.

"Almost done. Looking for Spence's assistant. Or nurse. Whatever her title is. Gal's got kind of an ephemeral quality. Everywhere they say she is, I get there, and she isn't. Already getting sick of this case, and it hasn't even been a day. But the games people play? Make me sick." He cleared his throat. Said, "Being in a hospital always makes me cough. I've got one more place to check, then I give up. Be there as soon as I can."

A pause. Then, "What's up?"

"A closet full of boxes to go through."

"On second thought, maybe I'm too busy."

Kyle growled into the phone, then hung up. "He'll be here. Looking for a witness who's playing hard to get."

"I think we'll see a lot of that," Burgess said.

They went back to searching through boxes. Kyle got another from the first stack. More photos. Burgess finished checking his box, set the files that looked most relevant aside, and grabbed another box. More old files, none that appeared helpful to understanding Dr. Spence or someone with a motive to kill him.

The next few boxes were the same. Old financial records. Old tax returns. Old correspondence. Insurance and benefits information from prior employment.

Beside him, Kyle was also moving from box to box. "Boring. Boring. Boring," he said. "Man definitely had a type. Beautiful, slender brunettes with sexy mouths. Quite a lot of them, if these are all girlfriends and not just pretty women who modeled for him so he could take their pictures. I wonder if the late, enshrined Lenore ever saw these. If she knew he had boxes of other women stored in their house?"

"Maybe he stopped photographing other women while he was married to her," Burgess suggested. "Maybe she was enough?"

Kyle snorted. "Guy with an obsession like this? I doubt it."

"Maybe he had a storage unit?"

Obsession. Obsessed. The word kept coming up. Obsessed with beautiful women. Obsessed with neatness. Obsessed with secrets. Obsessed with security. The picture that was developing was a complicated and disturbing one.

Eventually, Stan Perry returned. He was in a distinctly bad mood. "When I find that woman, who knows I've been looking for her, I am going to give her a piece of my mind. What the fuck's up with that, anyway? I know cooperation with the police can be iffy, but these are the same people who call us all the time, needing our help with difficult patients and dangerous situations. Why the heck isn't it a two-way street?"

He huffed out a breath. "I am sick of hearing how everyone is busy. Like we're not busy?"

"Busy staring into boxes." Burgess handed him a box to go through. "And don't assume there's nothing there, okay? This guy has secrets. Lots of secrets. And he likes to hide things. So, take it slow."

Perry looked at the box Kyle was going through. "Am I getting a box of babes? Because I wouldn't mind that at all."

"Dunno," Kyle said. "I'm kinda burned out on babes myself. Like I told Joe, it's like eating too much cake or something. After a while, they're just so much white noise."

"No way," Perry said. He gloved up and opened his box.

"Sweet Jesus!" he said, stepping back. "What the heck is this?"

Burgess and Perry leaned in. There were a number of sealed plastic bags in the box. In the one that was visible on top, they could see what looked like a silky blue nightgown, lavishly trimmed in lace and marred with reddish-brown stains that looked like dried blood.

THIRTEEN

"Looks like a nightgown," Kyle said. "A bloodstained nightgown, if I'm reading those stains correctly." He shook his head. "You called it, Joe, when you said this guy hid things and had secrets. But what is this about?"

They weren't supposed to jump to conclusions, but Burgess had a theory. A weird theory without much to back it up. He said, "Maybe this is crazy, but I'm thinking this might be the nightgown his wife was wearing the night she died."

"Who the fuck would keep something like that?" Perry said.

They often got on him about his language. Right now, they were all on the same page. Who *would* keep something like that? It wasn't always the gory or horrible things that creeped cops out. It was things like this. Things people saved that no one ever should. Things that, in some cases, were trophies, sometimes reminders of guilt they needed to carry.

Burgess didn't know enough about Dr. Spence yet to speculate. It was hard to put the memorial wall together with boxes of photographs of so many women. To understand the devoted husband and the man Deidre Lovejoy saw as her future husband, with the housekeeper's tale of the women he entertained. Hard to fit the roll of cash in the freezer that looked like he was planning for a quick escape, and the gun in the drawer, with the meticulous professional devoted to his patients.

People were complex and contradictory. He knew that. This case still presented some unusual challenges.

"Let's see what else is in the box," Perry said, carefully lifting out the top bag and setting it aside.

The next bag held what looked like a pair of fancy satin slippers. Silly little blue satin slippers, wedge-heeled, with nothing more than a strap over the toe—a strap decorated with downy white feathers—to hold it on.

"If she was wearing these," Burgess said, "it's no wonder she fell downstairs."

"I think I'm missing something here," Perry said.

"Me, too," Kyle said.

Burgess realized he'd been alone with her when Deidre Lovejoy had told him the story of Spence's wife's death. He shared what Lovejoy had reported about Spence's wife, Lenore, dying in a fall down the stairs. About the phones left out of the bedroom. Spence's exhaustion and failure to hear the phone. The unusual slippery patch at the top of the stairs. "She says he blames himself. That he's driven to save lives because of the guilt he feels over not saving her. Something he might have done if he hadn't been asleep and had gotten to her sooner."

He looked at the box. "Want to guess what's next?"

"No need to guess," Kyle said. "We've got her nightgown and slippers. It will be her panties. And that is just sick."

Of course, Kyle was right.

"We're making a lot of assumptions here," Burgess reminded them.

Kyle shook his head. "What else would this be? Unless we dig into his past and find a whole series of dead wives and girlfriends. That the man is…what was the guy in the old story called? Bluebeard?"

"Dr. Bluebeard?" Stan suggested. "It has kind of a ring to it."

"Let's get this done and get out of here. I need some sunshine and fresh air," Burgess said. Usually, they were eager to get out of places because of the filth or debris or stench of decomp or even sadness for the victim. This was different. Here, there was a dark pall that lay over everything despite the elegance and cleanliness of the place.

There was a murmur of agreement as they each bent to a new box. They'd toiled without speaking and without any new finds for half an hour when Rocky called them back into the closet.

"You're going to want to see this," he said. "This is from last night."

They lined up behind his chair, peering over his shoulder at a small screen. The video showed a woman at Spence's door, first ringing the bell, then pounding on the door with her fists. The video hadn't recorded sound, but it was clear that she was yelling.

"Deidre Lovejoy," Burgess and Kyle said together.

"She told me she never saw him last night," Burgess said. "She said they had a date. Reservations at a fancy restaurant. She was dressed to go out, and he stood her up. Called and said he couldn't make it. She said she called him several times. First, he said he was busy. After that, he didn't answer."

"Well, he answered his door," Jordan said. "See."

They saw Spence open the door, blocking her from entering. They saw the two of them exchange a few words, her gestures clear that she was very angry, and then saw her stalk away. The door closed. Then, they saw her come back, take something from her bag that looked like a bottle of wine, and smash it against the door.

"So, she was lying," Kyle said.

"I knew there was more from the way she was behaving," Burgess said.

"She's done a good job of demonstrating she has a temper, that's for sure," Kyle said. "This and then hitting Remy. Bet she never thought we'd see this, though."

"And someone cleaned up the wine and the broken glass," Burgess added. "There was no sign of that when we got here this morning. Hopefully, Rocky will find that on the recordings as well."

"Rocky hopes so," Jordan said. "He likes to be helpful."

"Looks like he's being very helpful." But Burgess had a question. "Are there separate feeds from each camera? Are you going to have to go through each of them, one by one?"

"Sadly, yeah. I think so," Rocky said. "Not that I mind. I've already done the garage. Recorded Spence coming home. No sign of anyone else arriving, though. Unless that someone was hiding in Spence's car. And then the camera goes off. The inside cameras might have something for us. When I get there."

Burgess, always impatient, wanted to say "hurry up," but just like their searches couldn't be hurried, Rocky's careful review of camera footage needed close attention.

He and Kyle went back to searching boxes while Jordan went on perusing the videos. "I'm back to his college days, I think," Kyle said. "Looks like Spence was always doing this, although the women in these early photos don't look like they're enjoying it so much. Maybe he refined his technique?"

Burgess wasn't finding anything of interest. Based on the style and furnishing of the condo, he wouldn't have taken Dr. Spence for a packrat, but there were an awful lot of papers that seemed to have no value, yet they were saved. Beyond the memorial wall, he also hadn't seen signs of sentimentality. But maybe Spence had been sentimental and was trying to move away from it. Or maybe he'd just been too busy since he moved here to go through all this old stuff.

After a few minutes, Burgess heard Jordan swear loudly. Then he appeared in the doorway. "Looks like, after the visit from Ms. Lovejoy, he turned all his cameras off. I'll check the rest of them, but the front door feed goes dark."

"Keep looking," Burgess said, though he wasn't feeling hopeful. It sounded like Spence had been doing something last night he didn't want recorded. Maybe he never recorded on the evenings he entertained women other than Lovejoy. Or maybe there was something about this visitor that was different. From what Lovejoy had said, Spence didn't normally cancel on her, and she knew when he was going to be away skiing or engaging in some other activity she wasn't interested in. But had Spence really been skiing or golfing?

He was thinking that in a prosperous area of dwellings like this, it was likely that Spence wasn't the only person with surveillance. If Spence had turned his system off—a peculiar action from a man who'd shown in so many ways that he was paranoid, or at least hyper-vigilant about security— someone else might have caught Spence's visitor or visitors, and his killer, on their cameras.

"Christ, but this is boring," Perry said, standing up and twisting around to straight out his back. "I thought being a detective was an exciting job."

Burgess waved a hand at the box with the bloodstained clothes. "You don't think that's exciting?"

"More like unusual. Or perverted. Though, I do wonder how he got them and why he kept them. I mean, did he strip them off her while she was dead or dying and hide them away or somehow persuade the authorities to give them back once her death was determined to be an accident? Pity we can't ask him."

Perry checked his watch. "You guys know what time it is?"

"Time to finish this up and move on," Kyle said.

"Time for me, like Superman in the phonebooth, to change from detective to daddy," Perry said. "I promised Lily I'd—"

"She doesn't know she married a detective who's wedded to his work?"

Kyle asked. "Sweet Lily thinks that now that you're married with a baby, your schedule will suddenly become regular and predictable?"

Perry shrugged, looking morose. "She does kinda think that. With the baby and all, she's feeling pretty overwhelmed."

"Oh, I know how that is," Kyle said in a high-pitched voice. "Why, with all these boxes, and a dead guy, and no obvious suspects, and two kids and an impatient fiancée who shouldn't have to care for my kids, I am feeling pretty overwhelmed as well. Aren't you, Joe?" He added, "Joe's got three kids. And one of them in trouble at school, which can be a huge distraction."

Perry waved him off. "Your sympathy and understanding underwhelm me, Terry. I thought you guys were going to have my back on this?"

"It may not look like it, but we do," Kyle assured him. "It's just that how you approach this from the beginning sets the tone for how it will be going forward. So, if you let Lily think that from now on because you have a baby, you can blow off work no matter what the situation so you can show up at home like a guy with a regular job, that's what she's going to expect. Which will often mean you can't do your job. Our job. Because our job takes as long as it takes."

It was the speech Burgess would have given if Kyle hadn't stepped up. They all struggled with balancing personal lives and work lives, but given the work they'd chosen, personal often had to take a back seat. Still, Stan had only been a dad for a few weeks. He understood that could be over-whelming.

He looked at the stack of boxes. They only had a few more to get through. That was a good stopping point. They could gather back here later, after family obligations were done, to do a quick canvass of the street.

"Six more boxes. Two each," he said, "and we can all break for dinner."

They each quickly finished their boxes and grabbed another.

Nothing in Burgess's first box. Nothing in Perry's. Nothing new in Kyle's. Just more pictures. They were each on their last box, with visions of outside air and driving home and maybe a good meal dancing in their heads, when Kyle said. "Uh-oh" and spread a handful of pictures that looked like they'd come from an Instamatic camera out on the floor.

There were naked women in these pictures. Well, girls, actually. The pictures weren't posed, or at least, the subjects of the photos weren't posing. To the three cops studying them, the girls all appeared to be unconscious, drugged, or intoxicated, and the pictures had been taken without their knowledge. There were pictures of a dozen different subjects.

Silently, they studied the pictures until Kyle said, "If I'm reading these right, it looks like our guy was a serial date rapist. Why the hell would he keep these? I wonder if these girls were aware that he was taking their photos? Or if he used these pictures to keep the girls from reporting what happened to the police? Or if there are police reports? If anything was ever done?"

He looked at Stan Perry. "How old is Dr. Spence?"

"Forty-four."

"So. More than twenty years ago. Or longer."

Kyle was the father of two teenage daughters, and cases where girls and young women were sexually abused really pushed his buttons. He stood up and stepped away, saying, "I know. Maybe I'm jumping to conclusions. But aren't you both seeing these the same way?"

"Maybe he's still doing it," Perry suggested. "And that's why the camera was turned off. Why there's no camera in the bedroom."

"Looks like we need to know more about his past," Burgess said. "I'm sure the hospital must have his CV, and we can see where he went to college and medical school. Check with police departments there."

He kept staring at the pictures and thinking about how pictures like these found their way into the internet, shared by pornography collectors. Pictures of girls as young as these, maybe eighteen but looking younger, might find their way into the hands of child pornographers, where they would live and be traded forever.

But why keep these? In particular, where had they been during the years he was married to and seemingly devoted to Lenore? Had they lived in a box in a closet in their house in Weston?

He thought, with no basis beyond instinct, that this crime was related to something from Spence's past. He knew from the lawsuits he'd found in the drawer that Lenore Spence's family was angry. He knew a lot of doctors had angry patients by whom revenge might be considered. It would have to be explored.

He made another note in his book, closed his own unfruitful box, and got to his feet. "We're done here for now. Let's go." He leaned into the closet, where Rocky was still scrolling through videos.

"We're off. Call me if you find anything. And don't work too late. There's always tomorrow, and none of this is going anywhere."

He hoped. They tried to process crime scenes as quickly as possible.

The first twenty-four and all that. But they'd had occasions when they were too exhausted to finish a scene, and before they could get back, someone had torched the place. That didn't seem like a likely scenario here, but you never knew. It was a chance he was willing to take.

He handed Rocky Jordan the keys, then pointed to the boxes they were taking with them. "If you two can take these, I'll get the stuff from the desk, and we are outta here."

"Eight?" Kyle said.

Burgess nodded.

"Here?" Perry said.

He nodded again.

They headed downstairs. Kyle and Perry left. Burgess got a box from his truck and put the materials from the desk, the dressing room, and the kitchen into it. He finished filling out the inventory that would accompany the returned search warrant, put a copy on the dining room table, and left.

FOURTEEN

Burgess stowed the materials he'd collected in the back, then sat in the driver's seat for a few minutes, shifting his mind from assessing the crime scene and the victim to being present for his family. Since there was a lot of cash in that roll from Spence's freezer, as well as valuable jewelry, he decided he'd drop off the boxes of evidence before heading home. Whether it was necessary or just a stalling technique, he didn't know.

As he was leaving 109, he gave Chris a quick call to say he was on his way and ask if she needed anything. "We need you," she said. "That's all. Nina is in a state, Dylan is ready to commit homicide, and Ned is feeling left out because he doesn't know what's going on. And I had a horrible day at work and am ready to quit. So, brace yourself. You're going to find us quite a delightful bunch."

Burgess was never sure when or how he'd signed up to trade his monastic state for domestic bliss and domestic chaos, but he had. He said, "See you soon," and headed into the scrum that was Portland's rush hour traffic. People from other places found it laughable when Portlanders complained, but there were a few times of day when crappy intersection design, oblivious pedestrians, the homeless, and the crazies, along with some timid elderly, made a simple journey anything but.

By the time he pulled in beside Chris's car, he'd passed on the chance to give out at least five tickets. Their lucky day. An irritated Burgess could be pretty intimidating.

He passed through the construction zone that was their ground floor and went upstairs. Chris was in the kitchen, with Ned helping her by peeling some carrots. Something in the oven smelled deliciously like baking chicken. He kissed her and went into the living room. Nina was curled up in one corner of the couch while Dylan loomed on the other. The kid seemed to have grown another inch and widened to match.

Burgess couldn't remember going from a scrawny thirteen-year-old to a hulking sixteen. It had just happened, as baffling as everything else that had happened when he was a teenager. Between his father's increasing intoxication and violence, his mother's despair, and the pressure of sports and school, there was so much complex stuff going on he couldn't focus clearly on any of it. He could remember his sisters' fear, though. It had been seeing his two sisters crouching in their darkened bedroom, trying to avoid their father's explosions, that had prompted him to step forward and take action.

When his father had raised his fist against his mother once too often, Burgess, seeing her cowering in the kitchen trying to talk his father down, had realized that he was the bigger, younger, fitter man. His size and his determination to avoid replicating his father's violence had kept him in check until that moment. His control snapped then. When he was done, it was his father who was cowering in the corner, bloodied and whimpering. Through the shock of what he'd done, Burgess had managed to declare that his father's violent days were over. He would terrify the family no more.

He'd grabbed his father by the shirt and shoved him out the door. Then, he gathered his mother and sisters in his arms, apologized for what they'd seen, and promised there would be no more violence going forward.

Though he rarely lost it, he'd lived with the fear that he'd inherited his father's temper all his life. He didn't want his son to inherit it as well.

Stepping into the room, he said, "What's going on with you two?"

"I said I was going to beat the crap out of Dexter Wiggins, and Nina doesn't want me to," Dylan said. Arms folded. Sullen.

"It will only make things worse, Dad," Nina said. "Can you tell him that, please? Dylan will listen to you."

Maybe Dylan would listen to him. He sat in an armchair facing them as he searched for the right words. This might have been easier if he'd had fifteen or sixteen years of interacting with them to build up to this.

"Everything go okay for the rest of the day, Nina?" he asked.

She nodded. "A couple of my friends said they wished their dads were like you. Sara's dad thinks the school can do no wrong, and Allison's dad makes her mom show up. I'm just…you know…waiting to see what happens tomorrow. Dexter is only in that one class. But there's out of class, too, and he's such a sneak."

"But Dad," Dylan interrupted, "if he thinks he can get away with it, he won't stop. He might not bother her in class, but he will find ways to do it outside of class. I know him. He's a jerk. He's an idiot. He's also someone who doesn't listen. Won't take no for an answer. They tell us he's got mental health issues, but I think he's just figured out that if he plays the mental health card, no one will do anything to stop him. I guess you could say he's a clever idiot. I'm not letting him try anything with my sister."

My sister. Burgess loved the way his son stepped up for Nina and Ned and regarded them as his siblings. His true siblings—half-siblings—had been left behind with his mother's husband after his mother died. Dylan had been close to them, but their father made little effort to keep them in touch with their brother. As Dylan might have put it: an idiot and a jerk.

Burgess said, "I appreciated your standing up for Nina. I've met with Dr. Jorgensen, and I hope the result of that meeting will be that the school enforces its own rules and this boy leaves Nina alone. We have to give it some time to see how that plays out before we take further steps." Reminding his son of the earlier episode, he added, "And you don't need any more trouble yourself. Dr. Jorgensen is supposed to be a professional and roll with this rather than bear grudges. But we don't know that she will. So, now is not a good time for you to pick a fight with Wiggins."

He watched his son carefully. Saw stubborn resistance. Before Dylan could respond, he continued. "You two should also know that the department will be looking into Wiggins. Checking to see if his behavior is on our radar. I've got Andrea Dwyer, our juvenile officer, meeting with Dr. Jorgensen and Mr. Harrison to be sure they understand what to watch for."

"What to watch for?" Nina said. "They need someone to come in and tell them that? Isn't that part of their jobs, to keep an eye out for students who pose a risk to others?"

"It is," he agreed. "But sometimes, people need to be reminded. It can be complicated to balance the rights of a troubled kid like Wiggins, if indeed he does have mental health issues, with those of the other students. But as you've shown with those recordings, Nina, his behavior goes far beyond what might get him cut some slack."

"You better believe it does," Dylan said, sitting up straighter. "He's sneaky. He does stuff when he knows no adult is going to be watching."

"There are things we should know about?" Burgess said.

"Oh, yeah. He's…well, he grabs at girls. Grabs at their breasts and their asses when their hands are full, and they can't protect themselves. Then he laughs like a jackass about it. The teachers know, and they won't do anything about it. I don't know whether it's because his father is one of the school's directors or if they're scared of Dexter. He's an intimidating guy." Dylan threw up his hands. "I've heard his parents are super protective."

Ah, Burgess thought, *as he'd suspected, Dexter had a connected parent.* The "my dad is important" card got played all the time. Often used to get cops in trouble. Combined with hyper-protective parents, it could be a nightmare. Maybe this was what had paralyzed Dr. Jorgensen?

From the door, Chris said, "I thought that was something from my era. I can't believe girls still have to put up with that."

"Not this girl," Nina said.

"What happened? What did Nina do?" Ned asked, worming his way past Chris and coming into the room.

"We can talk about it at dinner. Which is ready," Chris said. "Ned has fixed us some lovely carrot sticks."

"Way to go, Little Bro," Dylan said. "Maybe you'll grow up to be a famous chef."

He stood up and rubbed his lean stomach. "I am starving. I am always starving. Good thing we have Chris and Ned to keep us fed." He grinned. "And that is a very bad rhyme."

"I'm not hungry," Nina said. "I'm too upset to eat."

She looked at Burgess. "Dad. Tell them. I've had a very bad day."

Before he could respond, Chris said, "Then you can just sit and watch the rest of us eat," which made Burgess wonder if they had had a disagreement before he got home. Nina had many genuine reasons for stomach issues, given her past trauma, but she'd also learned to use her issues for sympathy or to get her own way. It had been a hard day for her, so she got some slack, but she wasn't sitting out family dinner. Especially not when he'd made the time to come home.

Oh. Right. Of course, everything was about him. He shook himself and headed for the table.

The golden roast chicken in the center of the table reminded him how grateful he was to come home to this instead of driving through a fast-food joint and rushing back to the conference room at 109. He looked at Chris. Saw that she was watching him.

He said, "I have got to be the luckiest man alive. A lovely family and a perfect roast chicken." He raised his water glass and said, "A toast to the cook."

Chris's tense face softened, and there was her smile. The smile that was like a sunrise. The smile that hooked him from the day he met her. Despite the conflict between his kids and the unpleasant specter of Dexter Wiggins, this made the dark, secretive world of Dr. Eliot Spence retreat. His home life might not be perfect, but it was normal. Conflict was normal. Raising teenagers was going to be fraught. That was okay.

No one pressured Nina to eat except Ned, who insisted that his sister eat some carrots. Once she'd nibbled on a carrot and seen that no one was going to force her to eat, she took small helpings of mashed potatoes and chicken and began to eat.

When the golden bird had been significantly denuded and everyone fed and relaxed, he returned to the discussion he'd been having with Nina and Dylan. "About this Dexter Wiggins," he said. "If there are things he's done that you know about, you should tell me. It will help us keep things from accelerating and help keep his potential victims safe."

"Who's Dexter Wiggins?" Ned asked.

Right. The problem with discussing teenage problems, including sexual harassment or worse, in front of a curious ten-year-old.

Chris was grinning, waiting to see how he'd handle this.

"A boy at school who's been being mean to Nina," Burgess said.

Ned, who was sitting next to his sister, gave her a hug. "I'm sorry someone's being mean to you," he said.

"I could back him off so easily, Dad," Dylan said. "He's as big as me, but he's lazy and flabby."

"And maybe get yourself suspended just as easily in the process. I understand the impulse. I was very protective of my sisters at your age. I'm just asking you to hang on for now. Give it some time. See if things can be worked out without—" Burgess considered how to say this. "Without resorting to violence. That's all. Nina knows she's lucky to have a brother who will stand up for her." Thinking about Ned's arm around his sister, added, "Two brothers."

He thought he could see Dylan relax, pretty sure Dylan understood that what he'd said was permission to act if things didn't change. They'd have to talk more about that, of course. He didn't miss Chris's raised eyebrows, either. Much more talking to be done. But for now, Nina was eating,

97

Dylan's air of suppressed violence was gone, and he hadn't had to discuss the ugly details of Dexter Wiggins's behavior in front of Ned.

He pushed back his chair. "I hate to leave such delightful company, but we had a homicide today, and I have to get back to meet with my team. Even though..." A quick look at Chris. "Even though I believe there might be apple pie." Smiles around the table. "And I hope you'll leave some for a tired old detective."

They laughed at him. Which was okay because he was happy if his family didn't see him the way he saw himself, as a grouchy old dinosaur lumbering toward extinction. He helped clear the table. Brought Chris a glass of wine to sip while he served the pie. Family settled, he hoped, Burgess headed back to the world of Dr. Eliot Spence and his secrets.

FIFTEEN

K yle was waiting. Stan hadn't shown up yet. A typical meeting of the three musketeers. Often, it meant that Stan Perry had larked off on a mini-investigation of his own, but it was too soon for that. Not enough was known. There was still a cop on the door of Spence's condo, and Rocky Jordan's car was still there, but the news trucks were gone, and only a handful of the curious remained.

Burgess parked and went to join Kyle. They stood with their backs to the building, the heat off the brick contrasting with the cool evening air, surrounded by the scent of the sea and the endless sloshing of the waves. The gulls had gone quiet. Lights were on inside the buildings, but no residents appeared outside. News traveled fast, and no doubt the neighbors were buttoned up inside, where they felt safer from killers who struck in the dark. That wouldn't last. People had short memories, especially of things that impeded their movements.

Often, the brass held press conferences in which they announced there was no reason for the public to be concerned without sharing any of that reasoning. The reason here was that the killing looked personal, and Spence's security had kept him well guarded. But they couldn't know that for sure, and the brass couldn't share it.

They stood side by side, not speaking, as they waited for Perry. After a while, Burgess said, "How was family dinner?"

"The usual. Older daughter burbled happily about school while my

99

younger ate in silence. She's unhappy about something and won't tell us what it is. I hope it doesn't mean she's being bullied at school. She's kind of behind the other girls, development-wise, and middle school girls can be awfully cruel. Yours?"

"Chris roasted a chicken, and there were mashed potatoes and an apple pie, so kind of heavenly. But Nina's upset about that incident at school, and Dylan, being the protective brother, wants to go beat the crap out of the kid who's harassing her. I think I've got things settled down for now. But who knows?" Burgess shrugged. "I just hope Dylan can keep a lid on it. Depends a lot on how the school responds. If the school responds. I've put Dwyer on the case."

"She's good," Kyle said.

Burgess agreed. She was. "Not Dwyer, I'm worried about. It's whether Dr. Jorgensen gets it. Whether she actually conveys her…and our concerns to the teachers so they keep an eye on this kid. You know how they can be. If we're not there in their faces, making them pay attention, it will be eclipsed by the next crisis and forgotten about or ignored. But the boy, Dexter Wiggins, is a ticking bomb. The question is whether he gets defused before he goes off." He shrugged. "If he hasn't already, and we just haven't heard about it. A young girl who's been assaulted might not report it."

Burgess sighed, a sigh born of so many years of testosterone-driven young men going off the rails even when they *were* on someone's radar because vigilance took work.

"Nina has a cell phone, right? And keeps it with her?" Kyle said.

Burgess nodded.

"And she knows she can call you anytime, whatever the school rules are about cell phone use?"

"She does."

"Remind her again."

The two dads leaned back against the brick, thinking of years of boys like Dexter Wiggins and how little they could do to keep something bad from happening. Dark thoughts to go with the deepening night. With the scene from earlier today.

After a bit, Kyle said, "So, Spence? Quite a piece of work, yes?"

"Gonna make some calls tomorrow. Try to catch up with PD down in Weston. See what they can tell me about Lenore Spence's death. About why her family might be suing him. And read those legal papers, see if there's any enlightenment or it's all just generic legal BS."

"If they'll talk."

"Right. Big if." Police departments could be incredibly helpful or deliberately unhelpful. There was no telling which way it would go until he called.

"I assume Dr. Spence had a lawyer to defend those suits. We might learn something there," Kyle said. "Though, of course, lawyers can be as bad as some of our fellow cops when it comes to sharing information. Even once we tell them Spence is dead, murdered, and their information might be critical to finding the killer."

Kyle looked toward the road leading to these waterfront condos. "I expect young Stanley was about halfway out the door when Lily asked him to change the baby before he left. Which led to a little this and a little that. Anything to keep him from leaving."

Burgess made an affirmative sound. "She's not going to make it easy. I missed those years. Mostly, I'm not sorry, but having more history with my kids might make dealing with them easier now."

"Probably not. Teenagers, you know, it's like aliens have kidnapped the kids we knew and left strangers in their place," Kyle said.

"That's damned reassuring."

"It was meant to be."

At long last, when Burgess thought his feet had grown roots down into the pavement, Perry showed up.

He was a youngster. The one whose bouncing energy they always envied. Tonight, he looked beat. He opened his mouth to explain, studied their faces, and instead said, "Sorry. What are my marching orders?"

"Stan, you will take the places to the left of Spence's. Terry will take those to the right. I'll start with the places across the street. Ask about any unfamiliar people or vehicles, anything that seemed out of place. Whether they have security cameras. Whether they knew Dr. Spence. Whether they've ever witnessed Spence have a confrontation with anyone."

He didn't have to tell them not to take "no" for an answer. They already knew how reluctant people could be to get involved, even when the questions were about a homicide.

They split up and went to work.

Burgess rang the doorbell of the condo across from Dr. Spence's. A sour-faced woman in her late fifties answered the door, ready to send him on his way.

"Detective Sergeant Burgess, Portland police, ma'am. I need to ask you a few questions about your neighbor, Dr. Spence."

She hesitated, the hand on the knob and the shifting of her feet a sign she wanted him to leave so she could shut the door. She said, "We really didn't know—"

"Just a few moments of your time," Burgess said. "It's important."

She huffed out an "Oh, all right" and stepped back to let him enter, then left him standing just inside, saying, "Wait here. I'll get my husband."

This place, very much like Spence's condo, was decorated the way he'd expected Spence's to be. Natural wood floors, white walls, lots of blue and white in the furniture, and a denim blue and white rug under a white cottage-style coffee table. There was a small room to his right that looked like a TV room. It had a large window that faced Spence's door.

He heard a murmur of voices, and then the woman returned, followed by a man in a coral polo and chinos who looked like he ate sour pickles for a living. Burgess figured mid-sixties. The woman said, "My husband, Alex Grundwald. And I'm Theresa. If you'll come this way?"

She led Burgess into the living room and gestured to a chair. The Grundwalds sat across from him, a few feet apart, and waited. Clearly, they weren't going to volunteer anything. Not a problem. He was good at asking questions.

He got out his notebook, balanced it on his knee, and clicked his pen. "Were you acquainted with your neighbor, Dr. Eliot Spence?" He looked for one of them to the other. The couple exchanged looks. He didn't yet know what that meant, but he would find out.

"We weren't friends," the man said. "We knew him to say hello to. That's about it. Why? Are you investigating Dr. Spence for some reason?"

"Eliot Spence has been killed," Burgess said.

They already knew that, he could tell, but he was happy to keep up the pretense that this was news to them if it might get better cooperation. "We're looking into the circumstances. Often, neighbors have observed people or events that are helpful in our investigation."

"Killed how?" the woman said.

Burgess shook his head sadly. Managed a regretful tone as he said, "I'm afraid we can't comment on that at this point. Keeping those details close. I'm sure you understand." He waited for their nods, then continued. "If I might just ask a few questions, and I'll be out of your hair, and you can go back to your evening?"

Across the room, he could see a computer screen open to a Scrabble game.

He waited.

The man nodded his assent to some questions. The woman didn't reply.

Burgess started with the security camera question. They didn't have one. Couldn't see why they'd need one in such a nice neighborhood.

"Our son thinks we should get one," the man said. "I told him fine if he buys it and installs it." He looked at his wife. "We're not very good with technology."

"Those homeless do wander down here occasionally," the woman said. "So awful. I suppose a security camera might be useful for that. We always call you."

Probably more awful to be homeless, Burgess thought.

They exchanged glances with every response. Burgess decided it wasn't that they wanted him gone, just that they were chronically crabby. Also, as a surprise after her initial unfriendliness, he thought they really did want to share what they knew, but they didn't want to seem like nosy neighbors. It was better if they made Burgess work for it, as though making a detective push for their information got them off the hook. He hoped they had something worth working for.

He said, "Have you noticed any unfamiliar cars or persons in the neighborhood recently?"

Shakes of their heads. Another glance exchanged.

"What about visitors to Dr. Spence's condo? Does he have any visitors that you've observed?"

When they hesitated, he added, "With his door directly across from yours, you're bound to notice things even if you're minding your own business. Can't help it, right?"

The man nodded. "He's got a girlfriend who's there quite frequently. A real looker. Tall, slender. Long dark hair. She wasn't very happy with him last night, though."

Burgess waited for more. Another nod and the woman spoke.

"Her name is Deidre Lovejoy," she said. "She's...I don't know what you'd call it." She looked at her husband. "A socialite, if Portland has them. We wouldn't know. We're content to keep to ourselves. Anyway, she's Spence's girlfriend. And as Alex says, she's a looker. Wears those super high heels and business clothes that are almost too sexy for business. She's been seeing him for—" Again, she stopped and looked at her husband. "I guess eight or nine months."

The husband nodded.

"Anyway. She was here last night, all dressed up. Knocked on his door and then—" Another glance, like she was only going to continue with her story if he approved. Or if he didn't want a turn to speak. Burgess saw a faint nod. "And then he wouldn't let her in."

"They argued?"

She nodded. "I'll say they did. She pitched a fit. I mean, there she is, all dressed up like a model or something, and she's screaming like a fishwife. Everyone on the street must have heard it. Then, he went back inside and shut the door, and she started to walk away. Then she came back, pulled out a bottle of wine from her bag, and smashed it against his door. Then she left."

"Do you recall what time this happened?"

She said, "Around eight. Eight-thirty."

She looked at her husband. "What else about last night do we remember?"

Her husband stroked his jaw thoughtfully as he considered. "There's that man...or boy, he's youngish. Dark hair. Kind of furtive, if you ask me. You know, the kind who wears a hoodie even when it's summer and hot so you can't see his face...he was here. You know the one I mean, Theresa?"

She nodded. "The little creep," she said.

He continued. "The guy...he hangs around, mostly across the street, watching the condos. It's creepy. Well, we think it's creepy, but he hasn't done anything that merits our calling you guys. Yet. We watch, though. We watch. Someone has to be responsible for the neighborhood safety."

"Vigilant citizens like you two are so valuable to the community," Burgess said, hoping he wasn't laying it on too thick.

"Thank you," she said. "Dr. Spence didn't share your opinion, I'm afraid. He was always peering about like he was afraid of something. Or someone. Yet, he had the audacity to accuse us of spying on him." She gave an irritated shake of her head. "As though we weren't supposed to be paying attention. It's our neighborhood, too."

"This is very helpful," Burgess said. "Can you tell me anything more about the person in the hoodie? You've said young. What about height? Weight? Did you get a good enough look to guess at ethnicity?"

Alex Grundwald nodded. "He's white. About...maybe five-eleven. Skinny. Skinny and wearing those stupid pants with the crotch down around his knees. I may not have had a good look at his face, but I can tell you that he wears Calvin Klein cotton boxer briefs."

"Which," his wife added, "is not something you really want to see on the public street. Or know about a stranger."

This was helpful, so Burgess tried not to laugh. A laugh would have shut off the faucet of information in a hurry. "You said he wore the hoodie even when it was hot, so he was around in the summer. About how long has he been here? And, if you know, how frequently?"

The man said, "We first spotted him about a month ago. He could have been here longer, though, because we were on vacation for two weeks and not around."

"Was he around often? Daily? Weekly? Was there any regularity to his schedule?"

"Maybe once a week," the man said.

"Or twice," the woman said. "Always in the evening. Not during the day."

"Mid-evening, like around eight," the man said.

"You say young. Could you estimate his age?"

They shook their heads.

"Can you describe his behavior? Did he walk or sit? Appear to have any chore or job to do? And how long did these visits last?"

"You think he's a suspect?" she asked.

Burgess shrugged. "Too soon to tell. At this point, we're still building a picture. But strangers are always of interest to us. So. His visits?"

"He'd just appear," the woman said. "Come walking down the road until he was nearby, and then he'd just..." She turned to her husband. "How would you describe it, Alex? Loiter?"

The man nodded. "He'd loiter. He didn't smoke. He didn't read. He didn't walk. He just leaned against that short wall that separates the walkway from the street. Lean against it or sit." He shrugged. "I've never understood how anyone could be idle like that."

"When is the last time you saw him?" Burgess asked.

This time, they spoke together. "Yesterday."

Burgess figured he'd exhausted that subject and moved on. "What about other visitors to Dr. Spence? Have you observed any besides Ms. Lovejoy?"

The couple looked at each other. Exchanged nods. Then he said, "The blondes?"

"The blondes?" Burgess echoed.

They nodded again in unison. "About once a month—" she began. Looked at her husband and got a nod. "About once a month, Dr. Spence would have a woman spend the night. They were always blonde. They always wore sexy clothes. Arrived by Uber, I think. Well, some car dropped them off. They didn't drive here. They were pretty in a kind of sleazy way. We always wondered if Ms. Lovejoy knew about them. She doesn't seem like the type to be accepting of something like that." She looked at Burgess. "You know what I mean?"

He said, "A woman who believes she's in a serious relationship doesn't want to be with a man who plays around?"

They nodded.

"Any other regulars?"

"Besides the cleaner?"

"Yes."

"There's a ginger-haired man. I think they must do some sport together. Golf, I think. He comes by sometimes and picks up Dr. Spence. They're usually gone for at least four hours. He drives a fairly new Audi SUV. Silver."

No wonder Spence accused them of spying. Burgess figured if he asked, she could give him the plate number.

"You've been very helpful," he said. He gave them one of his cards. "In case you think of anything else we should know."

Before he left, he tossed out one last question. "Was Deidre Lovejoy the only person who visited Dr. Spence last night?"

Glances were exchanged, and two heads shook. "There was one of the blondes," he said.

"You saw her arrive?"

A nod. "She came in a green Subaru."

"Around what time?"

"Maybe eight or eight-thirty? Shortly after Ms. Lovejoy."

"Did you see her leave?"

Two heads shook again. "She was still there when we went to bed."

"What about the smashed bottle and the spilled wine? It was gone this morning. Did you observe Dr. Spence cleaning it up?"

"Oh. That wasn't Dr. Spence. That was the housekeeper. She's really good. We tried to get her to work for us, but she said her schedule was full. It was a disappointment," the woman said. "We've never seen anyone who is a harder worker."

He thanked them again and moved on to the next house. An older man this time, leaning heavily on a cane, in a place that, despite being fairly new and nicely furnished, needed Dr. Spence's housekeeper and smelled faintly of cats. The man shook his head when Burgess introduced himself and explained why he was there. "Sorry, Detective. I'm afraid I'm of no use.

I've been away for about five weeks. Rehab facility. I had a fall. So, I'm kind of out of touch with what's been going on around here."

That explained the dust and stale air and why the cat scent was faint. Someone else must have taken the cat.

"I'll be quick, then," Burgess said, wanting to check a few things before he was dismissed. "Were you acquainted with Dr. Spence?"

"Acquainted is an interesting word, Detective, as it does suggest a casual relationship. I'm afraid ours was more distant than that. We nodded in passing. I'm a retired physician. When he first moved in, I rather hoped we might become acquaintances, if not friends. Perhaps have the occasional conversation about our mutual profession. A neighborly glass of wine or Scotch. It never happened. I made a few overtures, but he never showed any interest." He smiled. "About the only thing I've noticed him showing an interest in is women. Beautiful women."

The man, a Dr. Fellowes, broke off. "I apologize. I do not wish to descend into gossip about a person I didn't know. I observed the women, but for all I know, they could have been relatives. He could have had one stunning dark sister and several less classy blonde sisters. Beyond that?"

A shrug. "If I were to assess a person with whom I didn't really have a relationship, I'd say he was a cold man and damaged somehow. Showing signs of paranoia. He was unusually cautious in his comings and goings, as though he was expecting to be confronted or attacked, although I never saw anyone around who might be threatening him."

He broke off with an apologetic nod. "You see what I am doing here? I say I don't know the man; we never had any sort of relationship, and yet I am analyzing him like I did know him. But of course, as physicians, we are constantly making those sorts of assessments. These days, well, in my case, before I retired from practice, we had to do that because the system barely gave us time to do anything else. Sadly, as I am sure you know in your profession as well, snap judgments aren't always correct."

He fell silent. Looked around at his dim condo and shook his head. "I apologize. The place is rather a mess right now. My cleaner was supposed to come in before I returned from rehab, but she had a family emergency. She won't be here until tomorrow. So, for now, I put up with this. Afraid if I break out the vacuum myself, I'll end up back in rehab. But you are welcome to sit down if you don't mind a little dust."

He had no idea the kind of places Burgess had been in. Places where sitting down wasn't an option because all the chairs were broken, covered in debris or feces, or occupied. "I'm fine here or sitting. Whichever is better for you," Burgess said.

"Sitting, then. I'm just getting back on my feet. Literally. I'd rather not push it."

He led the way into the living room, switched on a few lights, and gestured for Burgess to sit. "I'm sure you have other questions," he said.

"I do. Were you here last night?"

Dr. Fellowes nodded. "My first day back. You're wondering if I observed Dr. Spence last evening? His comings and goings? Whether he had company?"

Burgess nodded.

"I'm afraid I may not be helpful on that score. I did hear a commotion across the way, but I didn't get up to see what was happening. Just didn't have the energy. A man and woman were arguing, and I recognized Dr. Spence's voice. As I said, I didn't get up to see who was arguing, but I believe it was Dr. Spence's girlfriend. A rather beautiful brunette, though not a very happy one, I think."

He gestured toward a tray on which there were some bottles of expensive liquor and a few glasses. "I don't suppose I can ask you to pour me a short Scotch? The Oban, I think. Rehab is a bit like being in jail, the way they monitor one's consumption. After weeks of lousy food and no drink, I could really use one."

Burgess got up and went to the tray. "Ice or water?" he asked.

"A couple of cubes would be nice. And now that I think about it, maybe not so short. Maybe a decent drink for a parched man?"

Burgess fixed the drink, went to the kitchen for ice, and gave the glass to the doctor.

"Thank you." Fellowes raised the glass. "Sure, you don't want one?"

It would have been nice, but Burgess shook his head. "On duty," he said. "So, anything else from last night?"

"A bit later, after the fight, I did see a young woman arrive, maybe around eight-thirty or a little later. Pretty. Blonde. Like the others, rather skimpily dressed for a cool evening. I happened to be up just then, limping to the bathroom. After that, I lay down on the sofa to rest. The prospect of climbing the stairs to my bedroom seemed daunting."

A shrug. "Sorry, I can't do better."

"Not a problem," Burgess said. "What about strangers or strange cars in the areas?"

"There was that odd boy who seemed to be watching him. I observed him a few times before my enforced incarceration in that rehab place, and he seemed to be back yesterday. I say 'boy' because he seemed young. Moved like a youngster. Had that hunched-shouldered, trying to disappear air that some of them have."

"Can you tell me anything else about him, about the boy? Height, weight, ethnicity, how he dressed?"

When the doctor didn't reply, Burgess said, "If you can."

"As I said. Young. Skinny. Maybe five ten or eleven. White. Dark haired. Black pants and a gray sweatshirt with the hood pulled up. He seemed to have some sort of handicap. That is, it seemed like the movement of his left arm was somewhat impaired. I say maybe. It could just have been an odd way of holding himself. Or a temporary injury."

"This is very helpful. Other than Dr. Spence's many sisters, did you observe anyone else who was a regular visitor?"

"His golfing buddy. What the English call 'a ginger.' The housekeeper, of course. A woman about his own age who looked nervous about meeting him. Slim, well-cut dark hair, very well dressed, and handsome rather than pretty. Carrying a briefcase. But she was here at least a month ago. She came twice that I saw. I think once there was a man with her, but I didn't get a good look at him. Spence didn't seem pleased to see her, but he let her in, and they were inside for quite some time."

He broke off. "I sound like quite the voyeur, don't I? It's not intentional. He's practically right outside my door. I can't help but see things."

Burgess thanked him and gave the man his card. "In case you remember anything else. Thank you for your time. And don't get up. I can see myself out."

"Good luck," Dr. Fellowes said. He raised his glass to Burgess, then took a drink.

Burgess always hoped he wouldn't need luck but often did. He let himself out of the condo and paused in the doorway, breathing in the fresh sea air. Across the street, he watched Kyle come out of a door, pause, and head for the next one. He looked around, in case the loitering youth was there, but saw no one. He kicked himself back into action and rang another doorbell.

SIXTEEN

Normally, canvassing a neighborhood would be a job for uniformed officers, but he and his team often kept the closest neighbors for themselves when there was time. As he rang the third bell, he had a brief vision of decades of ringing doorbells, of a much younger Burgess on a hot summer night, sweaty and tired, getting door after door slammed in his face.

The public's feelings about cops ebbed and flowed. They were the oppressors. The bad guys. The man. They were heroes. Rescuers. Part of the glue that held society together. Opinions were like an elastic band that stretched and contracted. Right now, cops were the bad guys again. People who didn't want to cooperate, who railed against police brutality, rarely asked themselves the question: Who are you gonna call if there are no police?

Two rings brought no response. He was debating between ringing again and moving on when the door was opened by a girl of about thirteen. Wild dark hair and deep brown eyes. Wide-eyed. Looking wary. She opened the door only the length of a chain as she said, "I'm not allowed to let anybody in, Mister. Please come back another time."

He showed her his credentials. "Detective Sergeant Joe Burgess," he said. "Portland police."

She looked at his badge and up at his face. Said, "It's important, right? About that man across the way who was killed?"

Burgess nodded. "It is. But if you're home alone and you're not supposed to let anyone in, I can come back when your parents are home."

The girl laughed. A kind of sad laugh. She said, "Well, good luck with that."

"I'm sorry," he said. "What do you mean?"

"I mean, my father is on a business trip. He's always on business trips. And my mother...stepmother, actually...is out with her friends. She's always out with her friends. Hold on."

She closed the door, and he could hear her fumbling with the chain. She opened the door and said, "You might as well come in. You won't find a time when they're home any time soon unless you want to wait outside all night until The Wicked gets home."

She wore gray sweatpants and a Rosie the Riveter tee shirt. Her feet were bare, her toenails a pale pink with glitter.

"The Wicked?"

She grinned. "As in wicked stepmother."

Standing next to her, he realized she was tall, an easy five foot ten, and fit, like, young as she was, she was an athlete.

Stepping aside so he could pass, she swept an arm toward the interior. "Do come in, Detective Sergeant. Straight on into the living room, if you please. And excuse the mess. I was going to do a bit of tidying up after I finished my homework."

So many kids in this city were raising themselves. People tended to think it only happened in poorer neighborhoods, but plenty of people with lots of money also prioritized their lives, work, and pleasure at the expense of their children. This girl seemed to be handling it well, but the single plate and glass beside a stack of books on the dining table looked lonely.

"I'm Kristin," the girl said when he was inside. "Kristin Daggett. I'm thirteen, which is old enough to be left home alone, in case you were worried. I am not beaten, starved, or neglected, except perhaps emotionally. But I think I'm probably better off on my own than with either my dad or The Wicked, and my mother has abandoned me to their tender care and moved to Florida with her new boyfriend."

She gave him a sly grin. "Sad story, huh?"

"I'm here because I—"

"Am investigating the death of my neighbor, Dr. Eliot Spence, right?"

"Right. Did you know Dr. Spence?"

Burgess stopped. This was wrong. He shouldn't question her without an adult present, no matter how mature she seemed or how valuable her information might be.

He held up a hand to stop her. "I appreciate your willingness to talk to me, Kristin. But we've got rules, and one of them is not questioning a minor alone." He didn't add, especially a minor female. Nor that he'd broken those rules when absolutely necessary.

He said, "I'm going to call a colleague and see if she can join us. If that's all right with you?"

The girl shrugged. "I believe rules are mostly made to be broken, but hey…do what you've gotta do. Call a colleague. A friend. An army. I don't care. I'll just—" She waved a languid hand toward the table. "Go back to doing my homework, and we can try this again when your colleague is available."

Kids these days. Adults often despaired of them, but the truth was, there were plenty who were competent, savvy, and ready to step up to save the crappy world that was being left to them.

He took out his phone and called Andrea Dwyer.

She answered with, "No, Joe. I'm busy." Then laughed. "Twice in a day? Really? To what do I owe the pleasure? And no, I haven't got any information about Dexter Wiggins yet. But I will."

"Not about Wiggins." He explained the situation. "It would be great if you could come down here and help me out with this, but I'll understand if you're too busy."

"Like I often say, never too busy for you. Plus, what I'm busy with right now is folding my laundry, which can wait. Who cares if I show up on the street in a wrinkled shirt? As long as I don't meet the chief, that is. Give me the address and about…" she considered. "Twelve minutes. That work?"

"Brilliantly."

He disconnected and told Kristin that he and his colleague would be back in about fifteen minutes.

"That was fast," she said. "I bet your colleagues like you."

Burgess smiled, thinking about the ones like Cote, who wished he'd get hit by a truck, and said, "Some of them, at least. I'll be back."

He stepped out into the rapidly cooling evening. It was sweater weather now. These last summer and early fall days were like that. Cool mornings, hot middles, and cool evenings. Chris complained it was hard to know how to dress and was always nudging Nina to take a sweater or a sweatshirt. Part of that was Nina's propensity to wear skimpier clothes than either he or Chris would have liked. They were what all the girls were wearing. But

Burgess knew what guys were like. Skimpy clothes on lovely young bodies, no matter how much women were entitled to dress as they pleased, could be like red flags to a bull.

He walked to the next condo and rang the bell. There were lights on inside, and he could hear the sound of a television, but despite ringing multiple times, no one came to answer the door. More of that eroding sense of community. The belief that everyone was entitled to their personal free-dom, but to hell with civic responsibility. What if he was ringing the bell because there was an emergency and someone needed an ambulance? Not their problem, he supposed. What if he was ringing the bell because the place was on fire?

He sighed. Stepped back and looked at the row of smart brick condos with their white trim, their balconies, and their flowerboxes newly redone with mums for fall. It looked like such a pleasant place to live. He turned and looked back toward Spence's condo. Saw Stan Perry come out of a door and lean back against the building to scribble some notes in his book.

Were Stan and Kyle getting the girlfriend, the blondes, and the ginger-haired friend, too? The lurking teenage boy? Were they getting the woman with the briefcase? What about others who had come and gone? Did those who shared walls with Dr. Spence have more to add, and would it be anything that would illuminate the situation? He hated tying up three detectives like this when one of them—perhaps all of them—should have been back at 109 reading through the materials from Spence's desk and closet. But this had to be done while memories were fresh and before anyone's memories were tainted by whatever the newspapers could ferret out and print.

He sighed and walked past the places he'd already visited to the condo next door to the Grundwalds. The place was dark. He rang the bell anyway. No one answered. He moved along. The next place had a more occupied look. Adult bikes in the small, private space outside the door, along with a small pink child's bike.

He rang and waited.

After a moment, he heard footsteps, and a harried-looking man who appeared to be in his mid-thirties opened the door and stepped out, care-fully closing it behind him. He put a finger to his lips. "We've just about got Melodie settled, which is something of a miracle. You're a cop, right? Inves-tigating what happened across the way?"

Burgess nodded.

"We didn't know him. Dr. Spence. I'm sorry. So there isn't much to tell.

My wife, Elaine. Lainey. She tried. She's a neighborly sort, and she thought we ought to know the people around us. But Spence? He was a cold fish. She took him cookies. He said, 'No, thank you, I don't eat sugar,' which was so rude. After that, we'd wave and say hi when we saw him, and he'd kind of tuck his head into his collar and pretend he hadn't seen us."

The man shrugged. "Oh. Sorry. I'm Peter. Peter Trask. And my wife is Elaine, and our daughter, Melodie, is almost three."

Burgess nodded. "Besides your interactions with Dr. Spence, which I gather were minimal, I have a few other questions if you have the time?"

The man glanced back over his shoulder, then nodded. Evidently, if someone else settled the difficult Melodie, that was all right with him.

"Have you noticed any strange vehicles or strangers in the neighborhood lately?"

Trask looked up and down the street, as though searching for the answer to Burgess's question. Then he said, "There's the kid," and described the same young man in a hoodie that others had described. "I asked him what he was doing here since he didn't appear to live here, work here, or be visiting anyone here. He told me it was a free country and none of my business."

Burgess asked for a description and got a version of what others had said, with the added information that the kid had a noticeable overbite and a sad attempt at a beard. Also, a tattoo on his right arm that looked like a work in progress.

"Kid always wore a hoodie, but he had the sleeves pushed up," Trask said. "I think it's supposed to be an eagle. A pretty pathetic one."

"Anyone else? Anyone coming or going at Spence's?"

Trask shrugged. "Besides the women? Because everyone must have mentioned them. It's become a kind of neighborhood sport. It wasn't nice of us, I admit, but we'd been waiting for the time when he got his schedule mixed up, and one of those tacky blondes showed up at the same time as perfect Ms. Lovejoy." He shook his head. "It never happened. Well, except it almost happened last night. Guess he must have gotten his calendar mixed up or something. Lucky for him, the blonde of the evening showed up just after Lovejoy made her scene."

He stopped. Put a hand to his lips. "Sorry. That wasn't nice. Especially since he obviously wasn't lucky at all, was he?"

"Anyone else besides the women and the kid?"

Trask shook his head. "We're mostly away during the day; we both work, and Melodie's at preschool, so I can't say who might have been here then. There was a couple who visited him about, maybe, three weeks ago. I say couple, but they looked like brother and sister. Tall, lean. About my age, maybe? Mid to late thirties. They looked professional. You know. Briefcases and business attire. Other than that, no."

"Did Dr. Spence appear to be someone who was quite rigid about his schedule? Regular departures and arrivals? If you know."

Burgess got a shrug.

"Ever observe any commotion over there? Anything like a fight or argument?"

Another shrug.

"Last night, did you observe the altercation between Dr. Spence and Ms. Lovejoy?"

Trask laughed. "It wasn't much of an altercation, I'm afraid. She knocked on his door. He wouldn't let her in. She yelled at him. He went back inside and closed the door in her face. She smashed a bottle of wine on his door. And then she drove away."

"But it appeared Dr. Spence was expecting another woman at the time? One who arrived shortly after Ms. Lovejoy's departure?"

"One of the blondes."

"Around what time did this occur?"

Trask considered. "I'd say it was around eight-thirty because Melodie was asleep, and Elaine and I were enjoying a glass of wine to celebrate."

Burgess turned so he could see Spence's door. Then, he turned back. "Did you see the blonde woman leave?"

"It's funny, you know," Trask said, "but we never see them leave. We see them arrive, at least when it stays light later, and he lets them in through the garage. But we never see the women leave. Lainey was remarking on that last night. She asked if I thought Spence murdered them and buried them in his basement."

"Does he have a basement?" Burgess corrected himself. "Do these condos have basements?"

"Nope. It was a joke."

"So, you've seen these women arrive, but you've never seen one leave?"

"Nope."

"Ever see Dr. Spence leave on an evening when one of these blondes was visiting?"

"Once or twice, but he always seemed to be alone in the car. Of course, they could have left after we went to bed. We're generally asleep by eleven."

Burgess figured he'd gotten about all he was going to get here but asked, "Do you think your wife might have anything to add?"

"She might. She's very observant, while I tend to be thinking about my work and then run into things. Scientist, you know. We really can be absent-minded. I can ask her and have her give you a call if she thinks of anything. But I am not calling her away from Melodie in the middle of our bedtime ritual. Just not. Sorry."

"Not a problem," Burgess said, fishing another card from his pocket. "My numbers are all on here. She can call me at her convenience if she thinks of anything. You both can. Thank you for your help."

He headed back toward the unit where he'd met Kristin Daggett. Dwyer should be here soon, and he was looking forward to hearing what Kristin had to say. Even if it was mostly a reiteration of what others had told him, she had such an amusing style of reportage it would be a refreshing change from the weary professor or the gossipy Grundwalds.

He stopped near her door and looked up the road leading down to the condo complex. Dwyer's neon green Jeep was heading his way.

SEVENTEEN

S he parked and gave him a mock salute. "Reporting for duty, Detective Sergeant." The comment was delivered with a grin.

Dwyer was among Burgess's favorite people. She was great at her job, wonderful with the kids in the city, and never sulked or showed attitude when she was asked to do something not entirely within her job description. She was also wonderfully easy on the eye, though Burgess figured even thinking something like that could get him in trouble with the anti-harassment crowd. It seemed that only dinosaurs like him didn't get it that they couldn't admire women for their looks, only for their brains. Well, okay then. Dwyer had an impressive brain, topped by glossy dark hair and perched atop a trim, athletic body. Oops. Probably, he shouldn't think about her body.

Could he use as an excuse that bodies were part of his job?

"So, what am I supposed to do here, Joe? Just be a chaperone while you ask the questions?"

"Unless you think of questions of your own. Then, you can ask the questions, and I'll be the chaperone. Deal?"

"Deal."

"So, I need to interview Kristin Daggett, who is thirteen, home alone. Dad is on a business trip. Stepmother, Kristin calls her 'The Wicked,' is out with her friends, apparently often out with her friends, and the mom has decamped to Florida with a boyfriend. Our homicide victim from earlier today lives right across the way, and I am betting—or would if I were a betting man—that Kristin can tell us a lot about his comings and goings."

"So, let's go," Dwyer said. "Don't want to give my clothes too much time to wrinkle."

They walked to the door, and Burgess knocked. When Kristin answered, she said, "Fifteen minutes. Wow! A man of his word." She grinned at Dwyer. "And this is?"

"My colleague, Officer Andrea Dwyer."

Dwyer held out a hand, and Kristin shook it. "Pleased to meet you."

"Likewise," Dwyer said. "What's your sport?"

"Soccer," the girl said. "I am an absolute fiend for soccer."

"Good choice. And you play?"

"Guess."

"Forward."

"Got it in one. So why don't you both come into the living room and sit down. Can I get either of you a coffee or tea?"

"I'm fine," Dwyer said. "Just finished dinner a little while ago. The Detective Sergeant would like a coffee. Black."

Burgess gave Dwyer a look, which she ignored.

"I'll just be a minute," Kristin said. "We've got one of those thingies that makes coffee with pods." She disappeared into what Burgess assumed was the kitchen. He and Dwyer sat down to wait.

It was fast, as promised. Served in a cheery yellow mug that proclaimed, "Every day you are my sunshine."

The girl grinned, and Burgess refrained from comment.

"So, when I was here earlier, you were starting to tell me about Dr. Spence," Burgess said. "How long has he been your neighbor?"

"Well, I think he's been here for about two years. But for much of that, I was living with my mom until she took up with Sleazeball Marty, and they decided I should live full-time with my dad."

"Which was?"

"At Christmas. Because, of course, kicking your kid out of the house at Christmas is exactly what Sleazeball Marty would think was appropriate."

"So, you've been here about nine months?"

She nodded.

Burgess could have asked specific questions, but he wanted Kristin's unfiltered take. "Tell me about Dr. Spence."

She nodded. "Well. For starters, I call him 'the oyster' because he was always such a cold fish." A grin. "I supposed oysters aren't really fish, are they? Anyway, as you've already guessed, I'm an outgoing, talkative sort of person, so I tried to be friendly to Dr. Spence like I would to anyone. I'm great friends with Dr. Fellowes next door. You might not have learned it in a short visit, but he's a very wise man."

Burgess nodded. He waited while Kristin pulled the elastic from her hair, smoothed it, gathered it up, and secured the elastic again. She bounced a few times in the chair as she settled.

"So. Dr. Spence. Either there's a hired killer out to get him, or the man is seriously paranoid. My vote is for paranoid, but maybe him getting killed changes things. Maybe he did have reasons to be worried about his safety. It's just that…well, the way he scurried around, always looking over his shoulder? It was kind of pitiful. He was this good-looking, fit guy with that beautiful hair, and he acted like a scared rabbit."

"Can you describe his behavior for me?"

"Sure. So, he'd come home in his nice car, and the garage door would open, and he'd sit there, staring into the garage before driving in, like he was checking it out. Then he'd drive in, get out of the car, and check the garage one more time, then come back to the opening and peer up and down the street. Only then would he close it."

"Anything else? Any other behaviors that seemed strange to you?"

"There was the girlfriend."

"Having a girlfriend seems strange to you?"

"How he treated her. Handled her. I don't know. She would show up and ring his doorbell, and then he'd make her wait like he was checking who it was. Then he'd open the door very quickly and almost pull her inside. Before he shut the door, he'd look up and down the street to be sure there was no one else out there and only after he'd done that would he shut the door."

She gave a little bounce. "She didn't like it. She thought she ought to have a key of her own so she didn't have to go through that whole scrutiny business. I know because I heard her say it. My room, you see, is just above the door, and I have a window seat where I like to sit and read, and if my window is open, I can hear pretty much anything that goes on out there." She gave a mischievous grin. "Which I like because it's kind of like being a spy. Oh, the things I could tell you about the people on this street."

She broke off. "Sorry. I know. You want to know about the oyster. So, the pretty, dark-haired woman who is his girlfriend—she doesn't look very friendly, by the way—isn't the only woman in his life. Well. Actually, I don't think the others are women in his life so much as they are...uh...paid companions."

She looked down at her hands, blushing slightly. It reminded Burgess that this girl was only thirteen, no matter how mature she seemed.

"This is just speculation, okay?" she continued. "I don't know for sure. How could I?" She described the frequency and arrival of the blondes as the others had.

"They came in cars...that is, someone drove them...and they were dropped off?"

She nodded.

"Did you see them leave?"

"Past my bedtime," she said. She hesitated. "Except the other night, the night before he was killed or, at least, when Lena found him dead, I did see one of them leave."

"Tell me about that. If you can," Burgess added, reminding himself that he was asking a thirteen-year-old girl about women who might be prostitutes.

"She was a little older than the others. More like thirties than twenties, I think. But she was really beautiful. The others were...uh...well, you know, sexy. Lots of styled hair, makeup, and tight clothes. This one was—" She hesitated, looking for a way to describe this woman's difference. "She was classier. Better dressed. More like someone who'd be his real girlfriend."

"Who else visited Dr. Spence?"

"His golf buddy. The guy with the reddish hair? Not a friendly guy, at least the couple times I said hey to him, but not paranoid."

"Can you tell me what the golf buddy drives?"

"Navy Audi SUV."

"Other visitors?"

She considered. "A few times, a woman, or a woman and man who looked like they were there on business. Very professionally dressed, if you know what I mean. Dark suits. The housecleaner. She's nice. The Wicked tried to get her to clean for us, but she says her schedule is full. I figure she's a good judge of people and knew that The Wicked could never be pleased."

There were cops on the force who weren't as observant as this girl.

"Anyone else?"

She tucked one leg up in the chair and rubbed her knee with her hand.

"Knee hurt?" Dwyer asked.

A nod.

"You iced it?"

Another nod. "But it still hurts. Big girl on the other team did a slide tackle and wiped me out."

"That's illegal. Did the ref call it?"

"What do you think? They still have trouble understanding that girls can be as fierce as boys. It is such a pain." A moment, then a grin. "I got her back."

"Good for you."

Burgess had forgotten that Dwyer was still on an adult soccer team and coached a girls' team in all the spare time she didn't have. Maybe that's why there never seemed to be a boyfriend or girlfriend. Dwyer was too busy.

The girl looked at Burgess. "I haven't forgotten your question. I'm thinking. There's something...I just can't seem to remember...oh. Yeah. So, you know how I said that Dr. Spence was kind of paranoid. Although, they say that it's not paranoid if someone is really after you, right?"

"Right."

"Well...a couple...or maybe it was three or four weeks ago. It was late, and I woke up because I heard two men arguing down in the street. I opened my curtain a tiny bit, and I could see Dr. Spence and another man. Dr. Spence must have come straight from the hospital because he was wearing scrubs, which he never did. The other man had his back to me, so I couldn't see his face. His voice was deep and gruff, almost a growl, so I couldn't hear most of what he was saying. But I heard Dr. Spence say, "Forget it. I am not going to pay you off. I owe you nothing, and you're getting nothing. You come around here again, and I'm calling the police and telling them you're trying to blackmail me.""

This was definitely something new. "Can you tell me anything about the man?"

"It was dark. And I only saw his back. He was bigger than Dr. Spence. Well, taller, not wider. Dark hair. No hat. And he was wearing a suit, which was kind of weird if he'd come to threaten someone."

She shook her head, and her elastic fell out again, suddenly framing her face with dark curls. She said, "Oops," gathered it up, and secured it again. "That's all, really. I can't think of anything else to add. Unless..." A hesitation. A sly grin. Her grin was adorable, and when she showed humor, she seemed much younger. "Unless everyone's been telling you about that boy who's been hanging around. Have they?"

"They have. Do you know something about him? Do you know him?"

"Of course, I know him. He's my brother Aaron. He also got thrown out when my mom and Sleazeball Marty took off for Florida. Only while Dad and The Wicked were willing to take me in, on account of my age and me being a girl and all, Dad the Jerk…did I mention that my dad is a real jerk? First, he abandons us to take up with The Wicked, and then he does this. I mean, I guess they're both jerks. When you've got kids, you're supposed to take care of them, which he totally doesn't get. But Aaron is only seventeen, and basically, they've left him to fend for himself on the street."

She stared down at the hand that was rhythmically rubbing her sore knee. "Aaron is clever. He's got Mom sending him money so he can pay for someplace to live, and he has a job, and he's finishing school, all of that. But he likes to come down here and hang around and remind Dad and The Wicked of his existence. Of what total jerks they're being not to let him live with them. With us. I think Aaron scares the Grundwalds. They're nosy as hell but also kind of timid. And that cute little family a few doors down with the bratty little girl? They're really spooked by him."

She rubbed harder, winced, and stopped. "He really spooked Dr. Spence, too. They had words a few times. Aaron can have a bit of an attitude, which, given that he's been abandoned by his family, makes sense. So, when Dr. Spence tried to send him on his way, he wasn't having it."

She straightened suddenly and looked at Burgess. "You know. I see plenty, but you should really ask Aaron about people coming and going. He can be kind of invisible but he's often around."

"Good thought," Burgess said. "How do I find him?"

She got out her phone. "I can give you his number and the address where he's staying. He won't be around now. He does cleaning at night, so he'll be working. But tomorrow after school, you should be able to catch up with him. He's staying with a friend named Sam."

How was it that these kids were virtually—and literally—abandoned by their parents, yet they'd turned out pretty well? At least, if Kristin's information was to be trusted, her brother was doing an awfully good job for someone whose parents were so wrapped up in doing their own thing they didn't have time for their children.

"My Granny Sal," she said, as though she'd read his thoughts. "Our parents are both crap, but my mother's mother, Granny Sal, always had time for us. Time. A snack. Cookies or a freshly baked pie. And along the way, she taught us about manners and about rules and discipline. About treating people well. It's funny, you know, how it didn't stick with my mother. Granny Sal used to say that she'd done her best, but then my mother's true nature came out. And it wasn't a very good nature."

Dwyer reached out and stopped the hand that was frantically rubbing the knee. "Have you taken ibuprofen?" she asked.

Kristin shrugged, looking sad. "I would have. But we're out of it."

"No problem." Dwyer rooted around in her bag and pulled out a bottle. "I never leave home without it. I play in an adult soccer league, and things can get pretty rough sometimes." She gave the bottle to the girl. "Go. Take it. Right now. You can keep the bottle. And tonight, sleep with a pillow under your knee and a cold pack. You know about RICE, right?"

"Rice?"

"Rest. Ice. Compression. Elevation.'"

"Never heard that."

"Well, you have now. Take it from Coach Dwyer, it helps."

"Thanks."

"We should be going," Burgess said. He took out a card. "If you think of anything else we should know. Or if you have questions. Or you need me or Dwyer for anything. Call." He looked at the girl who sat rubbing her knee. Her poise was deceptive. She was very young. "I mean it. Call us."

Dwyer held out a card as well. Kristin took them both and said, "I thought this was going to be scary, and it wasn't. Thanks."

They left, walking a little way down the street, and stopped.

"I'd like to smack those parents upside the head," Dwyer said.

"We both would. It's a miracle she's doing so well."

"If she's doing well and not just putting on a good front for us," Dwyer said.

"Probably for everyone. I think it's important to find the brother, sooner rather than later. Because I have an uneasy feeling about that. That maybe he's not as invisible as he thinks he is?"

"Right. I have the same concern." Dwyer started toward her car, saying, over her shoulder, "Back to my laundry. You be careful, Joe. Sometimes, the prosperous types who live in places like this can be very dangerous. And sneaky."

As though, after decades on the job, Burgess didn't already know this. But it was kind of her to worry about him. He headed across the street, where Kyle and Perry were waiting.

EIGHTEEN

Before Burgess could ask how things had gone, Kyle said, "Can we do this over coffee? If I don't get a jolt, I'm going to doze off right here in the street."

That wasn't like Kyle. He wasn't showy, but he was a dogged worker, one who never flagged. It was Burgess who'd been the flagger lately. So tired he'd considered retiring until Dr. Cohen over at the ER had decided he needed those pills for his thyroid. Still, if any one of them was tired, it was no wonder, with all they had on their plates.

"Sure. Great idea."

They headed for their cars. Before he followed, he looked up at Dr. Spence's condo. Lights were still burning downstairs. A cop was still on the door. He couldn't see any lights on the second floor, but if Rocky Jordan was still there, toiling away, he wouldn't. There weren't windows in that closet.

Over coffee for all, a slice of pie for Kyle, a burger for Stan Perry, and an apple cider donut for Burgess, they shared what they'd learned. Unsurprisingly, the neighbors' observations were pretty similar. Everyone had mentioned the girlfriend, Deidre Lovejoy, and how Spence used to make her wait before answering the door. Many had observed the parade of sexy young blondes in skimpy dresses. One neighbor had considered calling the police. There had been the golf buddy. The odd kid in the hoodie who hung around. Spence's coldness toward his neighbors. Only Kristin and one other had seen the couple with the briefcases, and no one besides Kristin had overheard Spence arguing with someone in the street.

Several people had remarked on Spence's paranoia, or at least his extreme concern for who might be around him, including his ritual for driving into the garage. One person had shared Spence's ritual for starting his run, which was similar.

Given how cautious the man had been, Burgess was surprised he'd gone out running at all. Something to ask about when he did a follow-up interview with Deidre Lovejoy. Right along with why she hadn't mentioned showing up at Spence's door and being sent away.

"The kid in the hoodie?" Burgess said. "He's the brother of a girl I interviewed." He shared the story of Kristin's self-indulgent parents and how they'd basically put the brother out on the street. "I got Dwyer to come and sit in while I interviewed her. She's very mature, but she's only thirteen."

"Turn over a rock, and you never know what you'll find," Kyle said. "The next-door neighbor on my side wasn't home. There might be something there, but we'll have to come back."

"It's strange, you know," Perry said. "People at the hospital, with the exception of that one female doctor, were unanimous in their praise of the guy. Wonderful colleague, great with patients. A chorus of 'Such a good man.' It's kind of like he's a Jekyll and Hyde type. Great at work and changes into someone cold and paranoid when he's at home. Of course, I still haven't caught up with his assistant, the one who keeps hiding. Who knows what she'll say."

"Maybe he felt safe at the hospital," Burgess suggested.

"Possible. But wouldn't he have had bad days? And why not carry his paranoia into his workplace?" Burgess said.

"Or they're all lying to us," Kyle said. "The old 'put on a good front for the cops and we won't be embarrassed' kind of thing. One thing we know from experience is that doctors don't like to be questioned."

He stood up. "Don't know about you two, but I am sick of thinking about Dr. Spence. I'm going to go home and enjoy a little time with a functional family. At least, I think we're functional. And young Stanley here has probably got diaper duty."

"He does," Perry agreed.

Burgess would love to have gone back to his functional family, especially since he wanted to check in with Nina before school tomorrow and, perhaps, lay a cautionary hand on his son's shoulder, but he needed to spend a few hours when the department was quiet, looking over some of the papers they'd collected.

Back at 109, he went to evidence to retrieve the legal papers from Dr. Spence's secret hiding places and took them into the conference room that would be their command center while they worked the case. There were whiteboards and a large, empty bulletin board waiting to be filled.

He sat at the large conference table and began to read.

He'd originally thought that the lawsuits involving Lenore Spence's siblings were filed to challenge her estate and wrest it from her husband. As he read on, though, he saw that these were wrongful death suits, accusing Spence of killing his wife and, thus, depriving her siblings and parents of her company and companionship and seeking compensation from him. Like too many lawsuits, the allegations were so worded in legalese that he wasn't able to get a clear understanding of what was being alleged beyond the obvious assertion that Dr. Eliot Spence had been responsible for the death of his wife.

On his waiting legal pad, he wrote the siblings' names and addresses and those of their parents, as well as the names and addresses of their attorneys and the courts where they had filed. Although Lenore Spence had been dead for more than two years, the lawsuits were fairly recent, having only been filed back in the spring.

The responses filed by Spence's attorney presented multiple and varied defenses, including the assertion that only one person could file a wrongful death suit. To Burgess's untrained eye, it looked like the brother had filed first, and a week later, the sister had filed her suit.

Interesting. Competing, then, instead of being on the same page?

He wondered if the sister was the woman with the briefcase a few witnesses had seen and whether the brother and sister had been there together? If the brother might have been the man Spence was arguing with? He might be able to find pictures of them online. It seemed like everyone was online these days. He was deciding whether he had the energy to do that search tonight when an idea suddenly struck him. The cop's gut at work. An idea that pulled him to his feet, already checking for his gun, his phone, and his cuffs as he headed for the door. He and Dwyer had discussed finding Kristin's brother Aaron sooner rather than later. It was thinking about Aaron that pulled him to his feet.

If everyone in the neighborhood had noticed Kristin's brother hanging about, then wasn't it likely the killer might have, too? Just as Aaron had been hanging around and watching, the killer might have as well. A killer stealthy enough to have escaped notice by everyone who lived there. A killer who might worry about being spotted. A killer who might have followed Aaron home and knew where he lived.

He kept thinking killer despite having no known cause of death. That bottle was too defiant a sign for it to be something done after a natural death.

That's what he thought. Not what he knew.

He hurried down the stairs, fumbling out his notebook as he went, looking for where he'd written down Aaron's address.

He was in his truck and on the road with a speed he didn't know he still possessed. En route, he called and asked for backup. Just in case. On TV, detectives never called for backup. Never told anyone where they were going. Walked into absurdly dangerous situations totally unprepared. It was one reason real-world cops couldn't watch TV cop shows. Dr. Lee, the medical examiner, said there were shows he couldn't watch because the crime scene and lab procedures were so deplorable. Like a DNA lab in an open corridor with random people walking in and out.

Why was he thinking about this? Because he didn't want to think his gut might be right about Aaron being in danger. He trusted his gut. Cops did. But he didn't want to begin and end this day with bodies. Especially not the body of a seventeen-year-old boy who'd already dealt with so much cruelty and neglect.

He drove through the city with a recklessness he would have condemned in others. But it was a necessary recklessness, and he was a good driver, even at high speeds. He pulled to the curb at the building where Aaron Daggett lived, jumped out, and ran to the door. As was way too common in buildings with low rent and transient occupants, the front door was unlocked, propped open with a brick. Unlike many of the unlocked doors he encountered, that door led to a foyer with mailboxes and another door that was locked.

Inside, Burgess scanned the board for Aaron's name. He wasn't listed. He thought about what Kristin had said. She thought he was staying with a friend named Sam. She'd also said that Aaron worked nights, so he might not be home, and this might all be a wild goose chase. A wild gut chase?

He scanned the board again. One of the apartments was rented to an S. Melendez. S for Sam? He tried the buzzer. Got no answer, so he did what everyone did when they needed to get inside a building: he rang the bells for other units. On his fourth try, someone buzzed him in.

S. Melendez lived in apartment 204, which he figured was on the second floor. He climbed the stairs, trying to move quietly, telling his bad knee to just shut up and wait; there would be ice sometime in the future.

Apartment 204 was at the end of a long, dark hall. Dark because half the lights were out and the other half pathetically dim bulbs trying to illuminate stained, brownish walls. The hall and the building smelled of age and neglect and cooking odors. He paused outside 204 and inhaled. Nothing besides those smells except something faint and sweet, which might be good news. Even fresh death has an odor, and blood definitely does. He raised a fist and knocked.

No one answered, but the unlocked door swung halfway open from the force of his knock. Crap. That wasn't good. The room beyond was dark. He got out his flashlight, pushed the door the rest of the way open, and stepped in, calling, "Police. Is anyone home?"

No one responded.

He found a light switch and turned it on. That was another thing about cop shows; they were always searching places in the dark instead of turning on the lights. It made it far easier for the bad guy who was hiding to jump out, never mind the risk of trampling all over a crime scene.

He was in an untidy living room. Untidy in the manner of single men. Beer bottles, soda cans, pizza boxes, and fast-food bags obscured the coffee table. Against the wall by the window, there was a desk with schoolbooks. It, in contrast, was neat. To his right, beside the door, were two pairs of shoes. One a men's size nine, the other men's size thirteen. Odd that anyone who lived with such clutter would be careful about that, but maybe both occupants had grown up in households where leaving shoes at the door was the practice.

The furniture was shabby.

To his right was a kitchen and dining area. To his left, a short hallway with a closed door at the end he assumed was a bathroom, and doors on either side he thought led to bedrooms. The bedroom doors were closed.

He hoped that if he knocked on those doors, he'd find the roommate, S. Melendez, asleep and Aaron Daggett's room empty, with Aaron out at his night job. Hope, like wishes, wasn't often met with success in his business.

He called again, "Police. Is anyone home?"

No one answered, but he thought he heard a faint sound. Could be from this apartment or somewhere else in the building. He crossed the room carefully, watching his step in case there was something to be concerned about disturbing. In the hall, he paused and listened. It sounded like someone moaning.

He opened the door on his right, flicking on the light to reveal a bedroom as untidy as the living room. Clothes and shoes were strewn about. The bed was unmade but empty. A quick search of the room confirmed that no one was there.

He stepped across the hall and was opening that door when a giant came out of the bathroom, spotted him, and headed toward him with a roar. A giant wearing only boxer shorts, his massive bare chest covered in a thicket of dark hair.

"Police!" Burgess yelled, backpedaling and holding up one arm to block the attack while he fumbled for his gun with the other.

The man was easily six foot five and broad, with a halo of dark curls, a face hidden by a beard and mustache, and dark eyes. He also looked half asleep.

"Police," Burgess repeated loudly. "Here to do a wellness check on your roommate, Aaron."

It took three repetitions before his words penetrated the giant's brain, and he came to a halt, saying, "Police?" in a confused voice.

By then, Burgess had his gun out and ready in case his words never penetrated.

"Detective Sergeant Burgess. Portland police. I knocked and announced myself," Burgess said. "The door was open. Are you Sam Melendez?" The guy looked more dazed than dangerous, but Burgess wasn't relaxing his guard yet.

"Open?" the giant said. He had a deep voice that rumbled in his chest. He ran a hand through his thatch of dark hair. "Door's not supposed to be open."

They were making progress, Burgess thought. *Melendez had moved from single words to simple sentences.*

"Are you Sam Melendez?" he repeated.

"Oh. Yeah. I am Sam."

It sounded like something from a children's book.

"I'm here to check on your roommate. Aaron Daggett." He took a step away from Melendez and said, "I'm going to put my gun away now. Is it safe to do that?"

Melendez nodded. Said, "Aaron's at work. Works nights."

"I'd still like to check. Make sure he's not here. Did you see him leave for work?"

The giant shook his head. "I was asleep." He waved a large hand toward the door Burgess had been about to open. "Gone. See for yourself."

Burgess opened the door and fumbled for a light switch. He stepped in, the giant so close behind him that he could feel the man's body heat.

"Give me some room," Burgess said. The giant backed up a step, and it felt like he could breathe again. Burgess was used to being one of the biggest men in the room, but this guy made him feel small.

Once it was illuminated, he could see he was in a room whose neatness matched the desk by the window. No clutter and few belongings. The bed was unmade and empty.

"See," Melendez said. "He's not here."

Not in bed didn't mean not here. Burgess had found bodies in bedrooms in lots of places other than the bed. He stepped farther into the room. As he moved past the foot of the bed, he saw a figure lying on the floor. The head was bloody, and there was a pool of blood under it. As he kneeled down to check for signs of life, there was another moan.

Alive, at least. He told Melendez, who was looming over him, to back up again and bent over the slight, pale figure to check the pulse. Weak. He said, "I'm a police officer, Aaron. Help is on the way."

Behind him, Melendez said, "Jesus, what happened to him? I've been here all night and didn't hear a thing."

Burgess had questions for Melendez, but first, he got out his phone and called for an ambulance. Then he called Kyle.

When he got a sleepy, "Kyle, investigations," he said, "I just found Aaron Daggett in his apartment with a serious head wound. Still alive. I could use your help here."

"Give me the address." No hesitation. Why he always wanted Kyle to have his back.

He gave the building's address, then called for their crime scene techs and disconnected.

"As soon as they've taken Aaron away, we need to talk," he told Melendez.

"Sure. But is Aaron gonna be okay? He doesn't look okay."

"We probably won't know until they've examined him in the ER," Burgess said. "He's got a pulse. He's breathing. And sometimes, head wounds can look worse than they are because of all the blood."

Trying to reassure this giant who'd slept right through an assault on his roommate. That was a hell of a sound sleeper.

He had a growing list of questions, but first, he needed to secure this building and start the process of gathering information from the tenants.

"I've got to go downstairs, check with patrol, and meet the ambulance," he told Melendez. "You need to step out of this room and not touch anything."

"I want to stay with Aaron."

"I understand. But this room is a crime scene, and we need to be careful not to disturb anything that might be a clue to what happened here. You understand?"

Melendez shook his head. He didn't understand. "I don't see how this could have happened."

"You didn't hit him over the head, did you?"

A slow shake of the shaggy head. "I wouldn't. Aaron is my friend."

Burgess thought Melendez, with his odd combination of huge stature and simple nature, might not have very many friends.

He'd learn more when Aaron had gone to the hospital. When he could work the apartment and question Melendez without interference. For now, he needed to protect his scene, or at least this room.

"If you didn't, we need to do all we can to find out who did, and that means leaving this room undisturbed."

But Melendez had moved on to something else. He said, "If someone came in and attacked Aaron, why didn't they attack me?"

Burgess didn't know. Maybe because Melendez was such a heavy sleeper, he didn't pose a threat? And maybe the would-be killer had taken a peek at Melendez and moved on, hoping he'd stay asleep. That said balls or a lot of sense. Or both.

He herded Melendez out of the room, reminded him to stay out, and went downstairs to find the backup he'd requested. Backup could search the building and keep anyone from entering or leaving. He told an officer to wait for the ambulance and where to send the crew when it arrived.

Then, before EMTs and a stretcher, with their focus on saving lives, not saving clues, could disrupt things, he went back upstairs and took quick photos of the living room, then scrutinized the floor for anything that might need to be preserved. Hard to tell among the clutter. Whoever had done this had been careful. There were no footprints, and nothing seemed to be disturbed. Not that it would be easy to spot a disturbance in all the mess.

He moved on to the bedroom. The bedroom was different. Aaron was neat, so Burgess looked for anything out of place. Unlike in Spence's condo, there was clearly something out of place—a lamp with a heavy black metal base had been pushed under the bed. It might be something. It might be the weapon the assailant had used. He photographed it in place.

It was late. He was tired. He wished his damned cop's gut wasn't so good sometimes. Still, he had to be thankful that his day hadn't, as he'd feared, begun and ended with bodies. Always assuming that Aaron Daggett survived.

NINETEEN

Burgess was kneeling beside the bleeding boy, murmuring reassurance that help was on the way when Kyle arrived. Kyle had had farther to go than the ambulance, of which there was still no sign. He came into the room in his usual fast, silent way, reminding Burgess, as he often did, of a stealthy cat. A big cat.

He stopped in the doorway, cold blue eyes surveying the room. Said, "Hanging on?" in a low voice.

Burgess nodded.

"He's just a kid, isn't he?"

Burgess nodded again. Before he inherited a family, he'd been better at detachment. Cops tried not to get emotionally involved. But interviewing Kristin, a girl a bit younger than Nina, and then finding this boy, Dylan's age, a kid who'd tried so hard to survive on his own, it got to him. He shouldn't let it.

"Hell of a strange day," Kyle said.

"You've got that right."

"This is the kid who was hanging around down at those waterfront condos?"

Burgess nodded.

Kyle switched gears. "How did you know?"

"To come here and check on him? Instinct."

"Civilians don't believe in it, you know. They think the cop's gut is something we make up to explain why we do what we do. Explain or excuse."

The boy moaned softly, and Burgess put a hand on his shoulder. "It's okay. You're going to be okay. Help is on the way."

Help that seemed to be coming from somewhere in Outer Mongolia.

"That giant out there is the roommate?" Kyle asked.

"Yeah. I haven't had a chance to talk with him yet, but he seems to have slept right through the attack."

"Maybe not the sharpest tool," Kyle said.

"Maybe. Could just be sleepy. Or stoned. We'll see." Burgess shook himself. Too busy to acknowledge how scary it had been when the giant came at him. A lifetime of adrenaline spikes like that had taken a toll on his body.

"What do you want me to do?" Kyle asked.

"See if you can tell how he—" He paused. "Or she got in. The attacker. Any signs. I've got the B crime scene team on the way. We'll see what they find. That room out there...all the clutter...it'll be hard. But sometimes our perps get careless, and there's no reason why they'd expect us to come here or connect this—"

He broke off. Kyle knew what to do. And just as he'd thought Spence's killer might have noticed the kid, there was no reason why that same killer wouldn't expect the cops to connect the dots. In the world of wishful thinking, he was wishing someone in this building had seen whoever attacked Aaron Daggett. Wishful because in places like this, people kept their heads down and played see no evil, hear no evil, speak no evil. Usually, because there was a fair amount of evil about that was hard to unsee or unhear.

Who knew? Maybe they'd get lucky.

"I've got patrol talking to people in the building. It's late, though, and people aren't inclined to answer their doors at this time of night if they're ever inclined at all."

"You are such a pessimist," Kyle said.

"Not at all. As soon as I am done here, I am going rain skipping. During which exercise I will sing at the top of my lungs."

"That would be a sight to see," Kyle agreed. "Only, in case you haven't noticed, it isn't raining."

"Guess I'm off the hook, then."

"Probably a good idea. Your bum knee wouldn't take kindly to rain skipping."

"Even if it would help my bum attitude?"

"Even if. Sorry."

They were conversing quietly, not wanting to disturb the injured boy. Humor was what kept cops going on long, crime-filled days like this. Usually dark humor. They tried to keep it away from the tender ears of the public.

"I'll go look for clues," Kyle said.

"Call Sage Prentiss, will you, and have him wait for Aaron at the hospital. We need to know the minute this kid wakes up…assuming he does wake up…and what the docs can tell us about his injuries."

"On it," Kyle said. He headed out into the living room.

Burgess could hear him on the phone, then moving around, and hoped he was finding something. It wasn't likely. If it was the same perpetrator as down on the waterfront, the person was very careful. But there was always Locard's Rule, which said that in any contact between two people, something was always left behind. Often, though, that something was very small and might only be found by an astute and careful crime scene team or a very fine detective.

Of course, Kyle *was* a very fine detective.

Time passed. Burgess found that his breathing had synchronized with that of the boy he kneeled beside. As long as there was breath and pulse, there was hope the boy would survive. He hoped for survival for many reasons—obviously for what the boy might be able to tell them about his attacker and about those coming and going at Dr. Spence's condo. Equally obviously, because this was a young life with so much ahead. Also, because he didn't want to have to tell Kristin that her brother had died. From what she'd said, neither parent would be that upset; they were too wrapped up in themselves, but she cared deeply. Burgess thought they were close, and Kristin needed someone she could be close to.

As he kneeled in the room, he noticed something that didn't seem to belong—the same thing he'd smelled outside the door—the very faint scent of something sweet. A bath product or shampoo, maybe. Something that didn't fit in this bachelor pad.

Had there been something similar at Dr. Spence's, something he'd over-looked in his focus on other things or something masked by the stronger scent of cleaning products?

There had been a number of people in there since this morning. Probably, it had dissipated, but weird as it might sound to someone outside his world, going back to sniff a crime scene wasn't a crazy idea.

After an eternity, there was a commotion on the stairs, then in the corridor, and a knock on the open door announced the arrival of the para-medics and a stretcher. Burgess said, "The paramedics are here. They'll take care of you." Then he stood and backed away to give them access to the boy.

Soon, Aaron Daggett was loaded on a stretcher and carried away. Finally, Burgess's focus wasn't divided, and he could concentrate on what else this room had to tell him.

Daggett had been wearing black jeans, a gray hoodie, and a faded tee shirt from some band Burgess had never heard of. He'd had shoes on, so he wasn't settling in for the night. Across the room, on a chair, was a backpack he'd probably been planning to take with him. Burgess hadn't asked Kristin about her brother's schedule beyond learning that the boy worked nights, but he assumed that Daggett probably went directly from work to school. Though maybe, given Aaron's presence down by the condos, it might be later. He hoped something in the room would tell him where the boy worked so he could check on Daggett's schedule. Or the roommate might know. He wondered if their killer had staked this place out and learned Daggett's schedule? Had they expected the roommate would be gone?

He photographed the backpack in place and was about to check its contents when a new commotion from the other room suggested that the crime scene techs had arrived.

He went out to meet them.

Burgess was used to working with Wink and Dani, but recently, the powers that be had decided there needed to be more personnel available to work scenes, figuring that it was cheaper to have more people than to pay so much overtime. Tonight, he would be working with Lonnie Rich and Tonya Kilgore. Kilgore and Rich sounded like a law firm to him. He was reserving judgment until he'd seen them work.

With the giant, Kyle, Kilgore, and Rich in it, the cluttered living room looked awfully full. The giant had risen to his feet when they came in and was looking agitated. Agitated enough that Kilgore quickly retreated behind Lonnie Rich.

"It's okay, Sam," Kyle reassured him. "This is our crime scene team. They're here to look for evidence that will help us identify the person who attacked Aaron."

When Melendez didn't move, Kyle took his arm and steered him toward the door. "Let's step outside for a bit and let them work," he suggested. "I know it's your place, but if we stay out of their way, they'll be done more quickly, and you can get back to sleep."

"I don't like this," Melendez protested. "I shouldn't have to leave my own place." Then, as though he'd just remembered why all these people were present, he turned to Burgess and asked, "Is Aaron going to be okay?"

"We don't know yet, Sam. Can't know until they evaluate him at the ER. But we hope so. I'll be going to the hospital when we're done here, and I can call and give you an update if you'd like."

"I would like that." Melendez looked at Rich and Kilgore. "Don't you be messing with my stuff. And stay out of my room. That's not involved in what happened to Aaron, and I don't like people touching my stuff."

"That's fine, Mr. Melendez," Lonnie Rich said. He was looking at the cluttered room, and his face said he wished he'd stayed back at 109. Not that any of them had that choice when a crime had been committed.

"Do you mind if we move a little bit of this...uh...clutter?" Kilgore asked. Her voice was literally shaking.

To everyone's surprise, Melendez grinned. "Little lady, if you wanna clean up my place, feel free. There's trash bags under the kitchen sink."

"That's not what I meant," she began. At a nod from Kyle, she shut up.

Melendez let Kyle lead him away.

Over his shoulder, Kyle said, "I'll do a quick interview in my car."

Burgess nodded.

When they were gone, the room felt huge, as though suddenly more oxygen was pouring in.

"Wow," Kilgore said. "That's about the biggest man I've ever seen. So, what would you like us to do here, Sergeant Burgess?"

Burgess described what he needed and said, "Bedroom first, as that's our crime scene. And mark yourselves a path, okay? Even though there have been people through here, sometimes you can still find something."

The two techs went to work.

He stepped out into the hall to call Chris and say he didn't know when he'd be coming home and almost bumped into a patrol officer half leading, half dragging, a skinny woman by the arm. She looked to be in her fifties, and she was definitely not there because she wanted to be.

She glared at him. "Are you the bastard I'm supposed to talk to?"

Burgess wasn't a bastard, as far as he knew. He smiled at her and said, "Why yes, ma'am, I believe I am."

TWENTY

B urgess asked the officer to take her down to his truck. He followed, stealing a moment on the stairs to call Chris. "Sorry," he said. "Got another crime scene. Kid Dylan's age. Victim of an attempted homicide. Might be a witness to this morning's. I don't know when I'll be home."

Sorry was becoming his most frequently used word, at least with his family.

"Hope the boy makes it," she said. "We'll leave a light on for you."

"I was hoping to talk with Nina before school tomorrow."

"I know. I wish you could. At least they both seem calmer. I like that Dylan feels protective toward Nina. He thinks of her as his sister. But I really don't want him in trouble at school again, and he seems..." She hesitated, then rushed on. "He seems to have inherited his father's need to protect people. Not that it's a bad thing, but it takes judgment, and few teenagers have one that's well-honed. Maybe you can drive them to school tomorrow if your schedule permits. Remind him about caution and self-control one more time."

A good idea. He thought his schedule said he had to be in Augusta for an autopsy tomorrow morning. "Probably not. Have to go up to Augusta. But I'll try to see them before they leave."

A silence, during which he read a suppressed "Dammit, Joe!" Then she said, "Good night. I'll miss you."

"I miss you, too." Not he would. He did. She didn't know how much she meant to him.

During the more monkish phases of his life, Burgess hadn't minded sleeping alone. Even thought he preferred it. But living with Chris had changed that. Now, the prospect of climbing into bed and finding her there gave him something to look forward to when the rest of his life was full of the awful things people did to each other. Filled with liars. With people who deliberately failed to see what was in front of them. Filled with evil and greed and unchecked anger and mental illness and other forms of ugliness and indifference.

Downstairs, he found the officer had put the woman in his front seat and was standing outside the car, waiting for him, an alert, watchful air about him that Burgess liked.

Burgess tipped his head toward the woman. "What have we got?"

"Maybe nothing. Maybe something. Before she clammed up and decided to make a scene, she said that she'd seen something earlier in the evening. Someone who didn't belong in the building, and she thought it was odd."

The officer cleared his throat. "She says that there are always people in and out, but this person stood out because he was a well-dressed, prosperous-looking man. She said they didn't see so many of those, especially not at night." He shrugged. "She'll tell you if she's done pitching her fit. Wanted to shake us down for some money in exchange for sharing what she saw." He sighed. "I'm sick of it, Sergeant. The way people always want something in exchange for what they ought to do because their neighbors or fellow citizens matter."

He was young and fit, with gym-built shoulders so broad they barely fit in his uniform. He was also neatly put together and clearly took pride in his appearance. Despite all that, his face looked old and weary, like the job was sucking too much out of him. He was the kind of cop they needed and the kind they were losing from the job because of the constant criticism and pressure from the public.

"You did well to find her and talk her into cooperating," Burgess said. "We both know how people can be."

The big shoulders rose and fell. "Thanks. Don't know about that cooperation, though. You'll see."

"You got a name for me?"

"Sybil, with a y."

Weren't Sybils some kind of ancient prophetesses? Burgess tried to remember. Couldn't. And was damned if he'd look it up on his phone, as was becoming increasingly common. People buried in their phones walked into traffic and fell down manholes, as well as being rudely antisocial. This conversation would either be helpful to their investigation or leave him wanting to punch something, an impulse he'd have to control.

"Thanks. I'll take it from here. You guys done with the building?"

The officer, whose name tag said "Cyr," said, "Think we've tried every door now. Maybe a third or more didn't answer. Maybe not home. Maybe not answering. Probably be the same if we were trying to tell them the building was on fire. Dunno." A smile came and went. "Maybe I'll try that next time."

Cyr hesitated, ready to head back inside, then asked, "The one who was attacked. He was just a kid?"

"Just another kid turfed out by his parents and left to fend for himself. Doing a pretty good job of it. Until this."

"He gonna make it?"

Now, Burgess shrugged. "Can't say. Have to wait for the ER docs to figure that out. We just find 'em and send 'em along."

"And look for bad guys when the world doesn't want to help us out."

This kid was definitely on Burgess's wavelength. But he seemed too young to be so cynical. "Afghanistan or Iraq?" Burgess asked.

Surprised, Cyr said, "Iraq. Left me cynical as hell."

"Yeah. I get that."

"So, you need me here anymore, Sarge, or am I done?"

Burgess considered. There had been three officers checking the building. "You're done. I need someone on the door. Doors plural if there's a back entry. Otherwise, you're good to go. If you could leave me a list of the units that weren't checked?"

"Not a problem." The kid got out his notebook. Wrote something down on another page, tore it out, and handed it over. "I'll check with Streeter and Orion and get their data. And we'll figure out who stays."

Burgess wanted this kid to stay because he was clearly very observant. He was also tired and eager to be gone. Probably pulling a double and needed the rest.

"That's great. Thanks. You look like you could use some sleep."

Cyr drew himself up like he'd been insulted. "It's not supposed to show. Not supposed to matter."

It mattered. A weary cop could miss things. Be provoked into anger too easily. He kept that to himself. Cyr had his pride, and Burgess respected that. Plus, Burgess had worked many a time when he was beyond exhausted. Sometimes, the job called for it. He turned to the woman in his truck. Her face was glued to the window, watching them. He went around and got in. Turned toward her. "Sybil your first name?" he asked.

"It is. It was my grandmother's name."

"It's unusual these days."

Silence. Then she said, "Yes. And I like that."

Despite the fuss she'd made with Cyr, when she was calm she had a pleasant voice. For both their sakes, Burgess hoped she'd stay calm.

"Right. So, Officer Cyr says you saw someone in the building earlier tonight, someone who doesn't live here. Can you tell me about that?"

"What'll you give me?" A wheedling tone. One he figured she used often. Constantly making bargains with life without expecting them to be kept.

"We don't pay for information, Sybil. You know that. But I could treat you to a meal at the all-night diner if you'd like."

Another form of bribery or payment for information, he supposed, but also something he did for hungry teens, street people, pretty much anyone who looked hungry, and Burgess had the time. He'd lost some weight, which was good for his bad knee. He wondered if part of that was needing to be home with his family and, thus, eating fewer meals at the diner.

"I'd like that," she said.

"So, talk."

She talked.

"I was coming back from the Big Apple after picking up some things. He was outside the building; looked like he was waiting for someone." A shrug. "He didn't look like he was waiting for someone in this building, not dressed like that. Unless he was an attorney or an awfully well-dressed social worker. Not that we get many of them. It's not a family building. Maybe someone there to serve papers? They can be pretty sneaky."

"Not someone you've seen around here before?"

She folded her arms across her chest and said, "Nope."

She wore a brown fleece over a mustard-colored tee shirt. Neither fit her very well. But the rings on her fingers, a wedding ring, a diamond engagement ring, and another ring with a blue stone looked genuine. Interesting.

"Anything you can tell me about him? Age? Race? Height? Hair color?"

She grinned, revealing teeth sadly in need of dental care. That seemed to be true of half the population he served. Cling to the jewelry that belonged to a former life but abandon the routines of self-care. "Late thirties or early forties. Around six feet tall. Medium build. Dark hair. White. He was wearing a hat. And he had kind of a high voice. Unpleasant."

Sharper than he'd expected if any of this story she was telling was the truth. "Do you know if he entered the building? Did you see him go inside?"

She shook her head. "Nah. He tried with me. Said he was there to see someone named Georgie." Another head shake. "There ain't no Georgie that lives here. Not that I told him that. Then he tried to slip in behind me, and I slammed the door on him. But people always let someone in. They don't care about anyone else. About security. Not me, though. I don't let people in. Figured he'd try that on someone else and that someone wouldn't have bothered to know who lives here, right? Because we've got a lot of younger people now, and they've always got friends who need to party or crash or whatever. I don't like it. It ain't much of a home, but it's my home, and I like to feel safe here. Can't feel safe if anyone can get in, can I?"

"So, you know everyone in the building?"

She said, "Pretty much," proudly. It *was* something to be proud of in a world where people ignored their neighbors.

"Did you know the boy who was attacked? Aaron Daggett? Sam Melendez's roommate?"

"Oh, sure. Aaron's a nice kid. The kind who'll carry my groceries or ask me how my day was. He's a hard worker, Aaron is. Working nights like that and still keeping up with school. Melendez isn't so nice; that is, he doesn't really notice the people around him. But he's not bad. He's quiet and doesn't have a lot of rude friends." She twirled her fingers in front of her ears. "Melendez has some mental thing going on. Maybe on the spectrum?"

He wondered how she knew so much about Aaron, so he asked.

"Oh. I dunno. It's just…he seemed kind of sad and lonely when he first moved in, so I made it a point to talk to him. Before I fell…before I got sucked into the bottle, that is, I used to be a teacher. Not good for much anymore. My brain's kind of foggy. But I still care about kids, and I could see that he was hurting."

Don't jump to conclusions about people. It was a lesson Burgess learned, forgot, and relearned over and over again. There were plenty of damaged people who crossed his path, and their stories could be heart-breaking. He didn't have time to take on Sybil's heartbreak right now, but he wouldn't forget her.

"So, you never saw the man inside the building?"

"Nope. I came inside, went to my apartment, and stayed there. Didn't hear anything, either. And by the way, if you hear me say 'ain't?' I do that to fit in. I can speak perfectly proper English if I need to, for instance, if I have to deal with the bank or the electric company or something. But the casual language? It helps me stay invisible. And staying invisible is impor-tant for survival."

She saw him look at her rings.

"I know. It's dumb to wear them around people who'll steal anything that's not nailed down. But my husband. My late husband, Hugo, gave me those, and I feel as though if I took them off, he'd vanish from memory. People we've lost, Detective Burgess, they need to be remembered. Don't you think?"

He did think and told her so. Asked, "Anything else you can tell me?"

She considered. "I don't think the man I described is the only person who got into the building tonight who doesn't belong here. I mean, obvi-ously, that happened. Someone—either the guy in the suit or someone else—attacked Aaron if it wasn't Sam, and that's not very likely. Sam's so scary he doesn't need to attack people. I didn't see anything, but I did hear someone on the stairs a while after I got home. My apartment is right at the top of the stairs, so I hear people coming and going."

He waited for more. For anything that might be useful. Just when he was about to give up and move on, she said, "I didn't open my door to look, but I could hear someone coming up the stairs, and whoever it was, they were light on their feet. Not like the man I'd seen earlier. He was a slap-his-feet-down type."

Again, he waited, hoping for one more little bit of information. After a bit, she sighed and said, "A while later, I heard someone again. This time, going down the stairs. Rushing down the stairs. When I looked out the window, I saw what I think was a young man, built kind of like Aaron, medium tall and slender and dressed in black pants and a black hoodie, running away. I say young man, but I really don't know. The hood was up. But the hips were slender, and the legs were long. The shoes were sneakers, and the person moved fast."

Her shoulders rose and fell. "That's all I got."

"When this person was running away, did you see them touch anything?"

If she thought this an odd question, she didn't show it. She said, "As he got to the corner, he paused, leaning against a light pole, arm wrapped around it, and looked back at the building. Regret, maybe? I don't know. Then he unwrapped and rushed away."

TWENTY-ONE

Burgess thanked her and told her that she could go. She grabbed the door handle and then looked back at him. "Thought you said you were going to buy me breakfast?"

"I will. Just not tonight. I'm in the first twenty-four of a homicide."

Her suspicious look said he might have just undone whatever connections he'd been building.

"Aaron's dead? I thought he was just injured?"

"Not Aaron. We had a homicide this morning that led us to Aaron as a possible witness." More than he'd ordinarily share, but she'd been helpful and clearly cared for Aaron Daggett.

"Oh. Well, if you get a chance, let me know how Aaron's doing." She gave a phone number, then stepped out of the Explorer, lowering herself carefully from the high seat. "I'd appreciate that."

"I'll try," he said, writing her number down.

A smartass would have replied that Burgess was very trying. Pleasing people was not high on his list of priorities, especially with a homicide and a serious assault demanding his time. She wasn't a smartass, though, or even that difficult, despite the fit she'd pitched to Cyr. Just testing the waters. Cyr would learn if he stayed on the job. People did a lot of testing.

Burgess hoped he would stay on the job.

She mouthed a "thank you" and headed back inside.

Burgess followed. He'd had Cyr's report but wanted to check with the other officers about their results. It was a whole lot of nothing. As Cyr had said, a lot of people hadn't answered their doors, and those who had, other than Sybil, had nothing to offer. The only thing he had to add to his list was that one person on the top floor had buzzed someone in around ten. Well, he thought ten. He wasn't sure.

It might be something.

Burgess went back to the apartment to see what Kyle had learned from Melendez. That, too, was not a lot. Aaron Daggett usually left for his cleaning job around ten-thirty. He worked in an office building on Congress Street and was part of a crew that cleaned the building between eleven p.m. and five a.m. and was faithful to that obligation. Sometimes, he'd come back to the apartment, have breakfast, and head off to school. Sometimes, his work ran longer, and he went straight to school. He'd sleep when he got home from school but wasn't getting enough sleep.

Melendez was a repairman for an internet company and usually left the apartment around seven-thirty in the morning. He had eaten a pizza for dinner and played video games, but after he'd smoked a joint, he'd been sleepy and had gone to bed early. Aaron was out when he went to sleep. He admitted that he was a very heavy sleeper, especially after he'd been smoking, and likely wouldn't have heard anyone come into the apartment. He was sure, though, that he'd left the door locked. He liked the building because the rent was low but said it was the kind of place where anything that wasn't locked up might get stolen.

He didn't worry so much about that as some people since because of his size, few people tended to mess with him. But recently, he'd installed a surveillance camera in the living area because someone had taken a game controller, and he wanted to see if, in his words, "the little fucker would come back and steal something else."

"And that," Kyle said, "is as far as I got. You learn anything?"

Burgess shared what he'd learned from Sybil. The guy in the suit who claimed to be coming to visit Georgie, maybe some footsteps on the stairs, and the kid in the black hoodie. Not a lot to go on. "We'll have to send someone back and talk to the people in those other units."

"Who will be so forthcoming?"

"We might get lucky."

Kyle made a disparaging noise. They'd become such cynics. Sometimes, though, they did get lucky.

As Kyle made his report, Melendez was sitting on the sofa, staring into space. People who could just sit and do nothing were a mystery to Burgess.

"Sam," Burgess said, "was your surveillance camera on last night?"

"Sure."

"Can we see if it recorded anything?"

Melendez shifted his bulk to look at them. "Oh, wow," he said. "Good idea. Maybe it caught something. Someone."

He pushed himself up and crossed the room to a shelf where a small brown teddy bear shared space with a stack of video games and a balled-up green sweatshirt. "Teddycam," he said, patting the bear on the head. He checked that it was working, then went to his bedroom and got a laptop computer. He fiddled with the keyboard a bit and then leaned forward toward the screen. "Oh, yeah. Yeah. Look at this."

He turned the screen so Burgess and Kyle could see it. What they saw was a shadowy figure in a dark suit and wool cap moving through the dark living room. The figure paused and listened, then moved quietly out of sight. The picture went dark.

"It only records when there's movement," Melendez said. "We should see him coming back."

Before they moved on, Burgess wanted to see it again. "Can you back up and play it again?" he asked.

"Sure." Melendez fiddled with the keyboard, and the movements of the stealthy figure were replayed. Burgess, impressed by the dexterity of those large hands, reminded himself that the guy fixed things for a living.

When the video was done, he and Kyle exchanged glances. "Okay. Go on," Burgess said, wishing there was sound so he could at least track the intruder's movements deeper in the apartment. The next movement it captured was Aaron Daggett coming into the apartment. He crossed the living room and went to his bedroom.

They waited to see what happened next.

When the shadowy figure returned, it sidled through the room with its back to the camera, which was odd unless it knew the camera was there. Burgess realized it was watching the window. Then, for a moment, it looked back as though worried that the sleeping Melendez might have been roused, giving a very blurred sight of a face. It crossed to the door and was gone. Tall. Lean. Dark hair.

Burgess was about to ask for a replay of that when Melendez said, "Wait. There's more."

147

Another shadowy figure, also dressed in black and wearing a hoodie with the hood up. This figure dashed through the room, head down, and disappeared from sight. When the figure returned, it moved through the room head down and a hand over its face. Almost running as it left the apartment. Maybe it was wishful thinking, but Burgess was reading regret in the person's retreat, in the hunched shoulders and lowered head.

They watched that piece again, too, and Burgess asked if there was a way Melendez could share the videos. There was, and he did.

"Dammit!" Melendez said. "Wish I didn't sleep so sound, you know, insteada snoring while he attacked poor little Aaron? I could have knocked that little fucker out so easy. Both them fuckers. And Aaron's such a good kid. Works so hard to finish school, and all after his lazy, dumbass parents abandoned him like that. I mean, who does that? Who kicks their kid out in his last year of high school when he hasn't even done anything wrong?"

Burgess could have told him dozens of stories of far worse things parents had done. He practically subscribed to the school that said people ought to have to get a license to reproduce.

"But why are there two of them?" Melendez said. "That first guy, who was bigger, and then the little one? It doesn't make sense."

Burgess and Kyle exchanged glances again.

Burgess said, "Do you know if Aaron had any enemies? Had he quarreled with anyone? Rubbed someone the wrong way?"

"Aaron? You gotta be kidding. He keeps to himself. Keeps his head down, just trying to get by, you know? Besides, he's too busy to rub someone the wrong way."

Burgess thought about the solitary figure in the dark hoodie hanging around down by Spence's condo and the way his watchful presence freaked out the people who lived there.

"What about a girlfriend?" he asked. "Does Aaron have a girlfriend?"

Melendez shrugged. "Not that he ever told me. Like I said, he was too busy for a girlfriend. Not that he's a bad-looking guy. Just...I dunno...he seemed happy to spend his spare time playing games with me. Or visiting his sister."

"You ever meet his sister?"

"Maybe once. Aaron was kind of secretive about her. I guess because she had to live with his dad and the new wife. Can you believe they actually call her The Wicked? Like something from a kid's book or something? Crazy, huh?"

Burgess thought the nickname was apt.

Nothing more to learn here. The B team was ready to search the living area, so Burgess encouraged Melendez to retire to his room. He and Kyle left, but not before asking them to look for fingerprints on the light pole, Sybil had pointed out.

Out in the hallway, he and Kyle paused. "You thinking what I'm thinking?"

"That it wasn't a guy?" Burgess said.

"Yup. Second one definitely wasn't a guy. Harder to tell with the first one. But was that second one trying to pass himself off as the kid who hung around near Spence's condo? If the killer was watching, he would definitely have seen the kid."

"Could the second one be the sister? Kristin?" Burgess wondered aloud.

It seemed so unlikely. Why would she want to hurt her brother? More likely, if it was Kristin, the attack on Aaron had already taken place, and Kristin had found him the way Burgess had. But young as she was, he couldn't see her leaving him like that. She cared for her brother. She would have called for help. Unless she thought he was dead and had no idea how to deal with that. It was true that sometimes even the wisest cops got fooled by people. But he hadn't been fooled by a thirteen-year-old girl. Of that, he was sure.

Now, he was torn. He needed to check on Kristin. He needed to let the family know about the attack on Aaron. Before he did that, he needed to know Aaron's condition, something a call to the hospital wouldn't necessarily tell him. Hopefully, Sage Prentiss would. That was why he'd sent a detective to the hospital. In his experience, dealing with hospital bureaucracy to get an update on a patient's condition could be a painful waste of time. Before he did anything else, he needed to be sure they were finished here. As happened far too often, he needed to be in three places at once.

He called Sage and got a brisk, "Can I call you back, Sarge?"

He turned to Kyle. "Are we done here?"

Kyle gave one of his rare smiles. "We were done, or at least done in, before we started. But the answer to your question is no. I think two clever detectives need to check this building's dumpster and the trash cans on the street nearby and see if anyone has shed a briefcase, a suit jacket, or a dark hoodie. Don't you?"

"Every time I think my dumpster diving days are behind me."

"A man can dream," Kyle said.

They could get patrol to do it, but they'd just sent the officers they didn't need away. It would take time to call them back. Besides, he and Kyle could do it quickly and efficiently. They were experts at searching people's trash.

It was a hell of a thing to put on a resume. "Let's do it," he said.

TWENTY-TWO

I t had been late evening when Burgess decided to check on Aaron
Daggett. It was a lot later now. As he and Kyle stood on the sidewalk,
he could almost hear the slow breathing and occasional snores from the
buildings around him. Lots of cops didn't like the night, even if they
weren't afraid of boogeymen under the bed. There was plenty to be afraid
of in their line of work. He'd always liked it. The quiet, the solitude, the
time to be alone with his thoughts. Not that he was alone tonight. He took
a breath of salty night air and followed Kyle to the back of the building.

The building's dumpster was large and rusty and sat only a foot away
from the building's brick wall. There was a rasp of protest as they lifted the
lid, as though it, like the sleeping denizens of Portland, wanted to rest
undisturbed.

Two flashlights probed the contents, looking for signs someone might
have hastily discarded clothing there. The assembled black trash bags lay in
the haphazard way they'd been tossed in. None of them had been torn
open by someone looking to hastily discard a disguise. No bits of cloth
appeared to have been shoved beneath them. Burgess was debating with
himself whether one of them ought to climb in and do a more careful
search when Kyle's light picked up something brown and unbagged. A
briefcase.

"There," Burgess said, pointing it out with his own flashlight.

Kyle stepped along the side and plucked it out. A plain brown leather briefcase with a zipper and two side pockets. Not a cheap one, either. Quality leather without a lot of scuffs, dings, or stains. They scrutinized it for initials. None. Unzipped it to check the contents. Empty.

"Just a prop," Kyle said. "Maybe we'll get fingerprints, though."

They stared gloomily into the dumpster. Finding the briefcase meant they needed to look further. Shift some bags around and see if the person had discarded anything else as well.

"Rock, paper, scissors?" Kyle suggested.

"How about you're younger and don't have a bum knee? You can toss a few bags my way to check, of course."

"Remind me why we didn't get patrol to do this?"

"Because we are gluttons for punishment? Because we trust ourselves more than we trust anyone else?"

"Because we're idiots who never learn," Kyle said, putting his hands on the edge and vaulting into the dumpster. He dumped about ten bags down at Burgess's feet, then another five or six, and began to rustle around himself.

Burgess tucked his flashlight in his armpit and opened the first bag. Stinky kitchen trash. He set it aside and opened the second. Newspapers and junk mail. He went on like that, his bags seeming to alternate between smelly trash and paper trash until bag number eight. Inside, he found a man's suit, a flat black wool cap, and a white shirt, men's size sixteen. Perhaps the oddest of all? A black man's wig.

"Got something," he said. "I think I've got the clothes that Sybil said the man who tried to get into the building was wearing."

"Then can we stop now?"

"Yes, we can stop now."

Kyle vaulted out of the dumpster, landing quietly on the asphalt beside Burgess. He bent to examine what Burgess had found.

"This is what your witness described the man who tried to get in was wearing?"

"She said a man around six feet tall in a gray suit, with a black cap, and carrying a briefcase."

"Aren't we the clever ones, then," Kyle said.

"Yes, Ter. I think we are. You want to slip inside and get someone from the B team to come and collect this stuff?" He was wondering what the purpose of the disguise was and why the wearer had discarded it. No easy answers to that question.

"I do. Then I want to go home and get some sleep before Detective Sergeant Burgess calls a team meeting. That Burgess guy is relentless."

"Just wait until I retire, and people start saying the same things about you."

"Never happen," Kyle said. "You are going to live as long as Methuselah and no one will ever let you retire."

"Are you kidding? Captain Cote probably dreams about my retirement every night."

"Nightmares, in his case. Who would he try to bully and push around if you weren't here?"

"You?" Burgess said.

Kyle's grin was evil. "Little does he know," he said. "I'll go get an evidence tech. Then let's both go home."

Burgess nodded, and Kyle walked away.

He returned the bags that weren't evidence, then closed the smelly dumpster and stood in the quiet darkness, waiting for a tech to appear. A few feet away, there was a scritching sound, and a rat appeared. Before the advent of his family, Burgess had probably spent more time with rats—of the human and animal kind—than with anyone else. Except maybe Terry Kyle. He and Kyle had been keeping each other supported and focused for many years.

Of course, when he was done here, he wasn't going home. Not until he knew more about Aaron's condition, and not until he'd checked on Kristin and given the news about the attack to her father. If her father was home. Otherwise, to the stepmother. He'd have to bite his tongue not to call her The Wicked.

Eventually, the tech appeared. Burgess gave a quick summary of what he wanted and then left.

Sage Prentiss hadn't called back, so once he was in the truck, Burgess called him again. Got an embarrassed, "Sorry, Sarge, I meant to—"

"Can you give me an update on Aaron Daggett's condition?" Burgess said.

"Skull fracture and concussion. A nasty wound that took a lot of stitches. No need for surgery, they think. But they'll be watching him closely."

"Conscious?"

"Not yet."

"Can you stay with him?"

"I can."

That was a relief. Burgess hated hospitals, and sitting around waiting for a victim to wake up when he had so many other things to do made him restless and irritable. "Update me if anything changes."

"Will do. The hospital wants to know about notifying his family."

"Right. Kind of dysfunctional. Like many of our customers. I'll take care of it."

"I'll let them know."

Burgess thought about that. If hospital personnel had contact information for Aaron's parents, they'd call and deliver news Burgess wanted to deliver himself. He wanted to see the reaction from the father and the stepmother. "Don't," he said. "At least, not yet. I'll let you know when it's okay. I want to speak with the parents first."

"Understood," Prentiss said.

He was coming along well. An asset to their team, which was often stretched too thin. "Call me if anything changes," he repeated, a nudge because Prentiss had failed to call him back.

He got another "Sorry, Sarge," acknowledging the lapse.

He drove down to the waterfront, parked near Spence's condo, and got out.

There were no lights on inside. There was still a weary cop on the door.

Rocky Jordan hadn't called to say whether he'd found anything else they should know about. Probably waiting until morning, assuming that Burgess and his team were asleep. Would that it were so. But the cop shop, like an all-night diner, never closed. And there really was something to that first twenty-four.

A first twenty-four that was rapidly dwindling.

He turned away from studying Spence's condo and walked to Kristin Daggett's. He found her huddled on the doorstep, looking as dejected as a human could look.

"Kristin?" he said. "What are you doing out here at this time of night? Aren't you cold? Don't you have school tomorrow?"

She raised a tear-stained face to look at him. "Aaron's dead, and I'm such a pathetic sister that I didn't even call for help. I just got scared and ran away and left him there. What kind of a person am I that I would do that?"

Burgess sat down on the step beside her, feeling the chill from the granite. He put his arm around her shoulders. "Aaron isn't dead, Kristin. He's at the hospital, being treated for a concussion and a fractured skull."

"You're just saying that to make me feel better. I saw him there on the floor. He's dead, Sergeant Burgess. He's dead."

"Is your father home?" he asked.

She shook her head.

"What about your stepmother?"

"She's home. But you know she won't care. If Aaron's dead, that's one less thing for her to think about."

A shuddering sob shook her body.

"Do you have a phone number for your father?"

"Of course I do. In case of emergencies. Not that he'd consider Aaron being dead an emergency since he was willing to let The Wicked toss him out like dirty laundry."

He got out his phone. "Give me the number."

She got out her phone, her hand shaking, probably with a combination of cold and grief, and gave him the number.

He dialed.

It was two-thirty in the morning, a time when the only phone calls most people got were the emergency kind. He hoped Mr. Daggett was one of those people and would answer.

After four rings, he went to voice mail. He disconnected and dialed again. It took three tries before he got a sleepy, "What the hell do you want?"

As expected, the man was a charmer.

"Is this Stephen Daggett?"

"Yeah."

"Detective Sergeant Joseph Burgess, Portland police," he said, "calling about your son, Aaron Daggett."

Silence. Then, "Yeah?"

"Your son is in the hospital with a skull fracture and other injuries. Someone attacked him earlier this evening. His condition is serious."

Burgess waited for the questions a normal, concerned parent would ask or the sullen "yeah" that seemed to be Daggett's preferred response.

What he got was nothing. Silence. What the hell was wrong with this man? In the background, he heard a woman ask, "What's going on, Stevie?"

Stevie? Something The Wicked probably didn't understand: a man who will cheat on his wife with you is equally likely to cheat on you with someone else.

Beside him, Kristin said, "May I talk to him?"

Burgess gave her the phone. "Dad? Aaron's in the hospital. He's been attacked. Hit on the head. He may die. Please come home. Come home right now. I need you. We need you."

Burgess waited for a response. Kristin waited for a response. Eventually, the man sighed and said, "Kristin, honey. I can't. I'm busy here. Maybe tomorrow I can finish up and—"

"Never mind," she said. "You're a shit dad, and you know it. Aaron might die, and all you can think about is yourself. And I know you're there with another woman. When The Wicked finds out, she's going to tear you apart."

She handed the phone back to Burgess. Focused on the call, she hadn't heard the door open behind them and was unaware that her stepmother was listening. Burgess didn't clue her in. It was easier for Kristin if her step-mother overheard the conversation rather than having to find a way to tell a woman she intensely disliked that her father—the woman's husband—was screwing around again.

"Mr. Daggett, do I understand you are not willing to be here for your son despite the fact that he is gravely injured and needs the support of a parent?"

He gave Daggett a moment to respond and got nothing but a heavy sigh. Then Daggett said, "Aaron is emancipated."

Legally emancipated or simply abandoned, Burgess wondered. "You mean you threw him out. You and his mother. I'll give the hospital your contact infor-mation. Maybe they can update you about Aaron's condition going forward. If you care. Likely, you'll still be responsible for his hospital bills."

Daggett was sputtering some protest when Burgess disconnected.

"How can he be like that?" Kristin said.

It was a fair question. Burgess tightened his arm around her shoulders as a voice behind them, the kind of shrill female voice that made Burgess's ears hurt, said, "Kristin. Who was that on the phone? What are you doing out here in the middle of the night? And who is this man with you?"

Burgess whispered, "Let me handle this," and stood to face The Wicked. As he did so, he realized he didn't know her name. Whether she was Mrs. Daggett or Ms. Something Else. Ms. Wicked didn't seem diplomatic.

"Detective Sergeant Burgess, ma'am, Portland police. Here to notify Mr. Daggett that his son is in the hospital, having suffered grave injuries in an attack earlier tonight."

"Mr. Daggett's not here, I'm afraid." From her tone, he thought that after she'd given her stepdaughter the third degree, she'd probably be taking steps to ensure that Mr. Daggett wouldn't be here permanently. Of course, despite her reported propensity for hanging out with her friends and her having urged her husband to push his teenage son out of the nest—all hearsay, of course—she might still be the "come home, all is forgiven" type. Her sour expression said probably not.

"It would be good if you could be in touch with him, ma'am," Burgess said. "The situation is grave, and of course, the hospital is looking for an adult to authorize treatment."

"I'll call and let him know," she said, "but it's not my problem. They're his kids, not mine."

Yup. People should definitely be licensed to have children. Of course, Burgess hadn't had a license and had had a child for almost fifteen years before he knew of the child's existence. Dylan's mother had abruptly moved away without telling him about the pregnancy.

He shrugged off the crazy musings in his head—they came sometimes when he was very tired—and looked at the woman in the doorway.

"Kristin's very upset about her brother. An appropriate reaction under the circumstances. I expect you'll be taking her to the hospital to see him as soon as possible."

Was that bafflement on the woman's face? Could she be genuinely surprised that a sibling close to a brother in serious condition would need to visit him?

"I really don't see how—"

Burgess cut her off. "How? You have a car, don't you?"

She nodded.

"So, you get dressed, you and Kristin get in the car, and you drive to the hospital. Nothing complicated about that."

"Except that I need my sleep."

No wonder Kristin and Aaron called her The Wicked. Though The Narcissist might be more appropriate. He waited to see what she'd say next. It was, and wasn't, surprising.

"Look, Detective. My husband's in bed with another woman, and you think I should interrupt my night's sleep—essential if I'm to function in the morning—to take one of his kids to visit another who's gotten himself beaten up somehow?"

Licenses for sure. Although this woman hadn't borne these children, by marrying their father and becoming their stepmother, she'd taken on a responsibility she now refused to fulfill.

"Never mind," Burgess said, way too tired to argue. "I'll take her myself."

TWENTY-THREE

He ended up leaving Kristin at the hospital under the watchful, if sleepy, eyes of Sage Prentiss. He hoped The Wicked would call one of the parents, either her straying husband or Kristin and Aaron's mother, and emphasize the seriousness of the situation. Burgess wasn't optimistic.

Prentiss was not pleased to have another kid added to his babysitting assignment. He had a baby at home and a wife who expected him to do his share. But Kristin needed someone to watch over her, and Burgess, being older, wearier, and more senior, won the lottery for who got to go home and get some sleep.

Not that there was much time left in the night for sleeping, especially if he wanted to be awake in the morning in time to speak with Nina and Dylan before they left for school. But he'd long embraced the "sleep when you can, eat when you can" philosophy of the job. He slipped into bed beside Chris, curled up against her warmth, and was asleep before he'd taken two breaths. Having Chris there, and a warm bed, certainly made his life better. Just before he fell off the cliff of sleep, he reminded himself to tell her that in the morning.

Miraculously, no one called him during those precious hours of sleep, and he woke if not refreshed at least somewhat rested. He dressed and came into the kitchen to find Nina, Ned, and Dylan all at the table, arguing about who got the last of the favored cereal and who would have to eat some healthy raisin bran instead. He arrived in time to hear Ned say, "Never mind. I'll eat it. I'm sweet enough already," which produced both laughter and affirmations that what he'd said was true.

"Morning, all," he said. "Everyone sleep well?"

Everyone reported having slept well, which was good.

Dylan fixed him some coffee, and Nina jumped up to put some bread in the toaster. He got himself a bowl, sat down next to Ned, and reached for the raisin bran. "Like Ned, I am already sweet enough." That got a chorus of laughter.

Now that he was here, the man who could speak to the evilest criminals or the most wretched victims found the words he needed for Dylan and Nina wouldn't come. He was too reluctant to disrupt this brief, pleasant family time to talk about Nina's ordeal or Dylan's temper or to urge them to be careful at school. Nina was so justified in what she'd done, and he loved that Dylan stepped up to be her protective brother. He just didn't want either of them to get into more trouble. Schools had a tendency to label kids, and he didn't want his labeled as troublemakers.

He drank his coffee, ate his food, and checked his watch. He was already late for his date with Dr. Lee and the late Dr. Spence and hadn't said a word. He hadn't said what he meant to say to Chris, either. He'd do that tonight.

"Gotta go," he said, standing up.

"Don't worry, Dad," Dylan said. "Nina and I aren't going to get into any trouble today. We promise. No one will get hit with books or cornered and threatened. Unless that jerk Dexter does something that requires a response."

"Not even then," Burgess said. "Let the school handle him."

"If they will."

"If they don't, you call me. Whatever the school's policy about phone use is, if you need me, you call." He moved his gaze from one to the other until he got nods from both of them.

"Okay. We'll call you," Dylan said.

"Yes," Nina agreed.

"Good. I mean it. If anything happens, don't hesitate to call me. Anything. Anyone. I hope I'm never too busy for my family."

Behind him, Chris said, "We all hope not."

She hugged him, and he and the kids left. He'd drop them at school and then go on to Augusta, while Chris would get Ned on the bus before she left for work.

It took an hour to get to Augusta, and he had fifty minutes. Less after he dropped off Dylan and Nina. He was rarely, if ever, late for an autopsy. He hoped Dr. Lee would wait for him. They usually got along, but Lee could be quirky. Sometimes, it felt like they were friends, and sometimes, Lee was fussily particular about his expertise and the perks of his profession. Burgess never knew what he would get unless it involved a child. Then he knew they were on the same page.

He drove north far too fast, occasionally using his lights and siren. Part of that was the necessity to hurry. Part because sometimes he still got a juvenile thrill from having traffic part before him like the waters of the Red Sea. Occasionally, someone doddering along in the fast lane seemed utterly oblivious to the lights and siren behind them. When he had time, he'd stop them and deliver a lecture on the requirement to pull over for public safety vehicles. This morning, none of them blocked his way, and he was grateful.

As he drove, he was making his to-do list for later in the day. At the top were to call Sage Prentiss for an update on Aaron Daggett's condition and whether any parent had surfaced. Then, to call the police down in Weston, Massachusetts, and see if he could get some background on Lenore Spence's death. He hoped that could be handled in a phone call, but it might require a visit.

He also needed to track down Spence's family and deliver the bad news. Reinterview Deidre Lovejoy about her movements the night Spence died, since her story was at odds with what witnesses had told them, and to get further details about Dr. Spence.

Those were at the top of his list, but the list went on. He needed to know more about Spence's brother-in-law and sister-in-law and, if possible, learn why they'd filed those lawsuits. He needed to fill out their picture of who Spence was and how he spent his time.

Though he liked to have two detectives at an autopsy, Burgess was on his own today. Partly because there was too much going on with the case to spare a second detective. Partly because the department was understaffed, and Captain Cote had made it clear two detectives couldn't be spared.

The phone rang as he was turning into the morgue parking lot. When he answered, Rocky Jordan said, "Found some more interesting things you'll want to take a look at. When would be a good time?"

"At the autopsy right now, and I don't know how long it will take. Let's say noon if that works for you? I should be back by then."

"Works for me," Jordan said. "See you." He hung up without waiting for Burgess's reply.

Burgess tucked away his curiosity about what Jordan had found for later. He parked and went inside, where he got a sarcastic look from Lee. Didn't look like a day when they'd be on the same page. His watch said he was only three minutes late.

Wink Devlin was there to collect Dr. Spence's clothes and any other evidence that turned up and to take photos. "Dani's back at the lab going over those clothes you found in the dumpster last night," Devlin said.

"Don't trust the B team?" Burgess asked.

Devlin only shrugged. He barely trusted anyone besides himself and Dani.

They gathered around the table and went to work. Undressed, Dr. Spence's athletic runner's body reminded Burgess of another doctor he'd seen years before. He resisted how memory wanted to drag him back to that case. It had been painful in too many ways, including the fact that the murdered doctor had misdiagnosed his mother's cancer, taking her from him far too soon. That loss was something he reflected on a lot lately. She would have loved getting to know Dylan, Nina, and Ned. That case had illustrated a difficult problem in a detective's life: he had to give the same meticulous attention to investigating the deaths of those he disliked as to the most innocent of victims.

He pulled his attention back to the cool autopsy room with its air scented, or about to be scented, with stomach contents and other smells people preferred to avoid. They could all be grateful that decomp wasn't advanced. That made these occasions even more unpleasant.

Sometimes, bruises on a body don't fully appear until later, and that was definitely true here. Yesterday, when they'd done their quick check of the body for signs of trauma and possible causes of death, Spence had appeared uninjured beyond a slight bruise on his chest and being violated with a bottle. Today, there were bruises on his wrists and shoulders, and the bruise on his chest was larger and darker.

Wink took photos of the bruises, and Dr. Lee went to work. He examined the chest around that bruise and said, "Might be traumatic bruising to the heart. A blunt cardiac injury. Sometimes, with sternal fracture. We'll see."

Eventually, the examination proved that speculation correct. Or, as Dr. Lee remarked, "We usually see this from an auto accident or a sports injury. Was he in an accident shortly before his death? Or did he play contact sports? Rugby, maybe? Could he have been hit by a baseball?"

The best Burgess could say was, "Not to our knowledge. He's a runner and goes to the gym. And plays golf. Could any of those activities lead to something like this?"

"Not normally. Sure there was no car accident?"

"None that was reported. His car is undamaged. Can you tell me more about this? It's called myocardial contusion?"

Lee nodded.

"What causes it? How could it cause a death?"

Burgess knew there was little Dr. Lee liked better than to deliver a lecture. Luckily for cops, who weren't always well-versed in medicine or trauma, Lee was a great explainer, a talent that played well in the court-room, too. Now, as he sliced and weighed and measured, and between dictations, Lee explained how a hard blow to the chest could break bones that pierced the lungs and, even without broken bones, could bruise and damage the heart. Severe enough, it could cause a tear in the heart or a heart attack.

"Often treatable," Lee said. "But not if you're home alone. Or unconscious."

But Spence hadn't been alone.

As they waited, curious about this unusual development, Dr. Lee paused to lean in and examined Dr. Spence's heart. "There's the tear," he said. "Must have been a heck of a blow. Sometimes, we see damage like this with only a slight bruise to the chest." He straightened. "Hard to imagine how this could happen at home with no signs of struggle. Maybe if you'd found him at the bottom of the stairs?"

A pause. He looked at Burgess and asked, "The way I saw him. That's exactly how you found him?"

As though what? The cops had staged that scene? Of course, someone had. "It was."

Burgess bit his tongue and didn't remind the ME that the body belonged to the Medical Examiner's office until it was released. True, there were cops who messed with bodies and mucked up crime scenes, but not on his watch. Not if he could help it.

"So, thoughts about how this could happen?" Burgess asked.

Lee turned away from looking at Burgess, back to the body, Dr. Spence's heart still in his hand. "Someone gave him a tremendous blow to the chest."

It didn't seem like something a strong, athletic man like Spence would allow to happen unless it took him completely by surprise. Or Spence had been drugged.

"Any way to tell whether Dr. Spence was standing or lying down when the blow was struck?"

"An interesting question, Detective." Lee turned back to the body, examining the heart, then the clavicle and the sternum. "Wish you'd asked me before we opened the chest."

Burgess bit his tongue again. Lee was a great medical examiner. He was also someone who didn't take kindly to getting too much direction from a mere policeman. At least they had Wink's photos.

After some further study, Lee said, "No worries. I think I understand what happened here. I believe he was lying down and…" Another pause. "It's almost as though someone stomped on his chest. Except the bruising doesn't suggest a foot or footprint. Maybe, knowing about this, you'll go back and find something obvious in the house."

Or not, Burgess thought. He'd go back and look, though. Of course, he would.

Lee made a sort of quiet humming sound to himself as he bent in with a light for an even closer look.

"Can't imagine anyone would lie still for this. I wonder if he *was* drugged before this happened. We'll see what toxicology has to tell us. Of course, some of the drugs they use for date rape? Sometimes, they're gone from the body so fast we can't detect them. Often, there's only about a twelve-hour window." He considered, then added, "We call them date rape drugs because that's how they're frequently used. But it's not the idea of rape in date rape drugs; it's the value of incapacity. Of rendering the victim helpless for whatever the perpetrator wants to do."

As though Burgess hadn't seen many date rape cases over the years. Definitely one of those days when he and Lee weren't on the same page. It happened. It was a warning, though, for him to pay close attention. If he let his mind wander the way it wanted to today, Lee might punish him by failing to mention something. Probably not, or not something important; Lee was too professional for that, but they were both human. Sometimes, the ME liked to pose little tests for the cops even though they both knew this wasn't a game.

Normally, Burgess was very focused on what was happening during an autopsy. Today, he had to struggle to gather together his thoughts. He bounced between being present and speculating about what to do next. He was never like this.

It was hard to keep his focus here, though, when what Lee was telling him meant it was increasingly important to know who had been with Dr. Spence the evening he died. When they'd arrived and when they'd left. Burgess wondered whether Deidre Lovejoy might have an idea. Had she merely shown up when Spence blew off their date, or had she been watching, perhaps suspicious about the existence of those sexy blondes? Aaron Daggett might have some ideas. If he was recovered enough to talk. Perhaps one of the neighbors who wasn't home when they'd done their canvass last night might have information to add?

Could they identify others who had watched the house? Other women Spence spent time with?

Except for the couple of doctors Stan had interviewed at the hospital, two male cheerleaders and a female nay-sayer, they still lacked a picture of Spence and his habits beyond what his girlfriend and his housekeeper had told them. They needed more.

The autopsy went on, punctuated by Lee's narration. It seemed like, aside from his bruised heart, Spence had been in very good shape. Mind wandering again, Burgess was thinking that death from a bruised heart was almost poetic. People really did die from broken hearts, though not in the way romances portrayed it.

Lee's narration continued as he worked his way down the body. He took swabs from Spence's penis and gave his opinion that the man had recently had sex. "Likely oral, vaginal, and anal." There were anal bruises and tears from the bottle he'd been sodomized with. "Perimortem," Dr. Lee said. "Around the time of death. If the killer meant to send a message to his...her...their...victim, they would have wanted him alive. Maybe a farewell? A coup de grace? Someone was sending a final message. And it is your job, Detective, to figure out what that message was."

Wasn't it always?

Burgess's bad knee was complaining about the hard cement floor. To distract himself, he asked, "You ever seen anything like this before? A myocardial contusion as a cause of death."

He checked himself and rephrased, "As a deliberate cause of death?"

"Can't say that I have. Pretty inventive, though, isn't it?"

"Would it suggest medical knowledge?"

Dr. Lee considered that. "Medical knowledge of some sort. But it could be an EMT. Or someone familiar with sports medicine. Or sports generally, since it happens to youthful athletes sometimes from a body blow or a base-ball strike, things like that. I guess it would require some experience with such an event or training to anticipate such an event. That gives you quite a wide field, I'm afraid."

Yes. It did. But Dr. Spence wasn't a kid playing sports, and he hadn't been in an auto accident. Burgess thought that narrowed the field. By how much, though, he couldn't say.

Finally, the autopsy ended. Lee summed up what he'd learned, and Burgess and Devlin were dismissed.

Out in the parking lot, Devlin said, "God, he was in a piss poor mood today, wasn't he?"

"I thought so. Just tried to keep my head down and let him finish. But yeah, he's usually much more collaborative. I wonder what set him off?"

"Nothing we did, Joe. Who knows what's going on in his life? Maybe Mrs. Lee and the little Lees are as difficult as Mrs. Wink can sometimes be. On the days when she's most after me to retire, I can get pretty prickly myself."

Burgess nodded. Wink was quirky at the best of times, something he overlooked because Wink was so good at what he did. Mrs. Wink, or more properly, Mrs. Devlin, had been after her husband to retire for the past two years at least. If Wink retired, Burgess thought he'd have to retire, too. He didn't see how they could do this without Wink's meticulous work and careful eye. Dani was good, of course. Wink had trained her. But she didn't have Wink's decades of experience.

"If you retire, I'll have to retire," he said. "Cannot do this without you."

"Think of all the fun we'll have. You can pursue your hobbies unimpeded by work, and I'll have all that free time for family events like baby showers, engagement parties, and luncheons with the ladies and—"

Devlin broke off. "I'd rather be run over by a truck."

Burgess nodded. He didn't have hobbies. He had work and family. Admitted to being one of those people whose self-image was defined by his work. Without work, he'd be lost.

"Maybe those clothes will tell us something," he said, nodding at the paper bags Devlin was loading. "I'm off to chat with Rocky. He says he's found something I should see."

"Rocky's one of us," Devlin said.

Devlin meant someone who put his shoulder to the wheel and kept pushing until he'd moved the case along. Burgess nodded. It was a characteristic they both respected. Far too often, it seemed, the younger cops, and, to be fair, some of the older ones, considered the job a nine-to-five thing and were reluctant to put in the hours that were needed to get break-throughs in their cases. Policing could be soul-sucking, for sure. It was also critically important work.

"He is."

They got into their cars and headed back to Portland.

TWENTY-FOUR

On the way, Burgess called Kyle. Got the usual "Kyle, Investigations," even though Kyle knew who was calling.

"What's going on?" he asked.

"Not a hell of a lot unless you count Cote sniffing around, trying to see if we're hiding anything."

"Haven't got anything to hide yet. I suppose you can't tell him that."

"Nope. So, I sent Stan to the hospital to relieve Sage Prentiss. Looks like Aaron Daggett is waking up, so maybe we'll get something from him. I've tracked down the two men Deidre Lovejoy told you were Dr. Spence's friends, Jeff Gilbert and Coleman Travis. You and I have an appointment to speak with one of them, Jeff Gilbert, at two today. One of the neighbors I left a card for called and said we can come by and talk around five, though he said he really doesn't have anything to tell us."

"They never know what they know until we fix our hard, cold eyes upon them," Burgess said.

"Sounds like something I would say."

"True. So that's it?"

"It's something, Joe. How was the autopsy? Learn anything about the cause of death?"

"Oh, yeah. It's a strange one indeed. Seems Dr. Spence died from something called myocardial contusion. In layman's terms, a bruised heart from a blow to the chest sufficiently strong to cause the heart to rupture. Dr.

Lee says these events usually result from car accidents, sports injuries, or falls. Beyond that? He says it's probable the subject was likely lying down and wondered how that might have happened. Whether Dr. Spence was drugged. We'll have to wait for toxicology to see whether that's the case."

"Someone with medical knowledge?"

"Lee says maybe, but that there are a lot of people around who, for various reasons, need to know how to recognize a possible myocardial contusion."

Kyle made a humming sound, as he sometimes did when he was processing things, then said, "That's a lot of news. Anything else?"

"Lee speculates Dr. Spence had a lot of sex before he died. And that the insertion of that bottle occurred around the time of death."

"So definitely a message?"

"He thinks so."

"Spence must have really pissed someone off," Kyle said. "Now, all we have to do is find that person."

"Although we've been told, or at least Stan has, that he was an exemplary doctor, and everyone thought very highly of him."

"By two of his colleagues. Two out of three ain't much," Kyle reminded him. "Though that third was pretty evasive. But he was sued by his late wife's siblings. They obviously didn't think so highly of him."

"You want to follow that up?"

"The siblings? Instead of poring over his financials, I'd love to. Admit to being better with people than numbers."

"Then have at it. The numbers things, you know, it's because numbers don't flinch when you fix your eyes on them."

"Nope," Kyle said. "With numbers, I do the flinching. Not that I'm bad at it. I just don't like it as much as scaring someone into coughing up the truth."

"What's Stan up to?" Burgess asked, then remembered. "So, Stan's at the hospital. I'd better give him a call. You know whether Daggett's sister, Kristin, is still there? She's too young for handling this on her own, but that family sounds pretty unsupportive. And a parent showing up could only happen if the stepmother called their mother or their father decided to bag his business trip and come home. She might not have done that if she was very pissed off since his 'business trip' seemed to involve another woman."

He thought of the stepmother last night. Stony face. Folded arms. And definite displeasure with the thought of her husband with another woman. But she'd taken the man knowing he had children, maybe taken him from the children's mother. She didn't get to abandon them now. Except it looked like maybe she had. So many times, the job made him want to shake people until their brains rattled. Constantly using self-control could be exhausting.

"I think Sage got the victim's advocate involved to give Kristin and Aaron some support," Kyle said.

"Right."

Burgess's focus had been on the Spence case. This conversation reminded him how many things from last night's attack on Aaron Daggett needed to be followed up. He had notes from Cyr and the other officers identifying apartments where they'd gotten no one to answer the door. He, or he and Kyle, could do that after they met with Jeff Gilbert, assuming something more urgent—like a trip down to Massachusetts—didn't bump it to another day. Maybe they should just send patrol.

"Back in thirty," he said.

"Roger that," Kyle said and disconnected.

Burgess made a quick call to Rocky Jordan to say he'd be there soon, then called Stan Perry.

Perry answered, saying, "I hate hospitals, Joe. You know that?"

Burgess hadn't known that. That is, he didn't know Perry hated them more than he or Kyle did. Cops spent too much time in hospitals, and a lot of it was with bad guys or victims. Neither made for very good company.

"Sorry to hear that, Stan, since we seem to be in a job that requires our presence at hospitals fairly often. So, Aaron Daggett. Bring me up to speed."

"He's awake. Groggy but awake. Scared out of his mind. He says he has no idea who attacked him. One minute, he's pulling on his hoodie and heading for the door; the next, something slams down on his head, and he falls to the floor. Nothing after that until you arrive."

"Nothing, Stan? He heard nothing? Saw nothing. Sensed nothing?"

"What he says."

"You in his room?"

"Yeah."

"Step out so you can talk."

"A moment, then," Perry said. "Okay. I'm outside."

"Think he's telling the truth or scared of someone?"

"Kind of both. I think if I pressed him, he might remember more. And I think he's scared. We know he kind of put himself in Spence's face down there by the condos. Not deliberately. The face he wanted to put himself in was his father's. But Spence might not have realized that, given how paranoid people say he was."

"But Spence wasn't the person who attacked Aaron."

Perry sighed. "Christ, Joe. I know that. I'm thinking that if Aaron was watching Spence, someone else who was watching Spence might have seen him and gotten worried that Aaron might have seen them."

"You ask him about that?"

"Working toward it. You know how these places are. Staff are never around until you need to ask a patient an important question. Then, they flutter in, and nudge you out of the way, and tell you not to upset the patient."

Perry had nailed it. Burgess couldn't count the times. Usually, they got along well with hospital staff, but when their missions clashed, they really clashed.

"True," he agreed. "So, when you get the chance, ask. Ask about everyone he's seen down there. The questions we asked the neighbors last night. Is the sister, Kristin, still there?"

"Yes. Another complicating factor. She's even more protective than the nurses and harder to push around. Poor kid. She's exhausted. She hasn't eaten. And she won't leave him."

"Still no sign of either parent?"

"What do you think?"

"Well, I think people ought to be licensed to have children."

"It's a good thought. I guess that means Lily and I wouldn't have Autumn, though. And, while I never thought I'd say this, she's a great joy."

It had been what? Four weeks? Six? Since Lily had had their baby. Burgess was pleased to see the wonder hadn't worn off. It was hard to maintain a sense of wonder in their world.

"Okay. Well, keep at it. See if you can learn anything from Aaron. I'll send Sage back after he's gotten some sleep. But—"

"But he's no Stan Perry," Perry interrupted.

"Exactly. No one is."

Burgess didn't add that that was both a good thing and a bad thing. Stan could be a real asset, and he could be a real pain in the ass. Lately, the asset side was winning.

"Call me if there's anything significant I need to know."

"Will do. And if I get a chance, I'll nose around and see if I can find others familiar with Dr. Spence. Like his assistant, who seems to be very adept at ducking me."

A car so tiny it looked like it would fit in his trunk suddenly swung into his lane. Burgess dropped his phone, braked hard, and leaned on his horn. If they stopped everyone who should be stopped for inattentive driving, cops would never get to do anything else. In response—a not uncommon one—the idiot who'd crammed himself into Burgess's lane slowed down. In the fast lane.

Burgess flipped on his lights and siren. The idiot slowed even more, as though a cop behind him was too much to process, then tried to move over into a space that was already occupied.

"Oh, for Christ's sake," Burgess swore. Irritated now both at the idiot in front of him and the person beside him who could have easily let the little car in.

He could tell this was one of those days when being a solitary hermit in a mountain cave was awfully appealing. He wondered if Chris would consent to conjugal visits.

Finally, the idiot beside him slowed to let the idiot in front of him move over. He accelerated, shut off the lights and siren, and left them behind.

Back at 109, Burgess managed to get to Rocky Jordan without meeting anyone who wanted a piece of his time. Maybe because even though his knee didn't like it, he took the stairs instead of the elevator. Captain Cote had a habit of staking out the elevator when he was looking for details the detectives didn't want to share.

He arrived at Jordan's office undetected with a ridiculous feeling of triumph. Eluding Cote shouldn't be necessary, but it was a fact of their lives.

Jordan was sitting at his desk, staring at a screen, something he could spend hours at without getting tired or bored. Burgess was grateful others had talents he didn't possess. He could never have done Jordan's job. He was a get out and shake the trees cop.

"So what have you got for me?" he asked, pulling up a chair and sitting where he could see the screen.

"Couple of things, Sarge," Jordan said, fiddling with his screen.

A fuzzy image of a person getting out of a car appeared on the screen. The person was a scantily dressed blonde. Tall. Wearing a skin-tight black dress and very high heels that showcased excellent legs. Long wavy blonde hair. Clutching a purse large enough to carry a small dog. One of the good doctor's hookers, Burgess figured. Unfortunately, while they got a very good view of her curvy backside, she kept her face away from the camera as though she knew it was there. Luckily, they did get the car's license plate, which Burgess wrote in his notebook.

"When was this?" he asked.

"Two nights ago. The night that Dr. Spence was killed," Jordan said. "Just a little after eight p.m. After she goes inside, all of the internal cameras are switched off. Guess Dr. Spence didn't want to be recording what happened during the evening." Jordan hesitated, then added, "Although the outside cameras stayed on. Which is why we got that video of Spence's girlfriend, Deidre Lovejoy, smashing a wine bottle against the door."

Burgess was trying to picture it. The woman is expected. Spence must be in his secret room so he can monitor her arrival. He checks the camera, sees that his evening's entertainment has arrived, and shuts the system off. But then he has to leave his closet, lock the door to the room, and go down and admit her. So, she must have been on the doorstep for a minute or two.

"No video of her standing at the door?"

Jordan shook his head. "She went in through the garage."

So, Spence had to open the garage door to admit her. "Weird," Burgess said.

"I know."

"What else have you got?"

"Well, if I go back far enough, I've got another blonde arriving about three weeks earlier. But that's not what I wanted to show you."

"Which is?"

There were footsteps in the corridor. With an instinct honed by long experience, Burgess got up and moved himself and his chair behind the door. He'd barely done that when he heard Cote's voice from the doorway. "Jordan, you seen Burgess around?"

Jordan shrugged. "Up in Augusta for the autopsy. He called and said he'd be here in about half an hour."

"Okay. Let me know when he gets here."

"Roger that, Captain," Jordan said. "Shall I tell him you're looking for him?"

"Yes. Do that."

Without a please or thank you, Cote walked away.

Burgess moved his chair back beside Jordan.

"Joe," Jordan said. "Captain Cote is looking for you."

"Thanks. So, what have you got to show me?"

"There's this," Jordan said. "From about two days before Dr. Spence died." He fiddled with his keyboard again, and another dark, grainy image appeared. This time of two people sitting in a car near Spence's condo. Both appeared to be tall and lean and dark-haired, though the driver appeared to be male and the passenger female.

Burgess thought they might be the couple Kristin had described, the ones with briefcases who looked like attorneys.

He thought of Sybil's description of the man who'd tried to get into her apartment building. Tall, dark-haired, wearing a baggy suit and carrying a briefcase. Of course, that description could fit many people, but if these cases intersected as they appeared to, the man in the car might be the same person. If she had her story, descriptions, and dates straight, which was a big if with many witnesses, particularly those addled by drugs or drink.

The clothes they'd found in the dumpster did suggest a tall person. But though they worked a lot with circumstantial evidence, this was only that. All the more reason to speak with those in the building who hadn't responded last night. Same with those who lived near Spence's condo who hadn't responded to their knocks.

"This is good stuff, Rocky," he told Jordan. "Is that it?"

"One more thing," Jordan said. He queued up another video. This one of Dr. Eliot Spence standing outside his front door, looking up and down the street. It was a visible illustration of what people had been telling them—Spence's paranoia in action. They watched the front door open and Spence peer out, then come out and stand four or five feet from the door, looking one way, straight ahead, and then the other. He repeated the sequence twice, then went back inside.

"From there, he goes back upstairs to his security set up," Jordan said. "Obviously, something spooked him."

"But we have no idea what."

"We do not."

About time to meet Kyle for their interview with Jeff Gilbert, and he hadn't made that call down to Massachusetts yet. He'd better see if he could squeeze that one in. Given the nature of interdepartmental cooperation, it might take some time to get the information he needed. He went to his office, hoping he'd get lucky and not run into Cote.

He wasn't lucky.

TWENTY-FIVE

C aptain Cote was at Burgess's desk, one generous buttock planted on the corner, looking like a fat bird of prey spotting something to eat. "Burgess!" he said, his head bobbing forward. "Finally. I need an update on the Spence case."

What you need, Burgess thought, *is to find something useful to do with your time so hard-working detectives can investigate unimpeded.* Aloud, he said, "Not much to report, Captain. I wish we were farther along, but this is one of those cases that's going to take a lot of leg work. A lot of interviews and reinterviews. It's like we've been given a jigsaw puzzle, but only half of the pieces are in the box. Our challenge is to find the people who have those missing pieces."

Cote shook his head. "Poetic but unhelpful, Burgess. I need something more concrete for the press."

As though feeding the press was the department's job, not solving crimes.

Burgess shrugged. "Well, sir. I wish I could give you that. Dr. Lee says we'll have to wait for toxicology to understand what killed Dr. Spence. To complicate things, we've got a possibly related attack last night on a teenager named Aaron Daggett. His family lives across the street from Spence." He shrugged again. "We don't know if the attack might stem from something Daggett saw or something someone believes he saw. Stan

175

Perry is over at the hospital now, waiting for him to be recovered enough to be interviewed. Other than that?"

He pulled out his desk chair and sat. Cote remained seated on his desk, looming over him. Being loomed over by a department captain might have unnerved some people. Burgess wasn't one of them. He was picking up the scent of Cote's lunch, which, from the smell of frying, he was pretty sure was fish and chips. Burgess hadn't had time for lunch.

He picked up a pile of pink message slips as he said, "Other than that, there appears to have been some bad blood between Dr. Spence and the siblings of his late wife, resulting in lawsuits. I'm about to call down to Massachusetts and see if I can get some details about his wife's death. Better details than his current girlfriend telling us that the wife died in an accidental fall down the stairs."

He gave it a beat and added, "If I don't get cooperation from the Weston police, I may need your help."

"Right. Happy to," Cote said. "That's all? That's not very much to feed...uh...brief the press. You don't have a cause of death?"

"As I said, the ME is working on it, sir. He'll update us as soon as he has those test results, I'm sure. You know how Dr. Lee is. He doesn't like to speculate."

The captain didn't like Dr. Lee very much, a feeling which was mutual. He also knew that toxicology results could take a while. He sighed in frustration as though this was something Burgess was doing deliberately.

Burgess did his share of deliberate obfuscation when necessary. He wasn't doing that now. He just wasn't ready to share Dr. Lee's information about the myocardial contusion until he'd been back to the condo, done some poking around, and done more interviews. He wished he could share, but Cote wouldn't wait for them to gather further information before blabbing details to the press. It wasn't something the investigative team wanted blabbed around until they had the whole picture. Similarly, they didn't want the fact that the victim had been sodomized with a bottle of a fancy Italian liqueur to get out. They were sure the assault was significant; they didn't yet know whether the choice of that particular bottle was too, but it was unusual enough to warrant suspicion.

Of course, if he wanted to, Cote could look at Wink and Dani's crime scene photos and learn about it for himself. Nothing they could do to prevent that. They were lucky that usually the captain didn't bother to explore beyond what he could get them to tell him. Occasionally, he would go through the murder book on Burgess's desk. Unfortunately, that sometimes resulted in details they wanted to keep under wraps being unwrapped and displayed to the press, the public, and the killer.

Investigations were often like hiking on a path strewn with boulders. They were used to that. It was tougher when the boulders were strewn by their own. Burgess tried not to waste too much energy on things he couldn't change.

Now, he sat clutching the messages, waiting for Cote to give up and go away, wishing a delicious sandwich would land on his desk. After another minute, Cote huffed again and hiked his rear end off the desk. "I want to know as soon as you do, Burgess," he said. "And don't try to play any games, okay?"

Burgess nodded. He supposed they were games, in a way. Just deadly games. Or necessary ones to protect the integrity of their investigations.

He thumbed through the messages, separating them into unimportant and important. Several he ought to return. Instead, he searched for a phone number for the Weston PD and picked up the phone.

After being shuffled around a few times to people who asked him to repeat why he was calling, he ended up with a detective named Norah Garcia. For the third time, he explained why he was calling and what he was looking for.

Garcia didn't shuffle him off. She said, "That was a sad one, Detective Burgess. Lenore Spence was a very well-liked member of our community. She was an active volunteer in a lot of community groups. A kind person and an all-around sweetheart. A lot of people were deeply upset by her death."

"What about Dr. Spence? Was he well-liked?"

"He was too busy with his practice to be involved the way she was. I don't know anything bad about him. There weren't rumors of domestic violence. He wasn't known to drink and drive. Just pretty much kept a low profile. There were a few people we spoke with after the accident—neighbors, mostly—who didn't have a high opinion of him. Apparently, he could be picky about things. Where people parked. Where they blew their leaves. How their landscapers behaved. Things like that. Our department was involved in sorting out those disputes a few times. But that's not unusual in a town like Weston. Expensive real estate and entitled people."

A pause. She said, "Forget I said that."

"Forgotten. So, there was nothing suspicious about Lenore Spence's death?"

"I didn't say that, Detective."

Burgess waited.

"We did a thorough investigation, of course. His story of the two of them keeping their phones outside the bedroom seemed a little off. Especially with him being a doctor who might be called in at any time."

She paused.

He thought she was scrolling through case reports online.

Eventually, she said, "There was a long-ago sexual assault allegation against Dr. Spence back when he was a resident. Nothing came of it."

"That's the only time there was ever a complaint about him?"

"To the police, other than those conflicts with his neighbors I mentioned. I can't speak for what might be in hospital records. What people who worked with him knew."

He couldn't be sure; she was keeping her tone very neutral, but he thought it was an invitation to explore Dr. Spence's past more thoroughly.

"As far as your department knew, then, the Spences were a happy couple? No trouble reported?"

"As far as we knew."

"Since Mrs. Spence's death, her two siblings have filed wrongful death actions against Dr. Spence. Were they involved in any way in the investigation of her death?"

"As two royal pains in the ass," she said.

Burgess was beginning to like this woman.

"Care to elaborate?"

Garcia sighed. "They were convinced, particularly her brother, that there was something suspicious about her death. That Spence had somehow caused it and should be held accountable. The thing was, by the time our officers and EMTs got to the house, Dr. Spence had moved her. Carried her to a sofa in the living room. We never had an opportunity to view the body in situ. That made it much harder to reconstruct what had happened. We had to work with what he told us, which was a bit garbled. Especially for a physician who ought to be used to dealing with emergency situations. And describing events in detail."

Another sigh. "Of course, this was his wife, and from all we learned about their relationship, Dr. Spence was very devoted to her. But, as I mentioned, her brother, and to a lesser extent, her sister, were convinced her death was the result of foul play."

"Did they say they suspected Dr. Spence had been responsible for killing his wife?"

"Not exactly. The brother thought that. The sister thought someone was trying to kill Dr. Spence. Kill or seriously injure. Neither of them was particularly clear about the reasons for their suspicions."

Burgess decided to come back to that. "We were told that there was an unusually slippery patch at the top of the stairs, which might have caused Mrs. Spence's fall," Burgess said. "Did you find that in your investigation?"

"We did. Some kind of furniture polish, perhaps? Their housekeeper denied using any such product. Swore she'd never use it on floors because it was too dangerous. We found no reason to disbelieve her."

"Any signs that someone else might have been in the house? Someone who might have wanted to harm either Doctor or Mrs. Spence?"

"Good question, Detective," she said. "That was unclear. They didn't have any kind of surveillance system in place. Just an alarm. But the alarm often wasn't armed during the day when Mrs. Spence was there by herself and rarely at night. He said there was too much coming and going, and she found it a burden."

"Anyone able to corroborate that?"

There had been humor in her voice. Now she laughed. "Not really. The housekeeper was scared silly. She's Brazilian. Here, legally, but still very uneasy in the presence of police. Beyond that? Mrs. Spence had good friends who often visited with her or stopped by to ride with her to various activities. None of them had anything to offer by way of illuminating the possibility of someone entering the house. We got a lot of 'This is Weston; things like that don't happen here.' Of course, you and I know things can happen anywhere. I tend to keep that to myself, beyond the usual admonition to be sensible about locking doors and using alarms. We're not supposed to scare the customers. Not even for their own good."

He bet she kept a lot to herself. He'd also bet Garcia was thirty-some-thing, attractive, and walking a cautious line between being effective and being considered ornamental. He was so lucky he'd never been considered ornamental, even if Chris did think he was attractive. A reputation for meanness had served him well.

He considered what else he wanted to know. "Were there any reports of suspicious people hanging around? Unfamiliar cars in the neighborhood?"

"There weren't."

"What about anyone who had a grudge against Lenore Spence?"

"Detective," she said, "By all reports, Lenore Spence was an angel. A woman as good as she was beautiful."

Definitely beautiful. He'd seen the pictures. "What about someone trying to get at Dr. Spence by harming his wife?"

"Nothing our investigation turned up. Doctors can be pretty tight-lipped, though. And clannish."

Things he knew from his own experience.

He'd hoped for more but couldn't fault the cooperation he was getting.

"Sorry to disappoint you, Detective," she said. "Wish we could help. It was a strange accident. Women so young do not normally fall down the stairs. Did your source tell you that she was wearing silly slippers with only a decorative toe strap to hold them on? Basically wearing high-heeled slippers while rushing to answer a telephone in the middle of the night?" She paused, then added, "Yeah, that definitely stood out for us. Who stops to put on slippers before rushing to answer a phone? But since the body had been moved, and since the slippers had fallen off her feet, we couldn't do anything with that. Couldn't even establish that she had been wearing them. But as I've said, we found no one who would have wanted to harm her. Including her husband, despite what her brother and sister said."

"Any more detail on what the brother and sister said?"

"Her brother, mostly," she repeated. "He was convinced that Dr. Spence had killed his wife for her life insurance. She was very well insured for such a young woman. But despite that assertion, he was never able to point us at anything that corroborated his belief. No texts, emails, phone messages, or anything else. Everything we found confirmed that Dr. Spence was devoted to his wife. And the insurance had been purchased a couple years before the event."

"Your take on the brother and sister?"

"He's an impulsive hothead who acts before he thinks. She's a lot more complicated. Silent and dark, and always looks like she's trying to choose the best place to stab you."

Very interesting. Burgess asked, "What about emails, texts, etc., that suggested anyone with a grudge against Dr. Spence?"

"He was a doctor. We both know there are always people with grudges against doctors. They very rarely act on them."

But Burgess had seen it done. "So, no one of particular interest? No one who was unusually persistent?"

"No. No. There wasn't."

He thought about the postcards he'd found saying *Unforgotten*. "Anything else unusual? Anything I should be aware of?"

"Nothing comes to mind. I'll take another look at the file and see if there's something I missed. But I think that's all."

"I appreciate it," Burgess said. "You've been very helpful."

"But now someone's killed Dr. Spence, and you have no idea who?" she asked.

"Correct."

"Does Detective Burgess always get his man?" Humor in her voice again.

"Or woman?" he said. "Usually, he does. Wish him luck."

"Good luck, Detective Burgess. Nice talking to you."

"And to you."

He'd been making notes as they spoke. Now he saved them, then printed them and put them in the pile waiting to be filed in the murder book. There was more here than he had expected. There might not be a murder, but there was definitely something. Something Detective Garcia had wondered about but never been able to pin down. He thought maybe that would have to come from Lenore Spence's siblings. He wondered how cooperative they'd be.

Time to meet Kyle for their interview with Jeffrey Gilbert. And still, no time to snag a sandwich. The policeman's lot was not a happy one.

TWENTY-SIX

As if he'd been summoned, Kyle appeared beside Burgess's desk, moving in that eerily silent way so that he was there before Burgess saw him approach. It was a hell of a skill. Burgess wasn't easy to sneak up on.

"Ready for a little excursion?" Kyle said.

Burgess logged out of his computer and stood. "Take me away from here," he said. "Please." He added, "I don't suppose you have a sandwich in your pocket?"

Kyle shook his head and turned toward the door. Burgess's phone rang. Stan Perry, calling from the hospital with an update. "Aaron Daggett's father has finally turned up. A total jerk. His first move, instead of understanding we probably saved his son's life last night or that his son was still at risk, was to insist that he didn't want the police bothering his son. The guy throws his kid out, leaves him vulnerable, and then acts like he's the good daddy just protecting his kid. He's called his wife to come and get Kristin. Supposedly, the wife is on her way. I'm definitely hanging around long enough to see that. I've always liked fireworks."

"Well, all that is a pain. We need Aaron's information," Burgess said. He'd put the phone on speaker so Kyle could hear, too.

"Hanging around is a good idea," Kyle said. "It probably won't be long before dear daddy decides that hospitals are not his thing and takes off again. Doesn't sound like he has much patience with fatherhood. We want to talk with Aaron; we just have to wait him out."

"Sounds right," Perry agreed. "I am definitely not leaving the kid unguarded. We've seen how that goes too many times. Relying on hospital security is like putting a newspaper over your head to keep off the rain."

"Dang, but that's poetic, Son," Kyle said.

What Burgess had been thinking. The image it conjured was awfully amusing. He thought the word for making things out of wet paper was "decoupage," but he wasn't sure. Maybe it was papier mâché.

"Keep us up on it, Stan," he said.

"Will do. Let's hope I am not driven to homicide. Some people just push my buttons. My cranky, sleep-deprived buttons."

"Do your best," Burgess said. "This case is going to push all our buttons."

"We getting together later?" Perry asked.

"Depends on what comes up in the next few hours. But probably. I've got some things to share from the autopsy and my chat with the Weston police."

"Oh. A chat, eh?" Kyle said.

"More collegial than I expected. Not sure yet what I learned or what I'm supposed to glean from reading between the lines."

He remembered that Kyle was supposed to be investigating Lenore Spence's brother and sister. "And maybe Terry will have something on Spence's late wife's relatives."

He looked at Kyle. Got a headshake that suggested no dice.

"We'll talk in a bit. We've got one of Spence's friends waiting on us. Don't want to keep him waiting too long."

"Later," Perry said and disconnected.

Burgess followed Kyle downstairs.

They took Burgess's truck. When they were on the road, he said, "This guy we're going to see. Gilbert. What do we know about him?"

"Guy's an accountant. Or a CPA. Something to do with money but not with investing it. He said he and Spence weren't that close but agreed to see us anyway. Reluctantly. Though that's nothing new. He sounded...I don't know quite how to put it...evasive, maybe? Like he agreed to an interview but was already ducking it before I got off the phone. That and how he would only meet this afternoon. Not this morning. And only today. I don't know if that was about him wanting to be in control or needing time to work on his lies."

"Why lies?" Burgess asked.

"Just a hunch, but I think he may have shared more with Spence than a fondness for golf. A fondness for sexy young women, maybe? Wild speculation, I admit, but I think he may have occasionally had the use of Spence's condo."

"That's pretty wild, based on nothing. Married?"

Kyle nodded. "Based on nothing but years of experience," he said. "And yes. Married."

"I see."

"Maybe you see. Wish I'd had more time to look into his background. But we've got to keep this case rolling. No time for deep dives."

Burgess changed the subject. "Lenore Spence's siblings. You shook your head. Does that mean you didn't learn anything or that you reached out to one or both of them and got blown off?"

"The latter. I started with the sister, figuring she might be the softer touch. She's like cold granite. Unless we can find a wedge that will give us leverage, we're not going to get anything from her."

"Sounds like the Weston detective's take. She said the sister was cold and secretive while the brother was a hothead."

"Sounds about right. I haven't caught up with him yet. We can hope a hothead might be willing to give up more, even if he doesn't intend to."

Gilbert's office was in a fairly new building in Westbrook. They took the elevator to the third floor and found the office easily. What they didn't find so easily was Jeff Gilbert.

The nervous young woman sitting at a desk outside Gilbert's office became practically tongue-tied when confronted by two large men with badges. She was small and thin with big brown Bambi eyes. After she'd studied her desktop and wrung her hands a few times, she gave up the information that Mr. Gilbert had left in a big hurry about ten minutes earlier without saying where he was going. When she'd reminded him that he had an appointment, he'd snapped that it was an emergency and she'd have to make his excuses.

"But he didn't get any phone calls saying there was an emergency, and he wouldn't tell me where he was going. It wasn't...well, it wasn't like him. He's very responsible about appointments. Uh. Usually, I mean." She ended with a shrug and went back to studying her desktop.

The nameplate on her desk said, "Ms. Meservey," so Burgess said, "You have no idea where he's gone, Ms. Meservey?"

She shook her head without looking up.

"Or when he'll be back?"

She raised her head. "Back?"

"When he'll return to the office. Does he have any other appointments today that you know of?"

Another head shake. "Usually, when he leaves this late in the day, he doesn't come back unless he has an appointment. Especially when it's good golfing weather."

Burgess and Kyle exchanged looks. It wasn't that late in the day. "Ms. Meservey, we have some important things to speak with him about," Kyle said, doing that thing where he loomed over the desk and stared down at her. "So, I guess we'll need his home address in case he's gone there."

She raised her head. "I'm not supposed to give out personal information," she said. She was flushed pink and looked about twelve years old. They tried not to be unkind to twelve-year-olds, but they needed to speak with Gilbert. A need that felt more urgent now that he'd ducked out on them. Ducking out on the police always raised red flags.

"Just to make it easier for us," Kyle said. "We're the police. Obviously, we can look him up if we need to. Be helpful to know the name of the club where he golfs as well."

Her body gave a little shake as she raised her head to her screen and typed something, then read off an address that Burgess wrote down. In a little girl's voice, she said, "You can call me Ruthie."

"We don't bite, Ruthie," Burgess said. "So, do you know where he usually plays golf?"

She nodded and named a local golf course.

"Thank you for your help," Kyle said, straightening up and backing away.

She seemed to breathe more easily when he'd moved away.

They'd turned and headed for the door when she asked, still in that little girl's voice, "Is Mr. Gilbert in trouble? I mean, is my job in trouble? Because, you know, I really need my paycheck."

"Not any trouble that we know about," Burgess said. "We wanted to ask him about his friend Dr. Spence."

"Oh my God!" she said, raising her head, those brown eyes wide and anxious. "And Dr. Spence is dead. If the police, I mean you, are involved, does that mean he was murdered?"

"It means there are circumstances that warrant further investigation,"

Burgess said. "It helps us to speak with his friends." He added, "They were friends, weren't they, Ruthie?"

"Oh, yes." She nodded vigorously. "Pretty close friends, I think." Then she clapped a hand over her mouth. "Oh. No. I'm sorry. My mom was very clear when I took this job that I am not supposed to gossip about my boss, and here I go—" A gasp, and then, "If he were to learn that I…"

"That you what?" Burgess asked. "What should we know about Mr. Gilbert's friendship with Dr. Spence? It's surely no secret that the two of them play golf together."

She pushed back from her desk as though she wanted to put space between them, then hunched over, her knotted hands between her knees. "It's because of Mrs. Gilbert," she said. "Mrs. Gilbert and Ms. Lovejoy. Things that they can't know. About when they say they're playing golf, but they aren't."

Burgess was wondering how this poor girl knew. What she knew and how she knew it, and whether Gilbert had been shockingly careless about his private life. Was it possible he was careless or lazy enough to let this child make his arrangements?

He and Kyle waited in the doorway to see what she'd say next.

"I've seen on TV," she said, "where someone should tell the police something, but they don't want to get into trouble, so they ask if the conversation can be kept confidential." A rather long pause while she twisted her hands and studied the floor. When they didn't respond, she said, in a very small voice, "So I guess that's what I'm asking you now. Whether if I tell you something about my boss and his friend, he'll never know you learned it from me."

"We can keep this conversation confidential," Burgess said, thinking, as he said it, of the many situations in which it might not stay confidential. No need to go into that now. It probably would never come up. He was also thinking that there was more to this childish-looking girl than the naïve youngster she appeared to be. He thought she wanted them to ask her about Gilbert's relationship with Spence so she could spill the beans. He wondered if Gilbert was fooled by her innocent child act.

He said, "What is it that you think you ought to tell us about Mr. Gilbert and Dr. Spence?"

"It's about girls. Or women. Or whatever they're called. Women who can be hired to provide sex for money. Sometimes, Dr. Spence and Jeff… Mr. Gilbert would get a hotel room and get a couple of girls in, and they'd—" She stopped as she searched for words she could use in front of strange men. Men who were cops. "They'd party. I mean, it was okay for Dr. Spence. He wasn't married. He was just…well, he called it letting off steam…but Jeff is married, and his wife is really sweet, and he has two adorable kids, and it's just not right."

How did she know about this? Had Gilbert asked his very young secretary to make the arrangements?

"I know what you're thinking," she said. "You're wondering if Jeff involved me in arranging these…uh…these events. Well, he didn't. He's just not particularly subtle about making arrangements, and well, frankly, Jeff has a pretty loud voice, and I was able to overhear some of the things he said. Some of the times that he—"

She broke off. "Okay. So, I'm nosy. I was curious about the stuff he was planning. It's, well, it's pretty far outside the range of my experience. Not that I'd ever—" She went back to studying her hands. An act, Burgess now realized. One of her cute little ways of appearing girlish and innocent. Again, he wondered if Gilbert had been fooled. Maybe he didn't care? A married man who partied with a friend and didn't care if his secretary knew about it? There was something particularly vulgar about that. And brazen.

He also wondered if something about these sexual encounters might have been related to Dr. Spence's death. Either these hotel room hookups or the women at his condo. It was a pretty expensive habit.

They definitely needed to speak to Gilbert. Soon.

He said, "So Mr. Gilbert and Dr. Spence would arrange to meet prostitutes in a hotel room?"

She nodded.

"Often?"

She lifted her head. "I guess that depends on your definition of often. It would be maybe once a month or so."

"He made these arrangements himself? He didn't ask you to make them for him?"

Her back stiffened, and she looked offended. "I wouldn't have. I like my job okay, but not that much."

Now Kyle had a question. "How long have you worked for Mr. Gilbert?"

She tilted her head as she considered, then tilted it back. "Nine months or so. I started back in January."

"To the best of your knowledge, these hotel meetings have been going on all along?"

She shrugged. "At first, I wasn't aware."

"As far as you know, they usually involved both Dr. Spence and Mr. Gilbert?"

"As far as I know," she agreed. "But it's all stuff I overheard, you understand?"

Burgess nodded. "Do you know with whom those arrangements were made?"

She shrugged. "I didn't make them."

"But do you know how they were made?"

Her cheeks got pink again. She shrugged. Did the staring down at her hands thing. Shrugged again. Said, "I don't know."

Burgess was sure she did. Even if her information came from eavesdropping on Gilbert's loud voice, she must have heard something. He suggested that to her, no longer so concerned about offending her girlish sensibilities. She glared at him and turned her chair so her back was to him.

"We're the police," he reminded her. "Your information, your truthful and accurate information, is important to an investigation."

"I really don't care," she said. "It was disgusting, and I don't want to talk about it. I was only trying to be helpful."

This interview reminded him of looking through binoculars. At first, everything was blurry and underwater. As the adjustment knobs were turned, the picture got increasingly clearer. It also reminded him that he was a dinosaur, as her offering and then retreating behavior brought to mind the term "cock teaser," which he was certain was absolutely forbidden and should be deleted from his brain. As though the brain wasn't a lot like an attic, where old, unused stuff was stored away.

As she did her demure staring thing and Burgess wrestled with his annoyance, Kyle stepped in again. "Can you tell us anything about their arrangements?" he asked.

"Not really. I mean, I made the hotel reservations because that was just business. I made lots of hotel reservations for Jeff and his friends. Jeff and his clients. He always wanted me to book a suite." She named a hotel near the airport. "About the girls?" A dainty shrug. "I know nothing."

And if Burgess believed that, he'd learned nothing in thirty years on the job. He didn't understand why she was being so coy or deceitful about that. Figured it would be hard to press her enough to get at the truth without taking an unnecessary amount of time. They had bigger fish to fry, and the clock was running.

Just in case the information might be useful, he asked, "Did you deal with anyone in particular at the hotel?"

She nodded and fiddled with her keyboard. "The woman I always spoke with was named Marni, with an i. I don't know her last name."

"Thank you, Ruthie," Burgess said. "We appreciate the help."

As they headed for the elevator, he wondered if she'd caught his irony.

TWENTY-SEVEN

"We check out that hotel? And Marni?" Kyle asked as they headed back toward Portland.

"We do. So, what's your take on that sly little Bambi?"

"That despite the air of demure innocence, she's a bit of a twisted sister who probably gets off on knowing all this stuff about her boss and very likely knows a whole lot more than she's told us."

"Exactly."

The afternoon traffic was thicker now, making the going slow. Burgess was thinking about Melina's meatloaf sandwiches and wishing they had time to stop and get some.

"I know," Kyle said, reading his mind. "I'm starving, too. Lotta cops, you know, they'd take the time to eat something. They wouldn't be scent dogs on the chase like we are."

"Agreed. But we have to take time for family. Can't take time for everything, you know. Not when there's an unknown killer out there, and people are still at risk."

The people still at risk included Kristin and Aaron Daggett, kids whose parents had abdicated the parenting role, leaving the cops to keep them safe. Well. He didn't know that, did he? He knew the dad had shown up at the hospital and put on a parental act. He assumed it was followed by a disappearing act. Knew the wicked stepmother was supposed to pick up Kristin. He doubted whether that had actually happened.

As if summoned—it seemed like there was a lot of that happening today, as though his thoughts were being broadcast on a billboard—his phone rang with a call from Stan.

"Dad's nowhere to be found, stepmom never showed, and now Kristin has disappeared," Burgess said, "Am I right?" He said it casually, but his adrenaline spiked. Kristin was a smart and mature kid, but she was also only thirteen, with no real-world sense of the risk a killer bent on remaining undiscovered might present.

"Right as rain," Perry said. "I guess you're not surprised."

"Fill me in." He put the phone on speaker so Kyle could hear.

"I tried, Joe. Really. The girl said she was going to the bathroom. Not a big deal. I didn't think anything of it until she'd been gone too long, and then it was too late. I couldn't leave the brother to go chasing after her. No one noticed her leaving. She isn't answering her phone. And yeah, the stepmom never showed. I called her, too. Went straight to voicemail. Same with the dad. Lotta deliberate unconcern there."

Perry sounded angry, and Burgess wasn't surprised. Stan was the most recent inductee into the world of worried parents, and it was hitting him hard. They saw it all the time, the many forms of parental negligence, but sometimes, it resonated more.

"We do what we can," Burgess said. "How's Aaron doing?"

"Like you'd expect. Wants to get out of here so he can look after his sister. Doesn't want to lose his job or get behind in school. He's a real good kid, Joe."

"What are they saying about releasing him?"

He could almost hear Perry shrug. "You know hospitals, Joe. They don't want to let him go unless there's someone who can look after him. And there isn't. So, they want to keep him a little longer, make sure he's really okay."

"He remember anything about the person who attacked him?"

"Says he doesn't. But he's scared, Joe. Like a lot of the people we deal with, he doesn't trust us to keep him safe, so he's going to sit on whatever he knows."

"Does he understand that he's not the only one at risk? That his sister is, too?"

Perry considered that. "No. I don't think he does."

"Well, you might try that as a lever."

Perry made a confirming noise and said, "What are you and Terry up to?"

"Got a tip on a hotel where our vic and one of his buddies used to have sex parties. Going to see if we can find the person who helped arrange them."

Stan Perry laughed. "Well, good luck with that."

"You doubt my investigative prowess? Or the effect of Terry's cold eyes?"

"Just pretty cynical about people's relationship with the truth."

Weren't they all?

"Call me if anything happens," Burgess said. "I'll send someone over to babysit Aaron soon, free you up for other work."

"Cote came by," Perry said. He sometimes liked to drop bombs at the ends of their conversations.

"What did you tell him?"

"As little as possible. But since I'm out of the loop, I don't know a heck of a lot, Joe, do I?"

"You're doing important police work, Stan," Burgess said.

"Sure doesn't feel like, especially when the kid's a clam, and his sister's gone missing."

Burgess couldn't help himself. He said, "Mama said there would be days like this."

"Mama can shove it."

Burgess sighed. He understood Perry's frustration. "I'll get patrol to send someone. Then you can go and look for the sister. Unless you want to try and track down another one of Dr. Spence's friends. His name is Coleman Travis. Supposedly a running buddy of Spence's. Runs a restaurant in South Portland."

Burgess gave Perry the address, adding, "We don't know whether he was a participant in Spence's sex parties or not. But we're looking for a general overview of Spence and his character and behavior. Like you were looking for at the hospital."

He considered. "So, the two docs you spoke with who told you that Dr. Spence was, how did they put it? Such a good man. You get any vibes from them that there was more they weren't sharing?"

"Of course. But doctors, you know. They're very good at not sharing, aren't they?"

"And the woman you spoke with? What was her name?"

"Taylor Hix."

"You ask her about other doctors or staff we should interview?"

Perry made a noncommittal sound, from which Burgess concluded that he hadn't. "Maybe you could follow up with that since you're in the hospital already."

"Sounds like a plan. Not like I didn't try, Joe. She was in such a hurry to get away she shut me down. I never got to ask the question. She had patients to see, and I was clearly a nuisance. Also, I could tell she wasn't comfortable criticizing a colleague, however much she disliked him. I'll follow up. And try again to nail down his elusive assistant."

A burning pain in Burgess's gut that wasn't hunger reminded him how having a family had changed his life. Dr. Spence's death was a case. A mystery to be solved. Yes, Spence was a victim, but he didn't draw an emotional response. Kristin and Aaron, on the other hand, did. They were kids at risk that the adult world had abandoned. In their case, Burgess and his team stood in for those who'd neglected them. The rule might be to never get emotionally involved, but sometimes, that wasn't possible.

As they parked at the hotel, his to-do list seemed overwhelming. So many places he needed to be, so many people he needed to talk to, and so many things to follow up on. Few cases were simple, but this one was such a maze. The information they were getting was so conflicting, never mind that people like Deidre Lovejoy and Spence's colleagues were trying their best not to cooperate. In Lovejoy's case, outright lying about her activities on the night Spence died. She needed to be called on that.

Along with that was the mystery of why Spence's late wife's siblings had sued him. Kyle had struck out with the sister, but there was still the brother. And they hadn't even gotten to reviewing the papers and photos they'd found, never mind assessing what they might mean.

As he opened his door to step out of the truck, his phone rang again. He debated letting it go to voicemail, but it was Chris.

A normally calm woman, she was almost hysterical. "Joe. Joe. Nina didn't come home from school. Dylan says he looked all over for her and couldn't find her. I called the school, and they were no help. She isn't answering her phone. What do I do?"

Whatever agenda he thought he had was about to be derailed. He hadn't had a chance to follow up with Andrea Dwyer, but he knew enough to know that Dexter Wiggins was dangerous and that his daughter had an unfortunate tendency not to back down when she should.

"Is Dylan there?"

"Yes."

"Let me talk to him, please. And Chris, I promise I'll stop what I'm doing right now and find Nina."

"Thank you, Joe. I'm just so worried. Will you call me? Will you keep me…how do you cops put it?…in the loop?"

"I will keep you in the loop."

She said, "Here's Dylan."

"Dad?" his son said.

"Tell me everything you know."

Kyle was watching him, absorbing his end of the conversation. He said, "Hold on," and to Kyle, "Nina didn't come home from school. There's a kid who's been harassing her. He's dangerously unbalanced. I'll fill you in when I'm done here."

To Dylan, he said, "Go ahead."

"Not much to tell. I saw her a few times during the day, and she seemed okay. I didn't see Dexter, but someone told me he was back in school. Then, when we were supposed to meet to catch our ride, she wasn't there. I searched the school. Asked everyone I know if they'd seen her, and no one had. But Nina wouldn't blow me off like that. She wouldn't go somewhere without telling me. You know she wouldn't."

"I agree. Did you speak with anyone in authority? Teachers? Office staff?"

"I didn't. Should I have?"

Even someone as confident as Dylan was hesitant about dealing with the front office, particularly after tangling with them when he'd protected a Muslim girl in a headscarf from a bunch of bullies.

"No. That's fine. Can you put Chris back on?"

Chris said, "Joe?"

"You called the office?"

"Of course."

"What did they say?"

"They said they have no way of keeping track of students once they leave the school building, even though we have no way of knowing whether she actually did leave the building. I could tell they didn't want to deal with this."

"Right. Okay. I'll start with the school and with that boy, Dexter Wiggins, and see what I can find out."

"Call me," she said.

"I will call you."

"I'm hanging up now. Go find our daughter."

Burgess took a moment to consider. Teenagers could be rebellious, even the good ones. But Nina knew they were concerned about the situation with Dexter Wiggins. She wouldn't fail to pick up a call from him or from Chris, and she wouldn't fail to meet Dylan without letting him know why.

He quickly finished explaining the situation to Kyle. He wished they'd brought two vehicles so that Kyle could stay here and finish the job they'd come to do. Now, he'd have to drive back to 109 so Kyle could pick up his car. A lot of time wasted when they didn't have time to waste.

"This Wiggins kid," Kyle said. "You think he's dangerous?"

"I *know* he's dangerous. Dwyer was going to look into him. See if he was on our radar. I've been too busy to follow up, but now, she's top of the list. You want to call her and put her on speaker. See if she's learned anything."

"On it," Kyle said, getting in the truck and pulling out his phone.

The pain in Burgess's gut was sharper now that there were two young girls at risk. He hoped Perry could look for Kristin and would call him when she was located while he looked for his daughter.

From Kyle's phone, he heard Andrea Dwyer answer. "Hey, Terry," she said. "Long time since you've called me. What's up?"

"Calling for Joe," Kyle said. "About Dexter Wiggins. You got anything for us?"

She sighed. "Wish I didn't, Terry. But he's a bad actor. Several incidents where he's been sexually inappropriate with young girls. He keeps getting second chances. Hate to say it, but without some serious intervention, we've got a serial rapist in that kid. And you know I don't label people lightly. I'm a big cheerleader for these kids. For most of my kids. Not for this one."

"Fill us in," Kyle said. He paused. "You have a home address?"

"Sure," she said and gave it to them. "What's up?"

"Joe's probably told you this already. His daughter had a run-in with Wiggins at school. The kid was harassing her with vivid descriptions of things he wanted to do to her sexually. She asked the teachers for help and got blown off, so she hit him with a book to make him stop. She also recorded the things he was saying. So, the school, unwilling to deal with Wiggins, suspended Nina until Joe intervened. Thing is—now Nina's disappeared. She didn't meet Dylan after school, and she's not answering her phone."

"Never mind the recitation of his past bad acts," she said. "Let's find him. I can fill you in later. We can start with his home, and if he's not there, I've got a few other places we can look. Sound good?"

None of it sounded good in the larger sense, but yes, it was a plan. Having Dwyer with them would be good. She knew where kids hung out and who to ask when she didn't know. Kids trusted her because she was on their side.

Burgess was driving over the limit, chasing his anxiety with his speed. He debated whether to go lights and siren or slow down. Decided to slow down a little. Just a little. If Nina was at Wiggins's house, he didn't necessarily want to alert the kid that they were coming. He figured Dwyer would reach the same conclusion.

The Wiggins house was on a dead-end street of largish, well-maintained houses with ruthlessly trimmed hedges and neat lawns diligently stripped of any fall leaves. There was a single car in the driveway, and none parked on the street in front of the house. Dwyer's marked cruiser was parked a few houses up the street. He parked behind her, and he and Kyle went up to her window.

"Anything?" he asked.

"No signs of activity. But that doesn't mean much. When mom and dad both work, the kids can get into plenty of trouble without alerting the neighbors." She glanced down the street at the house. "How do you want to do this?"

"Have you met Dexter Wiggins?" Burgess asked.

She shook her head. "His documented interactions have been with patrol."

"So maybe you could knock on the door and see if he's home? Say you're looking for someone?"

"While you do what? Sneak around the back and look in the windows?"

"I wouldn't call it sneaking," Burgess said. "But yes. Let's go."

TWENTY-EIGHT

There was no good way to sneak up on the house to get to the rear. The yard was too bare. No tall fence, thick row of trees, or foundation plantings to screen them. *Almost*, Burgess thought, *as if they expected to need the protection of those open spaces.* He hoped they could count on teenage obliviousness to allow them to get close. He'd sometimes thought when Nina and Dylan were involved in their music or their homework—often both—that Godzilla or a Yeti could walk through the room unnoticed. Ned would notice, though. Anything out of the ordinary caught his attention.

As Dwyer approached the front door, he and Kyle paused to plan their next move, then slipped along the sides of the house into the backyard. He hoped that no neighbor spotted them and called the police. That would be such a farce.

The rear of the house was more inviting than the sterile front. A large deck with stairs down to a stone patio with a firepit and chairs, a raised bed garden like the one Chris was working on, and a fenced-in swimming pool. The land back here sloped away so that beneath the porch was a lower level of the house with glass doors leading out to that patio. If the house was arranged in a typical manner, the downstairs room would either be a rec room for the kids or a man cave.

He was making a lot of assumptions, but based on experience, if Wiggins had Nina here, they would likely be in that downstairs room. From their opposing sides, he and Kyle approached the windows, thankfully uncurtained, and peered in.

Not a rec room or a man cave but a home office. No signs of life. No lights. No sounds. No people.

Dammit!

"Now what? Go up on the deck?" Kyle said.

Burgess shrugged, wondering if they should have gone to the school first rather than here. "We might as well exhaust the possibilities."

Moving quietly, they climbed the stairs to the deck. There were more floor-to-ceiling sliders up here, and the curtains were drawn back so they could see in. They could see right through an immaculate living room to a wide hall leading to the front door. Dwyer was at the door, speaking to a woman Burgess assumed was Dexter Wiggins's mother. The woman was shaking her head. They couldn't hear words, but even viewed from the rear, her body language said she had no intention of cooperating with the police. It was a response Burgess thought was well-rehearsed.

"Back to the truck," Kyle whispered.

They left the deck, slipped along the sides of the house, and met Dwyer at the street. They were silent until they were back at their vehicles. Then Dwyer said, "She says he's not home, and she doesn't know where he is. She also says—" She paused for effect, though they all knew what she was going to say. "That she wishes the police would stop harassing her son. He's a good kid, and it's not his fault if his actions are sometimes misinterpreted. He has, in her words, attention deficit issues that sometimes go unrecognized."

"Misinterpreted?" Burgess said. "Unrecognized? I wonder if she'd react differently if she heard the recording Nina made. There's no way that could be misinterpreted by anyone."

Dwyer sighed. "Like we haven't seen this a zillion times. As though parents protecting a troubled kid are doing their kids any favors." She shrugged. "So, what now? You want to check out some of the places he might be?"

"If you know of some, then yes," Burgess said.

"I'm the kiddie cop. Of course, I know where they hang out. A couple of places come to mind. There's an abandoned building over near the school. That's where I'd start."

Burgess gestured toward her cruiser. "Lead on," he said.

Before she opened her car door, Dwyer said, "That woman. So damned smug. So sure she was doing the right thing. As though protecting him until he does something that gets him sent to prison is the best course, rather than getting him the help he needs now." Another shrug. "Although it might be too late for that. It's not as though she hasn't had plenty of chances already."

She pulled away from the curb, and they followed.

"The 'my kid can do no wrong' thing gets awfully old," Kyle said.

"It does. Right now, we've got both sides of that coin. We've got the overprotective parent in Wiggins's case and the totally indifferent parent where Kristin and Aaron Daggett are concerned," Burgess said. "Sure, parenting is hard, but neither of those approaches has good results."

"You've got that right."

They rode in silence after that, Burgess trying to tell the monster in his stomach to calm down and let him breathe. Sometimes, the stresses of this job made him feel like he'd swallowed a hot knife. On the days when he most felt like retiring, he wondered whether the monster would go away if he quit or took a desk job or would just keep lurking and attacking him. The possibility of relief wasn't enough to make him seriously consider it, though. He had no idea who a retired Joe Burgess or a Burgess who sat at a desk and did bureaucratic things would look like. Instead, he sucked up the pain as the price he paid. Others might think that was crazy, sometimes Chris among them. He didn't care. He was like Popeye saying, "I yam what I yam."

"Are you growling?" Kyle said.

"Probably."

Someone else might have said a reassuring, "She'll be okay," but they were cops who'd seen too much that wasn't okay. Given too many hopeful parents bad news.

They retreated into silence again.

About five blocks from the school, Dwyer put on her blinker and pulled to the curb. They pulled in behind her.

Gathered on the sidewalk, she pointed toward a decrepit-looking building in the block ahead. "That's the place. Mostly, they're just kids, but some street people are also squatting there, so I'd suggest vests and weapons. Forewarned and all that. I've been in and out a few times without a problem, but I never count on that."

"Entrances?" Burgess said.

"Only two. Front and back. Supposed to be locked, but as fast as the landlord puts on padlocks, they're cut off. The layout..." She gave a quick description of the interior. "Downstairs is pretty open; the upstairs is more of a warren of little rooms. The kids who use it as a clubhouse? They've taken over a large room on the first floor toward the back." She pointed to a pair of grimy windows. "There."

"Any idea how many of them there are?" Kyle asked.

Dwyer shrugged. "Maybe a core group of five or six, with different hangers-on at different times."

"And Wiggins's role?"

"He thinks it's his place, and they are his…" She considered. "I wouldn't say friends because Wiggins doesn't exactly have friends. Maybe his crew? Only not like a crew that goes out and commits crimes or sells drugs, though they maybe do a little of that for shits and giggles. More like the guys choose to hang with him because he has some money. Some drugs. Some booze. He buys popularity rather than being popular, I guess you'd say."

Burgess wasn't surprised. "How should we approach this?"

"You take the back. Kyle and I will take the front. Just walk right in and see what's up. They aren't expecting us, so there shouldn't be anyone resisting, and it's not like they post lookouts or anything. Unless things are different this time, they'll just be sitting around drinking or smoking, listening to music, and saying dumbass things to each other."

The knife in his stomach stabbed. "But if he has Nina?"

"Then maybe he'll have taken her upstairs. There's only one staircase."

Taken her upstairs. Delivered as information. Like Nina was any victim and not his precious daughter. The knife plunged deeper. It didn't take much imagination to populate the scenario with bad things. Not with decades of bad things in his head. He didn't even know if Nina was here, and already, his anxiety and rage were rising like an incoming tide.

Kyle, his mind reader and best friend, put a steadying hand on his shoulder. "Take some breaths, Joe. You need to focus. If she's here, we'll find her. We've got this."

Kyle was right. Getting emotional didn't help.

Burgess nodded, then opened the rear of the Explorer so they could get their gear. Dwyer was at her trunk, also gearing up. That done, she and Kyle went toward the front door while Burgess headed to the back.

When he was in position, he texted Kyle. Then waited. An excruciating wait while minutes crawled past. Crawled so slowly that he thought he could feel them moving past him like something ancient and slow. Like a dying creature. When he heard a commotion of voices inside, he pulled the door open and stepped inside. The place stank of age and damp, of beer and unwashed bodies, of urine and garbage. The smells of poverty and despair and people who'd lost hope.

Sometimes, he wished he could bottle scents like that and take them to city council and state legislative hearings, where poverty and the desperate need for housing were too easily viewed as abstract. He'd stand there and pour out the reek onto the floor and say, "See. This is what happens when people don't have food and decent shelter and hope, and it's left up to us to clean up society's messes."

Never mind that if Dwyer was right, some of this scent came from careless teenagers. The smell was one he was familiar with from dozens of crime scenes. Maybe hundreds. Sometimes, he'd describe a place he'd been to civilians and get disbelief or laughter. The truth was often stranger than fiction.

Feet thudded toward him, several pairs, from the sound of it. He drew his gun and waited. Three teenage boys came around a corner and headed straight toward him. "Stop! Police," he ordered.

Wide-eyed, they braked to a stop like characters in a TV comedy, then turned and ran the other way.

Good luck with that, he thought.

He heard Kyle's voice echoing his command. One Kyle. Three boys. It was a fair match.

He didn't hear Andrea Dwyer's voice, so he walked toward the direction those boys had come from. Found Kyle standing in a doorway, gun raised, looking his best fierce self. As he approached, he heard Kyle say, "Not one of you moves unless I say so. Understood?"

A chorus of yesses.

Smart on the kids' part. If Kyle weren't his friend, Burgess would be wary of him, too, given Kyle's talent for going cold and still.

Burgess looked around. Five teenage boys in a room that was furnished with castoff chairs and a sofa, the world's ugliest coffee table, and a couple of tilted lamps. On the coffee table were beer bottles, a half-full bottle of gin and another of Scotch, and a hubcap that was clearly being used as an ashtray. The room reeked of beer and marijuana.

"Where's Wiggins?" Kyle asked.

The boys murmured among themselves, but no one answered the question.

"Wiggins?" Kyle repeated. "Where is Dexter Wiggins?"

Steps overhead told Burgess that Dwyer was up there, searching.

Finally, one of the boys said, "He went off in Jared's car."

"One of you Jared?" Kyle asked.

A red-faced, beefy kid who'd been trying to hide behind a much smaller kid said, "I am."

"You loaned him your car?" Kyle said.

"He took it, is more like." Smarmy tone and a face to match. A visual, if not verbal, "What's it to you?"

Like a bunch of half-drunk, bratty teens would faze Terry Kyle.

"What kind of car?"

Knowing Burgess was behind him, writing this down in his notebook, Kyle concentrated on his questions.

The car was an eight-year-old Corolla. Silver. Pressed, the kid coughed up a plate number, struggling with it as though he'd been asked to solve an algebra problem.

"He alone?"

That brought another silence from the group. Teenage male solidarity could be incredibly stupid sometimes.

Kyle raised his voice. "Is he alone?"

The skinny, dark-haired kid who looked like he might still have a few wits about him said, "He took that girl."

"What girl?"

"The one with the reddish hair who hit him with her book. That girl."

"You know her name?"

"Nina, something."

"How long have they been gone?"

The kid shrugged. "Dunno. Maybe twenty minutes? I wasn't paying attention."

"You know where he was going?"

This brought another silence. A complicit silence. They knew and didn't want to say.

"First one to tell me gets to go home without charges. The rest of you? It's breaking and entering, trespassing, underage drinking, drug use, and I am sure by the time we're done with you, there will be more charges to add to that," Kyle said. "So, do I have a volunteer?"

"You can't charge us with all that," the beefy boy said. "We're not doing anything wrong."

"Besides what I just listed?" Kyle said.

The kid, who seemed to still possess a brain, said, "He was going out to Evergreen Cemetery. There's a place across the street that used to belong to his grandma. No one's living there now. He won't let us meet there 'cuz his parents would have a fit, but he has a key."

Burgess got out his radio. Called for the patrol to come and assist with some arrests and gave the address.

Dwyer appeared from upstairs, looking frustrated. "Had to make my way through five rooms of squatters," she said. "Nina's not there."

"No. Wiggins has taken her off somewhere," Kyle said. He pointed at the kid who'd given them information. "This gentleman was helpful enough to tell us where. As soon as patrol gets here, the rest of these kids are going to have a trip to jail."

Dwyer looked at the kid who'd been singled out. "Allan, what in hell are you doing here?"

The kid shrugged. "Dunno, Officer Dwyer. I musta taken a wrong turn somewhere."

A smartass, but at least he'd been smart enough to see how his situation was going south.

"Indeed, you have," Dwyer said.

The kid shrugged his shoulders in a show of indifference. His shaking hands told a different story.

"Get the hell out of here," Kyle growled. The kid got.

Outside, sirens announced the arrival of patrol.

"I can handle this if you guys want to go look for Wiggins," Dwyer said.

"You can meet us there once you're finished with this crew," Burgess said.

"Right behind you," she agreed, then turned to the boys who were still in the room. "Names and addresses," she said, pulling out her notebook. "And your ages."

"It's not fair," the beefy boy who'd lent his car to Wiggins complained. "Why does Allan get to go?"

"Because he was willing to help the police investigate a crime," Dwyer said. She tapped her pen against her notebook. "Now. Names?"

Burgess and Kyle left.

TWENTY-NINE

At their vehicle, Kyle said, "Want me to drive?" and held out his hand for the keys.

"Why? You think I'm not safe to drive?"

"More like I think you have some calls to make. Maybe see if you can find out what house we're looking for. Who the car that Wiggins is supposedly driving is registered to. To Chris to give her an update about what's going on before she loses her mind. Maybe get some patrol out there for backup? Just a few details like that."

Burgess dropped the keys in Kyle's hand and got in on the passenger side.

"You might also want to check in with Stan and see if he's had any luck either getting more information from Aaron Daggett or in finding Kristin. Or is freed up to check in with the only doc who didn't give us the party line about what a wonderful guy Dr. Spence was, or look for Spence's assistant."

"Yes, Boss," he said.

Kyle laughed. "That'll be the day. Though I might relish inheriting the mantle of the meanest cop in Portland."

"You'll be good at it."

"You know that every time you hint at retirement, I get palpitations, Joe."

Good thing someone was keeping track of all the threads of this thing.

204

Normally, he was good at that. Right now, Burgess's head was entirely filled with a relentless loop of "find her before Wiggins gets a chance to do something awful to her." Nina had had enough awful in her short life. His job, his and Chris's, was to protect her from any more of that. To keep her safe. Right now, that task weighed on him so heavily that it was hard to breathe.

Despite the brief time they'd been in there, the stench of that building clung to his clothes. He rolled down his window to air himself out. Kyle did the same.

This time, they did use lights and sirens. Otherwise, the fecklessness of other drivers would have made Burgess's head explode.

While Kyle wove his way among the drivers who scattered helter-skelter before them, Burgess called dispatch and asked for data on the house they were looking for, for the registered owner of the car Wiggins was driving, and for patrol to meet them there when the address was found.

He hoped the grandmother whose house it had been was on the Wiggins side of the family. Otherwise, it would be a greater challenge. If he was at his desk, he could search obituaries. After the events at Nina's school, he'd looked up the Wiggins family, so he had the father and mother's names. Now, he gave those to dispatch in case they helped.

That done, he called Chris and gave her an update, trying to make it sound routine and keep his own anxiety from his voice. Here, three decades of keeping emotions in check served him well.

"Getting close, Joe," Kyle said, shutting down the sounds of their approach and slowing to turn onto the first road that bordered the cemetery. If dispatch didn't come up with an address or they didn't spot the Corolla, this could be like looking for a needle in a haystack. The cemetery was huge.

Slowly, they prowled along, each taking one side of the street while they searched for a small silver car. There were a lot of small silver cars and a lot of Corollas, but none was the right one.

Another turn. Another street. Burgess was sure that his resident knife had sliced right through his stomach when Kyle said, "There!" and stopped.

The irritated driver behind them gave a blast of his horn, pulled around them, and sped off.

To their left, there was a small house, almost a bungalow, painted a faded shade of green. Parked in the driveway was the silver Corolla.

As Kyle pulled to the curb and parked, Burgess called dispatch, gave the address, and asked for patrol, no lights or sirens.

They got out and approached the house. This time, Burgess took the front door, and Kyle went around to the back.

Burgess went up the steps, crossed the small porch, and hammered on the door. "Police. Open up!" he bellowed.

Nothing.

He pounded on the door again.

No answer. Without trying a third time, he kicked the door in. A lifetime of unyielding doors had taught him to use a mule kick.

He heard Kyle doing the same in the back.

He stomped hard on his desire to run through the house, screaming for Nina. Instead, he forced himself to slow down and move through the rooms carefully, observing what he passed. A dark living room with shabby furniture, the air stale and cold. No signs of habitation beyond a backpack dumped in a chair. To his right was a kitchen. An unlikely place to find Nina, but doing a thorough search meant checking it.

Like the living room, there were few signs of habitation beyond a bottle of vodka and two glasses on the counter. One glass was empty. The second appeared untouched. Burgess figured Wiggins had tried to get Nina to drink, and she'd refused.

Off to his left, he heard Kyle searching what he assumed was a first-floor bedroom. Leaving Kyle to that, he climbed the narrow stairs. At the top was a small landing. Straight ahead, a small bathroom. To his right and left, closed doors that likely led to bedrooms. He opened the one on his right. Empty. Not trusting that, he went in and checked beneath the bed and in the closet.

Nothing.

He hesitated a moment outside the next door, listening. What if they hadn't gotten here in time? He pushed the thought away. He needed to be wholly present, not distracted by the what-ifs, by concerns beyond those of safety and about what lay on the other side of that door.

He had his hand on the knob when Kyle joined him.

They stood together, as they had so many times, guns out, as Burgess, gun in his right, used his left hand to turn the knob and pushed the door open.

Nina was on the bed, stripped down to her underwear, her face tear-stained and terrified, while Dexter Wiggins, flabby belly over droopy Minecraft boxers, stood over her with a knife in his hand. Wiggins was a big kid, as big as Burgess. Next to him, Nina looked terribly small and vulnerable.

"Police officers. Drop the knife," Burgess commanded.

Wiggins did what so many bad guys did: he turned toward Nina, grabbing her and pulling her toward him to use as a shield.

Wiggins was at least twice her size. She didn't protect him from much. They could easily have shot him. The goal, if possible, was to get everyone out of here unharmed.

Burgess and Kyle separated, Burgess going to the right-hand side of the bed, across from Wiggins, while Kyle moved closer to him. Separating made it harder for Wiggins to watch both of them.

Time slowed down, distorted by tunnel vision. There was nothing else in the world beyond the boy with the knife and the girl on the bed. Nothing beyond other scenes with knives. Beyond training that said a man with a knife could get to you before you could fire your gun. Training, thankfully, Dexter Wiggins didn't have. Not that it would have helped him. If he got to Kyle, Burgess could still shoot him.

"Drop the knife, Dexter," Kyle commanded. "This isn't a game. You're inches from being shot. That how you want to end this? With your parents having to plan your funeral, knowing you'd kidnapped and attempted to rape a young girl? It's a hell of a memory to leave them with."

Wiggins had evidently watched too many TV cop shows. He pressed the knife to Nina's throat, saying, "Move aside and let me leave, or I'll kill her. I swear I will."

Nina's pleading eyes were fixed on Burgess, saying as clearly as words, "Save me, Dad."

"Letting you leave gains you nothing, Dexter," Burgess said. "We know who you are. We know where you live. What are you going to do? Get Mommy and Daddy to send you away somewhere safe? There is nowhere safe unless you want to go live in some shitty third-world country, which I guarantee you will not like. Don't make this worse than you already have. Do the smart thing and let that girl go. Drop the knife, and let her go."

Burgess moved a step closer, bringing his gun up and aiming it at Wiggins's head.

Kyle didn't move, but his gun was fixed unwaveringly on Wiggins's chest.

Meeting Nina's terrified gaze, Burgess nodded at her slowly. No fast moves that might spook Wiggins. "It's going to be okay, Nina," he said. "Dexter knows what he needs to do. He knows what the smart thing to do is. He knows otherwise he's going to get shot."

"You two back off," the boy yelled, a tremor in his voice. The hand that held the knife was shaking. "Back off. I'm telling you. If you don't, I'll…"

From downstairs, a voice, "Police. Is anyone here?"

"Detectives Burgess and Kyle," Kyle called. "Don't approach. We've got a hostage situation."

The officer downstairs went silent.

Suddenly, Kyle pointed at the window behind Wiggins. "Oh my God! What's that?"

Oldest trick in the books. Still in the books because it worked. Wiggins turned to look, and Kyle tased him.

Screaming and gasping, the kid released Nina and dropped to the floor, writhing and moaning as Kyle moved in and kicked the knife away.

Burgess held out his arms. Nina flung herself across the bed and into them. He wrapped her in the bedspread and carried her out of the room while Kyle kneeled and cuffed the squirming kid.

Downstairs, Burgess sent the waiting officer upstairs to assist Kyle, then dropped onto the sofa, clutching Nina to his chest, and called dispatch, asking for a supervisor and a crime scene team.

"Kidnapping and attempted rape," he said. "We've got the kidnapper. We'll be bringing him in soon."

In his arms, Nina sobbed softly as she wormed down into the quilt and refused to lift her head to look at him.

"It's okay, Nina," he said. "It's okay. Did he hurt you?"

"Oh. Dad. How did you find me? I was so scared. I hoped you would come, but I never thought you could. I wanted to call, and I knew you were calling me, but he took my phone. It's in his backpack."

He felt her trembling right through the quilt he'd wrapped her in and pulled her tighter.

Her voice was muffled by the bedspread, and her face pressed against his chest; she repeated, "I was so scared."

"You're safe now, Nina. You're safe."

He pushed away his anger toward the boy who'd done this, who'd terrified a girl who'd already had enough terror in her life. He concentrated on Nina as he tried not to think about the night he'd found Nina and Ned in that crypt, two foster kids tricked by a fake babysitting job, lured there by two young men with the worst intentions who were stoned out of their minds. While Nina had watched helplessly, fearing that they'd already killed her little brother, who lay unconscious on the ground, one of them had carved the other up like a slaughtered animal. She'd seen that. Seen what a disturbed man with a knife could do.

He couldn't push the memory away. That scene was in both their heads, accelerating her fears, fanning the flames of Burgess's anger.

Upstairs, he could hear voices as Kyle dealt with Mrs. Wiggins's good, misunderstood boy, the boy who'd abducted Nina and would certainly have assaulted her and perhaps killed her if they hadn't gotten here in time.

Cops were supposed to be dispassionate. No one could be dispassionate about this.

He called his boss, Lt. Vince Melia and gave him a shorthand version of the situation. Melia said he was on his way.

"Does she need to go to the ER?" Melia asked.

"No. I'm taking her home."

"We'll need pictures," Melia reminded him. "Wink and Dani are on their way. So am I." Melia hung up.

He didn't want to wait for pictures. The cop who wanted to preserve every essential bit of evidence at his crime scenes warred with the protective father who wanted his daughter out of here as quickly as possible, away from any reminders of this awful place.

"Pictures, Dad?" Nina whispered. "Why do they need pictures?"

"To create a record of what Wiggins has done. So, nothing goes wrong with prosecuting the case, and he goes free to do this to another girl. Maybe one who doesn't have parents who pay attention or a dad who can kick in doors."

"You kicked in the door?"

"You wanted me to wait outside and knock politely?"

A tiny laugh from the bundle in his arms. "That's so not you," she whispered.

"Are you okay?" he asked. "Are you hurt?"

"Bruised," she said. "From where he…" Silence from the cocoon. Then, "From where he dragged me to his car and then dragged me in here. From where he slapped me when I wouldn't drink that vodka he poured. Where he punched me when I wouldn't take off my clothes. Why would he do this, Dad? What is wrong with him?"

"Plenty," Burgess said, thinking of all the parents like Wiggins's who paved the way for their children to become monsters. It wasn't a silver lining to this dark cloud, but he was still thankful that Nina hadn't been raped or murdered. Of course, he was. He and Kyle had seen that too many times—young men who lacked consciences or boundaries, in part because their parents had given them the message that they didn't need to have them. That whatever they chose to do, no matter who was harmed, was all right.

Upstairs, there was thumping and the sounds of scuffing feet, and then Kyle appeared at the top of the stairs with the other officer, a sullen, scarlet-faced Dexter Wiggins between them, draped in a faded blue afghan.

Wiggins was loudly protesting that he should be allowed to put on his clothes.

"Can't do that. They're part of the crime scene," Kyle said.

"Wink and Dani are on the way," Burgess told him. "And Vince."

"Nina?"

"Bruised. Badly shaken. Otherwise, I think she's all right."

There was rustling in the quilt, and Nina's bright head appeared. "Thanks for rescuing me, Uncle Terry," she said. "I'm forever grateful."

Kyle shrugged. "We gotta take care of our kids, right?"

She murmured, "Right," and burrowed back into the quilt.

There was another officer at the door, and Kyle handed Wiggins off to the two of them and came back into the room.

"We sure do know how to time it, Joe."

Burgess nodded. They'd come so close to being too late. If traffic had been thicker or they'd taken a different turn. If Dwyer hadn't known where to find those kids, and they hadn't gotten the information about the car and this house? He shook off the what-ifs. "We got here, Ter. That's what counts. Got here, and Nina is okay, and that kid should be off the streets for a long time."

"Unless he runs into some bleeding-heart judge."

Their eyes met. Neither said anything, but there was a promise there that if Wiggins walked for any reason, Portland PD would be keeping a close eye and taking care of their own. He hoped it wouldn't come to that.

Kyle sat down across from him. Silently, the two of them waited for the cavalry to arrive. On TV, that was it. The guy gets arrested, and detectives ride off into the sunset. In the real world, there was a whole lot more to do to ensure that the bad guys didn't walk. That and making sure that the victims were cared for.

Once their lieutenant, Vince Melia, had arrived, been briefed, and could take over the scene, Kyle would go back to 109 and interview Dexter Wiggins, while Burgess would do the equally essential interview with the victim at home.

THIRTY

"Let's call Chris and let her know you're okay, shall we?" Burgess said.

The quilt rustled, and Nina's bright head appeared. "Do we have to? She's going to think I'm such an idiot."

"You're not an idiot," Burgess said. "He's twice your size and has mental health issues. But Chris is worried, and letting her know you are okay would be kind."

She whispered, "I thought I could handle him. I thought I could talk my way—"

Another silence except for sobbing. Then, "He said if I didn't cooperate and come with him, he would hurt Neddy, and I couldn't let that happen. Not again. Not after the last time. That was all my fault."

It was definitely not her fault, but Burgess expected if he protested for a lifetime, she'd still believe it was. It was her therapist's job to help her understand how to deal with guilt and forgive herself. She'd been very young when the lure of a babysitting job had put her and her little brother in such danger. That had come on top of witnessing her father killing her mother. Today's incident certainly wasn't going to help.

"Let's call," he repeated.

This time, she didn't burrow back into the quilt but waited while he made the call, got Chris on the line, and said, "Nina wants to tell you that she's okay." He handed his daughter the phone.

"Mom? Oh, Mom! I'm so sorry. I was so scared, and I didn't know

what to do, and it looked like it was going to be awful, and maybe I'd be..."
Her voice caught. After a moment, she went on, "Be raped or killed or
both. And then Dad and Uncle Terry kicked down the door and rescued
me and arrested that asshole Dexter Wiggins. I'm sorry for my language,
Mom, but honestly, that's what he is. He's a monster."

She listened for a moment and then said, "No. Honestly, Mom. I'm
okay. A few bruises. That's all. Dad and Uncle Terry are both here with
me, and as soon as their boss gets here, Dad will bring me home."

At that point, her control deserted her, and she started to sob. She
handed the phone to Burgess, who assured Chris that yes, Nina was okay
and yes, they would both be home soon. Chris said she'd leave work early
and meet them there. He reassured her that Dexter Wiggins had been
arrested and wouldn't be back on the streets as a threat any time soon.

He hoped he was right about that. Cops got pretty cynical about the
justice system, which they sometimes referred to as the injustice system.
Burgess frequently found himself saying, "We just catch 'em and bring 'em
in. After that, it's up to the DA and the courts, and the way they behave, I
can understand why Justice wears a blindfold. She can't bear to see the
mess that's made in her name."

"You're growling," Nina and Kyle said together.

"Got plenty to growl about," Burgess said. "Maybe you'd rather I chose
to sing?"

"I've heard you sing," Nina said. "Growling is fine."

If she could tease, he thought that was a good sign.

Burgess reminded himself to breathe. He felt as though he was being
drawn and quartered, at least mentally, with the demands of the Spence
case pulling him in several directions while he needed to be present here.

Predictably, he only needed to think about the case, and it would find its
way to him. It was Stan Perry, calling to report that he'd been relieved from
his post watching Aaron Daggett, that Aaron seemed to want to share
something with them but couldn't bring his brain to focus on it, and that he
was off to track down the doctor who'd tried to avoid telling them any
details about Dr. Spence.

Perry said, "I hear you and Kyle are off kicking in doors. Is Nina
okay?"

News traveled fast in cop circles, that was for sure.

"She's okay. We got here in time."

He heard Perry breathe out. He had a daughter of his own now, and
while it would be years before she could get into Nina's kind of trouble, he

was a seasoned cop with a head full of the world's evil, already looking down the road with trepidation.

"Good to know. Catch you later." And Perry was off.

"Does everybody know?" Nina asked.

"About you? That you're the victim? No. Just that there was a situation and an arrest. Most people still think I'm a surly old loner who lives a monkish existence. They don't know I'm a family man."

Nina laughed. "You try to be a family man. You're just torn between two families—the blue one and the one at home."

Pretty wise for fifteen.

There were footsteps on the porch, and Wink and Dani entered, followed by Vince Melia.

They stood in a semi-circle just inside the door, waiting for Burgess and Kyle to bring them up to speed on the case.

Burgess explained about Nina's trouble with Dexter Wiggins at school and how she hadn't come home today, then let Kyle take over to describe the events leading to this house and what had occurred here, including Dwyer's involvement and how her knowledge of Portland's kids had made the connection to the empty house. He described learning that Wiggins had borrowed a friend's car and that his grandmother had a house near the cemetery.

It was ironic how few sentences it took to describe the events. Their tense journeys, their confrontations, and the fear that had finally driven them here were only an underlay to the crisp, factual narrative.

But they all knew.

Melia directed Wink and Dani to start upstairs in the room where Wiggins had held Nina captive, then focused on Nina.

"We'll need your statement describing the events, but Joe...but your dad can get that at home. Are you sure you don't need to go to the hospital and get checked out?"

"Very sure, Lieutenant Melia," she said. "I'm okay. Really." Her voice was shaky again. Anticipation of having to talk about all this, even with people she knew. "He didn't get to—" She had to stop.

Melia was looking thoughtful, and Burgess knew what he was thinking. He was thinking that Burgess, being Nina's parent, shouldn't be the one to take her statement even though she'd be more comfortable with him. It wouldn't look good down the road, a father taking his daughter's statement, leaving it open to all sorts of challenges in court.

"Terry can do it," he said.

"I think that's better, Joe."

There were two versions of better. There was better for the investigation and better for Nina. Despite concern for her, ultimately, they had to choose the investigation. If Dwyer's information was correct, Nina wasn't the first girl Wiggins had tried something with. They would learn more as they dug in. In the end, the goal was to ensure that everything they did was by the book and the boy wasn't free to continue his predation. Predators who started young like this often escalated to homicide when the thrill of rape was no longer enough or when frustration with an unwilling victim dissolved any remaining fears or inhibitions.

"I'll stay a while, Joe," Kyle said. "And call Sage to get him working on a warrant for the house and the car. Vince can give me a ride back to 109."

Burgess was fine with that. He wanted to take Nina home and was comfortable with Kyle managing the scene.

To Nina, he said, "We'll need your clothes as part of the investigation and this quilt. Wink and Dani need to photograph them before they collect them."

Eyes wide, she said, "My clothes? Are you serious?"

"Almost always," Burgess said.

"But—"

"I've got a sweatshirt in the car. You can put that on. It'll be like a dress on you anyway."

She managed a faint smile and said, "I guess it's better than coming home in this ratty quilt. It smells like cigarettes and mildew."

Burgess set her in the chair and went out to the Explorer to get the sweatshirt. It *would* be like a dress on her, but that was a good thing.

She went into the downstairs bedroom to change and came out looking lost, dwarfed by the sweatshirt, her small bare feet looking so cold and white on the weary wooden floor. She handed Burgess the quilt. "Can we go now? Please?"

She walked to the door and waited.

Burgess took the quilt from her and set it in the chair. "We can go."

Nina hesitated. "Can I have my phone? Dexter put it in his pack."

Separating a teenage girl from her phone was torture, but she couldn't have it yet. "Not until it is photographed and processed," he told her. "We can probably get it later."

He'd had one more thought about processing the house and a reason to leave the quilt behind. Before he shared it, Kyle nodded and said, in a voice too low for Nina to hear, "I know. She may not be the first. I'll make sure Wink and Dani know that."

Burgess joined his daughter at the door. "Want to walk, or shall I carry you?"

She rolled her eyes. "I can walk. It's only like thirty feet, Dad."

Eye rolls. Faint smiles. Sarcasm. It was all good. He'd seen victims so traumatized they were mute. Some were never able to talk about it. Nina, despite her history, was a survivor.

He followed her out to the car, opened his passenger door, and helped her in. Because Kyle had been riding with him, he didn't need to clear away all the clutter that habitually lived on the seat.

He closed the door, backed the truck out of the driveway, and headed for home. Overhead, the sky was a leaden gray that perfectly suited his mood.

THIRTY-ONE

He pulled into the driveway beside Chris's car, and she, Dylan, and Ned were out the door before he was out of the truck. Ignoring him—he was just the cop bringing a beloved daughter home, after all—they clustered at Nina's door, barely letting her slide down off the seat before she was gathered into a group hug.

As he came around the car, he wondered what Chris had told Ned. He'd probably learn soon enough. Chris was a nurse and, like all experienced medical personnel, adept at the non-answer, the partial story. He trailed behind as they swept Nina inside and up the stairs. By the time he got inside, Nina and Chris were nowhere to be seen, and Dylan and Ned were back at the table, where Dylan was feeding Ned chocolate milk and cookies, and Fideau was waiting for cookie crumbs to drop.

That reminded Burgess that he still hadn't had any lunch. He dropped wearily into a chair and said, "Got some more of that for your old man?" When he sat, his faithful canine came and put his head on Burgess's knee and gave him a look that was pure sympathy. It was one clever animal.

"Sure thing," Dylan said, opening the refrigerator. "I'll make you a sandwich. Guess you've had kind of a hard day, huh?"

"Oh, no. I love going to autopsies and kicking in doors."

"What's an autopsy?" Ned asked.

Had Burgess never really told him about one? Before he could answer,

216

his phone rang. He took it into the bedroom, where he could talk without being overheard.

Kyle said, "When's a good time for me to come and interview Nina?"

"You already done with Wiggins?" he asked, though he knew that wasn't possible.

"Bastard lawyered up. Now, mommy and daddy and their lawyer and ours are all driving Vince nuts. I thought it would be a good time to make myself scarce around here."

"Let me check," Burgess said. "I'll call you back."

"Am I getting the brush off?" Kyle said.

"You're getting the 'it depends on whether Chris thinks Nina is up to it' instead of the cop dad's 'of course.'"

"Right."

"I don't like this any more than you do," Burgess said and went to consult with Chris.

She and Nina were huddled on Nina's bed, and she glared at him when he opened the door.

Ignoring the glare, which wasn't easy, he said, "Terry needs to interview Nina, and he needs to do it soon while everything is still fresh."

"You're kidding."

"Wish I weren't. I wanted to do it, but Vince said that might taint the interview since I'm her father. He wants Terry to do it, and he wants it done now."

"Well, too bad for him—"

Burgess cut her off. "Chris. This is a criminal matter. We need to make sure to cross our t's and dot our i's so that Dexter Wiggins can't walk away from this with a slap on the wrist."

He studied her rigid posture, her body protectively between him and Nina. Crap. This is not how he wanted things to go. "Think of this as the cop's ER. We have to treat things as urgent, Chris."

She knew. She just wanted to protect Nina, whatever that meant.

"Mom," Nina said. "It's okay. Really. I understand what Dad's saying. And it will be okay. It's not some stranger. It's Uncle Terry. He has daughters of his own. He's not going to be some big, scary cop. I wish…" She stopped, struggling for control. "I wish I didn't have to do this. Not now and not ever, but Dad's right. I don't want Dexter to get away with this, to be free to do this to some other girl."

Another pause before she said, "And neither do you."

Chris threw up her hands. "Okay. Okay." She narrowed her eyes at him. "But Terry had better go easy on her. She's been through enough."

He kept his temper in check despite wanting to respond. Instead, he said, "Of course," and went to call Kyle back.

"Good," Kyle said, "because I'm on my way. You wouldn't have something you could feed a hungry cop, would you?"

"Hoping the same thing for myself. I'll see if Dylan can scare up a sandwich for you. He's making one for me."

In the kitchen, he asked Dylan if he could make a sandwich for Kyle, then went downstairs to wait. Kyle must have driven like a bat out of hell because he pulled into the driveway only a couple of minutes later.

He looked like he'd been gnawed on by rats, his hair sticking up, his clothes rumpled. "Kid's goddamned mother literally attacked me," he muttered, tucking his shirt in. "Luckily, it's all recorded, and Vince is ready to charge her with assaulting a police officer. The place is a madhouse today."

Burgess nodded toward the stairs. "Dylan's making you a sandwich. You want coffee?"

"Need coffee. Christ, Joe. We've got a homicide to solve. We do not need this clusterfuck as well."

"Don't let Chris hear you say that. She's in full-on mama bear mode."

Kyle shrugged. "A policeman's lot."

They sat at the table and wolfed down sandwiches while Dylan made a pot of coffee. "I would have protected her if I could, Dad," Dylan said.

"I know you would. None of us expected this."

Dylan fell silent, but his posture was dejected.

This was what it was like to try and balance being a cop and having a family. You could never do enough or get it entirely right.

"Nina's in her room," he told Kyle. "You okay interviewing her there?"

"Not the first time I've been in a teenage girl's bedroom," Kyle said, giving him a look.

Burgess read the look as "And so have you. And yes, this *is* what it's like to balance family and the job."

They pushed back their chairs, and Kyle followed him to Nina's room. Burgess knocked, then opened the door. "Terry's here." He stood back and let Kyle enter the room.

Chris stood, still in protection mode, then forced a smile. "I'll leave you two," she said. She followed Burgess out as Kyle pulled out the desk chair and sat down facing Nina.

Outside the door, she threw herself into his arms. "He'll be gentle with her, Joe, won't he?"

"Of course. It's Terry. You know he will."

He held her, her head nestled into his shoulder, against his neck. Learning to be a parent was a challenge for her, too. Much as she wanted children, she was learning that it could be excruciating.

He pushed away all the things that urgently needed his attention, forcing himself to be present for her. For his family.

After a while, without raising her head, she whispered into his neck, "You got there in time."

"I try, Chris. I really do."

They stood there in an embrace. After a while, Ned wormed his way in, and then Dylan spread his arms around the bunch of them. No need for words.

When they broke apart, Burgess went back to the kitchen to finish his coffee while he prioritized his list. He needed to catch up with the woman named Marni, who'd arranged Dr. Spence's trysts with prostitutes at the hotel or at least booked the rooms. He and Kyle needed to pay an unannounced visit to Deidre Lovejoy. They needed to find Kristin and see if Aaron had remembered more about his attacker and was ready to talk. They still needed to catch up with Jeff Gilbert and Spence's other friend, Coleman Travis.

Too late now to catch Gilbert on the golf course. Visiting him at home would be challenging since he wasn't likely to tell the truth in front of his family. Of course, that could cut both ways. It amped up the pressure nicely. He wondered whether the sly Ruthie would tell her boss about their visit or whether her enjoyment of secrets would mean she kept that to herself. She was quite a piece of work.

He debated heading out but decided to wait for Kyle. Kyle was his sounding board, and he thought their next two interviews might need two detectives.

Across the room, Chris was exploring the refrigerator, pulling out ingredients for dinner. She withdrew her head briefly to look at him. "You won't be home for dinner, right?"

"Right. Got another missing girl in trouble. Lot of people to talk to who aren't too keen on talking to the police. Then Terry, Stan, and I need to meet up and prioritize our next steps."

"Right," she said again. "We'll leave something for you."

"It's always a treat to come home and find something delicious waiting," he said.

She gave him her sunrise smile and said, "Always a pleasure to cook for someone who appreciates it."

"Like the rest of us don't?" Dylan said, but he was teasing.

After what felt like hours, Kyle emerged. He looked worse than before he went in. Unsurprising. It wasn't easy to interview a girl you knew and cared about regarding a terrifying abduction and assault. He nodded at Chris. "She's good. She's okay. But she wants you."

Chris nodded and left the room. To Burgess, Kyle said, "We going to the hotel now?"

"Or looking for Kristin Daggett?"

Kyle shrugged and said, "Hotel," followed by, "What's Stan doing?"

Burgess matched his shrug. "Looking for reluctant witnesses, I hope."

Nodding, Kyle headed for the stairs, and Burgess followed.

Out in the driveway, they leaned against the Explorer while Burgess called Stan Perry. He got an instant, "Perry," and said, "Update me."

"Kristin Daggett is still missing. Aaron is still struggling with his memory. Both the doc I want to follow up with and Spence's assistant are pulling the disappearing act. And Lily wants to know when I'll be home. My frustration level is off the chart."

"Why don't we blow off this investigation, all go out for drinks and steak, and let the B team take over for a while?"

Burgess sometimes joked about bringing in the "B" team on investigations at those moments when they faced burnout. Unfortunately, it was only a joke. There was no "B" team, though there were some detectives who were being brought up to speed.

"Great idea," Perry said. "I'm sure Lily will understand if I blow off picking up diapers because we want steak and drinks."

"As will Michelle," Kyle agreed. "Hard-working detectives like us deserve a break."

Burgess looked at his watch. After five. He said, "Stan, why don't you take a break and go home for a bit, plan to meet up around eight?"

Perry exhaled. "That would be great, Joe."

As Burgess tucked his phone away, Kyle said, "Holy fuck!" He was staring over Burgess's shoulder at something in the road. Not a ruse. This time, he really was staring at something.

When Burgess turned, he echoed Kyle's astonishment. A large brown bear was ambling down the middle of the road. Over the years, he'd seen plenty of wildlife in the city, including several moose. This was his first bear.

"Just when you think it can't get any crazier," Kyle said.

"When did any of us ever think that?" Burgess asked. "Stan's gonna be really sorry he missed this."

He pulled out his phone, called Dispatch, and told them to send animal control and some officers and to call the Maine Warden Service. He took another moment to alert Chris and the kids. It was a rare enough event that they wouldn't want to miss it.

THIRTY-TWO

As soon as the first patrol officers arrived and were briefed, Burgess and Kyle took off. Soon, the scene would be a circus of professionals, neighbors, other gawkers, and news vans, and they had places to go and people to see. Captain Cote might assert that it didn't take two detectives to interview some clerk at a local hotel, but Burgess wanted Kyle with him. His cop gut might be aching from earlier in the day, but it still worked, and it was telling him that this wouldn't be the simple interview Cote would assume it was.

They drove in tandem to the hotel and parked, meeting up beside Burgess's car. So much time had passed that the woman they hoped to see might be gone for the day. Burgess thought not. He thought that someone who arranged hotel rooms for sexual encounters probably liked to be on scene in case something went wrong and that encounters like the ones Jeff Gilbert and Dr. Spence had enjoyed were more likely to take place in the evening. For Spence, at least. Of course, they knew of no encounters arranged for this particular day, but Burgess expected to get lucky if it was, in fact, lucky to be able to locate a witness engaged in facilitating prostitution.

The lobby was nice in a modern, impersonal way. Dark wood, light tile floors with faux oriental rugs, and dark leather furniture. The lighting was subdued and included some hanging lights with giant lampshades. Some of the couches were occupied by couples and singles, and there were a few tables where men, mostly in shirts and slacks, sat bent over laptops. The only individual who didn't seem to fit with a business hotel was a dark-haired young woman in a pink coat. The coat was short, her legs were long, her shoes were what Dani Letorneau called FMPs, or fuck-me pumps, and pink to match the coat.

He could be wrong, but he thought he knew what the woman's business was.

He looked at Kyle and got Kyle's very faint nod.

Instead of approaching the desk clerk, they sat down on an empty sofa near the door and settled in to wait.

They hadn't been waiting long when a woman with brassy blonde hair and a too-tight dress came through a door behind the desk and approached the woman. She sat down on the sofa and leaned in, whispering something. The young woman nodded, took the plastic room key the woman was offering, and headed for the elevators. Kyle followed. Burgess stayed in the lobby to watch for whoever she was meeting.

A few minutes later, the outside door opened, and a man in gray golf slacks, a blue polo shirt, and a tan windbreaker entered. His appearance matched the man in a photo on the wall of Jeff Gilbert's office.

How convenient. They were going to be able to kill two birds with one stone. Burgess texted Kyle: **Jeff Gilbert on his way up** and followed the man to the elevators.

Gilbert pressed the button for five and looked a little nervously at Burgess. "Me, too," Burgess said.

When they exited the elevator, Gilbert turned right while Burgess hesitated, like he was checking for his room number, then went left.

There was no sign of Kyle. Burgess figured he was either out of sight around a corner or already in the room. He turned a corner, then swung around and peered down the hall.

He watched Gilbert put his key in the door. It swung open, and the man stepped inside. Before Burgess reached the door, he heard Gilbert say, "Who the hell are you?"

He caught the door as it was closing, stepped in, and closed it behind him.

The young woman had shed her bright coat and was reclining on the bed in some very nice black lace underwear, a garter belt, and sheer black stockings. Burgess thought garter belts had gone the way of the dinosaurs, but he was a dinosaur who was still in action, so why shouldn't they be as well?

The woman had her hand over her mouth, her blood-red nails bright, shiny punctuation marks across her startled face.

Kyle loomed beside her. As Burgess entered, Kyle bent to the woman, actually a girl and a rather young one at that, and said, "Keep quiet." He straightened and looked at Jeff Gilbert.

"Detective Terry Kyle, Portland police, and this is Detective Sergeant Joe Burgess."

"I haven't done anything," Gilbert said.

Sometimes it was so damned predictable.

"You and your friend Eliot Spence haven't used this venue to meet with prostitutes?" Kyle said. "You aren't here today with this young woman to engage in sex for money?"

Gilbert blathered something incomprehensible, then glared at the girl and said, "And you keep your mouth shut."

"Fuck you, Jeff," the girl said, which pretty much confirmed a prior relationship. "You never wanted me to keep my mouth shut before."

"I said shut up," Gilbert yelled.

"Let's keep our voices down, shall we?" Kyle said. "We don't want to disturb the other guests."

"I don't give a fuck," Gilbert said and started for the door.

Such a charming fellow. Burgess blocked his way, pointing toward the room's single upholstered chair. "Sit down. We need to talk to you."

In response, Gilbert pulled out his phone. "I'm calling my lawyer."

"Not a good idea," Burgess said. "Because we want to talk to you about your friend Eliot Spence. You call your lawyer, and we'll be talking about charging you with engaging prostitutes, and I'm sure your wife won't be pleased about that."

"You aren't going to tell my wife about this," Gilbert said. "My lawyer—"

"Sit down and shut up," Kyle said. Then he got the name and address of the girl on the bed. Said, "You can get dressed and go. I just need to know how the arrangement with Mr. Gilbert was made."

"I can't tell you that," she said. "Marni will kill me."

Ah. Marni. The woman they'd come here to see.

Burgess had certainly been right about needing Kyle with him. Right now, things were going in so many directions at once he could have used Stan Perry as well.

He looked at Kyle and got a nod.

"You can go," Kyle told the girl again. "But not a word to Marni, you hear? We find out you've told her about this, and you're busted."

The girl smirked. "Yeah. Right," she said. "Or maybe you'd like a little of what Jeff was here to get? I'm fine with that. Fine with the both of you, if that's what you want. I just can't get arrested. Not right now."

He looked at Kyle. "Why don't you escort Ms...." He looked at the girl. "Your name?"

"Loreli. Lorelei Locke." She smirked again.

"Your real name," Burgess growled.

She tossed her hair. Long, dark hair with soft, shiny curls. "Wouldn't you like to know?"

Kyle picked up her purse and dumped the contents on the bed. Along with a wallet and some credit and debit cards, there was a phone, condoms, flavored lubricant, breath mints, and some other things Burgess didn't recognize.

"Hey! You can't do that. That's my stuff." Not so much a protest as a whine.

Kyle checked the cards and the driver's license and looked at Burgess. "Lisa Lockner," he said. He wrote the girl's address in his notebook. "She's seventeen."

"Oh fuck!" she said. "No. You can't come to the house. My parents will kill me."

Every minute, she was looking less like a sexy hooker and more like a scared schoolgirl.

Not a good day for anyone to look like a scared schoolgirl in front of these two detectives.

Kyle gestured to the stuff he'd dumped out. "Put your things away. Get dressed. And leave. And do not speak with Marni, don't call, don't text, or we will come to your house, and your parents will know about your little money-making gig. Got it?"

"Oh, God," she said. "You are so mean. The other cop wasn't so mean. He was just happy to get a..." She stopped, considering whether she'd said too much, while Burgess was making a mental note to check the daily logs and see who might have responded to a call from here and gotten himself a freebie. Plenty of time for that after this case was done.

God. He'd been so caught up in running around like a headless chicken on this case that he'd forgotten to check with Vice to see if this place was on their radar. Sloppy police work. He had to do better.

After a few silent moments during which he supposed the girl's pouting

225

was supposed to produce forgiveness or a willingness to avail themselves of her services, Lisa Lockner put on her clothes and her coat and flounced out of the room.

He and Kyle got out their notebooks, perched on the edge of the bed, and started in on Jeff Gilbert. Burgess let Kyle take the lead.

"Mr. Gilbert," Kyle said, "we're trying to build a picture of your friend Eliot Spence. It's what we do to give ourselves a deeper understanding of a crime victim and help us locate persons of interest. So...tell us about Eliot Spence."

Gilbert squirmed in the chair, staring at Kyle as though it was a trick question. He said, "You don't know who killed him?"

"Do you?" Kyle said.

Gilbert shrugged. "Probably his late wife's sister. They had a very bad relationship. You know that she was suing him to get her hands on Lenore's life insurance money?"

"As was her brother," Burgess said. "What can you tell us about his relationship with his sister-in-law?"

"It was bad," Gilbert repeated. "She and Lenore, his late wife, were very close. She never accepted the fact that Lenore's death was an accident. She truly believed that Eliot was responsible. She was angry."

"Angry enough to kill him?"

Gilbert shrugged again. "I don't know. But she's the only person who comes to mind when you ask who might have wanted to kill him. She's a very angry, bitter person. Plus, I expect she and the brother would inherit if...when...I mean, now that Eliot is dead, and they're both always bugging Eliot for handouts, especially the brother. They will inherit, won't they?"

Burgess didn't know. He hadn't found a will in his search through Spence's papers, but he hadn't had time to do a thorough vetting of what he'd collected. Unless a will specified otherwise, he'd expect Spence's money to go to Spence's family.

"So, the sister was angry and vindictive. What about the brother?"

"He's a total wimp," Gilbert said. "Does whatever his sister tells him to do. He just wants to smoke dope, play video games, and eat junk food. And take handouts from Eliot."

Gilbert seemed to be considering whether there were other possible suspects because he said, "It doesn't seem like something she'd do, but have you spoken with DeeDee? If she knew about Eliot's proclivity for hookers, she might have...I don't know...decided to put an end to that behavior."

Gilbert looked at them, his head tilted like he was curious. "Was Eliot's death very violent? There was nothing in the papers."

Burgess and Kyle exchanged a look. So, the imperious Deidre Lovejoy was DeeDee to Spence and his friend? Hadn't the cleaner said she'd specifically been told not to call Lovejoy DeeDee? "We don't give out those details," Burgess said. "So, you think Deidre Lovejoy didn't know about Dr. Spence's penchant for entertaining prostitutes?"

"She'd never stand for it. Too proud to share Eliot with paid companions. Eliot was trying to rein in those proclivities. He found it difficult."

There was, Burgess knew, such a thing as sex addiction. "Do you know how often Dr. Spence...uh...indulged in those proclivities?"

Gilbert shook his head.

"What about how often the two of you met with girls here?"

Gilbert didn't answer unless a squirm was an answer. So easy to fool yourself into thinking that you have a minor problem until you are forced to examine it.

"Once a week? Once a month? A few times a year?" Kyle asked.

"Maybe once a month."

"Were you aware that Dr. Spence also entertained women at his condo?"

Gilbert shrugged, then muttered a reluctant "Yeah."

"Did you join him on those occasions?"

"Nope."

"Never? You never used Spence's condo to meet prostitutes?"

Gilbert shrugged. "Maybe once or twice. But never the two of us together. There's only the one bed, see."

"Witnesses have suggested that Dr. Spence had a fondness for curvy blondes. In your experience, was that true?"

Gilbert didn't answer.

"Were there particular girls that you and Dr. Spence would request? Regulars?"

Gilbert didn't answer.

"If you know, did Dr. Spence ever have difficulties with any of the women he hired for sex?"

"Difficulties?"

"Women who might have been angry at their treatment? How much they were paid? Anything like that?"

"Not that he ever told me. But he wouldn't, would he? I mean, I think he treated them well enough. They came and did what he hired them to do; he paid, and that was that."

As though these transactions involved robots rather than other human beings.

"How long have you and Dr. Spence been using this hotel for your meetings?"

Gilbert tapped his forehead with a finger as though he was knocking the answer into place. His forehead was wet with sweat, and his carefully gelled hair was falling apart, revealing the beginnings of a bald spot. He was a paunchy man with a florid face. Stress did not bring out the best in him.

"I guess about a year. I'm not sure."

"His idea or yours?"

"His."

"Who arranged for the room?"

"I usually did."

"And for the girls?"

"One of us would call Marni, and she'd take care of it."

Like ordering a pizza or Chinese takeout.

"Did you know Dr. Spence before he moved to Portland?"

"Nope."

"How did the two of you meet?"

"Golf. Eliot was an avid golfer, as am I."

Burgess was wondering what else to ask when Kyle said, "None of the women you employed ever threatened to disclose your activities to your wife or Spence's girlfriend?"

Gilbert didn't answer with words, but his body language said a clear yes. Without waiting for a denial, Kyle said, "Tell us about that."

"It was nothing," Gilbert said. "Marni took care of it."

Speaking with Marni was definitely next on their list. Before they let Gilbert leave, Burgess had one more question. "Do you know whether Dr. Spence routinely paid for sex when he was married to Lenore?"

Gilbert shook his head. "From all that he's said, I believe Eliot was totally infatuated with Lenore. But..." A shrug. "It's hard to believe he could keep his compulsive need for sex in check all those years."

Burgess agreed. How likely was it that a man with a compulsive and expensive sex addiction like Spence's could leave all that behind for fifteen years? On the other hand, how would he hide the expense from his wife?

"Thank you," he said. "We may be back to you with follow-up questions, but for now, we're done."

Gilbert popped to his feet like a Jack-in-the-Box. "Just so my wife doesn't hear about this."

Burgess and Kyle, like a pair of twins, shrugged. They weren't in the business of harming marriages, but they would make no promises.

They watched Gilbert make his unsteady way to the door.

"That's a heart attack waiting to happen," Kyle said. "Glad it's not on our watch. Speaking of watches," he checked his. "We should find Marni and get that over with. I've got people waiting, and they aren't very patient."

"While we are the very essence of patience."

THIRTY-THREE

M arni Gleason, the woman they'd seen in the lobby giving a room key to Lisa Lockner, was now ensconced behind a cheap faux wood desk, cupped by an oversized blue office chair. She had a pair of red-framed cheater glasses on a string around her neck. She did not look happy to see them.

As he and Kyle took seats across from her, she pursed her mouth and sucked in air in a manner that told Burgess she was about to utter the familiar, "I didn't do anything." But she surprised him.

"You're here about Dr. Spence, I expect," she said. "The man was a royal pain in the ass. It's never nice to be happy about a person's death, but I will at least say it's a relief. He was a good customer but barely worth the effort."

"By which you mean?" Burgess prompted.

"That he had standards and demands that were difficult to meet."

"Elaborate, please."

"They had to be blonde. They had to be young. They had to be voluptuous. They had to have really great bodies. And they had to be instructed not to open their mouths except when he wanted them to. A lot of our girls are quite young and can get chatty when they're nervous. He once tossed a girl out into the hallway, naked, because he said she talked too much. That cost me a lot of money—calming her down, plus she needed to be paid, and he refused to."

It was astonishing, Burgess thought, how utterly calm she was, describing activities that were clearly against the law. He looked at Kyle and got a faint nod. They were both wondering whether she had—or believed she had—some kind of protection for her activities. That could wait. For now, they wanted to know what she could tell them about Dr. Spence.

"You booked the room and arranged for the women?" Burgess asked.

She nodded.

"Was it always Dr. Spence and Mr. Gilbert?"

Another nod. "But sometimes Dr. Spence wanted women sent to his home."

"Sometimes?"

Her smile was cynical. "Sometimes meaning at least once a month. It was an expensive habit Dr. Spence had."

"How did Dr. Spence find you?"

"Jeff Gilbert. He's got his own sex addiction, though, of course, calling it an addiction would be...uh...wouldn't put a very positive spin on my business." She leaned forward as though she was confiding in them. "If it weren't for people...for men...with an oversized need for sex, I wouldn't have my business, would I? Just catering to a need, like those for food or alcohol or tobacco or drugs. I'm a realist, detectives. I provide a needed service. No one is harmed by it."

Burgess thought about Jeff Gilbert's wife and the pain she'd feel if she knew about his extracurricular activities. About the money that he spent and whether his family went without so he could pay hookers. About Eliot Spence, now dead because of something that was probably linked to his sex life. About young women risking exploitation, disease, and violence when they used their bodies to earn money. He'd seen plenty of harm that came from the sex trade. He believed women had the right to bodily autonomy, but the system too often turned them into victims.

"Can you tell us who you sent to Dr. Spence's condo two nights ago?"

"I can give you a name and the phone number I used to contact her, but I think you'll find that they're both false."

He said, "I'll take that woman's name and number."

Marni opened a desk drawer, pulled out a notebook, and leafed through a few pages. "Here's what I have," she said and gave them the name—Alana Black—and a number.

He wrote the information down, already knowing it was useless. Burgess knew Alana Black. Knew her very well. A former hooker and one he believed he and Chris had set on a better track. He knew some other things as well: that Alana Black was neither white nor blonde and definitely not Dr. Spence's type and that the phone number wasn't hers.

"How did you find this woman?"

She shrugged. "She found me. A lot of them do. I've got a reputation as a straight shooter. Decent surroundings. Good pay. Someone around to call on if things go south or the man is trouble. The girls appreciate that."

"So, she contacted you, looking for work?"

"She did."

"Has she worked for you often?"

"She's new. The gig at Dr. Spence's condo was the first job she's done for me."

Now Kyle had a question. "How was she paid?"

"She wanted cash."

"Is that the usual arrangement?"

Marni shrugged. "We're mostly a cash business. No paper trail that way. The girls like it. The johns like it. I like it."

"Before you sent the girl calling herself Alana Black to Dr. Spence, I assume you met her so that you could assess whether she would suit the tastes of the man you describe as a fussy client?" Burgess asked.

"I did."

"Here?"

She nodded.

"When was that?"

"Maybe a week ago. Obviously, I have to meet the girls and assess their suitability before I can send them on jobs."

"What can you tell us about her?"

Marni tapped her jawline as she considered. "A little older than most of my girls. Maybe mid-thirties, but she had a spectacular figure. Big boobs. Long legs. A tiny little waist. And really beautiful hair. Long and wavy. Dr. Spence had a thing about hair. He liked it long. And, of course, blonde. She was very pretty and had done an excellent job on her makeup."

"Makeup matters?" Kyle said.

"Of course. Part of this is about sex. About the sex act. Getting their rocks off. But part of it, for many men, is about their fantasies. About getting to be with women they could never attract on their own."

"But Dr. Spence was an attractive man with a stunning girlfriend."

She nodded. "There's plenty of that Madonna/whore thing going on as well. The wives and girlfriends are the lovely, decent women. My girls are the whores. They can show a side of themselves to my girls they'd never show to their wives or girlfriends."

God, she was matter-of-fact. Her girls were viewed, and sold, as objects to satisfy men's lust. "What do your girls get out of this?" Burgess asked.

"Money. Better money than they can make in most of the jobs they're qualified for. Some of them are college girls looking for a way to pay tuition. Some are high school girls looking for some spending money. Some of them are young working girls looking to earn a little extra money. I've even got a few bored housewives looking to supplement their household incomes."

"So, this girl, woman, the one you most recently sent to Dr. Spence, she got in touch with you, right?" Burgess said. "And you arranged for her to come here so you could meet her? Is that your usual practice? You're comfortable having the girls come here, with knowing where you work?"

"It hasn't been a problem. I have something they want. They have something I want."

"Did this girl leave a message and you called her back, or did you speak with her the first time she called?"

Marni considered the question. "I think that she left a message, and I called her back."

"On your office phone or your personal phone?"

"On my cell."

"Is the number you called the one she called you from or the one she left in her message to you?"

If she found his questions annoying, she didn't show it. She said, "I think I just hit redial. I don't know. I suppose I figured I was just calling the same number she'd left."

Burgess looked at Kyle, who seemed to have some questions he wanted to ask. He said, "Just one or two more, and it's your turn." To Marni, he said, "So, you spoke with her once to arrange a meeting to vet her for the job. Then, there was a second time to arrange for her to visit Dr. Spence at his condo. Is that right?"

She shook her head. "It was odd, given how eager she was to get some work. I called her with another job a day or two before her appointment with Dr. Spence, and she said she couldn't do it."

"With Dr. Spence…did you tell her who her customer would be before she agreed?"

Marni nodded.

"Who makes the arrangements for the girls to get to their customers, you or the girls?"

"It depends. Some of the girls like me to do it. Others, like this new one, Alana, are comfortable making their own arrangements."

"So, you don't know whether she used Uber or a taxi or her own car?"

"I don't."

Burgess nodded at Kyle.

Kyle said, "Do you take pictures of your girls? Keep a kind of a Facebook in case your Johns want to choose?"

Why hadn't he thought of that? It made sense, given how businesslike she was.

"I do."

"So, can we see a picture of the girl you sent to Dr. Spence?"

She looked uncomfortable. "She didn't want her picture taken. It was kind of odd under the circumstances. She said she was fine doing the work, but she didn't like having her picture involved."

"So, you don't have a picture?"

Silence. Burgess was sure it meant she had a photo but hadn't been straight with the girl about that and wasn't sure she should share it with him. "As far as we know, she's the last person to see Dr. Spence alive," Burgess said. "If she's involved in any way in a murder, you don't want to be helping her get away with that. If she's not, she still may have information valuable to the investigation."

"You don't know that—" she began, then stopped. "Fine. You can have her photo."

She began to scroll through her phone. Burgess thought she would send them to a website, but maybe sharing pictures of all her girls was too much openness. After a minute of scrolling and frowning, she handed him her phone. The woman was, as described, very blonde and very beautiful. She was also at least a decade older than the girl they'd followed upstairs, probably more. Closer to forty than thirty. He wondered if that had been a problem for Spence.

He sent himself and Kyle the photo.

"The message where she gave you her phone number...the number you just gave us, was that in a phone call or a text?"

"Text."

"And that's the number you used when you contacted her to make arrangements to meet?"

She nodded.

"Did you call or text?"

"I texted."

Kyle held out his hand for her phone. "May we see that text, please?"

She hugged the phone to her chest and glared at Kyle. "You can't have it. My phone. I need it for work."

Burgess wondered how many clients she had. How many girls. How many rooms in this place were regularly rented for sex, and who in the hotel knew about it. Whether they were paid to turn a blind eye. Whether it had been on the police radar, just not on his or Kyle's. Questions to ask back at 109.

"This the only hotel you use for meetings with your girls?" he asked as she scrolled through her phone.

"What do you think?"

Getting snippy. He wondered whether she was having second thoughts about cooperating or whether she had another girl or another John to meet in the lobby and didn't want to keep them waiting. Or have one of them see her with two guys whose demeanor advertised "POLICE."

"I think you should answer my question," he said.

"I've got a business to run," she said.

"So do we."

She found the text and reluctantly handed her phone to Kyle.

Kyle read it, nodded, and then scrolled through all of her messages with the girl who called herself Alana Black. He made some notes and then checked her recent calls. A lot of recent calls. It must be quite a thriving business. On the night that Eliot Spence was killed, there was a call to her phone from the number that the girl had given Marni at around twelve-thirty at night.

He held the phone out to her and pointed to that call. "She called you at twelve-thirty on the night Dr. Spence was killed. What was that call about?"

She became fascinated with studying her nails as she said, "It's routine. I have the girls give me a quick call or text when they leave a job to confirm that all went well. Payment is done to me with a credit card. This lets me know that it's okay to send the girls cash to pay what they're owed."

He said, "The girls always call you?"

"It's routine," she said, which didn't answer the question.

"How did she sound when she called?" he asked.

"Fine. Normal. Not upset, if that's what you're asking."

Could be this woman wasn't the killer. Could be she was just cold.

Burgess hoped they weren't looking at a female serial killer, which would take this case in an entirely new direction.

He looked at Kyle, who was moving restlessly in his chair. There were more things they could try to learn here, but Kyle needed to get home, and Marni was on the verge of clamming up anyway. They'd probably gotten all they were going to get for now.

He stood, and Kyle followed suit. Burgess checked his notebook, read off a number, and said, "Is this the best number to reach you?"

She nodded.

"And your home address is?"

"You don't need that."

"We might need that."

With the two of them between her and the door, she decided cooperation was her best choice. She gave them an address.

"Any other phone numbers we could use to reach you?"

Reluctantly, she gave them her landline number.

"If this girl who calls herself Alana Black contacts you, please tell her we need to speak with her. And call us, and let us know she's been in touch," Burgess said. "Are we clear?"

"Yes. Dammit. You're clear. Now, will you please leave so I can get some work done?"

Kyle touched his forehead in a mock salute. "Until next time."

"I hope there is no next time," she said as she slid past them and into the lobby.

Across the room, a pretty young blonde girl perched on the edge of one of the leather chairs. Nervous as hell. Her skimpy coat suggested she wore little underneath it. She didn't look more than sixteen.

Burgess and Kyle exchanged looks. Marni's little business needed to be shut down and soon. But for now, they had other demands on their time. "I'll make a call to vice," Burgess said in a low voice.

They went out in the fall darkness to their cars and drove away.

In his car, Burgess got a call from Sage Prentiss. "I'm at the hospital with Aaron Daggett, Joe. I think you need to swing by and hear what he has to say."

THIRTY-FOUR

B urgess took time on the drive to the hospital to call the lieutenant who headed up vice and asked about Marni's little business at the hotel by the airport. He got a noncommittal "It's on our radar" and a little more. Sometimes, it seemed like they weren't one unified department working together to fight crime and protect the citizens of Portland but a bunch of people in individual silos more interested in protecting their turf than doing their jobs.

It was a battle he'd fought on various fields since he was a rookie and one he'd fight again. He didn't want to think about a fellow officer taking bribes to look the other way, but Marni certainly hadn't seemed concerned about police interfering in her business. He didn't have time to worry about it now.

He made a quick call to Chris to check on Nina, but the call went to voice mail. She was tied up, or they were eating dinner. Eventually, he hoped he'd be eating dinner, too, but it was way down the list right now.

He pulled into the hospital lot, parked, and called Prentiss to say he'd arrived. He got a gloomy, "Kid's changed his mind and doesn't want to talk" in reply.

Well, fuck that. A man was dead. Aaron had come close to dying, and his sister Kristin was still at risk, out there somewhere in a city on a cold night where darkness had fallen, and a killer might be looking for her. "I'll talk to him anyway," Burgess said. "Maybe he'll cough up a nugget or two."

It was an unattractive image.

He took the elevator. By this point in a long day, his bad knee liked to mess with him, and he didn't have time for the way pain could sap his energy. He took a few Advil and told it to settle down.

He found Aaron in bed wearing a sullen expression and Prentiss in a chair wearing an exasperated one.

"Detective Sergeant Burgess," he said to the boy in the bed. "I'm the one who found you after you were attacked. Do you remember that?"

The boy in the bed shrugged.

"We've been hoping that you'd recall more about the circumstances of that attack, and Detective Prentiss tells me that you have." He pulled the second visitor's chair close to the bed and sat. He made himself move slowly. A man at ease. No pressure. No sense of urgency. He got out his notebook. Clicked his pen. Said, "What can you tell me about that attack?"

"I got hit on the head," the boy said unhelpfully.

"Was the person who hit you facing you or behind you?"

Not a question the boy was expecting. He said, "Behind me."

"So, when you came into your bedroom, he or she was already there waiting for you?"

A shrug. "I guess."

Burgess nodded. "Do you have any idea whether your attacker was taller than you?"

"No idea."

"How tall are you, Aaron?"

"Between five nine and five ten, I guess."

The angle of the blow suggested someone taller, and Burgess made a mental note to see if he could learn how tall Lenore's siblings were. The woman who'd told them about a stranger waiting outside who'd gotten into Aaron's building had said the person was a tall man in a baggy suit. But she might not be a very reliable witness. And there had been a second person she'd referred to that she'd been vague about.

"So, the person hit you from behind, and you have no idea whether they were tall or short. Any idea whether they were male or female?"

"Had to be a guy to hit me that hard," Aaron said.

"You came into the apartment and went right to your room?"

A nod.

"You didn't stop in the living room?"

"Nope. Wanted to put some stuff in my pack, then I was going to grab something to eat on my way out."

"You didn't see your roommate?"

"He was asleep. At least, the door to his room was closed, and it was quiet."

"Do you remember anything from before you were attacked? Any strange noises or scents? Anything disturbed? Any sense that someone other than your roommate had been in the apartment?"

The boy considered the question, then nodded. "There was smell. A scent. Something sort of flowery."

"More like a woman's perfume or beauty product? A generic body wash or shampoo? Or more like a scented cleaning product?" Probably too many variables in that question.

The boy thought about it. Once he'd gotten going, he was answering Burgess's questions and seemed to have forgotten about his intention not to cooperate. He said, "Perfume. Or aftershave. Things are pretty unisex these days, and all the bodywashes and soaps are scented. And detergents, too. It was kind of like what The Wicked uses to do laundry." He paused, then corrected to, "What The Wicked has Kristin use to do the laundry."

"Your attacker didn't speak?"

Aaron shook his head, then clapped his hand to the side of his head. "Oh. Ugh! Shouldn't have done that."

"Right," Burgess agreed. "It can feel like your brain is sloshing. So, nothing from your attacker. After you were struck, could you tell if your attacker checked on you to see if you were alive?"

"I...uh...it's strange, but I think I could feel someone's breath on my neck, so I stayed very still."

"You're doing great," Burgess said. "This is all very helpful. Did you hear the person leave?"

Aaron Daggett considered. "Sorta. Quick, light footsteps, and then the door shut, and then I kind of drifted away. I was thinking I needed to move. To get myself some help. Only I couldn't. And then it was like I was gone, you know?"

"I know. Do you have any sense of how much time passed between when you got home and when I found you?"

"Nah. None. But I got home around twelve. What time did you find me?"

Burgess told him, then switched subjects. "Your sister. Kristin. She was here with you, and then she ran away. She hasn't gone home. We've been looking for her but haven't found her yet. It's concerning that she's out there on her own and at risk. Do you know of any place we should look? Somewhere she might go to hide? Someone she might stay with?"

Aaron looked confused. "I thought she went home with The Wicked?"

"Your stepmother left while Kristin was still here. She doesn't seem very concerned. And your father was also here and then left. Which means you and your sister are pretty much on your own. We've got someone watching you, but no one watching her. So, I'll ask again, in case you know, is there someone Kristin would turn to? Some place she'd go besides where your father and stepmother live?"

Aaron considered that. Started to shake his head. Stopped. Said, "Maybe one of her teammates? But I don't know who they are. It's difficult to keep up when I'm living with Sam and going to school and working, and she's there with them. The Wicked ought to know."

The boy sighed and closed his eyes. Neither he nor Burgess thought that was likely.

A decent person would have left him to rest then. The boy had been through a lot. But Burgess had to prioritize his investigation over manners. He said, "You spent some time down at the condos where your sister lives. People have reported seeing you there. Were you there two nights ago, the night that Dr. Spence was killed?"

This time, the boy knew better than to nod. He said, "I was there."

"Did you see a blonde woman arrive around eight?"

The boy snorted a laugh. "You mean one of Spence's hookers?"

"I do. What can you tell me about her?"

The boy's eyes closed again. Burgess was wearing him out. Well, Burgess was almost done. He waited.

"She was different from the others."

"Different, how?"

"Older. Taller. Beautiful rather than pretty or sexy. More poised and confident. Some of them practically creep into the garage, and the outfits they wear, they scream prostitute. This one could have been going to a fancy club. Sexy dress and shoes but not tacky, if you know what I mean. Like classy. And she was carrying what I'm pretty sure was a designer handbag."

"Did the others have handbags?"

"Yeah. But not like this."

Burgess asked, "You know about designer bags because?"

The boy grinned. "Because The Wicked spends a wicked amount of money on them. They haven't got money for me, and they treat Kristin like freaking Cinderella, but The Wicked spends like money comes out of the faucet. My dad goes apeshit over it, but she just shrugs."

"So, you saw this woman arrive. Did you see her leave?"

"I had to go to work."

"Right. So, you didn't. Have you seen her there before?"

"Coming to visit Dr. Spence? No. But I may have seen her another time, sitting in a parked car, watching the condo. But she's not the only one. I've seen a couple other people doing that, too. The tall ones. A man and a woman. They're always dressed in business suits like they've just come from work. I've seen them together, and I've seen her by herself."

"Anyone else who seemed out of place? Who didn't live there or who appeared to be watching Dr. Spence or his condo?"

"Oh, yeah. The ginger's wife."

"The ginger?"

"Sorry. Spence's golf buddy, the one with the kind of orange hair. Kristin says they're called 'gingers,' and I liked that, so I adopted it."

"But this was his wife? How do you know that?"

The boy shrugged. Carefully, so as not to jar his head. "Well, I mean, I assumed she was his wife. They've been at Spence's place for dinner with him and his girlfriend."

"This is a long shot, but do you know if Spence's girlfriend knew about his hookers?"

This time, Aaron forgot himself and nodded, then grabbed his head with both hands. "Oh God. Christ. Dammit, that hurts."

Burgess waited for the pain to subside, then nudged, "Spence's girlfriend. How did she know about the hookers?"

"Like everyone else, she sometimes watched the place."

A regular parade of people who were watching Dr. Spence. Burgess wondered whether Spence's security cameras had caught them or if they'd stayed out of range. Maybe Spence had good reasons to be so paranoid.

Burgess stood. Time to let the boy rest. "Thank you, Aaron. You've been a great help. Now, I'm going to go and look for your sister." He put a card on the table beside the bed. "My number, in case you think of anything else I should know."

He signaled for Prentiss to join him outside. "Seems like a lot of people might want to silence this kid. I'll get someone to watch him so you can go home and get some sleep."

"Thanks, Sarge. Appreciate it."

Burgess was lumbering away when Prentiss said, "I hope someday I'll be as good an interviewer as you are."

He turned. "You will." Then he took the elevator down to his car. It was definitely time for another interview with Deidre Lovejoy. Right now, though, he was going back down to the condos to see if Kristin had come home. If not, he'd have to look for her. And he didn't know where to look.

THIRTY-FIVE

I n the car, he called Alana Black. He couldn't think how the woman who'd gotten set up with Spence could know Alana, but he wanted to check. She answered with her usual, "Hello, Copman," followed by, "To what do I owe the pleasure?"

He didn't like it when she played games with him, so he was straight with her. "Murder down on the waterfront. Got a girl who was with our victim the night he was killed. The name she was using was Alana Black."

"It wasn't me," she said. "I've reformed."

"I know that, Alana. Just trying to figure out how she might have gotten your name."

"It ain't…isn't…trademarked or anything. I suppose it could really be her name. Probably there are dozens of us if not hundreds."

Burgess had met Alana when she was a sixteen-year-old, new to town. Gorgeous and sexy as hell, the other women in the game had decided she was too much competition. They'd beaten the crap out of her and left her naked and bleeding in a city park in the winter. Burgess had found her and taken her to the hospital, and that had been the beginning of an interesting up-and-down friendship. Now, she was a trained massage therapist and, he hoped, on the straight and narrow.

"What can you tell me about her?" Alana asked.

Burgess shared the little he knew.

"Not ringing any bells. Doesn't sound like someone I've met."

He was about to hang up—places to go and people to see—when she said, "Wait. There was a woman. Woman, not girl. Said she was a reporter doing an article on ladies of the night and wanted to interview me. Said she'd found me in an old article about that doctor who got killed. It was years ago. I said I couldn't help; I've been out of the business a long time. She was pushy and said she'd pay me for my time, so I agreed to meet her."

"You get a name? Check her ID, see if she was for real?"

"You're the cop, Joe, not me. Remember?"

He remembered. And sighed. A cop could hope, right? "You at least got a name, right?"

"Right. She said her name was Gwen. Gwen Sykes. And I did take her picture when she wasn't paying attention. She was looking for something in her bag. Money to pay me. She paid me very generously, by the way. Look, Copman. It has been way too long since we've gotten together. Why don't you come by and have some coffee? I'll tell you what I know, and we can catch up."

Even for a man as controlled as Burgess was—and he was very controlled—getting close to Alana Black was dangerous. Dangerous even with their boundaries well established. She was, bar none, the sexiest woman he'd ever met. She wore it like an aura; it followed her, trailing around her like an infectious cloud. He could be around her and resist it, but it took energy. Alana might have learned to hold the world of men at bay, but she sometimes couldn't resist trying to seduce him. Something that was true even though she'd spent time with his family and liked Chris.

"I don't have the time right now," he said. "In the first days of a homicide, and I'm looking for a missing thirteen-year-old girl who may be at risk."

"You're not just avoiding me?"

"Trying to do my job as best I can before I fall asleep on my feet, Alana. Can you send me the picture? And tell me whether there's anything else you know that might be useful?"

"She was a knock-out, if you like tall and blonde. A natural blonde, I think. Closer to forty than thirty but wearing it well. Nice clothes. Expensive clothes. Understated jewelry. Fancy purse. She drove a black BMW sedan."

"License plate?"

She laughed. "I don't have the number if that's what you're asking, but it was a Massachusetts plate."

"Was she a credible interviewer?"

That got another laugh. "Credible enough, I guess. She'd done some homework. She asked real questions about handling clients, about various sex acts, about pricing." He could almost hear Alana shrug. "I told her I was way out of date. She'd need to find someone still in the game. I put her onto a friend, and I don't know where things went from there."

"The friend's name wasn't Marni, was it?"

"Oh. Marni. I wouldn't send anyone to her. She runs a decent shop, I suppose, but she's a mean bitch who exploits kids. Young girls who don't know any better. Like I used to be, I suppose. I suppose…" She trailed off, then said, "I suppose I would have been better off if I'd had someone like Marni to look after me. But then, I probably never would have met you and gotten my life together. It's complicated, isn't it?"

It was complicated. He considered whether there was anything else he should ask her. Finally said, "Will you give me the name of the woman you sent her to? And how to find her?"

"I'll text you that and the photograph. Sure you don't have time for coffee? I make a wicked good one."

"I'm sure you do. I barely have time to breathe. When this is over, we'll do coffee, okay?"

"Promise?"

"I promise. Maybe you can come to dinner sometime. The kids would love to see you."

"Practically all grown up," she said. "And Dylan looking just like a younger you. The girls must be crazy about him."

Which was true, so he agreed.

"Bye, Alana. Thanks for the help. You stay safe, okay?"

"I always try, Copman. You know that. I could say the same to you."

"I always try, too."

She laughed and disconnected. A minute later, he got a text with a photograph, and right after that, one with a name, phone number, and address. Something else to follow up tomorrow. Compare Alana's photo with the one from Marni. Right now, he needed to look for Kristin Daggett.

He'd start at the condo, hoping she'd gone home after leaving the hospital. He seemed to be hoping a lot lately, even though it was often futile to do so.

He parked in front of Spence's condo, crossed the street, and rang the Daggett's doorbell. Nothing. He rang it again. Still nothing. He checked his watch. It was almost ten. He supposed The Wicked might have gone to bed. The Wicked and her errant husband? Well, too bad for them if that was the case. They might not care where Kristin was, but Burgess did.

He rang a third time, this time keeping his finger on the button for an annoyingly long time. If anyone was home, it ought to bring them to the door if only to make him shut up and go away.

After an irritatingly long wait, the door was jerked open, and a man in pajamas and a robe said, "What the hell do you want?"

"Detective Sergeant Burgess," he said. "Looking for Kristin Daggett. Wellness check."

The man shrugged. "Can't help you. Sorry. She's not here."

"She's thirteen. It's late in the evening. Her brother has been attacked and is in the hospital. Her safety is important. Are you her father?"

The man shrugged like he really didn't know, then said, "Yeah," without elaboration.

"Do you know where your daughter is?"

Another shrug. "Nope. My wife was supposed to bring her back from the hospital. She didn't. That's all I know."

"Sir, she's *your* daughter. She's very young. And that's all you know? What efforts have you made to locate her?"

The man's expression veered between annoyed and guilty, finally settling on annoyed. "It's late. I'm tired. I'm just back from a business trip, and I have an important meeting in the morning. I don't have time to track down a willful kid—"

"Willful child?" Burgess said, stepping closer to Daggett and forcing him back into the condo. "Your son's been attacked and nearly died. Now your daughter, who may also be at risk, is missing, and you aren't concerned about her?"

"My wife..." Daggett began, then trailed off with a shrug and fell silent.

Burgess figured this deliberately passive response was the man's M.O. Nothing to argue with or push against because there was nothing there. He said, "We need to locate her. Where would she go? Let's start with a list of her soccer teammates. Maybe she's gone to stay with one of them."

He stepped farther into the room, forcing Daggett backward.

"I don't know who they are," Daggett said.

"There must be a roster with phone numbers. You must have her game schedule. The name of her coach."

Daggett produced another shrug. "My wife is supposed to take care of those things," he said.

"Then let's ask your wife." Burgess was pretty sure that The Wicked, infuriated by her husband's infidelity, had decamped to somewhere else.

"She's not home."

"Then you can call her, right?"

"Look. This is my kid. My problem. Why don't you toddle off and harass someone else, Officer?"

"Detective Sergeant. Investigating a homicide and an attempted homicide that involves your son. Your daughter is a witness in a dangerous situation. I will definitely be notifying social services about the situation. In the meantime, I am not, as you put it, toddling off anywhere until you take whatever steps you can to locate your daughter. Try her cell phone."

He paused. "Does she have a cell phone?"

Daggett, unsurprisingly, shrugged. "I don't know."

Burgess repressed an angry, "How can you not know?" and said, "Who pays the phone bill?"

Mr. Shrug said, "I do."

"So, you can look at the bill and see what her phone number is, can't you?"

Mr. Shrug shrugged, then said, "All that stuff is at my office."

"Well, what about checking your phone? Has your daughter called you on your phone? Because there would be a record of that."

Mr. Shrug looked around briefly and said he didn't know where his phone was.

Burgess, patience sorely tried, suppressed the urge to rearrange the man's features and growled, "Look for it."

The man wandered off, climbed the stairs, and disappeared. For a minute, Burgess could hear him moving around, then nothing.

Had the asshole actually had the audacity to go back to bed despite a police officer waiting for him downstairs? An audacious asshole had an amusing alliteration. Smiling at that sentence, which lightened his mood, Burgess headed for the stairs.

Mr. Shrug hadn't gotten into bed but was perched on the edge of it, phone in hand, punching in a number. Burgess lingered in the doorway, listening. Shrug didn't seem to have noticed him. When someone on the other end answered, Burgess heard Shrug say, "Dammit, Kristin. Where the hell are you? I've got a cop here looking for you. What kind of trouble are you in anyway? Haven't I got enough trouble with your brother already? I don't need it from you."

Whatever she said in response didn't please him. He said, "Why didn't you come home? If it's my wife who's the problem, she's not here. You've pretty much seen to that."

Burgess could imagine Kristin's soft voice saying, "I've seen to that? I'm not the one who was in bed with another woman." But she probably didn't say that. She was probably trying to make her father see the illogic of what he'd said in a gentler way.

Whatever she said, it didn't please her father. He said, "Never mind. I'll let you speak to the cop. He's waiting downstairs." A pause, and then, "Yeah. That's the one. And no, he's not a nice guy. He's a pain in the ass."

Burgess retreated down the stairs to wait for Daggett. If the thud of footsteps on the stairs was any indication, Daggett was more displeased than ever.

He handed Burgess the phone with a sharp, "Kristin. She wants to speak with you."

It sounded very nose out of joint. Man doesn't want to be a parent but gets upset when someone else is concerned? What a jerk.

Burgess took the phone and said, "Kristin. Joe Burgess. Where are you? Are you okay?"

"Spending the night with one of my soccer teammates," she said. "And yes. I'm okay. I'm fine."

He fumbled out his notebook and opened it with one hand. Spread it on the counter and got out his pen. "Give me your phone number. And where you are." She did, and he wrote it down. "We need to talk again. But not now. Tomorrow after school work for you?"

"Sure. Unless you want to come to school and call me out of class and get everyone wondering what kind of trouble I'm in." There was humor in her voice. Like Nina, this girl was a survivor.

"Sure. If you want. Which school?" He wrote that down, too. "Okay. Get some sleep. Your brother seems much better, and we've got a cop in his room, so he should be okay. I just need to know that you are, too."

Again, there was humor in her voice as she said, "Thank you. I'm fine, and Shelby's mom will keep me safe. She's one of those dragon moms." Humor turned to wistful. She wished she had a dragon mom, too, he figured. Or any kind of a mom instead of some indifferent person correctly labeled The Wicked.

He disconnected and handed the phone back to Daggett. Without asking about his daughter, the man said, "You can let yourself out. I'm going back to sleep."

Back in his car, he studied the photo Alana Black had sent. Definitely blonde. Definitely beautiful. And not as young as Marni's girls. Then he compared it with the photo he'd gotten from Marni of the woman who'd called herself Alana Black. Neither photo was very good, but he thought it was the same woman. Something to follow up tomorrow. Right now, like Kristin Daggett and her idiot father, Joe Burgess needed to get some sleep.

THIRTY-SIX

O nce again, like a thief in the night, he shed his shoes at the top of the stairs and walked quietly inside. A quick scan of the downstairs showed that the renovation work had progressed a little, which was good for his temper.

In the kitchen, he was happy to find a note on the table indicating that a plate of food was keeping warm in the oven. Much as he'd like to reform his eating habits, the job, at least the way he did it, seemed incompatible with that. These days, with Chris and her cooking on his side, he consumed far fewer meals at fast food joints.

Tonight, he sat at the table and ate meatloaf and mashed potatoes. The peas had gotten a little tired while they waited, but it was a small price to pay for the rest. He washed his dishes and was heading for bed when Nina appeared.

"Dad? Have you got a minute?"

How could he say no?

He sat back down and waited while she poured herself a glass of milk and sat across from him. Without preamble, she said, "Are you sure that Dexter won't be at school tomorrow? Because no way could I face that."

He wanted to be reassuring and say, "Absolutely no way," but too many years dealing with the vagaries of the justice system prevented him. Instead, he said, "He shouldn't be. Those are serious charges. Sometimes, judges get too soft-hearted and give breaks to people who shouldn't get them, so I can't promise. What I can promise is that if, for some absurd reason, he is allowed to return to school, you call me, and we will get a restraining order preventing him from being in your classes or coming anywhere near you. I can almost guarantee we won't have any trouble getting that."

"But if he's there...Dad, what do I do?"

"You call me immediately, and I will take it from there."

God, what a world they lived in where a girl who'd been abducted and assaulted would have to worry about being forced to face her abuser at school. "I mean it, Nina. If he's there, you call me."

"Okay, Dad. I will." She said it weakly, like she'd just received another blow she was struggling to recover from. She finished her milk, put the glass in the sink, and wandered off to bed.

He sat at the table, staring into space as he tried to quell his anger. He gives his life to protecting victims and getting them justice, and then, they can't rely on the system for the protection they're entitled to.

True, he was jumping the gun. He didn't know that the system would fail her. He was just a cynic. And the product of experience. Nina here at home, and Kristin and Aaron, just kids, trying to navigate a world where responsible adults had abandoned them. The world was so fucked up.

Before he went to bed, he checked his phone in case there were messages he'd missed. There was one from Andrea Dwyer. A cryptic "Good news. Dexter Wiggins' parents are sending him out of state to school. Or will, if the court allows. Meanwhile, he's on house arrest."

Maybe it was good news, the out-of-state part anyway, though that might take weeks to reach fruition. The house arrest part required some parental attention and Wiggins's cooperation unless they had him wearing a bracelet. At least Wiggins wouldn't be in school. He thought it was a weak-assed result, given what the boy had done. Still, he felt lighter as he headed for bed. With luck, he'd get some sleep before the challenges, questions, and witnesses on his endless to-do list started calling his name.

Despite having resisted the impulse to imitate Dr. Spence and his wife and leave his phone outside the bedroom, the night was mercifully quiet. Unlike Spence—if the story about the phones was even true—his job required him to be reachable and responsive. When his phone, back in the kitchen by then, rang at seven-thirty, Burgess and his family figured it was likely to be Captain Cote and let Ned answer.

It *was* Cote, and he got a polite but firm, "I'm sorry, but my dad worked very late last night, and he's sleeping. May I take a message?"

Cote should be used to that by now. From the doorway, Burgess watched his younger son grin as he listened, then Ned said, "I'll give him the message," and hung up. Ned said, "See Captain Cote as soon as you get in. And Dad, he was not happy."

Which, knowing Cote, was an understatement.

Burgess ate toast, drank coffee, hugged Chris and Ned, and set off to drive Nina and Dylan to school. On the way, he updated what he'd told Nina in the night. "He's supposed to be on house arrest until he goes to a school out-of-state. If, for some reason, Dexter is there, you call me. Don't interact. Don't get drawn in. Just walk away and call me."

He got two affirmatives.

"I feel sorry for the kids at that school," Nina said.

"But they may be just like him. Or worse," Dylan suggested. "I'm hoping for worse. Maybe he'll get a taste of his own medicine."

Burgess dropped them at school, suppressing his urge to grab Nina and take her home. Things should be okay, and there was plenty of work awaiting him.

His desk, with its sea of pink messages, looked like it had been hit by a Pepto-Bismol bomb. He was sorting them when Kyle appeared.

"Caught up with Lenore Spence's brother," Kyle said. "He's a flaming asshole. Doesn't know why they filed the lawsuit. Isn't interested in talking about it. Just knows that Spence owed him. Owed them. Figure this was the way to collect."

"He tell you why Spence owed them?"

"In a vague and incoherent way. Seems he was pretty much living off Spence's tit, and the benefits stopped when Lenore Spence died."

"Anything about why he and his sister believe Spence was responsible for her death?"

Kyle shrugged. "Kinda, if this makes any sense. He said that he knew Spence was seeing other women and threatened to tell Lenore if Spence didn't start giving him more money. I guess Lenore was the glue that held them all together. Kept the peace between her husband and her siblings."

So much for his devotion to Lenore keeping Spence from whoring around, if what the brother had told Kyle was true.

Kyle pulled up a chair and sat. He looked like he hadn't slept.

"Pretty pathetic, isn't it, demanding Spence raise his allowance or he'd tattle?" Burgess said.

"It is. He said that he and his sister had…how did he put it?…paid a call or two on Dr. Spence to press their case for compensation and gotten blown off. I gather that Deidre Lovejoy arrived in the midst of one of those meetings, and seeing their sister replaced did nothing to help the relationship. Although he said Belinda kept her cool while he…his name is Mark Carlisle…broke a vase Spence said had been very expensive."

"And the sister? Belinda? Any idea why she'd file her own lawsuit rather than the two of them filing together?"

"Not really. He sounded kind of pissed that she filed her own suit. Thought he was the one who was aggrieved by Spence's conduct. But he says she and Lenore were tight, and she never believed Spence's story about how the accident happened. They believe Spence killed her because she found out about his womanizing. No question that both he and his sister actively hated Eliot Spence."

"This conversation took place when?"

"Jerk called me around one a.m. Definitely been drinking. It took well over an hour to gather much coherent information. Then he called back an hour later, said he hadn't meant it, and I had to forget everything he'd said. By that time, Michelle was awake and pissed off, and by the time I got her calmed down, I couldn't get back to sleep, so I moved to the couch and started running the whole business through my head. Which is why, in case an astute detective like yourself hasn't deduced it, I am tired as hell this morning." All delivered in a low-voiced monotone. "So, what's on our agenda for today?"

Burgess hadn't gotten a word out before Stan Perry arrived, looking wearier than Kyle. He mumbled, "Autumn cried all night."

Burgess led the two of them into the conference room and closed the door.

To Perry, he said, "You check on Aaron Daggett this morning?"

"Of course. The hospital is ready to let him go, but still only if there's someone to look after him. Which, as we know, there is not."

Burgess nodded. "Kristin Daggett spent the night with a friend. Father wasn't even concerned, although he didn't know where she was. We work so hard to keep kids safe, and then—" He broke off. He was preaching to the choir. He filled them in on what he'd learned from Alana Black last night and shared the photo she'd sent, then the one they'd gotten from Marni, which Perry hadn't seen. "We should show these to Kristin and Aaron, see if this is the woman they saw arriving at Spence's the night he died. And run down the phone number. It might lead somewhere."

"Calling herself Alana Black is a pretty good clue she's going to be hard to find," Kyle said. "Alana say how she knew the woman?"

"Doesn't know her. The woman, who called herself Gwen Sykes, contacted Alana and said she was doing an article on sex workers in Portland. Said she found Alana through an old newspaper article. Alana said the woman drove a black BMW with a Massachusetts plate and wore expensive clothes. Carried an expensive bag. She sent the woman to talk to another girl, Bambi Brown, who's still a sex worker. Alana gave me Bambi's contact info. Maybe she'll have something for us."

"If we can find her. Police aren't very popular with ladies of the night," Perry said. He slumped in his chair. "So, we've got the brother and sister of Spence's late wife. We've got the mysterious blonde who may have visited him on the night he died. We've maybe got his current girlfriend outraged because he was cheating on her with prostitutes." He hesitated. "Is it still called cheating when the guy is paying for sex?"

Burgess shrugged.

"Anyone else?" Perry said. "No aggrieved patients or colleagues? No one pissed off over a parking spot or a loud party? No possibility of a robbery gone wrong? Except we've got that bottle, which looks like it means something."

He looked at Burgess and Kyle. "What am I missing?"

"That pretty much sums it up," Burgess said. "We need to follow up with the name Alana gave us. Reinterview Lovejoy. See what more we can learn about Lenore Spence's siblings. Stan, you still need to track down that elusive assistant at the hospital and see if she has anything further to offer. Plus, there are all those papers we took from Spence's condo and the photos. They all need to be looked at."

He thought of something and turned to Kyle. "You ask the brother about those postcards?"

"Postcards?" Perry asked.

Had he not mentioned the postcards? He really was losing a step. Except they'd been running around so much, there hadn't been time for a full briefing. "We found a couple of odd postcards," Burgess said. "One in Spence's trash, more between a stack of tee shirts in his closet. All had only a single word: Unforgotten. Maybe someone out there seeking revenge was the reason Spence was so paranoid? Unforgotten fits Lenore Spence's brother and sister." He shrugged. "Or someone we haven't identified yet."

"But not Deidre Lovejoy," Kyle said. "What about Spence's other friend, Coleman Travis?" he asked. "We still want to talk to him?"

Burgess nodded. "So far, we have a muddy picture of Spence. He might be able to clarify that."

Kyle raised his hand. "I'll take Travis."

"And I'll go track down that assistant," Perry said. "And drop in on Aaron, see how he's doing."

Everyone, it seemed, was eager to get out in the field rather than sit with piles of papers. "Looks like I get the papers," Burgess said. "And the pleasure of trying to track down Bambi Brown." He knew one reason they were eager to get out in the field was to avoid being found by Cote, who would pry and prod and waste their time as though they were hoarding secrets. So far, beyond the bottle and Spence's sordid sex life, they had few secrets to hide. Maybe today that would change.

When they were gone, he called over to vice, got his favorite vice officer rather than the guy in charge, and asked if a girl named Bambi Brown was on their radar. He got a laugh, a "Wait a minute," and then the officer gave him a phone number and address and offered to send him a photo. "She's a piece of work, is our Bambi. Sweet as pie until you try to put the cuffs on, then turns into a wildcat. Pretty strong for such a tiny little thing. Good luck finding her, Joe. She moves around a lot. What's she gone and done now?"

"Nothing, as far as I know," Burgess said. "I'm looking for a suspect, and Bambi may know her."

"Well, if you do find her, bring donuts or cookies or something. Our Bambi's got an awful sweet tooth."

Moving on and wishing he, too, could have left the office, Burgess started in on Spence's papers. The lawsuits proved no more informative than the last time he'd read them. Hoping he might get more information, he called the attorney who'd filed on behalf of Lenore Spence's brother, Mark Carlisle. He met with the usual stone wall, even when he explained that the defendant was dead.

"Presumably, there's still an estate," the lawyer said.

Burgess hung up.

Frustrated, he left the pile of papers and went back to his desk, where he did a search for Gwen Sykes. There were plenty of women named Gwen Sykes in the world, but of those where there were also pictures, none looked anything like the photos he'd gotten from Alana and Marni.

Dammit! He felt like he was spinning his wheels in spring mud. Usually, the nature of the crime or the excitement of the hunt kept him going. This case made him think once again that it was time for him to take his dinosaur self home and leave the job to someone who'd still find it exciting.

Someone like Kyle. As long as Kyle had Stan Perry and could keep bringing Sage Prentiss along, the job would get done more than competently.

He was in that negative frame of mind when Captain Cote deigned to pay a call. Red nose. Peering eyes. Fat buttock planted on Burgess's desk. The predictable, "Where are my reports?" followed by "Bring me up to speed on this."

Burgess could spin a story with the best of them, but today, what came out when he opened his mouth was, "Far as we've gotten, Paul, there is no story. Vic was a doctor, and you know how cooperative that community is. The rest of the people we've talked to aren't saying much." Knowing it would send Cote in a different direction, one that might have him leaning on vice instead of personal crimes, he said, "We may have stumbled on a madam and her girls using a hotel out near the airport to service customers."

Cote brightened. "Yes. And?"

"And we've just started looking into that, but the woman in charge suggested she might have some kind of protection. She sure didn't seem concerned about being questioned by the police, and vice was awfully noncommittal."

Cote was positively glowing. "I need your report on that," he said.

"Working on it."

Miraculously, Cote left him to it.

Burgess wrote a quick report, leaving out some details like Alana Black's name, saved it, and stood up. Though he knew it needed to be done, he was too restless to sit with Spence's papers right now.

He was also too experienced to head out on what might be a wild goose chase. He sat back down and called the number Alana had given him for Bambi Brown. He went to voice mail. Then he tried the number of the woman who'd called herself Gwen Sykes. It rang as long as he would let it, but no one answered. He searched for photos of Mark or Belinda Carlisle. Found a couple that might be useful and printed them. Something to show Aaron and Kristin and Sybil, the witness in Aaron's apartment building.

Patting his monitor like it was a helpful friend—which so far it seemed to be—he opened up the photo Alana had sent and used Google Image to search for similar pictures. He got two blurry possibilities—a doctor and a lawyer, both in Boston. Though they weren't great likenesses, he printed them anyway.

Then he put all the pictures in a folder, grabbed his coat, and headed for the door. If he was a kid worrying about whether he was popular, this morning's lack of response from anyone was sending the message that he wasn't. You couldn't need to be liked and do this job.

THIRTY-SEVEN

B urgess found a space near the building where Bambi Brown lived and grabbed the bag of donuts he'd brought. Another building where the door was propped open instead of securely locked to protect the residents. The ambiance of the hallway was so familiar. The same gloom, dirty paint, and faint bulbs. He climbed a staircase that creaked and groaned under his weight and found the apartment. He knocked and was met with silence. Figuring someone who worked at night might be asleep in the morning, he knocked again. A puffy-faced, sleepy woman with uncombed russet hair pulled the door open and peered out at him.

"Do I know you?"

"Detective Sergeant Burgess, ma'am, Portland police," he said, holding out the bag of donuts.

"I haven't done anything," she said, reaching for the bag.

Without relinquishing it, he followed the bag inside, then let her take it from him. "Wanted to talk with you about a woman named Gwen Sykes."

"Who calls herself Gwen Sykes, you mean."

Not an entirely dumb Bambi, was she? He nodded.

She plucked a laundry basket off a chair and waved a hand. "Sit. Please. You want some coffee?"

"I wouldn't say no."

He waited while she bustled with the pot, pleased to see that her kitchen was clean. It meant the mugs probably were, too. Over the years, he'd been

258

offered coffee in mugs so dirty you could have started seeds in them, or in kitchens where his feet stuck to the floor and his elbows stuck to the table. He could tell, from the number of scoops she added, that she liked her coffee strong. That also pleased him.

While they waited for the coffee to brew, she sat down across from him, grabbed a donut, and ate it. "Oh, this is so delicious," she said, licking a smear of jelly off her hand. "My favorite."

She poured them both coffee and asked, "Milk or sugar? I mean, I might have milk. Haven't been to the store yet this week."

"Black is good."

"Probably for the best." She ate another donut.

Not knowing how far to go with the vice cop's suggestion about bringing something sweet, he'd brought half a dozen. He could see that wasn't overdoing it. Also, she wasn't planning to share. Fine with him. He'd been working on his weight these last two years for his knee and his overall health. He might be a cop, but that didn't mean he *had* to eat donuts. "So, what can you tell me about the woman who calls herself Gwen Sykes?"

Her grin was impish as she said, "Not a hell of a lot. She was looking for information from me, wasn't she?"

Not curious about how he'd found her or why he was looking for Gwen Sykes. Maybe Alana had made a phone call. "Do you know how this woman found you?"

She gathered her hair into a ponytail and secured it with an elastic. Sleepy, uncombed, and with bits of powdered sugar on her face, she looked about twelve. A twelve-year-old with very large breasts. "She said Alana Black sent her."

Another impish grin. "I guess you know Alana pretty well, huh?"

He nodded.

"She called me. This Gwen Sykes. Said she was writing an article about the sex trade in Portland, and Alana said I might be helpful. So, we met."

"Here?"

She shook her head, her curly russet ponytail bobbing. "No way. For two reasons. First, I don't like strangers knowing where I live, which I'm sure you understand. Second, if she was gonna pick my brain about my work, I was gonna treat her like a customer. At least get a good meal out of her, and hopefully some money as well."

"And did you?"

"Oh yeah. I definitely did. Fancy restaurant and a couple hundred bucks." She named one of Portland's best restaurants, and he was surprised. "I don't ever say no to lobster."

"Tell me about her."

She shrugged. "What's to tell?" But after he gave her a "don't play games with me" look, she said, "She's tall. She's gorgeous. A natural blonde, I think. Her clothes and her handbag say she has money. She was…it sounds odd to say this, but it was like she was on a mission, you know what I mean? Just so focused on what she needed to know. I mean, in my business—" She gave Burgess a lewd wink. "We have to get good at small talk. Make the guys comfortable, make it seem like fun, make it seem like the money part of the transaction isn't that important; they are. Some men like to feel sexy, to be admired. Some of them are nervous, and we make small talk to get them comfortable. Some of 'em, yeah, just wanna get down to business."

She shrugged and gave him that impish grin again. "Just like a therapist, I'm in a helping profession. And like you, I provide a valuable public service. Well. I'm getting off track. What I mean is that if you and I are getting together for a meal, we'll be interacting. We'll show some interest in one another, you get me? And she didn't. She shook my hand. Very firm handshake. She sat down, took out her notebook, and started asking questions. She barely paused to give the waiter an order. She was…I think the word is brusque. I took my time, partly to show her how it should be done, partly 'cuz I'm a friendly person. I asked questions about the menu. I asked about the drink specials and what he'd recommend. You know. Like someone who was enjoying a nice meal out."

"How did she react to that?"

"She drummed her fingers on the table. Which, by the way, gave me a chance to see that she wasn't wearing a wedding ring, though she had other rings that looked expensive."

"Who suggested that restaurant?"

"I did. I'm sure she wanted to take me to Dunkin Donuts or something. Not…" She slid a hand into the bag and took out another donut. "Not that I don't like donuts, as you can see. But how often do I get a chance to eat at a place like that? Never. That's how often. I'm not some high-priced escort or something. Just your everyday working girl."

"What kind of questions did she ask?"

"About my work. How I found clients. How to handle clients. I don't know. A lot of questions that sounded, despite what she said about writing an article, like she was thinking of getting into the business. It was pretty clinical. But she wouldn't have been good at it, except maybe for a very high-end escort, and probably not even that. She was too cold."

She poured him more coffee and said, "Oh. Something I didn't mention. She was strong. I mean, seriously, gym rat strong. She was wearing a short-sleeved blouse, and her arms were…I think the expression is cut if they use that for women? I mean, yes, she was gorgeous, and yes, she had a great body, and she wasn't just pretty, she was beautiful. But she was cold, hard, and harsh. If I were in a different helping profession, I'd probably say she was damaged. There was something off about her."

This was all fascinating. She was more observant than some cops he knew. Probably had learned to be to stay safe. He didn't have anything new to use to find the woman who called herself Gwen Sykes, though, unless there was something more that Bambi could tell him. She seemed both usefully nosy and observant, so he said, "How did she get in touch with you?"

"She called me. Said that Alana had given her my number."

"You still have that number?"

"Sure. It's in my phone. Got her license plate number, too, if you want that?"

"How did you get that?"

"Well, when we came out of the restaurant, it was raining. The valet brought her car around, a BMW, by the way. Black. She got in, and then… like she had an attack of conscience or something, 'cuz I'm still standing there, she rolled down her window and asked if she could give me a ride. I'm not stupid. I took it. Didn't have her let me off at my place, of course, but close enough. And as she was driving away, I snapped a quick photo of her plate. I'm not sure why. Just that we've all learned to be pretty careful, and, as I've said, there was something off about her. Something spooky."

She got up and went to her purse, where she took out a phone in a glittery pink case. "Cute, huh?" she said. "You want me to send you that plate?"

He got out his phone. "I do."

A little blurry but readable Massachusetts plate. If she was their suspect, this was bringing them closer.

"Going back to her name. Why do you think it's fake?"

She shrugged. "Instinct? And the fact that once, when her attention had drifted for a moment, I called her Gwen, and she didn't respond."

He nodded. Very observant.

"There's more," she said. "When someone a few tables away with a loud voice said, 'Heather,' she startled and turned. So, I think her real name is Heather."

"Sounds like a good possibility." Burgess stood. "I'll be going now. Thank you for your information. You're an excellent observer."

"Yeah. Maybe I should become a cop," she said. "But I don't think I'd like the hours, and all that equipment looks heavy."

"Very heavy," he agreed and walked to the door. When he looked back, she was happily eating her fourth donut. Amazing how someone with an appetite for sugar like that could stay so tiny.

You couldn't please all of the people all of the time, but once in a while, you could please one, at least briefly.

Two people were pleased, actually, because Burgess now had more to go on in locating the woman they suspected had been with Dr. Spence on his last night alive.

THIRTY-EIGHT

Burgess still wasn't ready to go back to 109. He knew part of his restlessness was worry about Nina. She hadn't called, and while no news was supposed to be good news, he wouldn't relax until he knew that she was safely home. She'd promised to call when she was.

So, what to do with himself? He figured it was a good time for an unannounced visit to Deidre Lovejoy. She'd given him her home address, which was also her office, so he drove there and went inside.

As she'd said, a part of her condo was her office, and it was furnished like an office and guarded by a secretary, or assistant, or whatever the current popular term was. She was a younger, less lovely Lovejoy clone. Same tall and slender build. Same carefully styled dark hair. Cheaper versions of Lovejoy's designer clothes. It was more than a little weird. He couldn't imagine why Deidre Lovejoy would want a Mini-Me.

He showed his badge and said, "Detective Sergeant Burgess to see Ms. Lovejoy."

"Do you have an appointment?"

"Police business," he said. "It's important."

"Well, it's just—"

"It isn't just anything," he said. "She's in, isn't she?"

"Well, yes, it's just—"

"Fine." He stepped around her desk and opened Lovejoy's office door. She had her bare feet up on the desk and was reading a design magazine.

Behind him, the clone said, "I'm sorry, Ms. Lovejoy. He wouldn't listen."

"It's fine, Hilary." Deidre Lovejoy dismissed her with a wave of the hand.

Today, the elegant Ms. Lovejoy was all in black. Black flowing blouse and trim black pants. Beside her chair was a pair of black stilettos. "Sit down, Detective," she said, her voice all honey and sweetness. "To what do I owe the pleasure?"

"Just a bit of follow-up," he said. "When we spoke the other day, you said that you hadn't seen Dr. Spence on the evening he stood you up. We now have witnesses who say you were knocking on his door around eight that evening. That the two of you argued. And that you smashed a bottle of wine against his door. You want to tell me what really happened that night?"

She shrugged. Tossed back her waves, then leaned forward, her hands tented above her desk.

"I'd just learned something shocking about the man I loved. About a man who I believed loved me, one I was going to have a future with. You can't imagine how awful that was."

Burgess didn't bother to tell her he'd seen a thousand shocking things and imagined plenty more based on what he'd seen. That wasn't why he was here.

"And that something shocking was?"

She gave him a "Do I have to say it?" look.

He nodded.

She said, "He visits prostitutes. Worse, he has them come to his condo. Presumably has sex with them in the same bed we sleep in. It's...it's disgusting, Detective. I was horrified to learn he was that kind of a man."

"How did you learn about the prostitutes?"

She shrugged and turned away, saying, almost in a whisper, "This is so embarrassing."

Burgess waited. He was supposed to be a gentleman and not press her on such an uncomfortable subject. Being a gentleman was something he could rarely afford.

She made him wait for it, but he was good at waiting.

"I was watching," she said. "When he called to cancel our date, I was angry. I'd had to pull strings to get that reservation, and I'd gone to a lot of trouble to get dressed, and then he just says he's sorry, he's busy. So, I went down to his place, and I watched, and I waited, and I saw that girl...that woman…arrive and go inside like she was expected. Then, I waited some more in case she was there on some kind of business other than the one she appeared to be on. But she didn't come out. So, I went and pounded on his door. And he did that awful, humiliating thing again."

"What awful thing?"

"The one where he makes me stand out in the street and be vetted before he'll let me inside. Like I'm just anyone and not his girlfriend. His lover. His partner. It just…well, it made me furious. It was so rude. He could be such a wonderful man, and then he could be so cruel. I didn't understand it. Him. Why he would be that way." She shrugged. "I guess I'm not as good a judge of men as I thought I was."

She folded her hands on the desk and looked down at her lap, not moving. A still black statue of grief.

That was supposed to be his cue to leave. Burgess wasn't very good at that sort of cue. Too many people were eager to have him gone.

"This business where he made you wait outside. He did this even when you were expected?"

"Yes. The bastard. Yes, he did. I asked for a key. I was there often enough. It wasn't unreasonable. But that brought out what I think of as his paranoid side. The one where he was always looking around as though he was expecting to be attacked."

"You ever ask him about that? About why he was so cautious?"

"Of course. It was such odd behavior. He gave me some throwaway line about an unbalanced former patient. That could have been true, right? Only then, why didn't he just get a restraining order? Have you found out who did this to Eliot?"

Burgess shook his head. "Still doing interviews. Sometimes, these cases can take some time. When you were there, watching Dr. Spence's place that night, did you see anyone else arrive or leave other than the woman you took to be a prostitute?"

She shook her head.

"The woman you saw arrive, you didn't see her leave?"

"After I smashed that bottle on Eliot's door, I was embarrassed, so I went home. Embarrassed and ashamed of myself. I don't usually lose control like that."

"You told us that you called him at intervals throughout the evening, but he only answered at nine and never after that. Is that true? Did you call him? Did you speak with him at nine?"

She shook her head again but stayed silent.

"Was that the first time you'd watched Dr. Spence's condo and seen women arrive?"

More silence.

"You say that you assume the woman you saw arriving was a sex worker. Can you tell me why you thought that? Why did you believe the man you were involved with was being visited by prostitutes?"

He got more silence. Then, reluctantly, she said, "Because of the way the woman was dressed, I suppose."

"Can you tell me what she looked like?"

"Attractive," she spat. "Very attractive. Blonde and tall and curvy and gorgeous. Not at all what I'd expect a hooker to look like. I mean—" She fell silent, debating whether to continue, then said, "As attractive as I am, which frankly pissed me off."

Burgess took out some photographs. The one Alana had taken, Marni's, and the two he'd found online. "Were any of these the woman you saw?"

She inspected them and handed them back, putting a thumb on the one Alana had taken. "Maybe this one. I can't be sure."

He got out the photos of Belinda and Mark Carlisle. "You ever see either of these people around, maybe watching Dr. Spence's condo?"

"Eliot," she corrected, "not Dr. Spence." Then shook her head. "Never saw them."

No help there. "Prior to that night, you didn't suspect Dr. Spence of using sex workers?" he asked.

She glared at him. "Of course not. Why would I? He had me. He was in a relationship with me. Why would he need someone else?"

Then her cool façade crumbled, and she burst into tears. "I'm not getting any younger," she said, "and I want a husband and a family. A quality husband, a husband worthy of me, which is what I thought Eliot was."

She spread her hands wide, then moved them up and down, indicating her body. "Do you know how much work it takes to keep all this up? The hours in the gym, the makeup, the colorist, the clothes? My biological clock is ticking. My looks will fade. And now, I've gone and wasted ten months on a lying cheater. Can you imagine how that makes me feel?"

All the women who looked at her with envy would not see Lovejoy's beauty as a burden. Burgess gave her one of the handkerchiefs he always carried, and she buried her face in it.

Burgess's phone rang. Terry Kyle. When he answered, Kyle said, "We might have a problem."

Which might have been the understatement of the year.

"Hold on," he said. "I'm with a witness. I'll call you back in five."

He left a sobbing Deidre Lovejoy, went down to his truck, and called Kyle.

"What's up?" he said.

"Just got a call from Lenore Spence's sister, Belinda. She says her brother is somewhere in Portland, he's off his meds, and he's looking for someone to blame for Spence's death."

THIRTY-NINE

"Where are you right now?" Burgess asked.

"Driving. Coming back from a frustrating chat with Spence's friend Coleman Travis. When it came to friends, he sure could pick 'em."

"Yeah. Just spent some equally frustrating time with the girlfriend, Deidre Lovejoy. She's still holding stuff back. Too humiliated about having a boyfriend with such sordid tendencies."

Kyle laughed. "If people didn't have sordid tendencies, we wouldn't have jobs. You wanna meet at Melina's? Grab some sandwiches?" Kyle said.

He was always up for killing two birds with one stone, plus he was hungry. "You bet. I'll be there in ten. You?"

"About the same."

They pulled in at exactly the same time, backing into their spaces and then pausing to look around. Chris said you could tell who the public safety people were because of the way they always backed in. They weren't the only ones, but cops backed in to be ready for a quick departure.

Melina looked up when they came in and smiled, her busy hands never pausing. "Ah, two of my favorite gentlemen," she said. "You look like you are hungry. You—" she pointed at Burgess, "you are always hungry, but that one—" pointing at Kyle, "he needs to eat more. He is running very hot all the time, never still for a moment."

"Oh, he can be still," Burgess said. "So still, you don't know he's there."

She laughed. "I can see that. So, two meatloaf sandwiches apiece, right? I have some cookies. Chocolate chip? Oatmeal raisin? Peanut butter?"

"Yes." They said it together, like a pair of hungry twins.

They got some drinks and went and sat at a table to wait. Burgess filled Kyle in and got Kyle's report on Coleman Travis.

"Travis thought Spence was an okay guy. Maybe kinda antsy sometimes, but otherwise cool. Classy is the term he used. He was jealous that Spence had such a classy girlfriend."

"He's the ginger?" Burgess said.

"Yeah. Like Prince Harry. Not bad looking if you like those ginger-haired, pink-faced types. He's got an excellent little, carefully groomed beard. Expensive haircut. Natty shoes."

"Natty shoes?"

"You know. Babyshit colored with white soles."

"Right. I've been longing for a pair of those." Burgess remembered Aaron's comment about a woman watching that he thought was the ginger's wife. "Is he married?"

Kyle nodded. "Yeah." Then, he gave one of his rare smiles as Melina arrived with their food. She set it on the table, then gripped Kyle's shoulder. "Now you eat it all, Terry. I mean it. You are too skinny. You are worrying off your food faster than you can eat it." She tipped her head toward Burgess. "Be more like him. A man needs some meat on his bones. Otherwise, you get sick, or God forbid, you are getting shot, and there is nothing to keep the body going."

"I'll be good," Kyle said.

He let few people scold him. Melina was the exception. They would put up with a little mothering for her great food.

"So," Burgess began when she'd left them, "what the heck do we do about finding Mark Carlisle, and who does he think he's looking for? If we can't figure out who killed his golden goose, how is he supposed to do that?"

Kyle shrugged, too polite to talk with his mouth full. After a moment, he said, "Beats me. I suppose we should stake out Spence's condo in case he shows up there." A shrug. "Though why he'd go to a dead guy's place to find the man's killer, I don't know. But people off their meds do not always act or think rationally."

"If he was staking out the place, as some of our witnesses have suggested—" He stopped. He hadn't had time to show the photos to Kristin or

269

Aaron or Dr. Fellowes, the neighbors who'd seen Spence's blonde visitor arrive. He abandoned what he was going to say and instead said, "I wonder if we should stake out Deidre Lovejoy, as well. And Aaron's apartment. Someone who kind of matched Carlisle's description was there the night Aaron was attacked. Someone who fit those clothes we found in the dumpster."

"Sure," Kyle said. "Let's tie up the entire department while we're at it."

"The sister…Belinda…she give us any other info? What vehicle he's driving? His cell phone number?"

"Yeah. For what it's worth. He's driving a silver Prius." He got out his notebook and read off Mark Carlisle's phone number. "She doesn't know his plate number."

"Mass plates?"

"Yeah. We can look it up."

Kyle's food had disappeared as though a magician had waved a wand. Now, he was into the bag of cookies. He held one out to Burgess. "Oatmeal raisin? Supposed to be sorta healthy."

Burgess ate it absently, his mind on their next steps, then went to the bag for another. He reminded himself to slow down. Eating too fast was bad for his already wrecked cop's digestion, and Melina's cookies were worth appreciating. The minute he started thinking about those who might be at risk, the knife that lived in his gut—mostly sleeping like a troll under the bridge—woke and stirred.

"Oh fuck!" he said and put the cookie down.

Kyle nodded. Got out his phone. He said, "We'll go down to the condo and take a look around. I'll call patrol and have them put a car on Lovejoy's place. And Aaron's." He waited while Burgess shared those addresses, then made the calls. "But Aaron's still in the hospital, right?"

"Far as I know. But the kid is slippery and scared." He got out his own phone and called Sage Prentiss. No one answered.

"Sage is supposed to be on the kid, right?"

Kyle shook his head. "He was going to find someone else to sit on Aaron so he could get some sleep, remember?"

"Right. But we don't know who that is, and Sage's not answering."

"Give it a minute and try again."

Like Kyle was the detective in charge, and Burgess was a newbie who needed to be led around by the nose.

He shook himself. This was not the moment to suddenly get sensitive about his position. He and Kyle traded roles all the time.

"Yeah," Kyle said, reading his mind. "Something about this one, huh? It's kind of like trying to wrestle an eel into a bottle. Of course, it's gonna make us doubt ourselves. Hard to have perspective when we've had our noses to the ground for days, right?"

"Right."

Melina approached with another bag of cookies. "These are for later. Or for Stan. He needs some treats, too."

"You take good care of us," Burgess said.

"So why not, when you are my best customers?" She smiled and made some shooing motions with her hands. "Go out now and find this killer so you can get some rest. You both look like you've been chewed by the rats."

They laughed and left.

At their vehicles, Burgess said, "So, down to the condos?"

Kyle nodded. Said, "You should check on Kristin. She might decide to come home while her stepmother…The Wicked?…is at work."

Burgess called and went to voicemail, though she should be out of school by now. The troll's knife began to stir.

The parking area around the condos was quiet at this time of day. People were either away at work or out doing errands. They rang Kristin's doorbell, but no one answered. Dr. Fellowes was out, as was anyone else they wanted to talk to. There were three silver Priuses, but none of them had Mass plates.

Burgess checked with patrol to see if anything was happening at Lovejoy's building. All was quiet. Same with Aaron Daggett's apartment. He said, "I want to check with the witness in Daggett's building who saw the man with the briefcase. See if she recognizes the photo of Mark Carlisle."

Kyle nodded. "What do you want me to do?"

"Swing by the hospital and make sure Aaron is there and guarded. Then, we should meet back at 109 and go through Spence's papers and photos. I'm getting a gut feeling that we may find some answers there."

"I should call Stan in as well?"

"Absolutely." Burgess looked around at a beautiful day he was missing. He badly wanted this case over.

They went their separate ways, Burgess hoping that his gut wouldn't fail him now.

FORTY

E n route, he called Kristin Daggett again and got no answer. There
was no call or text from Nina, who should be home from school by
now. Silence from some people he needed to talk to amped up his anxiety.
He shoved it into a lockbox in his brain and slammed the door. No energy
to waste on worry right now.

As before, the door to Aaron's building was propped open with a
cinderblock. Shaking his head, Burgess rang the bell for Sybil's apartment.
Nothing. Then a crabby voice asked, "Who is it?"

"Detective Burgess," he said.

"Come to take me to lunch?"

Funny what people remembered and what they forgot. "Not today," he
said. "Still trying to get this case put to bed. You have a minute to look at
some pictures?"

"Dirty pictures?"

"Afraid not. You want to come down, or shall I come up?"

"I'll come down. Got to get the mail anyway before some druggie
gets it."

He waited. After a minute or two, he heard footsteps on the stairs, and
she appeared. Looking better today. Her hair was combed, and her clothes
matched.

She smiled at his scrutiny.

"Clean up good, don't I? So, where's these pictures?"

He showed her the pictures of Mark and Belinda Carlisle. She studied them, then took a pair of glasses from her pocket and studied them again. Pointed at Mark Carlisle. "That looks kinda like the guy in the suit with the briefcase that I saw. That I told you about. This could be the guy. Although…" She studied the photo of Belinda again. "It could be her. They look almost like twins, ya know, with suits and dark hair? And it was night."

She was right. They did.

He said, "Thank you, Sybil. And I haven't forgotten our lunch."

She pointed at the folder he was holding. "What else you got in there? Anyone else I should look at?"

He shook his head. "Just some photos of a mystery woman we're trying to locate."

"I'm good at mysteries, Detective. My whole life is a mystery. May I see them?"

He handed over the photos of the woman who'd visited Eliot Spence the night he died. She studied them, then handed them back. "Sorry. I haven't seen her around here. Wish I could help."

She went to her mailbox, and he drove back to 109. On the way, he called Nina again. No answer. Kristin Daggett didn't answer, either. The knife in his gut stabbed. The four texts on his phone informed him Captain Cote wanted to see him. Not a priority right now.

He found Perry and Kyle already in the conference room, stacks of papers on the table in front of them.

Perry looked up when he came in. "You really think we're going to find the answer in here, Joe?"

Burgess shrugged. "Not finding it anywhere else, are we?" He said, "Terry, when you spoke with Belinda Carlisle, did you ask whether her brother is armed?"

"I did. He is."

Daylight was running out. A vulnerable kid was missing. An unbalanced man might be driving around the city, looking for someone to take revenge on. The brass wanted answers in the killing of a local doctor. Burgess and his team were weary, and nothing was breaking in their favor.

Burgess looked at the piles of papers, then grabbed the box of old photographs. He had no better reason to choose it beyond his gut. But what had his witnesses told him? That the woman was gorgeous but older. Not the age of Spence's other ladies of the night. That if it was the same person Alana and Bambi had described, it sounded like she'd been looking for Spence.

Was he jumping to conclusions? Assuming she'd gone looking for Spence because she'd refused a date with another man? It was all hearsay anyway. Was he making this assumption because once before, a woman bent on revenge had taken a similar route, something that could have been learned by reading old newspapers? Alana said the woman who called herself Gwen Sykes had found her through researching old newspapers.

Hold on. Impatience was making him skip steps. Possibly important steps. Something he'd yell at another detective for doing. He needed to slow down. Be methodical. Bambi Brown had given him a photograph of a license plate, and he'd forgotten to run it. He got out his notebook, said, "Back in a sec," and went to his desk. He pulled up the photo and then called dispatch, gave them the plate, and asked them to run it.

While he waited, he made more unanswered calls to Kristin Daggett and to Nina. He left Kristin a message to please call him back. He didn't want to scare her, but she needed to know she might be in danger. When Nina didn't answer, he called Chris. "Have you heard from Nina? She was supposed to call me when she got home, and she hasn't."

There was silence, one he filled with the worst possible imaginings before Chris said, "She didn't call you? She called me. Said she and Dylan were home, and they were going to go down to the park and toss a frisbee around because it was such a beautiful day. I reminded her to call you. I'm sure she meant to. Are you okay?"

"Other than losing another few years off my life? I'm fine."

"But you're angry." It sounded like she thought he shouldn't be. That Nina calling her was enough. It wasn't. They were close, but they didn't communicate telepathically.

"I am. Look. I've got to go. I'll see you at home. I hope."

She was starting to explain why he shouldn't be angry when he hung up. Too much to do here to spend time on pointless explanations.

He was about to give up and head back into the conference room when Dispatch came through with his information. The plate belonged to a Dr. Heather Benson, with a Boston, Massachusetts address.

He felt like the pieces were falling into place. A doctor who was about six years younger than Dr. Spence. Possibly a medical student when he was a resident? He needed to go back and look through those old photos. The ones where the subjects appeared to be unconscious. He might be wrong. He might be jumping to conclusions, but his mind was taking the pieces and putting together a picture of a man who'd used his position as a doctor to take advantage of unsuspecting women. A man with an addictive need for sex who, somewhere along the line, had started paying women instead of drugging them?

He went back into the conference room and told Kyle and Perry what Bambi Brown had told him. About her photo of the license place. About it belonging to a thirty-something doctor in Boston. Then shared what he hoped wasn't a crazy theory. "We have a name," he said. "Let's see if we can find a current photograph of Dr. Benson...and then..." He waved a hand toward the old photographs. "Let's see if one of these might be her."

Revenge could be taken in the heat of anger, or it could be, as the old saying goes, a dish best-served cold.

They spread the dozen or so photos of the naked women who appeared to be unconscious or drugged out on the table, placed Alana's photo of the woman who'd called herself Gwen Sykes beside them, and studied the array.

All of the women were blonde. With closed eyes and slack faces, it was harder to tell whether they were attractive, though all their bodies were young and sexy.

The three detectives stood in a row, staring down at the pictures. It wasn't as easy as Burgess had imagined. Then Kyle reached down and tapped one of the pictures. "This one," he said. "See the tiny scar?"

In sync, they all leaned in. Studied the scar. Picked up the photo Alana had taken. And nodded. This one.

Now, they needed to start digging into Heather Benson, starting with any photos of her online that were better than the ones they had.

It wasn't hard. Hospitals and practices usually posted photos of their doctors, and Benson's employer was no exception. The photos confirmed what they suspected—that Dr. Heather Benson looked like the woman who had approached Alana and Bambi Brown. Now, they needed to show it to witnesses who'd seen the woman arrive at Eliot Spence's condo.

"I'll take Deidre Lovejoy," Burgess said. "Seeing as we already have an established relationship. Terry, you can take Spence's neighbors, and Stan, you can see if Aaron Daggett recognizes her."

They were about to head for the door when Burgess thought about Cote, who loved to snoop through their files when they were out of the office. He hadn't found these photos when they were in the bottom of a box, but spread out on the table? He'd have a field day.

"I'm taking the file with Spence's old photos and Bambi and Alana's photos with me and burying the rest in the box. Anyone got a problem with that?"

Kyle and Perry shrugged. "Sounds like a plan," Kyle said. "But you sure you don't want me to take the file? What if you meet him on your way out?"

Which was not far-fetched. "Fine," Burgess said, handing him the file. "Don't lose them."

"Like I ever have?"

"Speak of the devil," Kyle said as Cote appeared in the window beside the door.

A hasty shuffling of papers and, all the materials disappeared back into the box or into Kyle's jacket and Burgess's pocket.

"What have you got for me?" Cote said, entering without even a polite "good afternoon."

"Just on our way out," Burgess said. "We've just gotten word that our victim's brother-in-law is somewhere in the city, off his meds, and looking for someone to blame for Spence's death. Apparently, Spence was supporting him, and he's angry that the money has stopped. We're checking out some places he might go."

A half-truth, at least, and more than they'd usually share.

Cote brightened. "You think he's our suspect?"

Kyle shook his head. "Dunno, Paul. We're more concerned with preventing another homicide, to tell you the truth."

Telling Cote the truth, the whole truth, and nothing but the truth was never a good idea. But they often told him shaded truths.

"We'll keep you in the loop."

Cote nodded. "You do that. You'd better do that." He glared at Burgess, who hadn't said anything that merited that glare, said, "I'm still waiting for that report about hookers at a hotel near the airport," and bustled away.

The three musketeers headed out before anything else could delay them. They'd put on a calm front before Cote, but all three were seized by a sense that there was a menace on the loose somewhere in their city. They hoped to head it off before anyone else got hurt.

FORTY-ONE

Once again, Burgess drove to Deidre Lovejoy's condo, relieved to see a patrol car parked outside. He could see lights on, and her car was there, but no one answered when he pressed the buzzer. After a few tries, he got out his phone and called her.

"Detective Burgess," he said when she answered. "I have some photos I need you to look at."

She sighed. "Not right now. Today has been hard enough. I just want to be alone. I want to rest and be left alone."

The slight slur in her speech suggested she'd been comforting herself with drink since his earlier visit.

"This will only take a minute, and it's important. Maybe critically important."

"I just don't feel like—"

He cut her off. "Let me in, Ms. Lovejoy. Now!"

She hung up, but a minute later, she buzzed him in.

She was waiting in her doorway when he got out of the elevator, her cheeks pink, her eyes a little glazed. She'd changed from her black business attire into deep purple satin pajamas.

He followed her into the apartment and got out the photos of Dr. Heather Benson. He put them on the coffee table and invited her to look. She picked up the first one and said, "This looks like the woman I saw going into Eliot's condo. Who is she?"

He said, "A doctor from Boston named Heather Benson."

Her look said, "Impossible." She asked, "Why would a doctor from Boston be dressed like a hooker and visiting Eliot? It doesn't make sense."

"I can't get into details at this point in the investigation," Burgess said. "But this does look like the woman you saw?"

She nodded.

"When we spoke earlier, you said you were unaware of Dr. Spence's fondness for hiring sex workers, correct?"

She nodded, watching him warily like he was going to spring some sordid new surprise on her. Unfortunately, he was.

"Did he ever speak about relationships prior to his marriage?"

She shook her head. "It never came up. Well, we decided we weren't interested in each other's prior dating history. Honestly, I think with my past bad breakup and his sadness about losing Lenore, we both wanted a fresh start." She tossed her hair back over her shoulders and studied him. "Why do you ask?"

"Among Dr. Spence's boxes, we found a number of photographs of women who appeared to have been photographed while they were naked and unconscious."

"Naked and unconscious? You can tell that from a picture?"

Cops could tell a lot from a picture. He nodded.

She literally moved farther away from him. "Goddamit! You keep bringing me more sordid revelations about a man I loved. How do you think that makes me feel?"

He could see how it made her feel, and he was sorry.

Before he left, because he didn't want to have to bother her again, he showed her the photos of Mark and Belinda Carlisle. "Have you ever seen either of these people around Dr. Spence's condo?"

"Eliot," she corrected automatically. Then shook her head. "I haven't. Who are they?"

"The late Lenore Spence's brother and sister."

"Why are you asking about them?"

He figured he might as well tell her. "Both of them filed wrongful death actions against Dr. Spence…Eliot…claiming he caused his wife's death."

She shook her head vigorously. "No way. No way. Her death was an accident."

Hating to have to give her more bad news, he said, "And they've both been seen visiting his condo or in the area watching it. We've received information that Mark Carlisle, who reportedly suffers from mental illness, has stopped taking his medication and has come to Portland looking for revenge for Dr. Spence's death—"

"Wait. Hold on," she interrupted. "You just said they'd filed wrongful death suits, which means they believe Eliot did something wrong. So why would he be looking to avenge Eliot's death? That doesn't make any sense."

Burgess agreed. He said, "People with mental illness often don't make sense. But if you're looking for a reason, it could be because it interferes with his desire to collect money from Dr. Spence, something he was doing before his sister's death." There was more he could have told her, but he had other things to do. He gathered the photos and put them in his pocket.

"Since you were involved with Dr. Spence, we're concerned that you could be among the people Mark Carlisle might target. I know it sounds absurd, but there's a risk. We've got an officer watching your building in case Carlisle shows up, so you should be safe. But if you see anything or if someone contacts you, please call me immediately."

He set his card on her coffee table.

"You sure as hell aren't being very reassuring," she said.

Burgess stood. "I'm sorry. I wish I could be."

She waved a hand without looking at him.

"Go. Just go and leave me alone. You've done your best to destroy my memories of the man I loved." She pulled her legs up and wrapped her arms around her knees. "I hope I never see you again."

FORTY-TWO

The feeling was mutual. She was lovely to look at but in a carefully crafted way. Nothing natural or spontaneous about her except, perhaps, her tears. He was definitely getting old if the sight of lovely women tossing their hair just made him want to sigh and say, "Get on with it."

Back in his truck, he gave himself a few minutes to refocus. Now that he had a pretty good ID of Dr. Heather Benson, it was time to take a closer look at her. What he learned would be sad, he expected. He imagined a scenario of a wronged woman—drugged, raped, possibly blackmailed into silence—finally driven by disturbing memories and lingering damage to take revenge. The method of Dr. Spence's death suggested someone with a knowledge of anatomy. The bottle spoke of revenge.

But while he might sympathize with her pain, he could never condone anyone allowing that pain to justify taking someone's life. He subscribed to the Harry Bosch theory of homicide policing: everyone mattered, or no one mattered. He'd solved cases where the world was better off with the victim dead, but society didn't work if killers got to designate themselves as good guys and make their own rules.

He checked his watch. Chris and the kids would be sitting down to dinner soon. He needed to call and confirm he wouldn't be there.

Chris sounded cold when he answered the phone. Hanging up on her, however justified he'd felt, was not good for their relationship. That tug between family and work was one reason he'd been single so long. The work took so much from him that there wasn't much left. "Sorry I was abrupt earlier," he said. "We've got a potential killer loose in the city. Need to stop him before someone dies."

She sighed. Echoes of Deidre Lovejoy. No one was happy with him today.

"Dylan and Nina home, okay?"

"They are. She's sorry she didn't call you."

He skipped "She should be" and said, "Wish I could be home for dinner, but I can't."

"Just be careful, okay. I mean, be very careful. We may not always show it, but we need Detective Joe Burgess here as well. And don't let Stan and Terry do anything foolish. Especially Stan. You know how he can be."

He did know how Stan could be. Having Baby Autumn might have settled him a bit, but he was still young and impulsive. He wouldn't be Stan if he wasn't.

"I'll try," he said. "I always try."

"Yes. You can be very trying."

Which he could. "Gotta go. I'll call and keep you posted."

Which was something else he could do and which would make her happy. Or happier.

Then he sat in the cold, dark vehicle a little longer and thought about the case. It was exciting that they'd identified a likely suspect. Far less exciting that it would be like beginning all over again, focusing the investigation on Dr. Benson and having to do it in another state.

Kyle called. "I'm down by the condo. No sign of Carlisle. Also, no sign of Kristin Daggett. The stepmom says she doesn't know where Kristin is and really doesn't care. You want me to hang on down here a while longer?"

"I do. The good news, I guess, is that Deidre Lovejoy identified that photo of Dr. Heather Benson."

Kyle sighed. Burgess sighed right back. Said, "I know, right? I'm going to call Stan and see what's up at the hospital."

"Right," Kyle said. "Call me back. I've got one of those feelings. One that says something's gonna happen tonight."

"I've got it, too."

He thought about Belinda Carlisle's information that her brother was off his meds and in Portland looking for revenge. Could be a plausible story, but it didn't feel right. Mark Carlisle looking to blame someone and harm someone because they'd interfered with his lawsuit against his former brother-in-law? When, as the lawyer had said, the lawsuit could still go forward against the estate. Would Spence's refusal to support his former brother-in-law be enough? He didn't know. Didn't know how Mark Carlisle had gotten along without support from Spence and for how long. Lenore Spence had been dead for more than two years.

He called up his conversation with the Weston detective. There were definitely assets. Lenore Spence had been well insured, a policy taken out a few years before her death when the Spences had decided to start a family.

The Weston detective had said that Mark Carlisle was a hothead. But who would he be looking for? And why? Witnesses had said they'd seen both Carlisles near Spence's condo. Together.

He kneaded his forehead, wishing the act would bring some clarity. He doubted that it would. Nor would coffee.

He called Stan Perry for an update.

Instead of "Hey, Joe" or "Detective Perry," he got, "This whole fucking case is a nightmare. It's like a twisted game of Whack-a-Mole. Only right now, I can't even find a damned mole to whack."

"Aaron?"

"Aaron is missing, and the cop who was supposed to be watching him didn't show up. No one saw Aaron leave. Of course. Because everyone thought it was someone else's job to pay attention. Can we please send in the B team? Lily's gonna lose her mind if I don't come home soon."

Burgess badly wanted to say, "Then, she'll have to lose her mind, won't she?" but he didn't. Perry was just getting used to balancing work and family, something Burgess was also learning. He said, "When was Aaron last seen?"

Perry laughed. "They've got no fucking idea. I've looked around. I've checked the security cameras. But one skinny youth in a dark hoodie looks a lot like every other one, and it seems this was 'skinny kids in dark hoodies' day at this place. What now?"

So damned frustrating to be the answer man with no answers.

"I think we need to do some brainstorming. Let's meet at Spence's condo. Terry is already down there, and it's a place Cote won't bother us."

"I really should go—"

"You really should meet us there," Burgess said. "With luck, this won't take long, and then you can head home." He called Kyle and said they were coming down. If nothing else, it would give Burgess a chance to sniff the air for that elusive perfume he'd smelled at Aaron Daggett's apartment. He'd never gotten back down there to do that.

Probably gone by now.

He still had the key, though, since Rocky had remembered to give it back.

He and Perry parked in an area just before the condos and walked to meet Kyle, who was waiting by Spence's door.

Kyle's mood matched Perry's, as his first words were, "You got some more wild geese you want us to chase?"

Burgess shrugged. "Trying to figure out which goose to chase and where to look for it."

He unlocked the door, and the three of them went inside.

Even though the place had only been vacant a few days, the air smelled stale. He waved a hand toward the living room. "Just want to check something upstairs," he said. "Be right back."

Even with his team, who were used to each other's eccentricities, he didn't say he was going up to sniff the air.

Upstairs, in Spence's sterile black and white bedroom, he stopped, closed his eyes, and inhaled. That very faint scent of perfume was still there.

Bad guys did all sorts of things to fool investigators. They wore shoes of different sizes. Left clues that weren't clues. But few Burgess had known wore perfume as a deception technique. He went back downstairs again.

Kyle and Perry were seated on Spence's luxurious couches. Both had their eyes closed. Burgess thought that if he'd been a little longer, they both would have been asleep. It was exhausting to have to be constantly alert and observant. To work days and nights and be on the seesaw of adrenaline. He hovered at the foot of the stairs and listened. Perry fell asleep first, then Kyle. He let them sleep. Even a short nap could help restore their equilibrium.

Burgess sat on the stairs, closed his own eyes, and let his thoughts flow. He'd learned that if he let it have its way and listened, his intuition would sometimes give him answers. So would his city. He'd served it so long that it sometimes repaid the favor, answers coming on the night wind or in a brilliant reflection off the bay.

Eyes closed and breathing slowed, he sent his questions into the ether. Who? Where? Why?

He was practically asleep himself when the thought stabbed into him like someone had flung a dart. A crazy thought that nevertheless felt right.

If Mark Carlisle was here in the city, he was here because he was seeking Dr. Spence's killer. If Spence's killer was here, it was because she still had some loose ends to tie up and hadn't been successful at doing that yet.

Tell that to a civilian, or, for that matter, to a rookie or someone farther up the food chain, and they'd think you'd lost your mind. Burgess thought his mind had probably been found. He had the who and the why. All he needed was the where.

He yawned and stretched and got to his feet. Went into Dr. Spence's fine kitchen and used the doctor's coffeemaker and expensive coffee to make a pot that smelled delicious. When the beeper said it was done, he set out three cups and went back to the living room. It was time to wake his sleeping companions.

FORTY-THREE

"Smells a lot like coffee," Kyle said as he stretched and got to his feet. "You been making free with the doctor's possessions?"

"I have. Smells good, doesn't it?"

"It does," Kyle said and nudged Stan Perry. "Wakey, wake, Stanley. It's coffee time."

Perry didn't bounce to his feet like Kyle had. He slumped where he was sitting and shook his head. "I gotta go home, guys."

"Soon," Burgess said, putting a mug of coffee into Perry's hand. "And don't spill this on Dr. Spence's nice couch."

When everyone was beginning to be caffeinated, he shared the thought that the universe had delivered and got nods from both.

"Pretty far out there, Joe. Still, it sounds more plausible than some guy off his meds looking to take revenge on our witnesses," Kyle said. "That always felt off to me." He sighed. "Got any great ideas about how we find this guy or the person he's looking for? Maybe stand on street corners with cardboard signs like our panhandlers?"

Perry stood and took a defiant step toward the door. "I'm going home. I'm going to change my baby and feed my baby and put her to sleep, and then I'll be free to think about this crazy business. Right now, I feel like my brain is splitting in half, and neither half is working."

Burgess was still formulating a response when Kyle said, "Go, then. Do what you've got to do. We'll let you know where we are and what we're doing. You can join us if your busy personal life allows."

Perry hesitated, then shook his head. "I'll be back," he said and left.

When the door had closed behind him, Kyle said, "I never expected that. Impulsive as he is, kid's always been a team player."

"Thought I was the meanest cop in Portland," Burgess said.

Kyle nodded. "You are. But I have my moments." He poured himself more coffee and looked at Burgess. "So. BOLO (Be On the Look Out) on Dr. Benson's vehicle? And then...assuming she's here...which is quite an assumption...who would she be looking for? The most likely prospects are the three people we know who saw her arrive at Spence's—Aaron and Kristin Daggett, and Deidre Lovejoy. Agreed?" He added, "Not that it isn't stupid for someone who's gone to so much trouble to commit a crime to return."

"They're the ones we know about," Burgess agreed. "And there was that attack on Aaron."

"But your witness said she saw one of the Carlisles at the building. At least, her description matched them. And someone in a hoodie leaving, a person we believe to be Kristin Daggett. Right?"

Burgess nodded, surprised at how easy it was to let Kyle take charge. "The clothes we found in the dumpster, though. That can't have been Dr. Benson. She's tall but she's neither lean nor dark."

Kyle nodded. "Though there was that wig. And the suit was baggy. What about Mark Carlisle? BOLO on him, too? Do we have a plate number?"

Burgess shook his head, and Kyle got on the phone to see if he could locate one. Burgess was thinking that it was time to get their lieutenant involved. Too much going on or about to be put in motion. There should be a supervisor in the loop. They trusted Vince, and Vince trusted them. He got out his own phone.

When he'd described the situation, Melia said, "This for real or two wild goose chases?"

"I wish I knew. What I do know is that if we sit on our hands, someone may get killed, plus a killer who might be caught here could slip away back to Massachusetts, where our investigation will get a whole lot more complicated."

"I'll come in."

"We're not at 109," Burgess said. "We're down at Dr. Spence's condo."

There was silence while Melia processed that. Then he said, "I'll come there, then," and disconnected. Like Kyle and Burgess, Melia was a cop's cop. He didn't waste time on chat, and while his job meant he had to pay attention to paperwork, he wasn't a paperwork fanatic like his boss, Captain Cote. Burgess thought Melia missed the days of a more active job and was glad for a chance to get some action. At least now that the lieutenant was back on his feet after a nearly fatal shooting.

He turned to Kyle. "Vince is coming down."

"He thinks we're nuts?"

"Kinda. But he's intrigued."

They sat in silence then, sharing the feeling that something dark and evil was moving through their city, and it was up to them to stop it. There was the day-to-day of the job, the tireless plodding and questioning and collecting of information. Then, sometimes, there was something bigger, something like a huge jigsaw puzzle they had to put together with lethal consequences if they failed. A puzzle that took hard work to unearth the pieces. It was hard to put "dark and evil" and "beautiful and blonde" together, but they'd seen it before. Evil, or the compulsive desire to do harm or take revenge, came in many forms. Damage could happen to anyone, and people could get so twisted up by what was done to them.

In their silence, they could feel the minutes ticking by.

"Dammit," Burgess said. "If only Kristin and Aaron weren't so damned pigheaded. Hard to keep them safe when they won't let us help them. At least we've got patrol sitting on Deidre Lovejoy."

"Until the officer is needed elsewhere. Or until she decides she wants to go out for some reason," Kyle said. "I didn't get the impression she was particularly amenable to reason."

"You've got that right. She's definitely the type to go out just to defy us even though we're only trying to keep her safe." How often had they seen that? "So…Mark Carlisle. Do we think he's looking for Dr. Benson? Do we believe he's really off his meds and running wild, or that he's on a mission?"

"Mission," Kyle said. "Somebody killed the golden goose, and he wants revenge. Though he could be off his meds. Did they mention meds when you spoke with the Weston police?"

"Nope. They only said hot head without amplification. I'm wondering why his sister would turn him in. Is it because she wants him stopped?"

"Can't really say, Joe," Kyle said. "I only spoke with her once, and all I got was a sense that she's a cold, hard person. If I had to guess, which we're not supposed to do, I'd say she might be setting her brother up for harm either by us or by Dr. Benson. Then she inherits that much more."

"Except why would either of them stand to inherit? Wouldn't Lenore Spence's death sever the connection?" Burgess shook his head. "The more we think about it, the crazier it gets."

Kyle agreed.

They often solved cases this way by playing a game of verbal ping pong, where they bounced ideas back and forth. Testing theories, challenging assumptions. Trying to make sense of a disparate bunch of information. Usually, it was Burgess and Kyle. Sometimes, the three of them. Often, as now, with an oppressive sense of urgency weighing on them.

"I'm going to call Deidre Lovejoy," Burgess said. "Remind her that it would be dangerous to leave her condo. Not that it will probably do much good."

He made the call, and it went to voice mail. He left her a message, hoping that her failure to answer was stubbornness and not that she'd gone out. Then, because he believed in belts and suspenders, he called dispatch to confirm that an officer was watching the place, only to learn the officer had been called to a more urgent matter.

He looked at Kyle. "The officer watching her condo got called away."

"Big surprise," Kyle said. "What do you want to do?"

They both knew what he was going to do. "We'll wait 'til Vince gets here. Then you can check out Lovejoy's place while I look for Kristin and Aaron."

"You think he'd go back to his apartment?"

"Where else is he going to go?"

"Kristin with him?"

"That's a wild card. I've called her cell and the friend she was staying with. No joy there. But if they're anywhere around here or at Aaron's apartment, I have a fresh new recruit to help me look."

Kyle almost smiled. "Would that recruit, by any chance, be canine?"

"Fideau is very good at finding people." Besides, though he didn't say this to Kyle, when he was working so much, he actually missed the silly mutt. It was nice to have one member of his household who didn't stare at him with reproving eyes. Fideau, the Crime Scene Dog, was unfailingly faithful and loving.

He called Dylan and asked him to bring the dog down to Spence's condo. While they waited for Melia, he went across the street to the

Daggetts' condo. A bit of relentless knocking brought The Wicked to the door, looking like she'd just finished a jar of sour pickles.

"She's not here, and I don't know where she is, and I wish you'd stop bothering me about this."

"Have you heard from her?"

She gave an indifferent shrug. "No."

Burgess had a lecture he could have given about the responsibilities she'd taken on when she married the children's father. He saved it for another day. Instead, he said, "I need a piece of clothing that Kristin has worn. Can you find one for me, please?"

She looked startled. "You're going to get the search dogs out? Do you think something has happened to her?" Like that had never occurred to her, despite the attack on Aaron? Despite Kristin being only thirteen?

Part of the lecture came tumbling out. "Jesus, Lady," he said. "She's missing somewhere in this city with no responsible parent to look after her, and there may be a killer on the loose. You know someone already attacked her brother. So yes, we're going to do whatever we can to locate her, and a dog can help with that." No need to tell her it was his own pet dog.

Dylan was there with the dog in a flash. Probably drove too fast, and Burgess didn't care. He hugged his son and took the dog's leash. Fideau gave him the canine version of "Oh my gosh, you've been gone so long, and I've missed you so much, and are we going to play now?"

"Definitely your dog," Dylan said.

"He thinks so," Burgess agreed. "How's Nina?"

His son shrugged. "She's okay. Can't stop blaming herself for what happened. Mom wants her to call her therapist, and she won't."

Burgess nodded. "She needs to do that."

"I'll tell her you said so," his smartass son said.

Then Melia arrived, took a look at Dylan, said, "A Burgess clone, for sure," and gave his son a hug.

"Gotta go, Dad. A ton of homework," and Dylan left.

Melia looked at the dog, waiting patiently by the door. He said, "The newest member of your team?"

Burgess nodded. "Fideau, say hello to Lt. Melia."

Fideau extended a paw.

Melia took it and shook it. "Pleased to meet you," he said. They had met the night Burgess acquired Fideau, but that had been such a crazy shit-storm it was hard to remember any particular details, beyond Burgess watching his son bleeding on the floor.

"So, what's the plan?" Melia asked. "What do you need from me?"

"We may need more bodies on this thing." He hesitated. "Live ones. We'll scout it out first and let you know. We need you in the loop. Someone taking point on this while Kyle and I are out looking for missing witnesses, threatened witnesses, and two people who may have them in their sights."

"Back up and fill me in," Melia said.

Burgess and Kyle gave him the background, identified the players, and described the threat.

"And we're here instead of at 109 because?"

"Because we don't need Cote getting in the way asking for reports and details when we're handling an urgent situation," Burgess said.

"What you *think* is an urgent situation."

Burgess patted his stomach, where for now the knife was slumbering, and said, "My gut," adding, "Because we don't want to spook the city reporting that there might be an enraged killer on the loose, and—"

He stopped himself. He didn't need to explain to Melia the risks Cote's compulsive need for media attention posed in a situation like this.

"Okay. You and Terry go and do what you've gotta do. I'm going back to 109, and you two keep me in the loop. If you need more people on this, don't fart around trying to be heroes." He looked at Burgess. "I mean it, Joe."

"Okay," Burgess said. "We'll keep you in the loop." He debated telling his boss that the department had already pulled the cop who was watching Lovejoy's condo. It sounded too much like playground tattling. The department was chronically short-staffed and had to prioritize risk.

Kyle and Melia headed out. Burgess made a quick call to Chris, saying he expected it would be an all-nighter, then offered Kristin's black tee shirt to Fideau. The dog sniffed the shirt, then looked at Burgess, nodded, and set off into the night, nose to the ground, nose to the air, nose to the ground. A long shot, Burgess knew, but Fideau had come through before.

FORTY-FOUR

I t was a cool evening, and despite a brisk ocean breeze, the air felt heavy. Burgess knew it wasn't what was outside of him. It was what was inside. His dark sense that bad things were moving through this night, and it fell to him and to Kyle to stop them. Maybe to an outsider or a compulsive watcher of TV crime shows, that would sound melodramatic. A moment when the music would get dark and sinister and thump beneath the actions of the characters. And then, there would be a commercial break. But in his real world, he knew there was evil. He knew about people bent on revenge. He knew how damaged people could have a distorted sense of right and wrong that made vengeance seem justifiable. He knew there were no commercial breaks.

He couldn't recall a time when they had two such individuals at work at the same time. Suspected individuals, he reminded himself. Plenty of times, cops said to each other, "Watch your back. Or watch your six," because there were threats out there. In truth, it was hard to watch your own back. He wondered if he was making a mistake, sending Kyle off on his own instead of the two of them working together. They really needed Stan Perry here to watch at least one of their backs. When it came down to death or diapers, he thought Perry had made the wrong choice. But hadn't he chosen Nina over the investigation?

Fideau headed toward the Daggetts' condo and sniffed at the door, then trotted off, Burgess following. He was learning to trust his dog. They might not find Kristin, but Fideau was definitely scenting something.

Fideau checked out the dumpster at the end of the condo block. A few parked cars. Then headed back toward the city, pulling eagerly on the leash.

Like Timmy with Lassie in the lead, Burgess followed, trying not to be too hopeful. There were some bars along here and a couple of restaurants. None of them places where a girl that young ought to be. He thought about Nina at that age. The trouble she'd gotten herself in by being young and hopeful and trusting.

He wished he knew more about this dog. Its past, its training. Whether he was expecting too much. They hadn't been together very long, but he had turned to Fideau in the past to locate a missing child, and the dog had come through for him. It was kind of a miracle the way the dog could trace Kristin's scent with all the other scents that must be carried by the wind.

After trotting briskly for a few blocks, the dog turned into a parking lot, mostly empty at this time of night. Had Kristin taken refuge in one of the boats docked at the end of this lot? That brought him back to another boat and another young girl who'd been too trusting, and those memories woke the slumbering knife.

Burgess had been knifed in the real world. He knew how it felt. His own internal knife wasn't so different. More than once he'd tried to throw it up but it wouldn't budge. It was as much a part of him as his arms and legs.

Looking right and left at the few cars still parked there, Burgess followed as Fideau trotted through the parking lot. No black BMW. No silver Prius. Fideau stopped, finally, outside a small shed-like structure. He turned and looked at Burgess and then back at the structure's door. Then he lay down on the ground and put his nose on his paws.

"In here?" Burgess asked, reaching for the door. Then he hesitated.

The procedures for approaching a suspicious door are drilled into cops from day one. This tired, battered door didn't look threatening, and he was here looking for a missing girl, not a suspected or would-be killer. Still, caution meant he didn't just reach for the handle and open the door. He stood to the side, then carefully reached out. The door should have been locked, but it wasn't. It swung slowly outward, the air rolling toward him carrying the scents of dampness and dust and something chemical.

At first, as he moved his flashlight around, he thought the shed was empty. Just snow shovels and paint cans and a pile of old canvas tarps.

Then he heard a shuddering sob and picked out what appeared to be a figure huddled in the corner, hidden by one of the tarps.

Could have been anyone. A homeless person who'd found shelter for the night. He said, "Kristin. It's Detective Burgess," in a low voice.

No answer.

He moved closer. Spoke a little louder. "Kristin? It's Burgess. I don't want to scare you. Just need to see that you're okay."

Suddenly, the tarp was pushed aside, and she rushed toward him, throwing herself into his arms. "She was chasing me. At first, she said she was just looking for directions, and then I got closer, and I saw it was her. The woman I saw going into Dr. Spence's condo the night he died. And I saw what she had in her hand. It was one of those sharp little knives that doctors use. A scalpel, I think they're called. And so I ran. She came after me, but I am very fast."

She broke off and buried her face against his chest.

"Is she out there? Is she still out there looking for me?"

There had been no suspicious vehicles in the lot when he entered and spotted the shed. But someone could have arrived. He summoned Fideau and said, "Fideau will stay with you while I check things out."

Slowly, reluctantly, she released her grip on his shirt and stepped back. She looked terrified. Fideau immediately put himself between her and the door.

"He won't hurt you. He's very gentle," Burgess said. "But he will protect you."

As she put out a tentative hand toward the dog, Burgess extinguished his light and stepped out into the dark, back against the building. He could feel rough boards as he stood there, very still, studying the lot. He reviewed the vehicles he'd seen on his way in and where they were parked. There was another vehicle near the entrance that hadn't been there before. In the dim light, all he could make out was that it was a dark sedan. Could be a black BMW. Could be anything.

He waited. Watching. No sign of movement in the car. He listened to the sounds of someone moving. Over the wind and the waves, he couldn't hear much. Slowly, he moved to the edge of the building and ducked around the corner, crouching over his phone to hide the light while he texted Kyle and Perry. He reported he'd found Kristin Daggett and asked for one of them to back him up.

Kyle responded immediately with: Can't. Watching a silver Prius. Carlisle?

Nothing from Stan, who was probably still doing baby duty. He texted Vince that he needed backup. No lights or sirens.

He didn't care if he was dragging patrol to a wild goose chase. This whole case involved chasing geese. Dr. Spence was the golden goose, and everyone else was after him or what was his.

He stepped back around the corner and studied the lot again. Nothing moving. Then, off to his left he heard a faint sound like the whisper of fabric rubbing against something. As he turned toward the sound, there was a rush of footsteps, and a woman in a dark coat burst from the shadows and came at him, her hand outstretched. Too dark to see what she was holding, but he wasn't waiting to see if this was Kristin's would-be attacker with a scalpel. He turned toward her and swung the heavy flashlight he was holding at the approaching hand. It connected just as the hand reached him.

There was a cry of pain and the clatter of something falling to the ground.

The figure dove for it. Burgess had his foot over it before his assailant could grab it. He said, "Police. Stand up and put your hands on your head."

She took off running. He went after her, yelling, "Stop. Police!" He had to say it. Protocol again. Few people ever stopped.

The black watch cap flew off, and a mass of blonde hair spilled out, catching some light before she disappeared into shadows.

Ahead of her running figure, he could see a patrol car crawling to a stop at the entrance to the lot.

He called, "Watch her. She may have a weapon."

Caught between him behind and the officers ahead, she suddenly veered off to the left, where a set of stairs led down to a dock where boats were moored.

Just what he needed. He accelerated, as did the approaching officer. The officer, being younger and faster, got there first. He commanded her to stop, and when she didn't comply, he tased her.

Excellent use of less lethal weapons.

She went down in a screaming heap.

By the time Burgess got there, the officer had her on her stomach and was cuffing her.

"Search her carefully," Burgess said. "She came at me with a scalpel. She may have more weapons on her."

Pulled to her feet, she glared at Burgess. "You've spoiled everything."
Lotta people felt that way.

FORTY-FIVE

Patrol took her away to be booked for assault on a police officer and resisting arrest, collecting the scalpel as evidence. Additional charges could come later.

Before returning to Kristin, Burgess took a moment to catch his breath. These spurts of intense activity with their adrenaline surges left him exhausted these days, and the night's work was far from over. When his heart rate was down and he was breathing easily again, he went back to the shed to collect Kristin and Fideau.

As he reached the door, he realized that he didn't know what he was going to do with the girl. He couldn't keep her with him. He could take her back to her condo, but The Wicked was no fit person to care for a girl who'd just been chased by a suspected killer and feared for her life. She needed to be able to decompress in safety.

Dammit! Why was everything so complicated? He could call social services, but they weren't right for a situation like this. Their remit would be to find her a bed for the night. He needed Andrea Dwyer.

Before he called Dwyer, though, he texted Kyle again: Dr. Benson in custody. Kristin safe. You?

He got back three words: Watching. Stan coming?

Meaning Kyle was still watching the silver Prius. Was Stan coming for backup?

He'd join Kyle as soon as he could. He called Dwyer.

"Suddenly, I'm so popular," she said.

"Of course you are. Got a job for you if you're available."

"Always available for you, Joe."

He described the situation and asked if she could come and get Kristin and give the girl a chance to debrief.

"Another of your waifs," she said.

"I do seem to collect them."

"You sure do. Maybe you should become the kiddie cop, and I can be the tough detective for a while."

"Job is yours if you want it."

"Joe. You will never retire."

Burgess told her where he was, and she said she'd be there in ten minutes. He went into the shed and found Kristin back in her corner, and Fideau settled on the floor in front of her. Guard dog on the case.

"It's okay, Kristin. The woman who was chasing you is in custody. You're safe."

She slowly unfolded from her crouch. "What do I do now? Do I have to go back to The Wicked? And what about Aaron? I think he's gone back to his apartment. Does this mean that he is safe?"

"Soon as we get you settled, I'm going over there to check things out."

"Settled?"

He told her Andrea Dwyer was coming down to get her and reminded her she'd met Dwyer before. "She's great. You'll really like her."

She gave him a semblance of her impish grin. "I thought you'd leave me in the care of Fideau the Wonder Dog." She put a hand on Fideau's head. "He's really great, too. It's…sounds funny, I know…but it's almost as though he can talk."

"I think he can."

That got another grin, which fell as she studied him. "Detective Burgess. Did you know you're bleeding?"

He sighed, choosing not to say, "Oh Fuck!" He said, "It's nothing," though he didn't know whether it was serious or not. He'd shed so much blood on the job. It sometimes seemed like he couldn't solve a case without a blood sacrifice. Not something this girl needed to know. Now that he was aware of it, his arm started to ache. But it was an ooze, not a gush. He probably had something in the truck he could use to wrap it. He had neither the time nor the inclination to go over to the hospital and get himself repaired. Not even if his favorite ER doc might be there. She took good care of him, but she was as sick of patching him up as he was of getting patched.

"Let's get out of this smelly place," he said, and they stepped out into the night. He was eager to be gone to back up Kyle but couldn't leave her alone.

Kristin was wearing only jeans and a tee shirt and was shivering. Normally, he'd give her his jacket, but it was in the truck, and his shirt was bloody. "We're a pathetic pair, aren't we?" he said. "Not a jacket between us."

"I had a jacket. It's in my backpack, but I dropped it when I was running. I can probably find it if I retrace my steps."

"We'll wait for Dwyer, and the two of you can find it."

"Okay." She crouched down and wrapped her arms around Fideau. Half for comfort, half to stay warm. The dog gave her his reassuring look. She looked up at Burgess. "Fideau's so smart."

Burgess watched Dwyer's cruiser turn into the lot, coming to a stop in front of them. Dwyer got out and said hello to Kristin.

"She's lost her backpack somewhere when she was running from an attacker. Maybe you can help her find it?"

"I can." Her gaze fell to his arm. "Another blood sacrifice, Joe?"

"Afraid so. Our subject is a physician. Armed with a scalpel. Thought I'd ducked in time, but I guess not. It's no big deal."

She laughed. "I know cops who'd consider that reason to take a week off. Guess they don't make 'em like they used to."

Like he needed reminding that he was a dinosaur? "I've gotta go," he said. "Kyle needs backup." He looked around. "Truck's down by Spence's condo."

"Want a ride?" she asked.

"Yes. Thank you. I do. Uh...we do." Couldn't forget Fideau, could he?

Kristin got in, and Fideau jumped in beside her. Before he got in, Dwyer leaned across the hood. "Got some news about Dexter Wiggins. Looks like the DA is willing to approve sending him to a special school out of state for adolescents with behavior issues. If they'll take him."

"Behavior issues? That's a new term for kidnapping and attempted rape."

"At least he'll be gone, Joe. Meanwhile, he's not going to be staying with his parents after all. Going to a juvenile facility. Someone convinced the judge he presented a threat to the public."

"Bless that someone. Thank you." He climbed into her car.

As they drove the short distance, Kristin said, "What about my brother? What about Aaron? Is he safe now that you've arrested that woman?"

"Aaron's gone back to his apartment, right?"

"He has. But is he—"

"He should be fine. But I'll head over there and check things out, just in case," Burgess said, telling the kind of reassuring lie cops often told.

But Kristin wasn't easily reassured. "But you said you had to go and back up someone named Kyle. Is that not about what happened to Dr. Spence?"

"Yes. There's another suspect involved," he reluctantly agreed. "But Aaron should be safe."

Enough "let it go" in his tone that she did.

Dwyer dropped Burgess and his dog at Spence's place and parked, and then she and Kristin headed off to look for the backpack.

Burgess called Melia and gave him an update. "Patrol is bringing in Dr. Heather Benson, our prime suspect in the killing of Dr. Eliot Spence. I'm off to back up Kyle. He's watching a vehicle we think belongs to Dr. Spence's former brother-in-law. The one whose sister says is off his meds."

"Keep me in the loop," Melia said. Necessary because it was his job to say it; unnecessary because he already knew Burgess would. "You need more people?"

"Trying not to spook him. More people might do that. We could use Stan Perry if he gets free—" Burgess stopped. He wasn't ready to share the reason for Perry's absence. Not yet. If it became a chronic problem, then Melia would need to know about it.

"You should know," Melia said, "that Cote sent someone to pick up that Madam or whatever they're called these days. Marni? She's flown the coop."

Burgess wasn't surprised. Her surprising candor made more sense if she was planning to run. He thought maybe she'd gotten a heads-up from someone in Vice that people were asking questions. When he wasn't on the clock with people at risk, there were things like this to ponder. But not right now.

Before he started driving, he got out his first aid kit and wrapped his arm. It was a nasty cut and should have stitches. Maybe later, when he wasn't busy catching bad guys. Chris would be furious that he'd gotten injured again. She was protective and worried about him. A good thing and a bad thing. It was hard to get used to being fussed over, even if she'd call it caring for him.

He texted Kyle: On my way. Park where? And got back directions. He parked the truck. Said, "Wait here," to Fideau and got a nod. Texted Stan to say where they were.

He grabbed his jacket, carefully threading his wounded arm through the sleeve. Kyle was sitting in his vehicle across from the building's front door. The silver Prius was parked about five cars down on the same side.

He climbed into Kyle's passenger seat. "You think he's inside the building?"

"I do."

"In Aaron Daggett's apartment?"

Kyle nodded. "We don't know that Daggett is there, though."

"Yes. We do. His sister told us."

Christ. A hostage situation with an already vulnerable teenage boy.

"What about Daggett's roommate?"

"Not home."

Maybe a good thing, but Aaron's giant roommate might have made short work of Mark Carlisle. Or gotten himself injured or killed in the process. Burgess knew firsthand that Melendez tended to act before he thought.

This should have been a situation for the SRT officers. They were trained to handle hostage situations. "SRT?" Burgess said.

"Let's give a bit. See what we can do."

Burgess nodded. He trusted Kyle's instincts.

They settled in to watch the door. A minute later, a woman Burgess recognized as Sybil came out. Tonight, she was back to her wildly mismatched garments. She looked up and down the street, then marched right to Kyle's vehicle, tapping on the window until he lowered it.

"There's a crazy man in Aaron's apartment," she said. "You need to do something."

Their responses crossed, with Kyle asking, "How do you know?" and Burgess asking, "Is Aaron okay?"

"Aaron's okay. He's at my place. Slipped out the window and came up the fire escape. He's a clever boy, that one. As for how I know about the crazy man? Aaron told me. But you know Sam is due home any time now, and then something bad could happen." She spun her fingers in the air near her ear. "You know Sam's not the sharpest tool, right?"

Burgess nodded.

"So..." She planted her hands on her skinny hips. "What are you gonna do?"

Good question, Burgess thought. "Do you know how long this crazy man has been in the apartment?"

She shrugged.

"Does Aaron have his phone with him? Could he call or text and tell Sam not to come home yet?"

She shrugged again. "I never thought of that. I think you'd better tell him yourself." She looked at Burgess. "You know my mind is a muddle. I might not get it right. You can come with me right now. Or whatever. I'll leave the door open."

Turning as abruptly as she'd come, she walked back toward the building.

"One of us better go," Kyle said. "And she trusts you."

"Unless it's a trap."

Silence in the dark vehicle. They had no reason to suspect it was a trap except for her sudden appearance and the way she'd headed straight for Kyle. How would she know they were there?

"Christ. I don't know," Kyle said. "We can't sit out here all night. If young Stanley were here, we could send him in, and there would still be two of us to pull him out if it was a trap."

"Oh no. We couldn't send Diaper Daddy into a trap." He felt mean the instant he said it.

"Diaper Daddy. We've gotten so cynical, Joe."

"Long ago."

A car they recognized came crawling down the street and parked almost across from them. "Speak of the devil," Kyle said.

Perry opened Kyle's rear door and climbed in. "So, what have we got?"

"A mystery," Kyle said. "We suspect that Mark Carlisle is in the building looking for Aaron Daggett. Probably in Daggett's apartment. Daggett's roommate is due home any time now. We know all this because a woman named Sybil, who keeps track of people's comings and goings, tells us that Carlisle is in Aaron's apartment, and Aaron is in hers. She says Aaron came up the fire escape."

"Is she reliable?" Perry asked.

"Maybe."

"We suggested she get Aaron to text his roommate and tell him not to come home. She thought that message was too complicated for her to deliver and suggested one of us do it. We were just about to flip a coin."

"Mark Carlisle being here doesn't make any sense if he's looking for the woman who killed Eliot Spence."

Burgess thought nothing about Mark Carlisle made sense, but this was nothing new. They'd dealt with plenty of people whose behavior didn't make sense.

"Sure it does," Kyle said. "He's looking for the people she'll target who can place her at Spence's the night he was killed. And oh, by the way, she's in custody. Spence's alleged killer. She was stalking Kristin Daggett. When Burgess intervened, she went after him with a scalpel."

"Bet that's a first," Perry said.

Burgess mentally reviewed the things he'd been stabbed or hit with. Thought a scalpel *was* a first. He saw the navy blue of his jacket was darker blue over his wound. Screw it. Nothing he could do about that now. At least it was his left arm, not his right. Cops had a saying: Sooner or later, everyone goes home hurting. In his case, it was sooner *and* later.

"I'm going in," Kyle said. "Joe, you remember which apartment our Sybil is in?"

Burgess told him the number. Said, "We'll all go, but we should tell Vince what's up."

"What we suspect is up," Kyle corrected.

Burgess gave Melia a quick heads-up. Got Melia's dubious, "Is this a good idea?" To which he only mumbled a reply. Melia might be pissed. He didn't have time to argue their case.

He put his phone away and nodded to the others. "Let's do this."

FORTY-SIX

They exited the vehicle quietly. No slammed doors. No conversation. Their footsteps nearly silent as they crossed the street. She had indeed left the door propped open.

They were operating with the vaguest of plans. Kyle would knock. If Aaron was there, they would instruct him to text his roommate to stay away, then move on to Aaron's apartment and try to coax Carlisle out.

If someone in Sybil's apartment was waiting for them and grabbed Kyle, they would be there for backup.

A million things could go wrong, but Sam Melendez's imminent arrival at an apartment where an armed man who might be unhinged was waiting made the situation urgent.

At least step one went right. Aaron Daggett, looking like he'd been dragged behind a truck and starved in a shed, answered the door. Kyle said, "Anyone else here besides you and Sybil?"

Daggett shook his head. Weakly, as though speech was beyond him.

They stepped into the apartment. The décor matched Sybil's outfits on a crazy day, but at least it was clean. A quick search said no one else was there.

Kyle stood over Daggett and tried to walk him through sending a text message to his roommate. After a few fumbles, Kyle took the phone and sent the message himself. The boy needed to be tucked into bed and fed chicken soup.

They waited for a response.

Crickets.

"Does he usually respond to your texts?" Burgess asked.

Daggett gave a feeble shrug. "I don't often text him. We just...you know...talk when we're home."

Great. So they didn't know if Melendez would register the text or respond.

"We've got to go down there," Burgess said. "Stop him before he gets to the apartment."

Daggett gave another weary shrug, as though lifting his shoulders was too hard, and said, "If it's not too late. Sam is a creature of habit. If he plans to be home at nine, he'll be home at nine. It helps him structure his life."

It was five past nine.

"I'm going down," Kyle said.

"I'm going down the fire escape," Perry said. He looked at Aaron. "You left the window open?"

"I did."

"When Mark Carlisle came into your apartment?"

Aaron Daggett didn't answer.

"How did Carlisle get into your apartment?"

"I..." Daggett put his head in his hands. "I was stupid, okay? He knocked on the door, and I opened it. I wasn't thinking. I expected it would be Kristin. She said she was coming over. That she couldn't stay there alone with The Wicked. She just couldn't." He broke off. "Is my sister okay? Do you know where she is?"

"We know where she is. She's with a very reliable police officer. And she's fine."

No time to go into details about Kristin's situation.

Burgess looked at Sybil. "Can you fix Aaron some tea?"

She nodded and headed for the small kitchen area in a corner of her studio apartment.

Perry slipped out the window.

Burgess and Kyle headed down the stairs.

They were too late. They could hear the confrontation between Sam Melendez and a man they believed to be Mark Carlisle before they got there. Melendez was saying, "What the fuck? You're coming at me with a gun in my own place? Where's Aaron? Is he okay? Because if he's not okay, man, then you are in deep shit."

Not intimidated by a gun, was he? Probably, a man his size wasn't scared by much. But Carlisle was a wild card. They knew next to nothing about him or how he'd react. He'd come here to make something happen, and he'd come with a gun.

They crept down the last few stairs and flattened themselves against the wall. Listening for something to give them a clue about how to proceed.

Carlisle said, "I've got no issue with you. I just need to find Aaron. Talk to him. I'm looking for someone, and I think he's seen her. I think he knows where she is."

Sounding so calm and rational.

They waited.

"Aaron's at work," Melendez said. "He's always at work this time of night."

They listened, hoping Carlisle would ask for an address and then leave. But Carlisle had seen Aaron when he answered the door.

"He was here," Carlisle insisted. "He answered the door, and then he disappeared. I think he went down the fire escape. Where would he go?"

"Sorry. Can't help you," Melendez said. "He doesn't tell me about his comings and goings. What do you want him for, anyway?"

"I just told you. I'm looking for someone, and he knows where she is." There was frustration in Carlisle's voice now. And anger. He was on a mission, and people were getting in his way. The situation looked to go south very soon.

Burgess realized that because of his size, Melendez filled the doorway, blocking Carlisle's view of the hall. He slipped around the corner, positioning himself beside the big man where Carlisle couldn't see him. Kyle slid in on the other side.

He worried that Melendez might react or say something, but the man remained firmly in the doorway. Sometimes, being stubborn could be a good thing.

Kyle reached in his pocket, and Burgess figured he was setting his phone to record whatever came next.

As though they'd communicated it to him, Melendez suddenly took a big step backward, and Burgess and Kyle, guns drawn, filled the space he'd left, pushing forward into the room and driving Carlisle back with the force of their charge.

Carlisle pointed his gun at them with a shaking hand. "Get out of my way!" he demanded. "I need to go and look for that kid. Or his sister. I need to find the woman who killed my brother-in-law. She had no right to do that."

Over Carlisle's shoulder, Burgess could see Stan Perry coming into the room. He said, "Are you Mark Carlisle?"

Carlisle nodded.

"Burgess. Portland police. I need you to drop your gun, Mr. Carlisle, before somebody gets hurt."

"I don't care if someone gets hurt. I've been hurt."

Faking sympathy, Burgess said, "Are you injured, Mr. Carlisle? Do you need medical attention?"

Carlisle shook his head and focused on aiming his shaking gun at Burgess.

"Why are you looking for this woman? The one you believe killed Dr. Spence?"

"She took something from me. Something I can't get back. So, I'm going to take something from her." He grinned. An abnormal, disturbing grin. "Her life."

He looked at Burgess. "You have to understand. Eliot was my friend. My buddy. He got that I needed his help and support. Lenore understood that, and so Eliot did what she wanted. It all would have been okay if Belinda hadn't gone and screwed up."

Calmly, like he was used to having conversations like this while facing a loaded gun, Burgess said, "Belinda's your sister, right?"

He got a nod.

"How did Belinda screw up? What did she do?"

That ghastly grin again, lips pulled back tightly against his teeth. "She killed Lenore. Of course, it was supposed to look like an accident, see."

Don't gasp. Don't show surprise. Don't let on how important this information was. He shot a glance at Kyle and got a nod. Assuming the phone could pick it up, this was all being recorded.

Burgess waited for Carlisle to explain. When nothing came, he said, "I thought your sister Lenore accidentally fell down the stairs."

"Oh no. That's what the police were supposed to think, and they didn't want to press for answers because Eliot's an important doctor. See, they would never consider that Belinda might be involved." He shrugged, and the gun in his hand dipped and lowered.

Guns were scary enough. A loaded gun in the unsteady hands of a disturbed individual was scarier.

"You filed a wrongful death action against Eliot. Against your brother-in-law. Why do that if you know your sister was the one who killed Lenore? Killed her own sister?"

Carlisle looked puzzled. "Well. Belinda was going to file a suit, and so I had to, see, so that I could get my share of the money. See, since Lenore was gone, Eliot figured he didn't have to pay me anymore. Only, see, I relied on that money. How else could I make my music or pay my rent?"

"I'm confused," Burgess said, trying to keep the tremble from his own gun hand. "Why would your sister Belinda kill your other sister Lenore? We were told they were close."

He thought he knew the answer but needed to hear it.

"Belinda was jealous of Lenore. Belinda wanted Eliot for herself, see. She'd met him first. She thought he ought to belong to her. Plus, you know, Belinda is attractive but Lenore she's...she was beautiful. Belinda couldn't stand it that Lenore had everything."

"Belinda caused your sister Lenore to fall downstairs?"

Carlisle nodded. Gave that sick grin again.

"Did she tell you how she arranged that?"

"Oh yeah. See, even though she thinks I'm a loser, Belinda always confides in me. She always has. We're just fifteen months apart. We always thought of ourselves as like twins."

Evil twins, Burgess thought as he brought his left arm up to brace his right. It hurt like hell. He was trying to keep other questions out of his head for now and concentrate on what Mark Carlisle had to tell them. On drawing out the essential information without getting anyone shot.

"How did she do it?"

"Well. She was over there earlier in the evening for drinks, and she put something in Eliot's drink so he wouldn't wake up. Then she put furniture polish on the floor near the top of the stairs, called Eliot's phone, and waited for Lenore to come out. We all knew about their crazy practice of keeping their phones out of the bedroom, see."

That sick grin again. Burgess wished he *could* put a bullet in it.

Carlisle seemed to be enjoying the story he was telling. "Belinda pushed her down the stairs and tossed those foolish slippers down after her. Then she went down the other stairs and drove home." He stopped. "She was so sure Lenore was dead or would die she didn't even stop to check. That's Belinda. She's very sure of herself, see."

"But why would you be okay with killing Lenore if it might mean your income would stop?"

"Easy. Because Belinda would marry Eliot, of course. Then, she'd make sure I got paid."

Who uses the word "easy" when speaking of a plan to murder his sister? Someone Burgess had been told was a lovely and generous person. Amazing, given the snakes her siblings were.

"But Eliot Spence didn't become involved with your sister. He moved to Maine and found a new girlfriend instead. Is that why your sister filed her lawsuit?"

"Oh. She just did that because I said I was going to file mine, and Belinda can't be upstaged." Not what he'd said a moment ago.

God. This was pathetic. Burgess looked down. His gun was practically a metronome. He hoped Kyle and Perry were steadier. Mark Carlisle didn't seem to notice. Between him and Kyle, Sam Melendez, who could have lost it and gotten someone shot, was steady as a stone.

"Did you know what Belinda was planning?"

Carlisle shook his head. "She was afraid I'd screw things up. I cared for Lenore, see. And I knew he'd never go for Belinda. She's my sister, and I love her, but she's a real cold fish."

Jesus. There was so much wrong with this. With this pathetic man. With his heartless sister.

"She told you later?"

Carlisle nodded. "Yeah. I assumed Eliot did it, see. Because of the other women, you know. Because he has…had an addiction. At least, that's how he explained it to me. He loved Lenore. He adored her. But he was a sex addict and couldn't help himself, and if Lenore knew, she'd leave him. She loved him, but she would never tolerate that. Well, I knew that Belinda had a thing for him, and when Lenore died, I told her about his addiction in case she seriously intended to move in on him. She said she didn't care, and that's when she told me about killing Lenore. She made it sound like a reasonable thing to do, see. She was the stronger one, the smarter one. She should have had Eliot if she wanted him."

He shrugged. "Crazy reasoning, see, but I don't argue with Belinda. She's scary."

That was pretty much the bottom line. Belinda Carlisle was scary, and if what her brother was saying was true, she had no qualms about killing someone to get what she wanted. He wondered why the Weston police hadn't taken a closer look. Wouldn't they have checked Spence's phone to see who'd made that call? To see if there had even been a call?

Plenty of time for those questions.

He pulled his thoughts back to the here and now.

They were fixed there, the five of them, in a frozen tableau of men with guns when Burgess heard footsteps on the stairs. It could be a resident of the building, but his instinct told him it was someone else. The steps sounded female, and if this were a novel, this would be the moment for Belinda Carlisle to make an appearance. Probably come to silence her brother, but who knew whether she'd be willing to kill police officers in the process? Had her call to the police been an attempt to get her brother killed, knowing he wouldn't act reasonably in a confrontation? Would that have left all of Spence's money for her if she won her lawsuit?

He nodded at Kyle, who nodded back, their mind-reading skills in play. Kyle turned toward the stairs and moved to the wall where someone coming up couldn't see him.

Carlisle, surprised by Kyle's move, turned his head to see what was happening. Perry used the distraction to grab him and throw him to the floor. Sam Melendez came to life, wrestled the gun away, and added his weight to the thrashing man, so Perry was able to cuff him.

One down and one to go?

Burgess turned toward the stairs and waited. His instincts hadn't failed him. Belinda Carlisle, all in black and looking so much like her brother it was scary, came around the corner. She was holding a gun, but it wasn't raised, just ready and waiting in case it might be needed.

How she'd known where to find her brother was a question that could wait with the others lining up for answers. What couldn't wait was subduing her and getting that gun.

She spotted Burgess in the doorway and raised her gun, giving a decisive jerk of her chin that said, "Out of my way."

Getting out of the way so bad guys could commit bad acts wasn't in Burgess's vocabulary. He pointed his gun at her and said, "Portland police. Drop your weapon."

She would have shot him as easily as she breathed if Kyle hadn't stepped out and brought his gun down on her outstretched arm. She screamed. Her gun clattered to the floor. She flung herself at Kyle like she was a hungry wildcat and he was prey. Burgess kicked the gun out of her reach and bent to help Kyle. She was all flailing arms and legs and bared teeth, and she was strong. Sorry, but he wasn't fucking getting bitten on top of everything else.

Together, they got her on her stomach and cuffed her. Then Burgess searched her. He found pepper spray, a knife, and disposable cuffs in her pockets. Jesus. Nothing like being prepared.

He got out his phone and called Melia. "We've got two suspects in custody, and we need patrol to pick them up." He gave the address.

"This is keeping me in the loop?" Melia said.

"This was doing a welfare check on a subject who might have been approached by our suspect and walking into a shitstorm. Gun party. Luckily, no one is hurt. If we're really lucky, Kyle's got it all recorded."

FORTY-SEVEN

M elia sighed. "You three," he said. "Do you need me there?"

"We need you to interview these suspects, once you've heard our reports. But save Dr. Benson for me."

Burgess didn't think writing reports was gonna happen anytime soon. He was beyond burned out. Gun parties did that. All that self-control and trying to keep everyone safe and pushing back against the tunnel vision that wanted to narrow his focus. Then suddenly, it was over, and they would be left like three popped balloons. Well, maybe not Stan Perry. Though Perry the Diaper Daddy was a whole new creature. Sleepless nights and big responsibilities had settled heavily on him and left him as drained as Burgess and Kyle were.

"Vince. We're fried," he said. "If you could send someone over to take witness statements. See if Sage Prentiss is available."

This wasn't like him. Burgess was a control freak. You had to be if you wanted successful prosecutions. Details mattered. Words mattered. Evidence and chain of custody mattered. You didn't switch horses midstream.

Kyle put a hand on his unwounded arm. "We've got this, Joe. Me and Stan. We can finish up here if you want to go get mended."

Melia, still on the phone, said, "Mended? What the hell, Joe?"

He didn't have the stamina to invent excuses. He said, "Down on the waterfront. The doctor we arrested…our best suspect in Dr. Spence's killing? She had a scalpel."

"Is it bad?"

"Just needs a few stitches."

"Crap. Just once, I would like you to solve a case without a blood sacrifice, Joe."

"We don't choose 'em, Vince. We just solve them." He handed his phone to Kyle.

On the floor by their feet, Belinda Carlisle was trying to eel her way to the stairs. He put a foot on her back—definitely police brutality—and said, "Lie still."

"I've got her, Joe," Kyle said. "Go sit down."

Burgess went and sat. He looked at Sam Melendez, who was sitting on the floor beside Mark Carlisle, one massive arm across Carlisle's back. Said, "You were great tonight, Sam. An absolute rock. We are so grateful."

Melendez looked at the floor and mumbled, "Thanks. So, is Aaron really okay? Because I'd like him to come home, so I know he's safe. And are you going to take these two people away?"

"We're going to take them away soon," Burgess said. "If you want to check on Aaron, he's upstairs with Sybil."

"Oh yeah." Melendez nodded. "She's kinda batty. She thinks she's his mother. Or acts like it. Which I suppose isn't so bad since the kid's own mother is such a loser." He withdrew the arm and stood. "I'll just go on up and tell him it's okay to come home."

This was what people did, Burgess thought. *When their own families failed them, they created new families to give them what they needed.* "Great," he said. "Thank you."

Melendez lumbered away.

Burgess closed his eyes. If he stayed here long, he'd drift off to sleep.

There was a thump as Carlisle tried to get to his feet.

"Don't," Perry said.

Burgess stood. Perry and Kyle had this situation under control. "I'm going over to the hospital and get sewn up," he said. He wondered how they'd feel if he brought Fideau into the ER. The poor pup had been patient long enough.

Downstairs, he let the dog out for a quick bio break, then drove to the hospital. It was the place where, to paraphrase an old saying, when you went there, they had to take you in. And you were usually bleeding.

He got lucky. His favorite ER doc, Sarita Cohen, was on tonight. In his experience, she was always on. Great for him when he needed stitching; bad for her because rest was important.

Dr. Cohen greeted him with her usual smile and led him and his canine companion into a cubicle. As she unwrapped the gauze, she looked at him. "This looks almost surgical."

"It was a scalpel."

"Your attackers are getting more professional."

"I hope not."

"So how are you otherwise? Energy coming back?"

"At a snail's pace."

"And your handsome son. Is he staying out of trouble?"

Burgess nodded. "This week, it's my daughter. Trouble not of her own making."

"Seems like it's getting harder to be young these days."

As she stepped away to get something, Burgess saw that she was pregnant. She was so tiny she'd probably be as big around as she was tall by the time her baby came.

"I see congratulations are in order," he said.

"I'm not sure. It was definitely a surprise to me. My husband is over the moon, though. We've been putting it off for years because of this thing and that. I guess fate decided for us." She put a hand on his shoulder and pushed him back against the pillows. Fideau was instantly alert.

"It's okay, Fideau," Burgess said. "Dr. Cohen is our friend."

They watched the dog nod and settle down.

"Wow!" she said as she numbed his arm. "That is one smart dog. Where did you get him?"

"Belonged to a bad guy we arrested. Guy went to jail, and Fideau decided to come home with me. My kids love him, but everyone agrees that he is my dog. I think he can talk."

She bent close, and he could smell the fresh green scent of her shampoo. He closed his eyes and let her work. Sleep was beckoning, eager to lure him in. He was headed toward its embrace when he found himself thinking about how to structure his interview with Dr. Heather Benson. After that, sleep was no longer on his agenda.

"Wow," Dr. Cohen said. "I felt that. It was like you were suddenly plugged in, and current was surging through you."

"That obvious, huh?" It was odd. With most people, he preferred to be inscrutable. With Dr. Cohen, he was okay with being read. He told her a bit about what they suspected regarding Dr. Heather Benson.

"He took so much from her," Dr. Cohen said. "It left her damaged forever. That happens sometimes. If she'd seen someone and gotten help, she might have been okay. But the same kind of drive that makes us doctors can make us reject seeking help. We're supposed to be the helpers. The strong ones." She smiled. "Kind of like you, Joe."

She finished sewing and bandaged his arm. "Chris isn't going to be happy about this."

"I know. I try. I do. I'm just a trouble magnet."

"More like a trouble seeker." She patted his shoulder. "Good luck with your suspect. And I don't want to see you…" She looked down at Fideau. "Or your dog in here again any time soon." Another of her gentle smiles. "Not that I don't enjoy your company."

His shirt and jacket were a mess, so she got someone to bring him a scrub shirt. Not the first time. He always hoped it might be the last. Burgess and Fideau thanked her and left.

FORTY-EIGHT

The woman sitting across from him looked tired. Tired and resigned, her shoulders slumped and her face worn as she waited for his questions. A lawyer friend had once told him that using the law to get revenge or satisfaction was rarely successful. The same could be said for using violence. And yet, it happened all the time. The damage that people did to each other could warp someone until they couldn't step outside and get any perspective on what they were thinking. That was for those whose actions were planned, of course. Plenty of their suspects had acted out of rage or passion or while intoxicated. That wasn't true for this woman.

Well. Maybe passion. A low flame nurtured for years.

Beside him, Kyle waited patiently for him to begin. Stan Perry would be in another room monitoring the interview. Two heads, or in this case, three, were always better than one.

Once he'd gone through the preliminaries, establishing her name, her address, etc., he asked Dr. Benson, "Did you kill Dr. Eliot Spence?"

She nodded.

"We need your voice, ma'am."

"I did. I drugged him. I killed him. I sodomized him with a bottle. Then I left."

"Why?"

"Because years ago, back when I was a medical student and he was a resident, he drugged me, raped me, and sodomized me with a bottle." She almost smiled as she added, "The same bottle."

She sounded calm. Sane. Cooperative. He didn't believe it or trust it. He thought even here, she might have a plan. All that meticulous planning to get at Eliot Spence. Wouldn't she have thought about what would happen if she was caught? Perhaps she planned to have herself judged mentally ill? Or perhaps, as they sometimes saw, the act itself was enough, and once caught, she was ready to confess.

"At the time you were assaulted, did you report the assault to the police?"

"I did. To the police and to the hospital. It was my word against his. They made me look pathetic and vulnerable. One of those women who got drunk and said yes and then regretted it. I am not alone, Detective. It happens to women all the time. Then. And still. After that, though, I knew who he was. I knew I wasn't his only victim. That he wouldn't stop until he was forced to stop. I...we, there were four of us who found each other... paid him a visit. We told him we would all file complaints with the hospital. With the medical board. We told him we knew there would be others, and we would find them. That it had to stop."

"He laughed at us. He thought he was untouchable. He had photos of us and threatened to share them. It was obscene and ugly. But we called his bluff. We told him to go ahead and share those pictures. It was evident to us, and would have been evident to the police, that none of the women he'd photographed were capable of consent. The pressure must have worked because, after that, I heard that he'd turned to prostitutes. Compliant women who'd let him do what he wanted without having to be drugged."

She sighed. "Could I have some water, please?"

"Water? Or would you prefer a soda? Or coffee?"

"Water is fine."

Interviews like this one, where the subjects wanted to tell their story, were rare. Fine with Burgess as long as they got what they needed to charge her.

When she had her water, Burgess nodded. "Go on."

"I followed him after that. Not physically. In the news. Wondering if he'd changed after his marriage. I saw the news about his wife's death and wondered if he'd done it. If she'd found out about the other women or his sordid sexual past and threatened to divorce him." She shrugged. "Not that I cared much. I followed his move to Maine."

She looked down at her hands, which were knotted on the table in front of her. Small, capable hands. "I realized that he…what he'd done…was holding me back from getting on with my own life. With forming a healthy relationship. I liked my work, but in personal relationships, I had serious trust issues. I could never get close to anyone. I was too scared of something happening again, and I understood that it was all his fault. He'd taken something from me that he wasn't entitled to, and despite therapy, I couldn't seem to get it back."

Her voice, powered by her anger, rose. "It was as though I'd been putting all my anger into a safe. Keeping it locked up. Working with a therapist, I opened the door to that safe, and it was like walking into a conflagration. I couldn't believe my body could hold that much anger. No matter what my therapist tried or what medications I took, I couldn't let go of the idea that I'd never move on until—"

She stopped. Drank more water. Looked at Burgess. "Until I was sure that he could never do to another woman what he'd done to me."

"The postcards that read 'Unforgotten.' That was you?"

She nodded. "I just wanted to remind him. Make him uneasy. Keep him on edge. Watching him, all those paranoid moves?" She smiled. "It worked."

"How did you kill Dr. Spence?"

"I'm sure you know the answer to that by now if you have a competent medical examiner. When he was unconscious, I laid him on the floor and slammed a sledgehammer into his chest."

"A myocardial contusion?" Burgess said.

She nodded, looking thoughtful. "I wasn't sure it was going to work. I had backup plans. But in a way, it was so elegant. Stopping his heart. When, of course, the man had no heart. At least, no heart in the sense of having feelings for others. Just an organ to pump blood through his body. And give him erections, of course. He was good at that."

"How did you do that without significant bruising?"

Another shrug. "I padded his chest with a towel. Once he was dead, I hauled him up on the bed and got out the bottle." A wistful smile. "I kept it all these years. I must have known I'd need it someday."

Burgess said, "You were at Dr. Spence's posing as a prostitute?"

For a moment, there was a spark of animation in her face. "It seemed like part of the perfect revenge. He didn't recognize me, which I found kind of amazing. But to him, the women he bought were nothing more than commodities. They weren't people. Just like the women he'd drugged and raped. We weren't people either, even though some of us were studying to be doctors. We were colleagues or at least future colleagues."

She shrugged, taking a moment to organize her story. "Once he'd ascertained that I met his criteria for beauty and body type, he barely noticed me at all. He ordered me around like I was a dog. It made what I'd come to do so much easier."

Burgess moved on. "The boy. Aaron Daggett. Attacked in his apartment." He gave the address. "Was that you?"

"That's where it went beyond what I'd planned. He'd seen me. He and his sister. I didn't know what else to do. I'd let Eliot Spence ruin my life once. I wasn't letting that happen again, no matter the collateral damage."

But she had let Spence ruin her life again. It made him sad. Sometimes, the killers were more sympathetic than the ones they killed. But Bosch's rule. Everyone mattered. Even the doctor from some years ago whose carelessness had killed his mother. That was the cop's job. They didn't get to play God.

He asked a few more questions and then let Kyle ask some more.

It was another day by the time they finished. A day when people, in particular Captain Cote, would be demanding reports. For now, though, he and his team were due a few hours to sleep. His arm was throbbing, and his eyes were at half-mast.

They were far from done, of course. Only on TV were cases solved in an hour. There were more reports to write. Mark Carlisle's information about his sister murdering Lenore Spence had to be shared with the Massachusetts police. And no way was he letting Aaron and Kristin's parents off the hook. Those kids needed to be cared for.

But that was for another day.

He, Kyle, and Perry met at his desk. They should be going home to sleep, but sometimes, there needed to be a time when they circled up and decompressed before they could do that.

Weary but satisfied that they'd done their job, however sad the underlying story, they headed out to their cars and drove to the diner for breakfast.

———

The End

DELIVER US FROM EVIL

A JOE BURGESS MYSTERY, BOOK 9

It was a habit Burgess had developed years ago. A nocturnal habit. At the end of a shift or if he needed some space with his thoughts, he'd swing by the park. Sometimes he'd stay in his truck and think. Sometimes he'd get out and walk into the park. He liked the smell of the earth, sometimes of fresh cut grass. Sometimes the fall scent of decaying leaves or, in winter, the sharp bite of cold air mixed with the salty tang of the sea. It was the place where, maybe five years ago, he'd found a young teenage hooker, naked, badly beaten, and left to die in the winter cold.

She'd survived and after some setbacks and missteps, had gone on to train as a massage therapist. Now, Alana Black sometimes came to dinner with him and Chris and the kids. She thought it was hilarious that she'd gone straight and ended up with a cop for a friend.

Tonight, even though a late November frost had turned the grass silver under a full moon, he was too tired to bother. A bad night's sleep and a long day at work had worn him out. He was planning to head home, where Chris would have saved a plate of dinner for him, but his truck had other ideas. When he told it to go left, it went right, rolling to stop where he always parked when he wanted to check the park. It was bad enough that his teammate, Terry Kyle, could read his mind. Now his vehicle was doing it?

Swearing, he grabbed his flashlight—the big, bright one that could sweep the park—and stepped out into the crisp night. The moist air had gathered around streetlights in nebulous halos and the frozen grass crunched under his feet. In the distance, an occasional car up on the highway sped past but down here he was alone. After a day of constant human contact, it felt good to be alone. Maybe his truck just knew.

His back to the highway, he stood looking out into the darkness, filtering out the traffic sounds behind him and focusing on anything that might not sound right. He might be annoyed but he was pretty sure he was here for a reason. Cops had instincts. They had gut sense. Just like he sometimes believed in divine intervention, Burgess believed that his city sometimes spoke to him. Tonight it wanted him here. Now he needed to know why.

Flashlight beam moving from side to side as he walked slowly into the park, he listened to the night, and there it was. A small sound, like the mewling of a kitten or the sobs of a weary child. Something out there was crying for help. He closed his eyes and focused on the sound, trying to tell where it was coming from. Thought he got a bead on it and headed in that direction, pausing every few steps to listen again. Another cry and then silence.

It might be some nocturnal animal. Might be. But Detective Sergeant Joe Burgess had been a cop for a long time and he'd heard hundreds, maybe thousands of cries of distress. He thought this was human. He continued his walk, stop, listen. But the sound had died away.

He stopped again, turning in a slow circle, and called out, "Hello? Is there anybody out there? Hello?"

The night only gave him silence. He shook his head, trying to tell himself he'd imagined it. That the ghosts of too many years were distorting his senses and throwing up boogeymen where there were none. Standing in the frosty grass, his feet were getting cold and his fall jacket wasn't heavy enough. Soon it would be time to switch up to cold-weather gear. Burgess believed in being prepared for the weather. There would be a warmer jacket back in the truck. He could go back and get it.

He could go back, start the engine, and drive home to good food and a warm, sleepy Chris in his bed.

Burgess turned, the breath he'd huffed out in irritation steaming around his face. His city had called him here but if it wasn't going to show him what it wanted, he was going home. As he turned back the way he'd come, he heard it again. So small and faint, and visions of the night he'd found Alana Black, beaten and bloody, came back to him. Whatever or whoever it was, he had to know.

He turned and restarted his slow walk and listened as he headed deeper into the park. "Hello?" he called. "Hello? Is anybody out there?"

This time the sound was clearer. A voice. A female voice, very faint and weary. She said, "Help me."

Surer of the direction now, he headed toward the voice. Toward her. Flashlight swinging from side to side, illuminating the darkness of bushes and the crisp gleam of the grass.

She was lying on her side next to a battered, rusty trashcan. Bloody. Naked. Her thin white body looking almost unreal in the silver moonlight.

Burgess hurried toward her, pulling off his jacket to cover her and getting out his phone. He gave his location and called for an ambulance. For officers to secure the scene and for evidence techs. He didn't know if this was a crime scene, a place where she'd been assaulted, or whether she had been dumped here, but there might be something.

Assured that help was on the way, he knelt beside her. "Police officer," he said. "I'm Joe."

Her body was more bruised than unbruised. Dark purple ridges circling her wrists and ankles said she'd been restrained. A prisoner. Held against her will while struggling to escape. She was young, probably not much more than his daughter's age. Nina was sixteen. Despite the bruises, he could see that she was pretty, with long, wavy dark hair and delicate features.

"You're safe," he said, keeping his voice low and gentle. "I'm a police officer. My name is Joe. Help is on the way, and you're safe." He took her hand in his and repeated, "You're safe."

Her eyes opened briefly. Eyes that were a startling emerald green. "Please," she whispered. "Please don't let them find me. Don't let them take me back."

Available in Paperback and eBook from Your Favorite Bookstore or Online Retailer

ABOUT THE AUTHOR

Kate Flora's fascination with people's criminal tendencies began in the Maine attorney general's office. Deadbeat dads, people who hurt their kids, and employers' discrimination aroused her curiosity about human behavior. Flora's been a finalist for the Edgar, Agatha, Anthony, and Derringer awards. She won the Public Safety Writers Association award for nonfiction and twice won the Maine Literary Award for crime fiction.

When she's not writing, Flora gardens in the writerly town of Concord, Massachusetts, and on the coast of Maine, and bakes when she gets stuck in writing a story. She's been married to a delightful man for more than forty years.

facebook.com/katecflora

x.com/kateflora

www.ingramcontent.com/pod-product-compliance
Lightning Source LLC
Chambersburg PA
CBHW030243030726
47493CB00023B/571